IN PINELIGHT

In Pinelight

A Novel

Thomas Rayfiel

TRIQUARTERLY BOOKS

NORTHWESTERN UNIVERSITY PRESS

EVANSTON, ILLINOIS

TriQuarterly Books
Northwestern University Press
www.nupress.northwestern.edu

Printed in the United States of America

10 9 8 7 6 5 4 3 2 1

This is a work of fiction. Characters, places, and events are the product of the author's
imagination or are used fictitiously and do not represent actual people, places, or events.

Library of Congress Cataloging-in-Publication Data

Rayfiel, Thomas, 1958–
     In pinelight : a novel / Thomas Rayfiel.
        p. cm.
     ISBN 978-0-8101-5236-6 (pbk. : alk. paper)
        I. Title.
PS3568.A9257I5 2013
813.54—dc23

2013002127

∞ The paper used in this publication meets the minimum requirements of the American
National Standard for Information Sciences—Permanence of Paper for Printed Library
Materials, ANSI Z39.48-1992.

This book is dedicated to my friends

David Harmon

Spencer Finch

Cliff Thompson

J. Anderson

IN PINELIGHT

Mean as ever that's what he used to say about her but who are you? You say I know you well I know a lot of people or did. They're all gone now most of them. You must have been a kid when I saw you last I guess you're all grown up now but grown up from what from who I mean? Where's Rebecca? Rebecca my? No she's not here she left years ago how do you know about? Yes when Mother died he expected her Father he expected Rebecca to take her place to run the household. Five years older than me but Mother dying made her practically a grown-up in his eyes. That's what she objected to all that drudgery. Of course at the time I didn't realize anything no not consciously. I just remember the fights. Once she even threw a plate. He hit her I remember that it stops the conversation that sound. There's this rise of voices back and forth faster and faster you try turning away from it under the covers that's where I was under the covers we shared a bed he and I after Mother died I was too old to be in the same room with Rebecca anymore they go back and forth the voices when it's a fight it's like they intertwine finish each other's sentence but not the way the other one wants the sentence finished. Then there was this meaty sound and. I pretended to be asleep. She didn't leave the next day no it wasn't like that. I think she just didn't want to cook and clean. I pretended to be asleep but you can't close your ears. No she never talked to me about it. All I knew was that

Mother was gone and that we couldn't ever have flapjacks again. We didn't talk I was too young she everyone said she was beautiful later after she left like that was some kind of explanation that her beauty took her away. I assume she is. She never came back never sent word by now she'd be but who told you about Rebecca? Local history there is no local history nothing happens here I mean things happen but they don't amount to much that's what Lebrun's wife used to say. She'd complain Nothing ever changes here all of you just sitting around like a bunch of stuffed owls. Stuffed owls that's what she'd call us a bunch of oh she was a live wire.

⁓

You'd ask Lebrun how his wife was and he'd say Mean as ever. What they saw in each other I'll never know. Well apparently he was handsome that's what they say. I'm no judge he was smart I can tell you that. He could make something out of nothing. He knew how to play the system knew there was a system which I didn't not until later. He saw the dam was going to be big. While the rest of us were busy complaining about it or gawking at it the construction I mean *Boondoggle or Salvation?* that's what Lawrence asked in the *Pennysaver* in his editorial while we were all asking ourselves that question he went and got himself a job there with the Black River Authority. I remember him in that pickup truck with the writing on the door always on his way somewhere always checking levels. Yes water levels. Well sure we were envious. The paper mill and the glove factory were the only places hiring those days and then he came tooling around town in that Black River Authority pickup but I don't know how it came about he was handsome. To me he just looked like. I think it was all wrapped up with that new truck new job the idea that he maybe had a future don't think women aren't taking that into account they'd be fools not to. In any event I know for a fact his real name was Lebrun. Brown that's what he went by. You say

4

it's a translation yes a translation from truth to falsehood Lebrun was his name he was a Canuck but he didn't have an accent not by the time I met him. How did I know I don't remember I just did Claude Lebrun that was his secret self the one nobody knew except me. Anyway handsome to women it's just another word for money. You say there are handsome men who are poor I don't know about that Ed Mosher I suppose he was handsome but when his father was alive and it looked like he would inherit the hardware store that's when people decided he was handsome later the handsome part just stuck it was a memory. Now Lebrun excuse me Brown was handsome in a forward-looking way full of possibilities or so I recall. It could all be colored by what happened subsequently subsequently yes I know my English three-and-a-half years of high school then I had to leave I had to go to work but Rebecca what on earth are you asking about her for? Of course I know there's a town under there. Conklingville. It was nothing don't let people tell you different I've walked its streets or its street rather that's all it was a wide spot in the road. When they decided to flood the valley no one objected money was hard to come by then. The Army Corps of Engineers did it they dammed up the river and flooded the place but it wasn't much to begin with. You think there are fish swimming through the halls of some underwater palace down there? The church the general store the feedlot. Go to the general store I suppose he did we all did although how you know about that surprises me. Nell owned it she had rooms in back. They were her cousins that's what we called them the girls who lived there. It only occurs to me now that they weren't. Cousins I mean. One was even part Indian but we assumed somehow she was still her cousin I guess we didn't want to know different it was nothing fancy no chandeliers or beaded curtains or anything like that. A dollar. Which was quite a lot in those days. I suppose he did but I don't know I never saw him there. She was careful not to have you see anyone else. Where was Nell from I have no idea she could have been born here or dropped from the moon for all I know. The Indian? Again I have no idea her cousin that's all. How could I tell by her hair of course it was long and black wait Gabrielle or am I imagining? I don't think so. I don't think I could imagine a name like that. So what if it's French I didn't name her anyway she was only part Indian half-breed that's what they called her not Lebrun he never you see that's the kind of remark he would never make he was very proper. I think he acted like that to get away from what people said about Canucks in general that they're unclean and can't control themselves. Especially down there. Can't control themselves down I don't think I ever heard a curse word escape his lips. Why do I think he went to Nell's well everyone did all the young men. He wasn't that different. You're only making him so by singling him out people always seemed to think he was special I didn't I thought he was just like us but more so is that the same as being special? Lawrence in the *Pennysaver* called him *a poet who used bricks and mortar instead of words* what do you think that means? Poet. He could barely write. None of them can. The ones that come down. We get their riffraff their leavings. The only poetry he had went into his shirts they were very white he put us to shame in that department shirts trousers appearance in general you could see it in the ladies' eyes. Gabrielle and him why do you ask? You take me for some kind of Peeping Tom? Braided yes a long single braid going all the way down her back all the way down to I could tell you stories but I'm not the kind that does.

⁓

The church the general store the feedlot and houses of course. Just regular houses. None very special. An attorney. First Calvary Baptist at the end of town or the beginning depending on how you approached. No I did not. My father told me a thing or two about that about religion in general well that it's a racket basically. He should know. It took him for everything he had. No we never attended not as a family I suppose I went in once or twice you can't avoid going in. The Reverend there he was typical acting like he knew best like he had some private line to Heaven Father told me all about them. Lebrun well I assume Roman Catholic Saint Anthony's up in Antone but he never talked about it. Religion it's all a scam if you ask me if you live close to the wild the way we do here you don't need a church or a man to introduce you to God. An attorney's office yes. Alice's father. Near the church. Lawyer Breckenridge that was his name. It was an ordinary little town had a stream running in back all little towns did that's why they were built where they were in the first place I don't consider a stream so special yes it was the Black River I suppose but there was nothing river-like about it then these names they come up with no one called it the Black River then it was just a runoff ditch behind the main road. The Army Corps of Engineers they're just a name too it sounds so impressive Army Corps of Engineers but really it was just a scheme that's what most of us thought at the time flood control for the people downstate as if those politicians ever showed any interest in the welfare of ordinary citizens before. Cement was what it was really about Lebrun told me later millions of tons of cement at I don't know how much a pound. Yes he confided in me or boasted I should say it amounts to the same thing got in on the ground floor he did I don't know how. Filthy Canuck they called him behind his back. It was such desperate times if they offered you money for your house you took it. Besides it was the state no one argued they named a price and it was ready cash so. Where Nell went after I have no idea most people moved to Antone after they flooded the town but her I don't think so. Retire no one retires here they put you out to pasture that's what they do and even that's a false picture skin and bones is what you're left with in the end then the bones poke through the skin and have you ever seen a dead horse? But no I have no idea where Nell went or Gabrielle could that really have been her name it sounds so unlikely or any of her cousins for that matter by then I'd met Alice and she wouldn't let me buy a penny's worth of nails from that store she regarded it as the gateway to Hell. Did she save me well I wouldn't be so dramatic. You can't be saved you can't save yourself things simply are that's what life has taught me. At the time yes I thought there were choices but now looking back for example Do you love her? Lebrun asked me once out of the blue. It's funny because we hadn't even discussed her. Alice and I had been very careful we thought no one knew but then Lebrun asked Do you love her? It wasn't even a question I had asked myself and I said Yes which strikes me as funny now. So he knew even before I did that I loved her that I loved Alice so where's the choice in that?

~~

We didn't tell anyone because of her father. He didn't approve. Represented I don't know what I represented to him what are you talking about? I was courting his daughter and he disliked me didn't think me fine enough for her represented besides he's the one who turned out to be the troublemaker. No it was all so long ago I don't want to talk about it. Oh so you know how do you know? Yes the court case. I didn't think anyone remembered. It broke Emily's heart. I'm sorry Alice. Alice's heart. It happens. I get names mixed up. We hadn't had Emily yet or if we did she was too young to understand. You ask me things you already know the answer to are you trying to catch me out in a lie? Why did he disapprove? Too good for me he thought that she was too good for me but I proved him wrong I provided I made deliveries in weather much worse than this this isn't even snow this isn't the kind of snow we used to have. Brown you mean Lebrun? Yes maybe once or twice but he was far below her in social standing. You see you totally misunderstand. He was a Canuck. Emily I mean Alice had nothing but contempt for his kind. The lines were much more clearly drawn then. Not like today when you pretend nothing matters where you come from or what you look like or how you speak that it's all some Brotherhood of Man. No that's all right it takes me that way just let me. There. I'm fine now. She despised him no that's wrong she didn't notice him enough to despise him not at first. That's a better way to put it. Alice. Men of course it doesn't matter as much with men we can talk to anyone it's all tied up with work yes he steered a few things my way I don't know why because we were friends I guess. But Gabrielle there was no way he could have known about Gabrielle and me I would never have talked to him about that some things are better left yes a single braid didn't I tell you already a black braid of course it swayed all the way down her I remember following it the path trying to follow one in particular those braided paths what would you call them strands? The braids within the braid. Do you think you could get me out of here? I suppose not. It's just that on a day like today I would like to smell the snow yes the snow it's one of those smells that aren't supposed to be that nobody talks about like blood. You don't smell blood sure you do you just don't know you do. Anyway by the time they flooded it town was all stripped. People salvaged things then not like today. Today there's nothing but waste. I took a walk the night before. There was a barricade but no one manning it soldiers there's a job for you in peacetime at least the Army Corps of Engineers what a joke they were all at The Triangle no one was guarding the fence they'd built at taxpayers' expense. Why because I wanted to walk the streets one last time. Well yes I never thought of it that way but since you bring it up I suppose my two loves were living within fifty feet of each other it's not so surprising the world was smaller then but there was also a depth to it that no longer exists because I don't know why because everything's gotten shallower I suppose wider but shallower. I saw him before he saw me he was carrying a lantern we still used kerosene back then. I watched him. You know they say most Canucks are part Indian themselves mixed blood it's the way they walk as if the ground and their feet have something in common very low and snakelike he didn't see me for quite a while so I watched him you can tell when a man is up to something. There were only foundations left wood bricks metal anything useful had been stripped away. He stopped at one building I couldn't tell which what had been there I mean they were just like broken stumps by then like old teeth with a hearth in the middle just a slab of rock he stood there a long time a house it was a house I don't know which one or maybe another store I don't remember it was eighty years ago all right sixty by then but even so what do you care? No not the church or Nell's or the feedlot I'm sure of that some other building it can't possibly have any significance now besides it's not where he was but what he did that I remember he stood there holding his lantern there was no moon and began kicking at the stone like it offended him. This big blackened hearth I remember the light from the lantern swinging back and forth getting kind of herky-jerky him kicking and some dust or dirt or ash flying up. All silently. Well I was surprised because he never displayed anger you see. He was calm. I mean even when he was mad at someone he was still calm the more difficult the situation the more quiet he became it was a characteristic but here where there was nothing but calm not a soul around he was kicking the stone so hard it looked like he was going to break his toe that's when I went over I called to him but he didn't seem to hear me so I grabbed him by the shoulders. Yes a white shirt what funny questions you ask. His eyes were turned back in his head I suppose it was some kind of seizure no there was no smell of alcohol on him no he never touched a drop many of them don't you know. The ones who can't handle it. They swear off completely. Even one sip and they go crazy it's another sign they might have mixed blood Canucks because of course Indians can't drink firewater can't digest it I don't know if that was true in his case but. Then he kind of woke up came to as if nothing had happened all he was concerned about were his new boots had he gotten them scraped. I said What are you doing? But he remembered nothing he thought I meant by coming and said Same as you I came here for the same reason as you. The funny thing is now I see it every day town through the waves. Yes Conklingville buried underneath the waves although you can't really be buried in water can you? Drowned I suppose but no not drowned either because there was nothing left no one living so if it's not living it can't be drowned. Submerged I see it every day submerged. They won't let me out of here because of last time. Only as far as the porch. It's frozen solid. I don't know what they're afraid of what they think I'll do but I see it even now even from here coming up from under the ice. Oh yes ice moves.

⁓

No there was no cemetery in Conklingville no bodies to move not that I recall. That's one delivery I wouldn't have made. Horses they won't let you they don't like corpses once we came across the scene of an accident Cole Byron his guts stretched halfway across the road just outside of Antone. Allure she stopped before I could even see. Fifty feet off at least. Well the smell of course as I said snow blood things that shouldn't smell do people just won't admit it. I couldn't get her to take a single step finally I got down from the cart with some notion of taking the bridle and tugging and then I saw it too quite a sight you take what's inside us unravel it and it can go quite a long ways from here to there. Flies? No no flies it was cold then like now the milk stayed fresh all the way back to Kathan. Then I had a story to tell. Turning the team around though even that was no picnic. The Byrons they're a law unto themselves there's too many of them that's the problem or there were back then nowadays I don't know I don't get out much. Allure that was her name when I got her it's nothing I would have thought of but it's bad luck to change a horse's name you know Allure and Firebrand seventy-five dollars the pair I went all the way over to Schuyler to get them. Yes I knew it was the end for horses but that made it all the more appealing somehow souls they have souls they're someone you can talk to you can't talk to a pickup truck. Allure and Firebrand I had quite a run with them for years it made more sense to hire me than one of those Fords that were always breaking down or getting stuck in the mud. Now of course they build roads like highways it's different now. Allure could pick her way through any sort of trouble. Alice accused me it was silly she accused me of liking horses more than her. I suppose I did like the silence Allure and I had. The silence of our conversations. Because they don't answer so you go on talking or thinking rather but the way you go on it's based on how the horse is silent somehow so your thought is put onto different passageways you know what I mean? Allure I found myself in talks with her going places with her in my mind that I could never have reached alone. Once we were going all the way to the base of the fire tower. It was wet I had to concentrate because the road there well it's hardly a road at all more like a path in disrepair but still we were discussing I don't know what and suddenly my father appeared yes he was dead by then I told you I left school because he had died well that was why if your father died you left school right away you were a man all of sudden whether you wanted to be or not anyway he appeared in front of me and Allure neighed or I wouldn't have even noticed I was so concentrated on the path always the path you have to be aware you can't drift can't nod off to sleep and there he was hands empty arms dangling shocked to see me like I was the ghost not him. I didn't even have time to give a cry and he was gone but that was the day before Alice and I. Married well married in the eyes of God you might say. Of course it counts as a conversation just because we didn't talk doesn't mean it wasn't a conversation the point is without Allure. Oh people still go there couples I mean if they want a bit of privacy it's a pretty spot that high up. And you don't get surprised. You can see others coming hear them climbing the trail. In summer the man would be up in the tower that was his job the fire-watcher it belongs to the Authority now it's part of the basin technically it's trespassing though I hear it's become a tourist attraction the tower. People go up for the view hikers picnickers there's no fire-watcher there now they use helicopters but I'll bet some people still go there to. My father? I don't think he ever took a day off in his life certainly not to climb a tower and look at mountaintops he was a demon for work no the point is my god you are dense aren't you he appeared and our eyes met and I realized it was time. Alice had been pestering me that's the wrong word pestering but she wanted very much to be married to be out of that house. They were already talking about flooding the valley and her father she and he didn't get along that would be the kindest way to put it so. Why was I reluctant I don't know I wasn't really just she could be quite annoying Alice she had a way about her. They say opposites attract. I suppose it shocked me seeing my father his eyes they told a story. The dead don't blink you know oh yes it's common knowledge. I don't know from where where does any fact come from they look at you the dead like they're the ones who are surprised as if you know something they've forgotten like you're this well. Yes a well that they're falling into. It's hard to explain you have to experience it anyway I went home and the next day we Alice and me. Water cooking supplies the usual stuff. He'd be up there all summer the fire-watcher. He couldn't leave. What did my father want? For me to move on most likely for me to get going with my life so he could get on with his. Well I guess get on with his life is the wrong word so he could get on with whatever it was he was doing instead so he could rest in peace maybe.

⁓

Nowadays I don't have a horse so there's no one to talk to. It's all gizmos now all machines you can't have a conversation with a machine it just sits there. If you leave say a television set alone in a room for ten hours and come back nothing has happened to it while you were away so it has nothing to tell you. That set right there for example I come in in the morning and it's got nothing to say to me it doesn't make my thoughts go anywhere I don't mean the channels I mean before I turn it on I mean just as an object but with Allure or even Firebrand not as much with Firebrand but in the morning when I would come to her we would have both slept both dreamed and so we had things to say to each other. Words yes I supplied the words but without her I would have supplied different words or none at all but a TV if a TV starts putting words in your head well then I would begin to worry if I were you because they don't have souls machines the way animals and nature do nature as in plants yes of course you can talk to plants trees there's a whole religion built around trees. Lawrence in the *Pennysaver* used to put his hand on an oak. Why? You would have to ask him wouldn't you? No he passed long ago but in his editorials he used to write about them sometimes the people what were they called in ancient Britain before the Romans they strung ivy from the branches of trees he wrote that was their church the whole forest he was a funny man Lawrence. We were proud to have someone like him in the community. I don't think he had any friends here but that was the way he wanted it. You'd find him in the forest sometimes he'd just go there and stagger as if there were all these difficulties on a flat piece of ground hills and valleys you couldn't see sometimes a complete barrier right in front of him like a wall. You'd come on him standing there all walled in and have to take his hand and lead him out of it but your TV if you hear that talking inside your head then that's your soul leaking out like the air out of a balloon. I haven't had a good talk in a long time not the kind I used to have with Allure. She died they all die. No you sell them before. They break down and then I don't see any contradiction I'm sure whoever's using me for whatever purpose will sell me

14

off to be made into pet food at the end of the day when my useful-
ness is ended it's got nothing to do with feelings. Alice well that's
different of course yes I cremated her and scattered the ashes right
out there. No not by the shore I went out in a boat the two of us well
three counting her. Lebrun he had that what do you call it a skiff he
used to go right up to the lip of the dam where the turbines are the
spillway I wouldn't want to go anywhere near there when the current is flowing but for Alice we went to the middle of the lake just
the three of us. She was in a little box from the funeral home a coffee
can really I mean the same size and shape. I had a hell of a time opening it and the wind was blowing or came up rather just as I so part
of her blowed back into the boat into our hair too it upset him all
out of proportion Lebrun I don't know why because he was Roman
Catholic I guess something about her remains her heavenly rest. To
me it was just mineral it's not really ashes you know it's more coarse
almost gravel no not like coffee at all what are you talking about he
tried to pick it out of his hair his clothes the bottom of the boat he
was frantic. Not like him actually. I didn't tell him this but I had a
bit between my teeth and rather than spit it out I swallowed it. A bit
of Alice. Why not? We were trying to drift right over town not over
any building in particular just where she had grown up where she
had been happy. You can see it from here I've told you you can see
town rising out of the water. Her father? I have no idea. He left after
the trial it was foolish him representing himself but of course no
one else would have. He won yes but it was the kind of victory that
makes you have to leave right after. He had angered too many people burnt too many bridges we all stick together here we solve our
problems privately maybe we hate each other but we don't do what
he did we don't drag in the law that's. He never collected a dime
of the settlement I don't think he ever intended to I think his aim
was to shame them Cochrane and Christopher and it was true what
they did was wrong but dragging them into court that way exposing

them it's only in the movies and fairy tales people gain by having the truth come out most of the time the truth is like radium radium what they have in bombs you know it glows and you can't touch it you can't even look at it you can only tell it's there when it blows up and then it destroys itself so it's not there anymore. He was a bit of a preacher that was his style in the courtroom The truth will set you free he said. Alice was ashamed. She was like me she wanted to fit in she was born here it means something maybe because she didn't have a mother that was a bond we shared. It set him free all right free to disappear we got postcards for a while from different places as far away as San Francisco I recall meanwhile those two continued their work as if nothing had happened. Tell me what the point of it was except to humiliate us. I suppose he felt he had to defend his honor. Delivered to them of course I did and Cochrane he made fun of me for it and so what? They paid. Now I'm here and they're gone I don't see where honor comes into it. Yes it buys you a penny postcard from San Francisco exactly. *Much Ado About Nothing* that's what Lawrence said in the *Pennysaver* he was very what do you call it very careful dealing with Cochrane and Christopher that whole business right up until the end then of course he got all. Why are you asking about this are they going to flood more valleys? Dam up all the rivers? It's not healthy you know. Things get trapped here things that should go out that should flow to the sea they get trapped here and grow too big for their own good fish yes and other things there used to be for many years here they talked about a northern pike who kept growing and growing vicious creatures they have teeth you know you have to use a metal lead on your line they can bite through practically anything no no one ever caught it it was just a legend that he was stuck here when they first dammed up the stream and grew massive. But I meant other things when you dam up a place not fish it's like how a body becomes swollen stopped up and then yes the spillway that's what it's there for to relieve the pressure the turbines take a certain amount and make power but when the level gets too high when there's too much snow and starts to melt it can be terrifying. I was in that little room with him once with Lebrun. The control room down past the gate so you're actually on top of the dam inside it really when they opened the runoff valve full and all the water went down the spillway and the whole structure shook. I thought we were going to die there was all this loose stone on the side and the water crested and swept it away whole boulders washed down into the basin you should have heard the roar. There's nothing more powerful than water water has a mind of its own.

~⌀

It changed everything the dam changed our way of life. How can it not when you look out your window one day and there are trees leading to a little runoff stream a ditch practically and the next day it's over your head it's what do you call it a reservoir no not a lake I know the tourist people say lake and that fake Indian name they chose for it none of us call it that. No window in particular not mine no I'm speaking generally. Gabrielle's window certainly yes I told you she was in back the girls had their individual rooms I don't remember any of the others but Gabrielle's she was on the second floor. No nothing like a bordello. The opposite. She kept her room neat as a pin. And her person too. What do I mean by that I can't believe I'm telling you this I mean no fancy unmentionables nothing like that she was a good girl Gabrielle I don't know why I'm crying you bring up the past like this and of course it unearths things. From her window the stream and then very steeply Mount Woodcock rising on the other side. Now it's the opposite shore. She had practically nothing these girls were not rich she had one picture of Him you know the kind where you can see inside His chest the heart all wrapped in barbed wire I don't understand why they worship a man they can't touch the heart of women but aside from that oh yes and her one

17

bit of decoration a piece of glass that was all triangular what is that called that breaks the light up it was in her window yes a prison just a tiny one but with a hole for a string it's funny what you remember it threw colors on the room on us once too. Yes we did it in the daytime why not? Of course it was before. I told you after Alice she wouldn't even allow me to buy a bag of nails from that store but before. Then we would talk Gabrielle and I it's really about the talk. The Chinese someone told me the Chinese form words together with their bodies that you can see it in their letters. Him here her there and together it makes a word in their language in their writing. I forget. Someone. No a horse doesn't tell you things like that I'm stating a fact Chinese people when they when they you know when they do it it spells out things that's what their alphabet is based on. Well you traveled so what it doesn't mean you know more. Like I said what you miss today is depth you skim over things you think it's all new but you really just skim over things make the same mistake over and over that's what life is the same mistake over and over then you see the error of your ways and that's when you know you've reached the end that's why it's funny all those hippies who used to come around here and live in the woods or scientists all looking for something some truth and then when they find it well like I told you then the game is over it's like radium it rots off your fingers burns you to nothingness truth. After? What became of Gabrielle after? I heard you. I was just. It's not clear anymore that time of my life it's like a smudge you know how when you look through eyeglasses and there's a bit of something oil or grease. I suppose she moved on no there was no place similar in Antone or if there was I didn't know about it being a married man by then. As a bachelor of course you're more noticing of that type of thing like I said for a while we were in a kind of bubble just we two Alice and me and then Emily she came along and so the outside world there was a blur. No I would never go to a place like that after I was married. Alice taught me to behave.

Before I didn't know my ass from my elbow you should pardon the expression looking back it's a miracle I didn't go crazy before I met her she had a strong moral streak she pulled me back from the edge you might say edge of what well she would have called it sin what she saved me from but I wouldn't go that far. Yes that's when I began doing deliveries with the money the state paid when they flooded the town that's what I bought my wagon with. Making deliveries is all about being reliable people could set their watch by me once I started making deliveries. It was the same with Lebrun he and I both we were wild you have to tame it you have to channel it for me it was into my business for Lebrun I suppose it was the job at first checking levels but really it was land owning land that was his passion. He would sit with me and I would drink that's when we talked oh yes I had quite a thirst back then before Alice made me stop it was a struggle how she weaned me from the bottle he would sit with me for hours usually outside when I had collected enough pennies to buy a pint of Old Gentleman that was the cheapest. He never spoke to others the way he did to me we were sitting once high up on Woodcock Mountain there's a stone outcropping just pine needles and moss he waved his hand around as if to indicate indicate what well the extent of his empire that's what. We were barely twenty but the vision he had he waved his hand from one end of the valley to the other and said it would all be his someday. I drank to it you know like it was some kind of pact we were making although what my part in it was I couldn't say we would kick at loose stones or throw them over the side wait it wasn't moss no it was lichen that green that soaks into the stone God's bones I've always thought those outcroppings the way they peek through they're God's bones the stone where it emerges. Sitting on sun-warmed stone it's one of my favorite things. It's all seabed you know the bottom of an ocean this was all flooded just like the valley the entire planet was under water I read it in a book you think I'm ignorant just because I drove a cart we have a library here. No I found Cole Byron on the other side near the Hollow that's where the Byrons live whole clans of them it's not the kind of place I would go they don't need deliveries they're dangerous people some of them hillbillies there's no good soil there it's the wrong side no sun. They hunt for small game do roadwork in the summer plow in the winter cut wood they're all handy with a chainsaw also more light-fingered stuff is how they make their money if you understand what I'm saying. None of their houses look fit to stand the winter but they always do. It's a terrible road a streambed really all rocks I would have had a time getting my team up there if I'd ever had cause to go which I never did but where we sat Lebrun and I looking down on the land looking down on the path that led to Conklingville he just kind of indicated with his hand that it was all his or would be someday that's how Lebrun thought of it even then that it was his empire.

$\sim$

Once. I got as far as Sparta. I didn't like it. Too busy. I was told to pick up a chest there it came packed in ice they didn't tell me what was inside and on the way home a truck honked and made Allure jump. She didn't like the busy roads all those vehicles couldn't get used to them. He did it to spook her I'm sure the driver he hooted his horn she jumped and the chest I hadn't packed it well enough it fell out and opened and when I went around to collect it there were all these at first I thought marbles skittering along the side of the road but then when I went to pick one up I saw they were eyeballs twenty or thirty of them all packed in ice rolling around on the ground. It gave me a turn I tell you the way they stared up. You try and make them into pairs your head does when you see a bunch I mean two here two there but the way they were gazing every which way and all different colors and sizes. I scooped them back up there was grit clinging to some but I didn't risk brushing it off I was afraid of doing more harm scratching them or whatnot so I put them all back in the chest and fastened the lid more securely weighted it down I didn't want that to happen again. To Cochrane and Christopher of course to their clinic. No they paid me fine they never mentioned the eyeballs but after that I think they got a man to come up from Sparta and make a special delivery it really was too far for Allure she didn't like the hustle-bustle she was a country horse for country roads and then they built the highway and of course that was that. What were they used for I have no idea human eyes who could imagine there'd be so many rolling around and looking everywhere even now I see them like they had a mind of their own. No I didn't tell Alice it would have upset her particularly after her father tried to stop them she would have made a stink if I'd told her. She didn't understand that if you just let things be nine times out of ten they go away but I regretted losing their business over that over the eyeballs because they paid that's how they were able to operate so long with what do you call it with punity because they paid their bills right away none of those next Tuesday or the end of the month excuses. Alice she kept my books she would go crazy seeing how everyone put me off but the clinic was cash on the barrelhead I remember hauling that chest off the back of the wagon and Cochrane coming out himself in that doctor's coat he always wore yes a lab coat very anxious he was I didn't say anything about the accident of course he paid me right on the spot took the money out of his back pocket I was never allowed inside one of his staff came to get the chest two actually those thugs they brought with them from the city to wait on the rich people the clientele anyway the two goons took the chest and he paid me and then he asked Any trouble? No I said but when I went to clean out the wagon that night I found one eye it had rolled into the corner it was staring straight up at me. I didn't know what to do. Bury it no I couldn't bury it. Could you bury an eye looking up at you it would be like burying a man alive I went back to the clinic at night and threw it over the wall I thought maybe they would think it had rolled free after they opened the chest and then they would return it to its fellows yes I chucked it over the side it was late past midnight but music was still coming from there dance music oh the rich people they had a fine time getting cured but Sparta no it's not my kind of place too many people. The patients? I had no dealings with the clinic's patients none whatsoever unless you count meeting one or two of them at the train when that fancy car of Cochrane's broke down which happened now and again. Those Chevrolets were pretty to look at I suppose but yes I could fit seats in the back of the cart well a bench it was a bit rough one of them called it rustic I remember. He would come with me of course Cochrane never Christopher you didn't see much of Christopher. Cochrane was more the public face of the clinic he would come out all hearty and hail-fellow-well-met to the clients or guests or suckers more like although who knows they always left seeming happy. I never heard a complaint except of course in the end when the whole thing blew up but Cochrane he would take their hand in both of his and clasp it he was a big man he would just engulf them it was unsettling to watch he would look them in the eye they were mostly skinny runty-looking people with fine clothes some would be limping or coughing coming off the train others you could tell from the way they looked around as if they were being watched or followed you could tell something was wrong inside between the ears you know. He would tell them all about the treatment on the way back they lapped it up all these scientific words. He had the gift of gab I suppose but to us to me certainly on the ride out for example he was a quiet fellow never said much of anything just glared at the trees I think he hated the countryside. Christopher now he was a different story. He didn't get out much but when he did he had all sorts of questions to ask oh about the bark of hemlock you know when you boil it down and berries those red ones that grow near Indian Pipes that sort of thing home remedies he was always asking about home remedies. Some-place like Romania Transylvania Bo-something Bohemia yes he told me once it looked just like here. I was shocked. I imagined all those places looked different but then when I thought about it it made sense a forest is a forest particularly pine pine's so ancient and ferns they're the most primitive of all he told me he wouldn't be surprised to see one of those woolly elephants come charging through the ferns yes a woolly mammoth I thought that was a funny thing to say somewhat of an accent but I understood every word. The eyeballs what about the eyeballs oh I have no idea. His experiments I suppose. Is that why you're here to find out about Cochrane and Christopher? They were partners yes but they fought like cats and dogs that's the way of partners often. I did like hearing that music out in the woods all that way miles from anywhere it had stopped the crickets so I don't know it changed the feel of the outdoors somehow made it more special. I told you dance music it was festive this little outpost surrounded by pines yes the contrast maybe because you can't even pitch a tent here that's what makes it so different try pounding in a stake the wood splits in half the stone is so near the surface not ev-erywhere of course but where there's any amount of soil the trees have taken it. Pine trees the roots they choke everything they shut out all growth but their own and the needles they're full of acid so there's no underbrush either no bushes or plants except ferns and sometimes in a clearing a few violets. Yes it's a dead world I suppose that's one way of looking at it but something well perhaps you have to grow up around here to appreciate it you can walk for example in almost complete silence because of the needles the carpet and there's something about the light because there are no leaves I suppose just needles so the rays of the sun are filtered they take on a kind of green stain and the smell of course that smell it's supposed to be healthy but it's not for everyone. It's funny wood pine it doesn't burn well it starts out with a sizzle the resin and the needles go up fast they crackle and glow but the trunks don't burn they just turn black they're full of creosote bad for stoves it's not good fuel so the forest even when it burns it comes back quickly you go the next spring and there's green all over. Sometimes you get a change birch and maple and oak they finally have some sunlight to grow in if the needles if the carpet has burned up too but it doesn't last usually. *Pine forest has one long life spent taking over everything in its path. From these trunks a thousand grasses will sprout. This will all be meadow in forty or fifty years.* Pretty isn't it? The *Pennysaver.* People didn't know what to make of Lawrence's editorials. I mean it was mostly ads and personal announcements. I would like to thank the staff of the hospital for the fine care they gave my husband stuff like that and then every week on the inside of the first page he would wax poetic. Or comment. Rebecca? No she never came back.

~

A World-Class Kitchen they called it in the brochure I'm telling you the clinic accounted for a great deal of business in the town. And they paid that was their great virtue it made up for all their sins well money will do that. The settlement? Yes but they got that overturned they got some smart lawyer or paid off a judge by then Alice's father was gone he didn't contest it it was made clear to him that the community valued the work they were doing Cochrane and Christopher. We made our pact with the Devil I suppose but at least we drove a hard bargain you got to give us credit for that not just food there were grounds to tend rooms to clean all kinds of staff although none or very few were allowed into the sanctum itself but altogether I would say twenty-five or maybe thirty people owed their livelihoods directly to the clinic that's a lot in a town our size. I wouldn't count myself among them no not directly I wasn't directly employed but as I said I did odd jobs for them and they paid they paid as soon as yes that's true I hadn't thought of it but places like

Norm's Hideaway and The Triangle benefited too they were much more lively at night because people had money to spend and the occasional clientele came even though they weren't supposed to leave the grounds but the occasional clientele would appear slumming more at Norm's than at The Triangle. The Triangle was a bit rough. Later it changed hands and became acceptable people even brought their wives there were tables they served spaghetti dinners but when I first started going to those kinds of places well if you saw a woman it meant she was you know. But Norm's Hideaway was more there would be the occasional clientele asking for a certain brand of whiskey or some cocktail I'd never heard of. A gimlet one time I recall this man in a suit a tight-fitting suit I don't know why that impressed me so much I'd never seen anything like it it was tailored I suppose his hands trembled he asked Norm for a gimlet and Norm just stood there for a minute then went back behind the bar and got to work. Ice. Shakers. Lemon peels flying. Bottles rattling and it came out green. I went to the library the next day and looked it up it's a tool with a screw tip for boring holes did you know that? A gimlet. It was rare though that I'd go to places like The Triangle I don't like a rough crowd people spitting on the floor and the fights I never could fight I never saw the point in it. Alone on a ledge overlooking the valley now that's how I liked to relax when I was having a nip or at the quarry yes it's still there where could a quarry go? That was my secret place I never saw anyone else there not at the time I went I went in the evening it caught the last light that's where I. It was a place to get my thinking done. I suppose I was a solitary drinker although as I said I enjoyed company if it was of the right sort Lebrun yes he would sit by me and we would talk not at the quarry I told you that was my private place. Gimlet-eyed I'd read somewhere and I thought because a gimlet is green because it has lime juice that gimlet-eyed meant green-eyed but then I looked gimlet up and I saw it was a screw-tipped piercing implement and realized gimlet-eyed was something else entirely. Alice's eyes? Brown. Gabrielle's? Gabrielle I don't remember. Eye color it's not really that important green blue brown it's more the way the gaze affects you. Lebrun for example his eyes they bored into you when he turned your way when he trained them on you but the thing is when people think they're seeing into you at the same time they're leaving themselves open that's what they don't realize that's what I discovered just when they think they're learning everything there is to know about you is the time when their own souls are the most revealed it's a two-way street. So Lebrun and I no never at the quarry. Oh you mean that rock face where they tore out the side of the mountain. That's just dirt and boulders where the mining company went bust years before where the birds make holes you mean? Swallows. Yes it's a kind of nest they have in the dirt it's so sandy no that's not the part of the quarry I'm speaking of no that's not where I went I went behind and up. There's a path. I could show it to you but of course it's winter and my legs but farther back the quartz pit that's what I meant by the quarry it's not more than ten feet deep but lined all on one side with rose quartz the kind that has a blush to it there's mica too on the ground sheets of it you can break it off. I used to sit there peeling off layer after layer never getting to the end kind of like an onion. My feet would dangle over the side and I would look into the quartz wall it's glassy like a mirror but not a mirror you can see yourself in. I never met another living soul there except once a geologist a rock hound he was just as much of a trespasser as me he must have heard about it somehow I don't know from who no I didn't offer him a drink I told you it was my private place we talked a bit he said it was a very unusual formation. How do I know he was really there well that's a strange question to ask how do you know anyone's really there how do I know you're really?

26

The Timberline Institute but we just called it the clinic. Of course I was inside. No not when there were patients the day before Thanksgiving before they closed the place up for winter Cochrane and Christopher would have a party an Open House they called it they were very clever that way everyone got to satisfy their curiosity the whole town came people from miles around they must have spent a pretty penny on it a buffet table cider no no hard stuff there was no drinking after all most of the people who came there were drying out but music too there was a dance floor outside. So what if it was cold the tennis court croquet shuffleboard it built up goodwill which came in handy when someone like Alice's father tried to. For that no Cochrane didn't wear a lab coat I don't think he was ever really a doctor either one of them. Christopher didn't even pretend although he knew more about medicine than Cochrane Cochrane was just a fraud that was proved later but Christopher he would be there too standing there so much smaller than Cochrane. Cochrane wore a big tweed jacket the kind with a belt sewn onto the back a hunting jacket but not one that you would ever actually use to go hunting or fishing in too expensive to get dirty. They greeted you at the door and then we'd all go in and gawk the women gawked at the food and the furniture the men gawked at what it all cost. The medical part where the treatments took place that was closed but I slipped in there once no that was before the eyeball incident I was curious that's all I saw Christopher come through that heavy rounded wooden door and then get distracted and forget to lock it so I slipped through. It was all white and enamel the other side with tiled floors and drains where the water treatments were and spigots coming right out of the wall there were machines too like in a dentist's office but scarier the real scary part though was when I heard the door close and realized he had come back and remembered to lock it the sound of that bolt sliding shut it echoed because there were no carpets or paintings on the walls nothing to muffle the sound. I realized I was locked in and had to keep going had to keep exploring except by then I wasn't looking for anything except a way out which I found eventually a staircase these narrow stairs leading up to what I suppose was where they lived the two Founders that's what they were called in the brochure the Founders Cochrane and Christopher. There was a bedroom a sitting room where they probably had breakfast a study for paying bills and then a little balcony a porch where I could see everyone see the whole town population dancing and talking the kids eating sweets playing games. Yes only one bed. That wasn't such a surprise I mean I had never thought of it before but when I saw it it kind of made sense. None of that is so shocking if you know nature ducks you'll see two mallards well they're not fighting each other I can tell you that and other species too it's not as uncommon as you think. But getting down of course that was the trick there was no way to get back down without being seen. Finally I went around to the other side and saw how by lifting the bedroom window I could jump. It wasn't that far onto some bushes that would break my fall it was only about fifteen feet or so but of course the window was still open there was no way I could go back up and close it no one saw but I did wonder later if either Cochrane or Christopher noticed. Probably not like I said it was before the eyeball incident. Christopher's laboratory where he conducted his experiments? No that was somewhere else no one ever found out where. People searched they looked for trapdoors sliding bookshelves the sort of thing you see in the movies. I remember Ray Eggleston he was the trooper the one who kept on the case the longest telling me he had picked up each vase and bust all those knick-knacks they had thinking maybe one operated a lever that pulled back a wall but no they never found where Christopher conducted his experiments conducted that makes it sound so bad I still have my doubts. Cochrane yes I would not be surprised to hear anything about Cochrane but Christopher I think he had some kind of serious purpose I know it's crazy what they said he was trying to do but it's also interesting in a way don't you think *an elixir of eternal youth* that's what Lawrence called it he was surprisingly nasty when it all came out usually he didn't judge he presented both sides fairly or picked some interesting point to discuss something you wouldn't have noticed yourself a different way of looking at it but it was as if there was all this pent-up anger he had at the two Founders he wrote mocking them using all those words from the brochure. I don't see who he was trying to shame. They were long gone. Ourselves I suppose for believing in them or for looking the other way. I don't see anything so bad about wanting to stay young forever it's the only time when things aren't. An elixir of eternal youth it would taste good don't you think like honey maybe but thinner and with a hint of some taste you remember but can't quite pin down that's how I picture it if you can picture a taste. I'm by nature more forgiving we all have our flaws I liked Christopher he didn't talk down to me didn't treat me like an ignorant carter. Delivery boy I heard myself called even though by then I was married with a child they acted sometimes as if I was an idiot because of that expression I get. Alice told me. Holding the reins but with your eyes pointed god knows where that's how she put it. I know exactly the state she was describing and it wasn't my being an idiot it was the opposite I was thinking things through. What most people never do. They only think as far as they can as far as the limits of their brain will take them then they stop they get all bewildered it's like trying to see past the dark beyond where the glow of a lantern ends but if you explore if you keep going feel with your brain into the dark well there are all sorts of things out there. I would be watching the road too because that's part of it. It's all part and parcel that's what most people don't realize seeing what's in front of you and seeing what's inside you I can't put it into words but that doesn't mean it doesn't exist it's a level of understanding and apparently when I tried reaching that level I would get an empty look on my face but I saw everything. If I was an idiot wouldn't the packages have gotten lost the milk canisters spilled wouldn't we have wandered into a ditch? I sewed that town together like a giant needle looping in and out of people's lives a thread not that they ever noticed but I never wanted to be noticed. The elixir? He never mentioned it no he just asked questions. I don't think you'll see anything now where the clinic stood you think there's still a secret room no one else could find with a jar sitting on a shelf a vial of something some precious purple-colored syrup? Is that where you're going after here? Everyone looked believe you me not just the troopers reporters came around from big city papers and after they left kids well teenagers used to go out there who wouldn't it was a tempting place to break into it had a history yes they'd have parties there beer and worse they made a fire on the floor in the middle of the big room that's what I heard. A fire out of I don't know what. The furniture was long gone maybe the molding they'd pried that off the walls maybe the wainscoting that's what you do when you're young and stupid and drunk. Beer I guess that's the real elixir of youth but the clinic what was left of it was a total loss. It was a blessing really someone could have been hurt it could have fallen down on them. No I wasn't close to Christopher in any way why do you say that? He spoke to me a few times asked questions about bark and berries that's all. The laboratory maybe it was in his room that nook upstairs I saw where they had breakfast. Everyone thought it had to be you know like in a Doctor Frankenstein movie with sparks and glass beakers and whatnot but the Elixir of Eternal Youth maybe it's just a simple thing an idea he came up with and mixed at the breakfast table maybe they had it along with their toast and coffee. No I'm just speculating I know nothing less than nothing of course if he did discover it it would explain how they disappeared so completely because if they took it themselves the elixir they would be unrecognizable. They were hardly young to begin with in their forties at least so if they took it took a lot of it I mean it would have sent them back in appearance wouldn't it? I wasn't going to drown myself I told you I just saw the outline of the town so clearly. The level goes up and down. They lower it in the fall empty out the basin so it will catch all the melting snow in spring. Lebrun explained it to me. What happened was I thought I saw town. The sun was going down over the mountain and there were colors purple red pink yes in a way like that glass Gabrielle had a prison turning it into some kind of I don't know steps they looked like steps of colors that I thought I could walk out on all the way to where town used to be. In any event Cecil stopped me more roughly than he had to it's not like I was about to put up a fight. Too much of a fuss was made over it and these restrictions well all I can do now is sit here and think let my mind go where my body can't. Emily had just begun kindergarten. She was too young to understand of course there was all this excitement a reporter tried to question the children at school can you imagine he had the nerve to wait as they came out and then asked them some nonsense about science run amok or human experimentation words they had never heard before and that weren't appropriate anyway didn't fit the circumstances. It's crazy what they do to kids nowadays not shielding them not letting them be. No I don't think it affected her. She was her mother's daughter always helping out. I tried to interest her in the horses but she was terrified I think that may have been Alice's doing unconsciously of course. A child can tell. The way she would flinch Alice that is if she heard Allure snort or neigh the barn was a good two hundred feet back but when a horse is hungry. And then there was that business with Firebrand he couldn't be held responsible for that it was Ira Gray's mare from two miles down the road I told Alice it was the mare who jumped the fence Firebrand was just grazing peacefully just minding his own business he was a quiet creature not talkative. Emily does recall that or claims she does. I think maybe she recalls her mother's reaction more. It was quite a spectacle no not seeing one horse mount another I mean how Alice she began screaming. Allure no she would have none of it certainly not with Firebrand or any of the other suitors they brought by she was a fine horse too good for the types around these parts. In the end she began to drift to one side I thought it was her vision at first and tried blinders but the vet the county agent when I finally got him out here said it was muscular some kind of degeneration affecting only one half her body so she it's as if she was driving herself into walls into posts it was painful I pulled so hard to try and get her to stay on course but she couldn't comprehend couldn't understand. When I didn't take her out anymore she kicked at the stall door or showed everyone her teeth tried to bite Alice which was the last straw I suppose. Alice overreacted but it would have happened eventually and you get a better price if they're not too far gone if they're still relatively healthy still have some meat on their bones although it's the hoofs actually the man told me that bring in the most money they make gelatin out of the hoofs so next time you're eating Jell-O.

We survived. When there was no call for horses anymore I found other ways it's not a place for handouts here you have to work. Alice no her job was to raise Emily just Emily just the one. Certainly we wanted more but Alice she called it God's will a doctor no what could he say it just happened or didn't happen rather God's will one was enough that's what I would tell her. She would cry. Would I have liked a son? I don't know it's not as if I was such a great pleasure to my father so far as I can remember but of course there was a certain loneliness. I don't know whether it was greater than what other people feel or not I'm no expert. She had a garden out back Alice it got bigger and bigger by the end I had to clear some of the woods so the afternoon sun would reach the last row. Tomatoes eggplants which I don't care for much squash a lot of things I don't care for much it occurs to me now beans lettuce bushels of lettuce we didn't know what to do with it all cucumbers nothing useful. She'd take them to neighbors or we'd leave them out on a stand in the summer the honor system a box for money people paid. If they didn't the stuff would have rotted anyway. Everything comes at once that's the problem. Farming's the hardest job in the world my father poured his life out into a plot of land that grew mostly rocks from what I could tell he had me breaking my back out there before and after school and all summer that's why I never took much of an interest but Alice she had a green thumb she could make a stick grow. Actually everything grew too much things went crazy we had watermelons the size of well the size of watermelons I guess but that's still pretty big. It's the only reason she tolerated the horses was because of their manure. I'd find her there at night after dinner picking caterpillars out of the broccoli she said her plants were better company than me of course she was joking but it's true I came home tired. Emily would help her she'd run up and down the rows. I would read. The librarian Miss Dick she called me her best customer. She saved things for me or got them from the other libraries she would request things she took an interest in my education she was very sweet an elderly lady well not really elderly she seemed that way to me at the time her mouth it had that puckery shape I don't think anyone but children and myself went in not on any kind of regular basis. It was surrounded by spruce trees fifteen or twenty of them so the windows well it might as well not have had any windows they were so blocked off just one big room in front where Miss Dick's desk was and then the books not more than six or seven rows. In back there was a room for children. That was brighter because of the carpet. The floor in front creaked you couldn't make a move without setting off the whole apparatus. History was what I was mostly interested in. Greeks and Romans. Nothing happens now that hadn't already happened back then. She sat at her desk all day sharpening pencils making little notations in a book I have no idea about what. There was an ink pad and a stamp I took Emily a few times at different stages but she never showed much interest except in the ink pad. Once Miss Dick and I were talking and she managed to reach up over the desk and stick her fingers into it we had a time wiping up all those smudges she managed to get them everywhere I'm sure there are still a few oh I could never punish her that was Alice's job it's the woman's job to punish. I tried to show her an alternative a different side but she was having none of it Emily I mean which is fine she's content to be what she is. No she never has not yet. I wish she would marry but the men here I can't say I blame her they leave or drink too much and drive their cars into trees. I don't know about Emily's love life or if she even has one she makes those sticky buns that seems to be her main relaxation she's always bringing them over. I give them to Cecil. After she's gone of course. Love there's love between us how could you even ask you must not have children yourself love that's what makes things so difficult if we didn't love each other it wouldn't be so well I don't know so hard sometimes but she's a good girl it's just that there's a gap that's all. Between people. You shout across it or talk without saying anything or if it's a man and a woman you you know that's when people think they're touching the most when they do it but there's still the gap. Then sometimes unexpectedly it's gone you don't even know what happened why it went away or when it's coming back. The strangest thing is it can be with a total stranger or with someone you know but don't really want to know all that well it's like a lightning flash unexpected you're always surprised you jump that's what it was like with Lebrun and me we really didn't have anything in common especially later as he became successful and I well I told you I managed but it wasn't like anyone was building me a new house the way they did for him yes it's demol-

34

ished now but that little road off the dam that leads to the area
where the maintenance workers park their trucks that used to be a
house the dam keeper's house built by the Authority. Nothing fancy
but solid with a separate garage. He convinced them that they
needed someone on site who could man the controls in an emergency. They even ran a phone line there which was very unusual at
the time not a party line a private line so he could well I suppose let
water in and out what else is there to do in a dam it doesn't sound
that complicated to me but I must tell you in that little room he
took me to the one that's practically inside the structure there were
a million dials and gauges it almost made me wonder if it wasn't just
the dam I was in. Yes I know there's a power station below the turbines but besides that maybe the dam it's a way of diverting our attention from something. Well I wouldn't know would I because my
attention it's been diverted but all those dials and gauges and that
private line maybe they had a small submarine I don't know I'm just
imagining. Things were far more secretive then. People were afraid
of the Russians of men from outer space of monsters from the deep
even that northern pike people talked about babies wading too far
out into the water and never being seen again. Still they built him a
house you have to wonder why. The Authority seemed to have un-
limited money he took me for a ride in his truck I have to admit and
I was no fan of trucks they were my competition but it was a beautiful machine so comfortable. Springs he told me fancy shock absorb-
ers. It was in that office actually that little brick room that's when it
happened I was complaining about something Alice and I had had
one of our little disagreements when he reached out and touched a
dial adjusted it slightly and it was as if my mood was connected to
that dial he made it go up just a little less than a quarter turn but it
was as if my heart was connected to whatever that dial controlled
because the next minute I was happy. I turned to him it was such a
surprise and we both smiled and I thought for that one instant he

knew everything. I felt his eyes I told you they were of that gimlet-screw-tipped-piercing variety and I saw through them back into him saw that he understood things what I was feeling and I saw that he envied me for feeling what I felt. That was the strangest part of all that he lacked something I had. Me. It's like for that brief flash we understood each other the gap was gone. After? Nothing it's not like I realized all that at the time it was only after talking things over with Allure that I was able to put it into something like words words I could understand. Alice why would I tell Alice no she didn't like any of my friends she didn't even like Miss Dick or my going to the library she regarded books with suspicion I don't know why. Miss Dick and me never oh no there was never any a hint of. Greek and Roman history. But it bothered her I don't know why and sometimes I went back to my old ways took a nip or two but that's to be expected life deals you blows it was nothing our marriage couldn't handle nothing out of the ordinary the gap with us well yes but that almost becomes a necessary thing the gap between two married people after all you need your distance in a marriage you learn how to pitch your voice around it or over it the gap it becomes a third party how it widens or narrows you can't have moments like the one I had with Lebrun with whoever's frying your eggs each morning with the one who sees you at your worst. You wouldn't want that you need to have some distance.

～つ

My father well that's a sore spot because he had that quarrel you know with religion he felt that he was it's not a word he would use not a word he would even know but he felt he was persecuted there was some financial dealing some way he felt he had been taken advantage of. He wasn't buried in Conklingville no. There's a church way up in back of the beyond you might say over the mountain near Indian Pipes it's all boarded up and abandoned the church itself just one room not even a steeple but the graveyard if you can't afford it or if they won't let you in anywhere else well for five dollars then I don't even remember who I paid it to one of those charlatans but for five dollars they let anyone in there. Some mealy-mouthed preacher in the rain just the two of us he made me hold his umbrella as if I was his servant hold it high over his head so his bible wouldn't get wet his precious bible and two men from the town I didn't even know their names they had dug the hole it was barely the right shape the rain was caving it in on the very outskirts the last row but inside the barrier before the forest began. He said I'd have to come back in the spring and buy a stone but of course I didn't in those days people were eating acorns you pounded them up fried them in lard if you were lucky enough to have lard anyway yes up by Indian Pipes it was less than a town really just an old logging camp where someone had set up a store a true Indian they said a full-blooded Cherokee. I suppose that's where it gets its name or maybe from the plant I don't know. Indian pipes they're these white plants that you find in the forest they grow right up through the pine needles white pipes I don't know if there's any up there in particular or if it had to do with who knows maybe some souvenirs he sold. He was dead long before. The store the Trading Post that's what it was called his widow had taken it over she was a round-shaped woman no not an Indian she sold cigarettes gum dry goods whatever she could stock I took one canister of milk up there a week this was before bottles she had an icebox no I never stopped and paid my respects. He's not there any more than he's anyplace else. In his mind everyone was out to get him I'm the opposite I don't believe the world notices me I don't think it singles me out especially one way or the other. Father to him it was all a conspiracy all these forces bent on his destruction it's all in how you look at things. The berries they grow there near Indian Pipes the ones I told Christopher about I don't know of anywhere else in the north country where they grow like that but you have to know where to go you have to go high it's an interesting place on Mount Natherne behind the town there's a logging trail and off that there's a property line a wire fence old-style barbed wire with just a twist or two of sharpened metal every few inches. It's completely buried in pine needles now except every once in a while it rises up to where it was nailed against a tree. They didn't bother with fence posts couldn't drive them into the soil probably so there's just a bit of wire left hanging off a nail. What makes it interesting is the trees it's nailed to. There must be something in the iron or the rust of the nail because each tree is twisted in the exact same way they don't grow straight but with the trunk running parallel to the ground kind of. You can sit on them or lie on one even I remember stretching out it was as wide as a bench and ended in a knob instead of branches I had never seen anything like it it's from the nails the nails they must poison it somehow. And if you line yourself up pretend you're the fence and find where the nail on the other side is even though there's no more wire there even though it's buried or disintegrated underneath you can see a tree just like the one you're standing at misshapen in the same exact way maybe fifty feet off. I spent a whole afternoon once tracing that property line and the strange trees it produced. Then it ended. Maybe a few of the trees fell down and there wasn't a trail anymore maybe they continued farther up I don't know I had to go back and get the berries. They grow all around there. Not for Christopher for myself I told you when business dried up when I stopped getting so many calls for deliveries I turned to other things I forget how I knew about the berries it was common knowledge that they aided the digestion I didn't even know their name they were just those red berries up by Indian Pipes no no one told me there was this floating knowledge then you could reach into and take whatever it was you needed. What's happened to it the knowledge you mean? I'll tell you what's happened to it everyone's watching TV instead. You boiled them if you didn't boil them the effect was the opposite your stomach would throw them right back out at you but boiled they'd stay down. I stirred them with sugar and B&B you know what that is Brandy and Benedictine. Lebrun would bring it to me from Schuyler. The bottles to put it in they were the hardest to find I wasn't about to pay for new ones besides if they were all the same it would seem like something you get in a store in Varney's Drug for example. I kept an eye out for trash or old houses that had been abandoned that were falling down. People kept them in their windows colored bottles kind of like stained glass and then there was the dump of course that was my great resource I cooked it up in back. Alice complained about the smell not the money though people swore by it they'd buy two three bottles at a time more than I could make. Word went out when another batch was ready it got so I would look behind me when I went up there to pick them to make sure no one was following me. No labels that was part of the I wouldn't call it charm it wasn't snake oil the stuff really worked but not knowing what it came in having each bottle be different a different shape the colors too that was part of the appeal. Women liked that brownish-tan glass that medicines came in men were more interested in the brighter colors blue or purple there was a brand of liniment that came in black that tickled them drinking out of a black bottle. Of course I washed them out boiled them too I didn't want anyone getting sick. For babies with indigestion or teething pains that was another use just a teaspoon of course it was quite a sideline for a while. No it wasn't an elixir just a remedy. Lebrun used to laugh he said it was a remedy looking for an affliction but those trees some-times I wondered if you could see them from the air if they would make some kind of path or shape I followed them as far as I could but. Oh I couldn't even show you if I wanted to I couldn't even get to the base of the logging trail much less up to where Indian Pipes that woman Mrs. Larsen that's what she called herself well that's a good question how could she be married to a Cherokee Indian if she didn't take his name well some of them didn't have names Christian names that is they'd just be Joseph and the rest was tribal. The white man wasn't supposed to know. Besides she couldn't call herself Mrs. Flies-with-Eagles or whatever his secret name was. She had a bicycle I do remember that. That was unusual back then. It was always propped against the side of the store as if someone had just come in and was buying something and then was going to pedal off again but it never moved from one year to the next. I suppose she took it inside in the winter and there was a totem pole too hand-carved. Yes a totem pole with faces rising up ten twelve feet. Her husband I assume. The Trading Post I haven't thought about that place in years.

∿

It all began to go downhill when the glove factory closed they did some dirty deal the lawmakers there was a law saying you couldn't import gloves oh everyone wore them then all the women you couldn't go out in the street unless you were wearing gloves there were shops whole shops just devoted to them but then some cabal some group of thieves they paid off the legislature to pass a law saying partially made gloves could be imported. Well partially made turned out to mean gloves with only one button missing so they'd ship these so-called unfinished gloves down from Canada then just sew on one button and overnight the industry disappeared the plant closed and Antone was never really the same. Ever since then town's had a kind of after-the-fact feeling. The only places that make money here are the liquor store and the funeral home. The paper mill still operates but just barely it's owned by some foreign company now. Kathan's better it has tourism at least Lake Kathan and all those bungalows. It's a prettier place what with the Green and the bandstand the houses have a kind of look to them with that gingerbread trim and all. I used to go to the concerts there everyone did Saturday nights in the summer the bandstand I remember they used to play Stars and Stripes Forever It's a Grand Old Flag why that brought on such a feeling I don't know the cymbals clashing and all those horns. There were fireworks on the Fourth of July the town still had money then and enough people for an all-volunteer band. Now you couldn't even find someone to organize such a thing. The bandstand itself is still there they've maintained that even though there's no one left to play it's a nice little town down to one intersection really where 9N meets the Greenfield Road. You've got Varney's Drug on one corner Red's Esso or whatever it's called now the gas station on the other then Walt's diner. That was quite a mistake he ordered a sign saying COUNTRY CORNER but I have no idea why it came reading COUNTRY CORONER. He didn't even notice until it was hoisted into place nobody told him I don't think he saw it himself for the first few days and by then well it was high up on the building not easy to take down I'd never seen anyone actually shake his fist before but there was nothing he could do the company claimed that's how he'd filled out the form besides he'd signed for it. It became a point of pride as if we had a fancy restaurant here not just another hash house he even said it Country Coroner when he answered the phone. I'm not sure he knew what it meant. Walt's gone and his sign too there's just the gas station and Varney's Drug. In the summer there are summer businesses the ice cream stand the man who rents rafts inflatable rafts but I don't count them because after Labor Day they disappear Miss Dick used to say after Labor Day you could shoot a cannonball down the street and not hit a soul. She kept the library open all year come hell or high water. There must have been days when nobody walked in and in the winter well you could actually feel the wood shrinking in on itself. I used to think there were less and less books on each shelf they never seemed to reach the ends when it got cold because they were huddled together. All Miss Dick would do is wear a shawl you could practically see your breath. There was a budget but from what I gather she spent most of it by October and that included her salary. They say she only bought soup canned soup though I ran into her at the North Country Market once and she had six bottles of birch beer which surprised me it was this nasty drink bright purple one of those fizzy sodas for kids. Maybe that was her secret vice. She got me to read all of Thucydides he's a Greek no not that kind of Greek an old-fashioned one. The wars between Athens and Sparta it's funny we have a Sparta here. If I hadn't had to leave high school. I used to sit with my book on Saturday mornings sit in the bandstand and read while Alice and Emily shopped. I suppose I count those among my happiest times I can't say why maybe knowing that they were about to return but not back yet and my being gone myself in my mind but also sitting there smack dab in the middle of Kathan my finger traveling across the page. There's no place like that in Antone. It's a mill town unless you go down by the river there is that little riverside park but it's more for children to swim in they don't mind the backwash from the mill it's green sometimes the water not a natural green green like detergent from the wood pulp they say but Antone's a real town at least it doesn't close up in the winter you've got the Leather and Lace you've got Hig's. I don't go anywhere anymore I told you I can't move except for when the van takes us into town. To go anywhere else I'd need help and well Cecil's job just between you and me Cecil's job is the opposite he's not here to help he's here to make sure we don't go anyplace. What's so great about staying inside? I ask him. It's safe he says. Shows you what he knows. I look around and all I see is danger. You've got to give death a moving target. Stay in one spot too long death it fixes its sights on you I don't mean you should travel halfway around the world no but you can't linger too long any one place in your mind you've got to be like those bugs on the water they go in spurts have you ever watched one with their feet pressing down little reflections little dimples where they must see themselves on the surface but always moving to no place in particular but never staying still. I don't say things like that to Cecil no he'd think I was crazy well he already does but there's the matter of food what he serves us I don't want him to think of me as a difficulty there are some people the difficult ones he mashes up pills in their dinners you can tell it's like they've sat too long in their bodies they become part of the chair their heads droop down and so I stay on his good side or I try to but secretly I keep my mind active. What do I think about? Well for example what if I'd followed Gabrielle's hair up instead of down to her head I mean where all those braids came from where they gathered and organized before becoming one and swaying down her back. I was a young man then I did one thing after another but now I think back and try imagining the reverse like one of those salmon going upstream. Dams are murder on them they can't figure out what's blocking their path they keep leaping it's a sight. Lebrun he was more fisherman than I I never cared for that part where you whack them against the side of the boat or slit their belly with a knife I could never but he took me in that skiff one day we carried it to the other side below the turbines where no one's allowed it's too close to the machinery but he it was springtime and there were hundreds of them hurling themselves out of the water like little torpedoes twisting splashing back trying again it was utterly hopeless we could see but they couldn't. There was well besides the elevation itself there were the turbines but they had a memory of where they came from when they were young of going over the spillway see it's easy for them to go down but back up again of course that's difficult impossible but it's all they wanted the rest of life's illusions had burned away and all they were left with was this desire to go back. I was upset by it by this desire to return to kill themselves basically. Lebrun he just wanted to make sure we weren't caught. It's illegal they're so unguarded you could have practically scooped them out of the water with your hand they were so exhausted their fins all tattered their gills working they were going to die anyway he said so why not catch a few? I did but in a very half-hearted way I tried not to hook anything I'd cast far from the mouth of the turbines where the water churned where you could see them jumping I pretended to be interested in the view craning my neck trying not to see what was happening right at my feet. He had the boat full they were wriggling and flopping all along the bottom he didn't even have time to kill them and even in their death agonies they were still trying to flop upstream. But Gabrielle. Sometimes I wonder if I had gone up instead of down. I suppose if you want to take the long view you could say they were the lucky ones the ones he caught because they did make it over the dam afterward that is after he'd collected them stuffed them in a sack and taken them back to his house that's on the other side only a few yards but still. Maybe they could sense it the ones who were still lingering before he put them out of their misery. That they'd crossed over. He was one of the first people in these parts to have a freezer.

∽

That's not the quarry. Kids they call that part you're talking about the Swallow Slides because of the birds. Kids break in well they step over that chain that blocks the road and then they slide down the mountain face. I was sitting in my spot once yes the quartz pit behind them and up when I heard a whole bunch whooping and hollering it distracted my thoughts so I got up to go when well I'm at the top you see they were all below me I was out of sight to them I don't know how many of them there were at first oh fourteen or fifteen years old I guess but by the time I came out of the woods they'd gone almost all of them there were just two left a boy and a girl. It was very awkward because I was right on top of them practically and they were talking. Well I'm no Peeping Tom or whatever a listener like that is called but you can't close your ears the way you can close your eyes that's the problem. I couldn't have been more than ten feet away but totally hidden almost directly overhead on the part of

44

the mountain where there's still soil while they were lying back on the sand where the birds nest the warm part the part that got the light. No they weren't. What a filthy mind you have. They were just talking they were kids. I heard her say how difficult this time had been the hardest summer of her life she said and I wondered what happened had some parent left or maybe it was a bad time in her you know development becoming a woman and all I don't know because of course I came in in the middle of it and also because I really didn't want to listen I couldn't move without them hearing me so I tried to just. It was more the tone of what they were saying than the words. I don't think they were boyfriend and girlfriend I'd say they were maybe friends although that seems unlikely at that age especially it's hard to be be friends a boy and a girl. But I couldn't really move I was trapped there I was afraid if they saw me or heard me I would ruin it for them I didn't want to ruin their moment this young couple if in fact they were a young couple. Brother and sister? I never thought of that. I stayed perfectly still except raising my pint of Old Gentleman to my lips every once in a while it's funny I can't remember a single other thing she said or what his answers were because he must have been saying something back I just remember crouching there trying not to make a sound and drinking more than I should have and the swallows how they couldn't go home their nests were right there but they were spooked by those kids they flew around and around making those cheeping sounds you know. When they're in a group like that they look like a brain a brain yes all the chemicals going back and forth that's all the brain is you know it's a flock of swallows a cloud of chemicals we get Science magazine here. The cover's ripped off so I don't know the date but news like that about the brain or the stars doesn't go bad certainly not from month to month. Anyway the birds they kept circling it was past their bedtime they can be quite nasty creatures when you get in their way get between them and their young ones but the boy and the girl

45

they were too busy talking no they didn't move at all no cuddling maybe they were brother and sister it never occurred to me before though certainly I never talked that way with Rebecca. Why did she leave well if you must know she left because someone offered to take her. Yes a man of course. It was a great disgrace at the time. I've come to take a more long view of it since like boys who go off to war I've come to think of it a woman going off with a man I mean how many other ways are there for her to get out? She left with one of those clienteles of Cochrane and Christopher she worked there as a maid first a laundress actually they let pretty girls work there that was part of their plan keep the clientele happy she even got promoted to the inner sanctum where Cochrane supervised the treatments hosing people down with ice-cold spring water is what it sounded like from what she told me which wasn't much she wasn't supposed to talk about it at all they swore everyone to secrecy. Some man from the city. She never talked about him. It all happened very fast god knows what it was or how long it lasted once they got away from here I mean maybe she thought they were getting married maybe they did I never heard another word I never met him so I never even knew the name under which she might be living. I came home from school one day and Father was out in the field later than usual working away to no point just like always. That's how he was. Not a successful farmer. He would put in the hours but it was almost like punishment punishing himself not with any sort of plan in mind and there was an envelope on the table it was already opened so he had read it. An envelope she had taken from the clinic it was fancy it had raised lettering but the paper inside she must have written the note here I mean at home because it was torn out of that journal she kept so maybe she hadn't decided until the last minute. What she wrote? Nothing meaningful. I barely remember. The journal Mother had given her that journal to write her thoughts. I went to the window and looked out. His shoulders the way he was attacking the earth it was. He liked those kind of hopeless battles pitting himself against impossible odds so he could lose I guess so he could say later that he lost with honor no we never discussed it. I don't remember who cooked dinner that night it's a good question. Her room? Neither of us moved into it it never occurred to us I don't know why it was tainted I suppose or maybe we thought she'd come back. After a while we filled it up with things junk implements trash neither of us went in there much we continued to share the one bed but he came home later and later. That's how I learned to drink from his example. At the quarry what happened was I got tired of waiting. I knew Alice would be upset. She worried sitting at the kitchen table all rigid-like. I retraced my steps I didn't want to disturb them the boy and the girl I tried blundering my way out through the woods. I knew where I was going but there was no path a branch hit me right across the face it didn't help that I had had too much Old Gentleman. I kept it in the barn Alice never went there. I'd bury it in the bottom of the oat bin Allure and I would trade a look. Anyhow I made it to the road. It's always strange when you come out from the woods in an odd place and the road is there. It doesn't look like it normally does because it's just a random section one you just pass by unknowingly if you're in the cart or certainly in an automobile. The boy and the girl? No I don't remember who they turned out to be the people who come after you they're never as interesting as the people who come before. Father for example. No I don't think I'm anything like him I told you he thought the world was out to get him he thought so highly of himself that the world noticed him moved itself to crush him like a bug I know I'm nothing nobody in the general scheme of things. That flock of birds that brain they didn't even notice me they saw the boy and the girl the young lovers the brother and sister whoever they were I was just invisible just part of the fabric of things. We all are part of the fabric but some don't realize it don't accept it. They tangle up the pattern try and stand out but of course it's impossible they make this big mess and call it an achievement. Lebrun with his empire what did it amount to? Eagle Enterprises that's what it was called. Well he looked like one they said an eagle from the side what would you call that his profile just his eyes I think is what they really meant and his attitude that he would swoop down and take advantage of the situation. Anyway he worked so hard and did so much and now who remembers him? Just me and pretty soon.

~~∽~~

Well that's the big question isn't it where did the money come from? I don't know not his salary no one got paid that kind of money then and the bank would never have loaned a Canuck anything. For what? To buy worthless land or what seemed like worthless land at the time. He spread his arm out indicating and then fifteen or so years later he owned no not all of it but chunks here and there built houses at first by himself and then with crews all while keeping his job at the dam so he could do both. Vacation homes with wide decks and kitchens that were part of the living room so you could drink eat do god knows what else all at the same time and glass whole walls made of glass facing the lake the reservoir so from the other side when the sun hit them they'd flash these glass walls. It was unsettling at first birds used to fly into them I remember early on going with him to one hearing him chew out the crew about something. He found these men I don't know where. They would live on the site no not from around here they were totally dependent on him shifty types they spoke Italian some of them I went with him to one of the sites and it was half-finished but the wall was up the glass wall and I found a hummingbird dead right by the sliding door. It was per-fectly preserved ruby-throated copper and green one of the prettiest things I'd ever seen you don't usually get to see them up close they're always in motion even though they're standing still in midair there's always that buzz around them their wings always going but this I'd never seen one so still. I turned it around looked at it from all sides it fit not even in the palm of my hand but the hollow. I could have made a fist around it with the bird inside and you wouldn't have noticed a thing not a part would have stuck out. Lebrun came up behind me I must have been staring getting that look Alice complained about he said You shouldn't touch dead things but I didn't want to just let it drop even back to where I found it it seemed wrong somehow now that I'd held it. I tried to show him how perfect it was. He finally took it from me I thought to look at it but then he just threw it into the forest. They were all around here that kind of house by the end. He bought the plans off some architect and then adjusted them to the ground to the terrain. Me I just brought bricks when it was up a trail when it was too hard for a truck to make a delivery or once he hired me to stay in one of his places overnight. It was only half-done but he had fired the crew I don't know why and he was afraid they would come back maybe burn down the place or at least damage it so I stayed there. Alice was OK with that she didn't mind. The money he paid me was more than I made in a oh I've never minded being alone there was no electricity but I brought a lantern and the fireplace worked not that I made a fire but it was there to look at that's always the first thing they put up after they pour the foundation. Freddie Seaborne he worked in the mill but he had this talent for stone he did the fireplaces on Lebrun's homes the stones all fit together he'd spend hours with this big pile he'd collect I'd watch him hold one up then another they all looked the same to me. Then he used lampblack mixed it in with the cement so it gave every stone an outline so you really looked at it the hearth the chimney all the way up. I liked his work. No we had an oil burner we needed it for heat not looks. That night he'd left me two chairs and I propped my feet up on one. If you've driven a horse-drawn cart no seat that's standing still seems hard. I was just about to drop off when there was a knock it was on the glass door. I slid it back and there was Lebrun he pushed past me and when I turned to follow him that's when I noticed the blood it was in drops on the brick floor. He headed to the sink so the water must have been hooked up just not the electricity he was holding his arm. At first I thought there was a bandage but when I looked closer it was just the sleeve of his shirt all torn and bloody. I asked what happened but for a long time he didn't say anything just washed the wound in the new sink probably the first time it had ever been used see that's an example of how cool he could be the hotter the situation the more cool he would get like by going so far in the other direction he could bring things back to the middle to normal somehow. I watched him strip off his shirt it was a ball of blood and wash out this long slash on his arm. He didn't say anything to my first question and I knew him well enough not to ask any more I just went over and held up the lantern so he could see better he had a handkerchief a clean handkerchief he was always very particular about that a big white flowing one he would never blow his nose into just use to wipe things off a doorknob or a glass at Walt's a water glass even though it was already clean he took out his handkerchief and I helped him tie it so after a while the flow of blood stopped it was still bad though I told him to go see Doc Harmon but once he got it bandaged he took the other chair and we sat in front of the fireplace just staring into the empty grate and him holding his arm. At first I thought it was some member of the crew he had fired taking revenge on him because some of those types I could easily see them with knives he laughed at that though the idea that any of those wops would have the courage. Ed Bailey he finally said. What about him? I asked. Ed Bailey was supposed to be in Sparta he said. Ed Bailey was the mill manager. A tough son of a bitch. He did go to Sparta a lot that's where the bosses were I suppose he got back late most nights then it all became clear of course his wife Maureen although I couldn't believe it at first because well because she wouldn't be my type not my first choice but of course in these matters that's when you realize that it's all a joke the idea that there's any such thing as beauty that it's transferable I mean from one person to the next the idea of beauty because Maureen Bailey she well who am I to say none of us is much to look at if you stare too long but I just sat with him. That's when he asked about Alice he was always what's the word caring a lot about our marriage taking its temperature I don't know why. If I would complain he would tell me how good she was which she was of course for all my complaining she was good which puts a strain on things. Lebrun was sensitive to that he's the only one who understood her saw how special she was except for Emily and me even though they had no contact and she well the feeling wasn't exactly mutual she would practically go into a fit if I mentioned his name she blamed him for all my missteps. I tried telling her he didn't drink he just kept me company anyway there he was holding his arm that bandage filling up he'd let his hair grow long by then so he looked more like an Indian eagle-like I guess and then it came out I don't know how it wasn't related to anything but he asked did I think there were men from outer space? Well it wasn't such a strange thing to talk about in those days this was before the moon launch or any kind of satellite little green men they were part of the folklore I suppose like elves and goblins used to be I said I didn't know and he said he thought sometimes they were living among us. I remember I asked who because he said it like he knew like he had someone specific in mind but he just smiled. Ed Bailey? I asked. I thought maybe that was the only way he could imagine a man getting the better of him but he frowned as if he hadn't even heard the name before as if it was another conversation entirely even though his arm I'm telling you it was all puffed up. Living among us doing what? I finally asked. Then he answered. That's how he was if what you said didn't go in the direction he was heading he just ignored it. Doing nothing he said just living among us. The funny thing is Ed Bailey the next morning we heard he'd had a terrible accident his car they said it was right when he got home he was driving home from Sparta and his brakes just as he was coming to the end of the driveway his brakes failed he was so bruised up two black eyes a few broken bones they had to take him back downstate in an ambulance that was the last anyone ever saw of him or his wife Maureen they were just gone. The house it sold I think without their ever coming back I don't know about their possessions maybe they had them sent for no one knew what really happened except me of course. I don't know why Lebrun was talking about little green men he had lost a lot of blood. He did eventually go to Doc Harmon but not until the next day and then he told some cockamamie story about a saw blade snapping. Alice she never suspected a thing she never realized he was on her side.

～

A tattoo no he didn't have a tattoo what kind of question is that? I don't know why people get those things. Why mark up your body it's like renting it out turning yourself into a billboard an advertisement for something. Ed Mosher he claimed when he woke up with his tattoo that it was none of his doing he didn't even know he'd got one until later because it was on his back. He was over in Schuyler on one of his binges he came back here and a few days later someone had to read it to him it still didn't make sense didn't ring a bell even when they spelled it out. Lorene. It's a name apparently though not one I've ever heard it got to be a joke around town strung from shoulder to shoulder like that in big letters. Hey Ed how's Lorene? people would call. Well there was no shortage of women to read his back I can tell you. They liked to take care of him mother him but little green men I don't know where Lebrun got that from maybe he'd seen one out there in the woods when he was dripping blood maybe you see them more when you're taken out of your element bleeding and such everything gets strange like that road I remember stumbling onto when I cut through the forest that time to avoid the boy and girl well it was just the road but I had no idea where I was I'd traveled it a thousand times before knew every tree and leaf but if you'd told me it was another planet I wouldn't be so surprised. Take one go ahead they live up to their name that's for sure sticky like flypaper. It's very nice of her to bring them she makes them by the hundred takes them all over gives them to everybody I wish she wouldn't. She's known as the Sticky Bun Lady that's what I hear yes I still hear things well there are the other residents they have visitors and the van takes us into town once a week I go to the luncheonette I sit at the counter there's a waitress Vera she gets me an egg sandwich that's all I eat anymore an egg sandwich and a cup of coffee. She's from someplace else everyone is now. People drift I don't know why. Back then it was only the hippies who came through like that and even they had a kind of purpose to them more than the people today they were after something. I didn't mind them not as much as some around here. It was funny the summer they first came because town Antone I mean was celebrating its sesquicentennial sesquicen it means one hundred and fifty years since the place was founded I don't know by who by someone who couldn't go a step farther anyway there was a kind of proclamation they posted everywhere that in honor of that all the men in town should grow beards to take us back to that time eighteen-whatever. So everyone grew a beard and then there were wooden nickels that had the town's name on it and a picture an artist's rendering they called it of how Antone used to look which was almost exactly the same as it did now it was redeemable this wooden nickel all through town at all the shops can you imagine? There was civic pride then. And organization. People cared. Nowadays cars just whiz through people stop for soda and gasoline get back in and keep going I have no idea where. Back then it was actually a home even if it wasn't yours you sensed it that it was a home to someone. Anyway that summer there were all these fes-

tivities a banner stretched across 9N and we began to notice kids
these kids who appeared with backpacks and sleeping bags or in
those big what do you call them buses a Volkswagen bus the kind
you could live in if you were a bum practically a hobo but all these
kids had beards too the boys the girls they looked even more like
pioneer women than our wives yes the wives were supposed to wear
long dresses and bonnets that never caught on as much as the beards
but these hippies they just blended in at first eating at the luncheonette or camping out at the KO Kampsite you'd be sitting at the counter scratching your hairy jaw and this kid next to you he'd look like
he'd stepped out of a log cabin. Except they had all sorts of you know
colorful touches which I must say I liked. Other people wanted to
hold them down and cut their hair off by force which I found kind
of funny grown men with full muttonchop side-whiskers themselves
grumbling about the filthy hippies how they never bathed and whatnot it was in the air you see what we did as a kind of historical thing
they playacted it even more tried to make it real. I didn't mind. I
thought they looked good. I still had Allure then and they went
crazy when they saw her. The town hired me to give children rides a
hayride we filled it up with hay in back and I nailed extra high rails
so no one could fall out it was part of the festivities but very few of
the local children took advantage I suppose a hayride seemed old-
fashioned to them. I think they were also a little afraid of Allure
because she I didn't know then but she was in her illness the start of
it and beginning to act up she'd make sounds not neighing much
more threatening than that like a growl but high-pitched it scared
children I remember one boy he before they even lifted him up he
started crying and struggling so much they had to but the hippies
once they heard about it they piled on. The town was furious of
course they'd paid me money and then all these outsiders took advantage. It looked like something out of a circus twenty or so long-
haired kids hanging off the sides climbing up to the very top singing

songs. One of them rode next to me sat on the bench Saara like Sara but with an extra a. She had long blonde hair almost down to her backside. She wore daisies in it and once butterfly milkweed yes the orange kind although I told her I warned her the milk you know that liquid that comes out when you cut the stem that's sticky but she didn't seem to mind. The route was through town from the river park to the cemetery. We'd turn around in that lot there I did it on the hour some of them took it two three times a day then they'd go back to the campsite and do god knows what. Saara she invited me there once they were having a party that night no but it was a very nice gesture. Well the sap whatever you call that stuff in milkweed it's sticky. To get it in such long fine hair. I suppose she didn't mind. It did look that orange against her long blonde hair it did look beautiful she might have been the prettiest girl I ever met. There were all these boys and girls but you couldn't tell who was what if you know what I mean. Saara didn't really belong with the rest of them they were always laughing smoking that stuff I could smell it behind me sometimes they would half-bury themselves in the hay so no one could see I was afraid they would light the cart on fire. Allure's ears would prick she was mad at me that and having a girl next to me on the bench oh horses know. She didn't need eyes in the back of her head for that. Her tail the way it would swish but Saara I think she wanted to get away from them sitting with me up front she asked about flowers and birds I even let her take the reins once but that was a mistake that's when Allure almost drove us into the filling station pump what's that brand called with the flying horse into the Mobil station yes. Everyone laughed but we almost toppled over that would have taken some explaining. Emily no she never came she was helping Alice in the garden or around the house it was a beautiful summer I took maybe it was the last time Allure and I ever went out together I took that bunch up to Indian Pipes. They paid me. I was as surprised as anyone that they had the money. They dressed so scruffy but one of them I forget his name with a beard of course their leader I guess I must have told Saara about Indian Pipes about the berries up there and the trees and she must have told him because he asked me about it what it would cost to take everyone up there for the day and when I named some ridiculous amount he reached into his pocket and took it out in cash. Swartz that's what it was a Jewish name but with the beard he looked just like everybody else. There was also I forgot to tell you a kangaroo court for men who wouldn't grow a beard. There were a few more than a few at first I don't know if it had to do with not liking being told what to do or not liking how they would have looked. One I remember John Fairchild he even said he couldn't do it for religious reasons which is just typical how you use it for whatever you want religion. But the pressure to not shave like I said there was a real feeling of community spirit not like now. They'd put up posters with their pictures the ones who didn't shave that's all the kangaroo court was really court of public opinion I guess they didn't hold an actual session or anything but tried to shame them by showing the ones without beards like they were criminals. One by one the holdouts stopped shaving until yes that's right how did you know only Lebrun his picture was on every power pole and taped up in the newsroom. It looked like he was running for office or something. He didn't seem to mind. You could even say it backfired that he seemed the most manly man in town clean-shaven staring out at you from all the signs while the rest of us were like a herd of sheep even looking like a herd of sheep all fuzzy you could barely tell us apart.

~

It must have been on a Sunday I took them up because there was no hayride Sundays Reverend Berrian insisted. They brought I was fearful actually I was afraid it would turn into a wild drinking party but all they brought was fruit. I know it was supposed to be like something out of eighteen-whatever with the hayride and the beards but looking over my shoulder I saw them eating grapes and thought it could be a scene right out of the bible. No I've never read it myself but from stained-glass windows and that picture Gabrielle had I sort of got the idea of how things looked back then. We went along fine at first it's fairly level until you go off the main road then Allure started pulling tricks on me. I shouldn't be so hard on her she was sick but I didn't know it or didn't want to see it she kept wandering to one side as if there was another road as if it sheered off into the woods. We were just outside of town. I passed my own house but Alice and Emily were out back they well Alice in particular wouldn't have approved especially on a Sunday I don't know where she got that from her father was hardly a model of religion maybe in reaction yes because he was so strange that's the word she always used strange it's as far as she'd go in criticizing him. She used the same word for me when I did things but with me she'd go further in criticizing I mean anyway we ran into trouble on the old logging trail it hadn't been well maintained and Allure stumbled a few times on stones. There was a lot of dirt blowing back. I like a dirt road and so did Allure most times. It's easier on their hooves and the color that light tan it's easier on your eyes especially in summer but that day she was getting hard to handle. Firebrand he was just clip-clopping along he didn't have as much personality as Allure he was a quiet soul but she was acting up making that growling sound. The kids they were smoking by then it smells like alfalfa to me no Saara wasn't sitting next to me she was with the others she'd moved to the back after our accident maybe they teased her about it I don't know by the time we got to the Trading Post my arms were ready to fall off. I got down and gave Allure a piece of my mind. She was having none of it she could be the orneriest creature her tail swishing in the heat like she wanted to whip you over the head with it they all piled out the kids. They hadn't been aware of anything. One had a guitar. Mrs.

Larsen she was still there she could barely walk had her hair up in a gray bun but she was still there they bought I don't know where their money came from they talked about free-this free-that but they certainly had spending money ice cream chocolate bars they had a feast on the field at the base of the path. Saara put some black-eyed Susans in her hair. I guess she was a flower child though I've never thought of her that way before. It was just as well we rested because I had to settle down Allure and Firebrand get them all fixed up. No I don't remember the bicycle what a memory you have I'm sure it was leaning against the wall outside the door just like always but I was busy horses it's not like you turn off the ignition key and slam the doors I got them settled and by then the kids I have no idea what I ate I must have brought something a baloney sandwich some-thing like that Alice would slap together a sandwich most days balo-ney liverwurst deviled ham but when the kids were ready we went into the woods. I showed them the berries I don't know why. Yes it was a secret but they weren't from here so I figured Swartz the tall one he seemed to know all about them or acted like he did he called them by some name I don't know a Latin name and said they had properties well everything has properties. They all nodded the others like it meant something. I took them up to where the first tree was the ones that are shaped funny. It was quite a walk farther than I re-membered steeper too and when they saw the berries they acted like I'd shown them a gold mine or something. I don't know why I warned them you couldn't just eat them raw you had to boil them or else your stomach. Saara then she took my arm and I guess it was the trees they had the same effect on her that they had on me she wanted to walk that line where the fence ran go from tree to tree the others they stayed behind. I was afraid Swartz was going to come with us I was beginning to see well with those flowers in her hair and the way she moved she could step so lightly it was like she didn't weigh any-thing I was afraid he was going to come with us I could see in his eyes that he wanted to but then he stayed stayed with the others and so we went off. I showed her how if you stood right where the nail was hammered into the tree trunk did I mention that before? I can't remember everything I've said. They weren't regular nails they were big rusty wedge-shaped nails the kind a blacksmith used to make almost like a piece of pie. I think that's how the rust from the iron must have gotten into the tree's system into its blood its sap or whatever because the shape was so unusual it must have pried something open. We tramped for at least a mile farther than I'd gone before. The other time I'd lost track of the trail but this time she had better eyes she stared and stared and found the missing link the tree I'd missed before when I'd given up. It was bent like the others but not as much maybe the nail hadn't I don't know like a bullet missing your heart it was misshapen just a little but then on the other side when we got there me panting she just bounding around I'd never seen her so happy that's true I barely knew her at all but I could tell she was happy she'd had a kind of sadness to her before when we got to the other side of this tree well there it was the next one about twenty yards off and with an actual section of the fence still leading away from it so we knew. Hear that? That's the Emergency Squad. Wonder where they're going. They can save your life if they reach you in time. Of course usually when they save you it's better if they hadn't. Because when they bring you back when they save you it's already too late usually part of you has already gone off due to lack of oxygen. Like Norm for example. He was never the same once they found him and stuck all those things in him electrocuted him basically from what I hear. Everyone said how lucky he was and on the surface well he walked out of this hospital his wife Cheryl I remember Cheryl saying what a miracle it was but then it was like a different person had taken over his body or worse than that that the real him was somehow coming out in a way it hadn't before like the leaves you know in the fall everyone says they turn colors but really

59

that's their true color coming out the chloroform that's what makes them green no I know what I'm talking about I read it in Science magazine the chloroform it knocks unconscious the true color and then when it goes away in the fall everyone says Look at the colors but really they were there all along underneath. Well Norm he was always the nicest man which is hard when you're a bartender but once he got out of the hospital he got this mean streak in him that was more than a streak. Cheryl eventually had to where does the chloroform go when it leaves I don't know how should I know? By then they'd turned it into a family restaurant just like every other place around here the roadhouses I don't know what happened there used to be all sorts of wild places here not that I ever. There are better ways to spend your money. She had to go live with her mother he holed himself up in that house no one dared go near it poking his shotgun out who was it some boy had a paper route and instead of throwing it onto his porch walked it up once because it was snowing so it wouldn't get wet you know tucked it in the screen door and well Norm took a shot at him or in his general direction. This was a perfectly decent man up until then it's like that part of him had left the part that makes us not kill each other. My true color you mean if I was a leaf? Well of course there are evergreens at least that's what I'd like to think I am green covered by green. Other people might tell you different. Norm? Nothing. I mean I don't remember. That's what happened to him what I already told you. The rest? Everyone passes that's not a story a story is what happens to you along the way. There are bends in your life like a pipe when you get to an elbow in a pipe and it goes in a different direction not just straight that was his that was the bend in his life his heart stopping and coming back and him not being the same after. I don't know what happened later I mean I do but it's not important he died of course there are you satisfied? Vera? She gives me an egg sandwich and a cup of oh Saara yes she was we followed it that's all until the end. Well it must have been some old-time loggers' line before they had surveyors we were getting near the top of the mountain and then there was this wall of saplings not saplings really but trees hundreds of them you couldn't get past. It was a growth I'd never seen anything like before. They must have shaved off the whole peak maybe forty fifty years ago shaved it clean because what grew there instead it's like nothing had a head start so all these trees at once started shooting straight up not even growing branches just bolting for the sunlight that's what they do it's a race so close together that's what I couldn't figure out I never saw anything like it a solid wall unnatural nothing like a true forest really almost like a garden planted by some I was going to say some evil spirit I don't know why. I didn't like it I wanted to turn back. For one thing I was exhausted I remember sitting on a rock the flies were bad and saying We have to go back but Saara of course she was much more well she was younger for one thing she just turned herself sideways basically and went through this wall disappeared on the other side of it. I called out her name I was worried. I couldn't see her after the first few feet but I also knew there was no way I could follow her in it was almost like a sieve the trees were packed so tight together I was too big I couldn't fit but I felt responsible like I was her father and started calling her name that's when that boy that fellow Swartz appeared. He must have been following us I didn't realize it at the time I was so busy keeping an eye on her he said he heard me calling but there's no way he could have come so fast we were too far up he must have been watching us although I don't know why it's not like I was going to try and no I never thought of such a thing I must have been in my well more than twice her age. He came right up behind me running and then he kept going into the trees just the way she did. He was a skinny little bastard pardon my French on a boy it's not as attractive he disappeared right between two tree trunks just where she had. I heard him calling her name. I didn't like the way he used it. More familiar. He was calling her and disappearing deeper

61

away from me and then I heard them find each other you could tell by the way he stopped and I heard just for a second her voice I think she was surprised that he had appeared and then they must have gone on maybe there was a clearing maybe they reached the top I don't know. I didn't hear them anymore. After a while I got tired of waiting and decided what with the trees and bits of fence they could find their own way back going downhill it's easier you just follow gravity basically so I went back to take care of Allure. The rest of them they had gathered a million berries. I was a little ticked off but of course it was my own fault I don't know what I expected. They grow back if you pick them early enough. Swartz I guess he ran a tighter ship than I give him credit for he had left them these burlap sacks they filled. I didn't know what they were planning to do. To aid the digestion yes but without the B&B I'm not sure if their medicinal properties really anyway he and Saara came down later maybe an hour or so they must have had a rough time of it finding their way because they were all mussed up burrs in her hair I noticed and the colored handkerchief he usually had looped in his blue jeans was missing. I asked them what it was like there beyond the wall of trees but they couldn't really describe it or rather they did but each said something different. By then Allure was giving me more cause for concern acting up again that's when I began to notice or began to realize rather that it was serious her condition. No Saara didn't sit with me on the bench for the ride home she rode in back with the rest just as well really I had a hell of a time.

~

I told you from the little park by the river up Main Street then veering right at the Mobil station a red horse with wings Pegasus yes but Allure didn't try and go there because of the horse no I don't think she wanted to. With the horse? With the picture of a winged horse on a gas pump? No that's a very funny idea but it was a muscular

62

degeneration the county agent said past the gas station and the bank then past Mosher's or whatever it's called now then south again up past the school and then that lot where the buses turn around after they've dropped off the children or the hearses park yes by the cemetery. I must know three-quarters of the families buried there I spent a fair amount of time at that cemetery that summer in particular I couldn't go back you see there was no place to wait the cart would have blocked traffic. Besides Allure didn't like having cars and trucks whiz by I can't say I blame her so at the end of the run after I dropped everyone back where I'd started I'd do it again but much faster with no people and sit there in that lot for twenty minutes until it was time to resume. Oh I'm not spooked by cemeteries it's bad soil you know that's why they put them there they choose the worst plot of land where all the stones are. Father used to joke well he wasn't joking really that he was digging his own grave tilling that soil that our fields were rocky enough to be a cemetery for the entire family. He was just joking. He had what they call a gallows sense of humor especially after he started staying out to all hours. A farmer drinking that's a bad sign other people shopkeepers mill workers the foreman at the glove factory he's drinking to get something out of his system but a farmer it's not a life that goes with late nights and carousing. Father he didn't have the temperament for it for either one actually farming or drinking I'd wake up and he hadn't made it all the way to bed he'd be passed out his trousers halfway down snoring like a two-man saw. Amethyst you know the purple stone the Greeks thought it cured drunkenness they used to get it out of the quarry here amethyst tourmaline pyrite that's fool's gold I don't think you ate the amethyst though I think you wore it if you were a Greek I mean wore it around your neck maybe or on a ring I don't know I could ask Miss Dick if she was still alive. I don't know how it worked if it stopped you from getting drunk so you could drink as much as you wanted or if it stopped you from wanting to drink. Why did I read so much Greek and Roman history well it's a way to see things. I could tell by the way people looked at me they thought I was just pretending even Alice she well she was jealous of Miss Dick which was crazy but she thought too that I just had a book of fairy tales with me that it was some never-never land Ancient Greece. I tried to tell her the Ancient World it's just like now it's as if the world has come back has made a full circle except a little bit up like a coiled spring and if you jump make a little jump in your mind from one coil to the next you can see what's happening in your own life so clearly by reading about what was happening back then. She didn't understand at all. Rebecca's? That wasn't a book for reading it was a book for writing in a blank book a journal. Mother gave it to her for her birthday. I never looked inside it might have even had a lock I don't remember I just know what the paper looked like that's all. It wasn't at all personal the note just an explanation saying how sad she was so Father wouldn't come looking for her. After that things got. I would catch him staring I could tell he was thinking of the three why is he why is the boy this simpleton why is he the only one left me? I can't say I blame him. No it never occurred to me to ask the same question why I was left with him. A son doesn't ask that question it's different between a son and his father I owed him too much. Once I almost drowned I was standing right next to him we had all gone to some pond I can't remember which. It was hot Mother and Rebecca were asleep he and I waded into the water it was pebbly not muddy I remember my feet on the pebbles so it must have been Brandt Pond yes not Lake Kathan that's where the summer people went this was back in the woods very small but deep deeper than you'd think and all stone on the bottom. My feet were squeezing the pebbles I must have been four or five years old when the ground just fell away a drop that's what they call it when it falls away suddenly like that a drop I must have panicked swallowed water because I sank straight down he was right next to me standing right next to me but not noticing. I didn't make a sound just disappeared like someone had pulled me under and then I was fighting for my life I rose but not all the way not high enough to splash I saw or felt his leg this column and tried grabbing onto it but my hands were so small they slid around it it was so thick and slippery I couldn't get a grip and then I went down again. It all probably took ten or fifteen seconds but it felt like a million years. I hit his leg the next time I came up didn't try and grab it just punched it clawed it anything to get his attention and then next thing I knew I was back on the beach coughing more like a barking sound all the water in my lungs rattling around oh I got terribly sick after. I spent the night under a sheet with a pan of boiling water my mother kept refilling it for the steam I was coughing and shivering I suppose you could say he saved my life so later no I never asked why was he the only one left me. Rebecca was like Mother Mother was raven-haired they called it she had that kind of skin that never gets red just gets darker in the sun Italian yes her name was d'Abruzzi before she met him I don't know how. At some dance. He worked for the railroad at one time. I never heard her use it in front of me Italian I never could make sense of it when those wop crews of Lebrun's spoke it. Father made fun of her that whole side of her teased her about it called her a well only when he was in a certain mood. Italian no she never taught it to us that was unthinkable it was forbidden she spoke it to herself she'd mutter in it or if she was happy she'd sing. He couldn't stop her from singing. Those songs her voice would rise up but that's nothing like what the crews talked I'd hear them sometimes talking among themselves it always sounded like they were plotting a murder. She her voice would rise to Heaven of course that's probably how I see it now in light of what happened but Heaven I don't believe in it myself but I believe in her belief if you see what I mean her belief was the strongest thing about her. Father he wouldn't let her pass it on. That's why neither Rebecca or I no we never. He kept us out not just out of

Saint Anthony's where she went but anyplace. We loved it at the time of course. On Sundays we could play while everyone else had to go to church but now looking back I wonder if. Because you end up with all those same longings but apply them oddly. Church for better or worse in church you get to work that stuff out of your system. Why am I here what should I do what happens when I die all that. It's like a roadhouse really a church from what I can make out for the soul or whatever you want to call it. People letting off steam singing and praying. We would play just the two of us because there was no one else around on a Sunday morning in a way it was church for two is what it turned out to be. Not that the alternative is any better going to some house of worship every Sunday I mean. Father after Mother died him trying to get her buried yes that was the cause of the whole complaint how he'd been taken that's what he kept saying been taken by the church all these monsignors and deacons whoever it was he dealt with at Saint Anthony's trying to get her buried there. Why was it so important well that was obvious if you'd known her if you'd heard her sing I mean just a plot in the Roman Catholic cemetery you wouldn't think it would be that hard to manage but because she'd married outside the church it turned out they were making him jump through all sorts of hoops needing all these special dispensations from Rome they made it sound like. That's when he took the second mortgage and began staying out at night complaining to anyone who would listen. They claimed all sorts of things that weren't true he couldn't find her records baptismal certificate or whatever he tried to show them this medal she wore I had never seen it before I remember him brandishing it waving it back and forth like it had magic powers it was the only time Rebecca and I were allowed in that church he must have brought us there for sympathy there was some fat priest and my father was waving this medal in front of him saying that she wore it next to her skin never took it off he claimed and I hadn't seen it before so I was staring at it the way it would flash in the light. We weren't in any back room no we had waylaid this preacher priest halfway down the aisle or whatever they call it I remember the medal passing in and out of this shaft of red from the stained glass I guess Father yelling and explaining he'd already spent so much money and the other one the preacher whatever you call him finally yelling back the two of them it was like they were fighting over her and Rebecca and me we were just clutching each other. You see? You can't get it off your teeth that's the problem. What I don't understand is why she draws attention to the fact calls them sticky buns to begin with. I'm polite though I always act pleased that she brings them not just to me I know she gives them to all the men at the Emergency Squad I think maybe it's that old saying that the way to a man's heart is through his stomach. She's known as the Sticky Bun Lady is that any kind of name to be known by? The way to a man's heart. Alice never cared about food one way or the other. Growing it yes if she'd been a man would have been a good farmer but serving it eating it no I don't know where Emily a man's heart they just want children women the rest it's not so important. It's not their fault. They're driven. It's out of their hands. What did she see in him you mean Mother? Well love of course as for him well he loved her too but he showed it more after she died when she couldn't feel a damn thing pardon my French. No it was hopeless. There's a place close by the cemetery outside but close by for those who haven't taken communion or officially rejoined the church. Not since she had been married. That's what all the fuss was about apparently she never whatever they wanted her to do confess beg pardon she never did it. So even though she went every Sunday in winter too they didn't consider her officially a member that's what infuriated him she even put money on the plate and went without not that I noticed at the time but I found out later he told me. She was a dues-paying member as far as he was concerned but of course he loved her but it wasn't enough it didn't make him happy it's not through the stomach I can tell you that the way to a man's heart.

～

Because of her father that's how I got to know Alice. He was an unusual man. Yes in the end he considered me unworthy but before before she and I began to go around then he was quite friendly. Father
had died and I was living at home. The bank let me stay until they
could sell it. As a kind of caretaker. No they didn't pay me they claimed
Father owed them it was out of the kindness of their own heart that
they let me stay on that was made clear I still had to go out and do the
same chores and I was working for Seraphim Washburn then. Oh the
less said about him the better he was a mean man Seraphim yes well
maybe they sensed it his parents right off and tried to combat it by
calling him an angel or maybe he hated the name got bullied for it in
school and decided to act the opposite I don't know. One day I had
just carried a block of ice into Nell's store I was staggering out and
Lawyer Breckenridge that was his name Dan Breckenridge must have
been watching me from his office he put his head out and called. I
remember thinking I was in trouble well I'd had enough of lawyers
the bank's lawyers the lawyers from the state trying to put me in an
orphanage an orphanage I was seventeen I had just left school it's
true though I wasn't really prepared. Washburn he took advantage of
me I see now but in a way that was good it toughened me up anyway
my back was aching and he told me to sit in the chair across from his
desk it was the softest chair I had ever sat in. Nell would never have
asked me to sit down. She was all right I suppose fair I mean she
wouldn't cheat you but she also wouldn't give you a straw hat in a
snowstorm. Breckenridge he must have been watching me out his
window oh everyone knew everyone's business back then people
talked that's all they did there was no TV no air conditioning you sat
outside at night the houses were like ovens and you amused each
other you talked. It was common knowledge what had happened my
mother my sister Father I still had that picture in my head of them
lowering him into that hole behind the church on the road to Indian
Pipes how it was already filling up with water by the time they got

around to shoveling the dirt. I probably still had earth jammed under my fingernails from when I tried to. Never mind. He asked questions how was I doing and such he was taking me seriously no one else had. I was just known for what had happened all around me not for myself. I was an unfortunate I remember hearing someone calling me a poor unfortunate one of the teachers said it when it came out I was leaving school early not graduating and I thought poor am I poor it never occurred to me we never seemed poor before even though I suppose we were. Put Father next to Mother no it was impossible even though she was outside the church not part of their little exclusive club he was so much more not one of them and he had made all those accusations no I never even asked besides I think she would have wanted some peace finally not to be next to him with all his agitations. I know it's a silly thought but you'd be surprised at what you find yourself considering. It was in his house his office was in the front room there was a sign ATTORNEY AT LAW he conducted business there. His wife had passed away I don't remember her at all I didn't really know them they were fancy people town-folk the office had these curios an eagle carved out of some black stone so it looked like it was about to swoop down from the top of the bookshelf a glass bell with something inside I only remember the bell for some reason not what was in it I'd never seen one before and a world the kind you spin yes a globe everyone had one of those all the rich people. And brass paperweights. He asked how I was getting on as if we knew each other maybe he was taking it upon himself a charity case you know he acted like we'd met before. It was a strange feeling that chair I knew I had to get out of that chair before it got too comfortable I was about to go to sleep and Washburn he would be screaming at me when he found out. Then just as I was leaving Breckenridge he suggested I come back. I was confused. I thought maybe he had a job for me we agreed I remember on Sunday afternoon. He knew I didn't attend. Him oh no doubt. A lawyer you wouldn't have gotten any business then if you didn't go to church. Everyone went. We were an oddity our family or the three of us rather and I was the only one left maybe the only one in the whole north country who didn't attend some sort of service Baptist Methodist Episcopalian Roman Catholic like I said if you don't get it when you're young the habit then it's hard later on you don't even know what to do really when to kneel which way to face but also the other things. What to do in your head. I said I'd come Sunday afternoon but I had no idea for what if it was a social call or if I should dress for rough work. God's judgment absolutely that's what they all claimed. What happened to us one after the other Mother Father Rebecca what happened to Rebecca that was worse than death in their eyes I felt it on me that they were all waiting for the other shoe to drop the final proof that I don't know that we'd been singled out for punishment. Sometimes though I think it was for the best I think I got it all over with early all the heartache what happened later well it was painful enough but it was more of the same I wasn't surprised really more what's that word they use in church when a girl when she wears a white dress confirmation yes it was more like confirmation. I've seen men get knocked sideways by grief but me I was a boy when it came I just took it in stride I assumed it was normal. So Sunday I arrived that day in a kind of mix of clothes not quite my Sunday best but. He showed me out back they had a little garden there and I thought yard work and began to roll up my sleeves when he motioned for me to join him instead they had a table sitting on some tilting ground and wrought-iron chairs the kind that look like they're made of vines and leaves the pattern I mean the shape but iron. It was the height of luxury then or it seemed so to me. But everything was a little slapdash a little off-center the way it was tilting down toward the river the table the chairs the pitcher of lemonade even it was almost slopping over where it poured out you could tell I recognized it from our own house as different as they were the lack of a woman's touch that was

70

the woman's job back then to make everything seem level and when she left died I mean any woman any wife or mother the household went askew. It's not true today because they wear pants and go to work just like us and meanwhile everything just slides all to hell back at home but then it was an art it was their job. We had no money none to speak of none for finer things but Mother made it so the house it rang kind of like when you tap a glass is the only way I can put it. Everything had a place. And this house the Breckenridges' which was miles above us in social standing but without a woman's touch it was the same the same feeling everything was about to slide off the table into your lap and the chair you were sitting in was going to tumble over onto the ground even the flowers were too big too tall they hadn't been cut you see they were drooping. Anyway we began to talk I was hardly at my ease I didn't know what I was doing there when he started speaking to me about my sister yes Rebecca you have to understand that no one so much as mentioned her name back then. What she had done I know it seems like nothing now when men and women are all over each other publicly when they act like animals in the street although animals have much more modesty than we do Allure for example but yes Rebecca he asked about her experiences at Cochrane and Christopher's he asked about the clinic just like you've been doing. Well I knew nothing about the lawsuit then didn't even know what a lawsuit was I thought it was idle curiosity and since she was gone had been gone for over a year I figured what's the harm? Not that she had told me that much like I said they swore them to secrecy the ones who worked in the sanctum but I managed to guess some things from clues she let drop. Hints. No I probably shouldn't have but I was so pleased to be addressed as well not an equal but as a person that's all. To be noticed. To be accepted into the community even as a young man trying not to spill lemonade on a rickety table in a garden that was going to seed. I told him what I knew about Cochrane and Christopher which was basically they combined science and God. Cochrane he was the preacher of the group the snake oil salesman Christopher he was more the one who gave it its what would you call it its mystery. On the surface yes it was just to cure people that's what the brochure said for the relief of physical and nervous ailments there was all this talk of mountain air and hydro-something spraying them with hoses you laugh but it was all the rage in those days hydrotherapy yes it's just as silly as what they do now nowadays they run. I see them. For their health they say jogging they call it believe me if you step back just one inch in time I mean it all seems as silly now as what people did before. They run. Run from what? Sometimes they have a heart attack and die right by the side of the road. For their health. Once they got the people comfortable they started talking about all the amazing discoveries they had made. That's where Christopher came in I told you he had a serious side to him he probably believed in what he was doing I can't say the same for Cochrane although you never know it's amazing what people can convince themselves of. Eternal youth yes your body is an alarm clock that's what they told them that's the only thing Rebecca ever let slip. I figured out the rest from that. He held up an alarm clock Cochrane or maybe Christopher and told them showed them actually how he could turn back the hands. It sounds like a joke doesn't it him actually turning back the hands they must have known who to talk to who to try it out on the most desperate I imagine. She was there for it all Rebecca. She had beautiful eyes. She aided in the treatment she calmed them she said because apparently what they did after was somewhat scary the procedure no I never knew she never told me. It frightened her I do know that I think that's why she ran off one of the reasons there were so many reasons I suppose there are always reasons to go off it's just if you act on them or not. Breckenridge no he wasn't interested in any of this that's what was so odd I tried to tell him or hinted rather at what I knew but all he cared about were rumors that the clinic was practicing white slavery. White slavery that's what they called it back then nurses and patients in the sanctum my sister of course she was the prime evidence. He wanted her to come back and testify he thought I knew where she was. The rest of it when I tried to explain when I tried to interest him that went right by him. He kept returning to he had a real bug up his ass about the white slave trade he kept calling it I wanted to say Have you ever looked out your window farther than your own sign ATTORNEY AT LAW and seen across the street? Do you think that everyone's buying candy and tobacco in there it doesn't take an hour to buy two penny's worth of molasses that's for sure and for that you don't have to button up your trousers after. I was getting more and more confused because he seemed to be deliberately missing the point when Alice came out. She asked if she should bring us more lemonade. She had been inside the whole time. The sun it shone through her dress you know when the light's at that angle and seems to pierce everything like an X-ray my chair was tilted I was off-kilter so I saw glimpsed really her whole body it just appeared in an instant as she was taking the pitcher back in I don't think he even introduced us. Of course he was using me yes but I didn't care. I was using him too. I felt there was now this way I could slip back into the community the sun it showed me how I got this glimpse. That's why I was always grateful to him even later when he made a fuss raised all those objections to Alice and my going around together and when he finally went off his rocker completely and sued the clinic sued them for slander for attacking his good name taking away what business he had left using their influence against him. Certainly he managed to show that there were all sorts of goings-on there but nobody cared they had too much money too much pull Cochrane in particular he was a frightening person to cross. In the end yes the downstate jury awarded him some money but then he had to leave town.

73

See when you fall through one layer of ice there's usually another one to catch you. That's what Cecil didn't realize. Well in his case it might not be so because he never met a sticky bun he didn't like if you take my meaning but when I went out there I knew what I was doing I know when the lake is frozen enough to walk on. It freezes in layers there's air in between that's why it groans that's why you get all those strange shifting sounds they're like planes of ice. Planes. No flat sheets planes not planes planes they move in and out of each other. You have to watch. You can't see it you have to watch. There's a difference you know. People see all the time but they almost never watch. Cecil he saw me going out there but I had watched I knew exactly what I was doing I knew it would hold my weight. Besides it's not such a bad way to go I've seen worse believe me. Cole Byron yes well that was more a family dispute from what I gather. They never. Ray Eggleston he investigated he went and talked to people in the Hollow I asked him about it after he said he'd never seen such conditions in all his life just the general poverty they're all church-going people though. Reverend Berrian he keeps them in line. Every Sunday. And on Election Day that old school bus his church uses drops them all at the town hall women you don't see from one year to the next mothers with six children the oldest daughter holding the youngest and the wife eight months gone again he tells them who to vote for and then their husbands get jobs on the road crew that's how it works. But Ray he never found anything. I went out there onto the lake because I was confused but I'm not senile you know people get confused in all phases of their life a man thinks he's in love with a woman leaves his wife and child for her and then realizes it's a mistake that's confused isn't it but you don't call him senile because he's only forty-five. I thought the way the ice heaves it had thrown something up and so I went to investigate. I would not have fallen through and even if I had fallen through another layer would have caught me. Cecil on the other hand but all that blubber would have kept him from freezing. Across the street yes the general store and then in back Gabrielle's room from her window she had that glass that made rainbows. The stream? No it was on Breckenridge's side he had the garden and then it sloped down to the water that was the problem. Ground always slopes down to water so everything is at an angle. Did I say Gabrielle had the stream out her window that's not true. I may have a memory of it but it's a false memory because the stream how could it be in two places on both sides? Love? I don't know. I suppose. Before Alice she was the only person who took note of me Gabrielle but you know I really don't want to talk about this the stream where it was or who I was passing time with it's really none of your business you're just like him like Breckenridge I try to tell you that there was some kind of cult operating not more than two miles from here that they practiced well you know what the later claims were when it all exploded all came out and you want to hear about some time back when the Black River was practically a ditch. Why would you have any interest in the milk truck? The milk truck doesn't have anything to do with local history yes it took away my business but by then I didn't mind it was all in bottles then the milk and they clinked so much that it drove me and Allure crazy and of course I didn't have refrigeration so even though I had ice and straw people started complaining. I personally like milk that's a little turned it has some bite to it some character that Dietz boy he was sick anyway if you ask me but his parents made a big stink over how they had to take him to the hospital and how he almost died all because the milk I delivered was supposedly a little too sharp. After that well Lebrun became my main employer plus the odd job like those hayrides and of course my elixir. Did I say that? See you're confusing me again. Not elixir medicine or remedy yes. The milk truck was run by a weasely little fellow what was his name I don't know not from around here he came up every day the dairies downstate once they had refrigeration refrigerated trucks they began to ship. Before I'd get it all locally. Then in the blink of an eye it all changed all disappeared every step here has been a step downhill the glove factory closing farms going under even the clinic closing nothing took its place. Only Lebrun saw the future. Vacation homes. People who had nothing better to do than sit around all day drinking and boating drive thirty miles to Schuyler to eat a fancy dinner there was even for a time a playhouse a genuine theater in Kathan. Where the old bank used to be the Mountain Trust they had a beautiful building limestone with wide steps all sorts of curlicues and decoration solid built like a brick shithouse and they gave it up said it was too cramped built some modern building outside of town instead. A low one just a box really with big windows and a place you could drive through so you didn't have to get out of your car. What's so terrible about getting out of your car? I tried just as an experiment going through that little underpass with Allure one day but they wouldn't serve me. Imagine. My own money in there and they wouldn't she left quite a calling card Allure right under the teller's nose. I would have done the same if I had the ability. Anyway they took over the old bank building this theater troupe and built a stage right where Petrides the vice president used to sit. He would sit there at this big desk and just shake his head. If you were coming in for a loan I mean. He'd see you at the door hat in hand and before you could even reach the little gate where his secretary was before you could even get that far he'd shake his head. He could tell. Well right there the theater company set up a stage and they had seats real seats the kind that bolt into the ground it was a very professional operation only a few seasons it lasted but no I never went it was for the summer people not for us still it kind of sprinkled fairy dust over the town having actors around. They were always building things the scenery you'd hear hammering they would leave the side door open and the costumes I remember sometimes you'd see someone wearing a costume running to The Town of Day Store if they needed a last-minute prop. Once they came into Walt's right before an opening and borrowed a bottle of ketchup. It was in the play. Walt he kept it in a special place after when they returned it like it was the star of the show this bottle of ketchup. Of course it had to do with the war. That's what keeps things going a war. Everyone spends money like there's no tomorrow. We had several fellows who went. There was talk of a monument in town in Antone not Kathan but that's all it was talk. There were only three who didn't come back. Four really but one of them was a Negro. Three they figured wasn't enough for a stone with a plaque I mean you could almost have statues of the three of them for the same price and the thought of that they were just schoolboys straight out of high school the thought of having statues of those boys nobody could quite picture it. Then there was talk of naming a park after them renaming it rather the one down by the river but the Elks who had raised the money for the park they objected so. But the war it gave everything I know this is wrong to say but it gave everything a holiday atmosphere. People for and against. Arguing all the time. Marching. Wearing buttons. I don't think anyone took it seriously it was so far away a place nobody knew how to pronounce Vietnam certainly not those boys they were just kids some recruiter came along there were no jobs here anyway and the next thing you knew there was talk of a life-size statue of them in bronze but that died down. *Cooler heads prevailed* I remember Lawrence wrote in the *Pennysaver* he actually got in hot water by questioning what was going on there people not just the parents of the boys but well there was a lot of patriotic sentiment you know people said he shouldn't be questioning. All he did was make a few remarks. But the theater that was part of it too. All those costumes. The same way you saw boys in uniform. People dressing up it's a sign of the times. Live long enough and you watch it will all come around again oh yes any minute now it's all going to happen again I may not be here but they'll all be back those same people.

No I never got to know the actors. I imagine they were pretty good you'd hear them rehearsing out the stage door that's what they called it even though well it was just the side door of the bank before it was always locked even in the hottest weather. They had a safe down there. They couldn't move that of course when they moved the bank it must have weighed a couple of tons. The kind with a big wheel and ten inches of specially hardened steel. You went by it on your way to the bathroom once they turned it into a theater the door was open left wide open for people to gawk at I wonder what Petrides thought of that his precious safe. He would just sit there in the new bank all day long smoking cigars. The whole place stank. I asked him once if he spoke Greek he looked at me as if I was trying to get at him trying to make fun of him maybe he got a lot of that growing up. It was about my reading I wanted to explain but I never got a chance he just looked at me even when he didn't have a cigar it was like he was blowing smoke in your face then turned away. Still I would have liked to hear when they say The sea The sea that's in Xenophon I would have liked to hear what that sounds like in Greek. Petrides he was one of the ones who objected most strongly to Lawrence in that editorial asking *What are we doing there? Why did these boys have to die? For what reason?* he acted like Lawrence was a traitor just for speaking his mind like he'd killed those boys himself with his words but the ties he wore Petrides they were just the same as those hippie clothes the peaceniks had. What's it called with all the different colors like a sunrise tie-dyed yes. He thought he was a real snappy dresser Petrides or you'd see a soldier dressed out of the Revolutionary War with a three-cornered hat and a flintlock rifle over his shoulder sitting on the green eating a tuna fish sandwich. With one of those buttons you know the peace sign or whatever you didn't know who was in a play and who wasn't it was in the air that sense that something was happening or about to happen or maybe had already happened and you just hadn't figured out what. Not like now. Now it's all shut down. It's winter. But not for long.

I have no idea what his first name was maybe Higgenbottom. Hig's was all anyone ever called the place with an apostrophe yes. It was a bar not a roadhouse because it wasn't outside of town I told you I didn't like places like that in or out of town you paid too much just for the privilege of sitting in some dark room listening to the trash they have on the jukebox but in winter there's no place else to go you can't sit outside so sometimes I'd. Higs. H-I-G-S. Why are you trying to confuse me? The sign had an apostrophe but his name didn't or maybe the other way around I don't see what difference that makes. The advantage was it had a back way a back door that led out onto the alley and from there you could just slip onto Main Street it looked like you'd come from the newsroom. Alice's friends that's who I had to watch out for no I wasn't supposed to be drinking and I wasn't drinking not most of the time see I never got credit for all the times I wanted to drink but didn't there'd be three or four times a day when I wanted to take a nip but didn't but then if just once I gave in it's not like that made the score four to one in my favor or anything like that. I tried telling her you spend all day staring at a horse's derriere even a horse as fine as Allure naturally there's a time when. Her father no Breckenridge I don't think he touched anything stronger than lemonade. He should have. He could have used a little liquid refreshment he was such a tightass so morally upright as he would have put it so morally upright he didn't see well never mind. No just that it's those people who are so high and mighty they don't ever see what's happening right under their nose or behind their back yes of course I mean Alice well nothing just that she had she had already. Yes before me I wasn't the first. She never talked about it not directly but I knew of course because of that time we what I call our wedding day. She never she'd blush if I even mentioned it later on but that time we became man and wife in our own eyes I could see that she'd already we never discussed it but I sensed she regretted it that it had been a mistake and there was Breckenridge going on about sexual license and loose morals at the clinic while at the same time his daughter. I considered it our anniversary our true anniversary although Alice she'd barely acknowledge anything happened before we went to the town hall but as I said if you don't go to a church when you're young from the start then you make your own church out of what's at hand so to me that was our true wedding in our true church even though no I'm not going to tell you where what business is it of yours? The important thing is that I undid the damage or so I thought. She needed caring for I sensed that right away even before I before I found out. What she saw in me I have no idea. Love? Love's after the fact. I try and tell Emily that in a nice way by reminiscing not as if I'm speaking about her life directly that the way to a man's heart isn't through sticky buns or whatever else she goes around handing out that it's well with her mother and me it was based on need we were both like two people drowning we were hanging on to each other. What's that you say that we'd drown anyway well then that's a bad example I guess. All I'm trying to say is love is after the fact. It's just this big blanket you throw over what happens almost like you don't really want to see what's going on underneath. No not the quarry. Not there either. I'm not going to tell you. No I could never get her to go back I told you she acted like it hadn't happened. And on the day of our true anniversary I called it even though I couldn't bring it up not directly but on that day I'd try and be extra nice to her. I don't know if she ever realized we never discussed it but her friends if they saw me coming out of the Leather and Lace by the time I got home I swear it traveled faster than me and Allure that's for sure all those biddies gossiping with each other burning up the phone lines she'd be waiting that's why later on I'd go to Hig's instead and go out the back door. Yes it covers a multitude of sins love that's what Lebrun once said to me we were going on well I was going on he was probably just listening I was going on about how she'd locked me out again and how despite it all I still we still loved each other but all it did was make us fight more and he said Yes love it covers a multitude of sins which I didn't really understand at the time but later when his adventures I guess you could call them with the opposite sex got more dangerous after Ed Bailey's wife and there were others believe me he got quite the reputation always rumors that he been seen jumping out a back window or coming out of somewhere he shouldn't I realized it was the danger he was after that was love for him. He had to be right on the edge almost getting caught almost getting worse than caught getting I don't know seen for who he really was. Because the individual women themselves there was nothing they had in common not that I could tell. It wasn't about them so much he didn't boast he didn't kiss and tell but he let slip references to where he'd been or where someone else had been like if Pete Chicoin for example had taken a camping trip to hunt for elk you knew that meant well not that I'm saying anything about Mildred Chicoin she's still alive so far as I know. The husbands had more in common than the wives now that I think about it they were all a certain type. Oh it's hard to say probably just the type who wouldn't have given him the time of day growing up but with Alice there'd be times when I'd get home and she'd have already heard from some meddling biddy that I'd been walking funny down Main Street. After a while I didn't even try talking to her through the keyhole what's the point I think it was as much punishment for her being alone there as it was for me not being allowed in I had Allure at least and Firebrand all she had was Emily. It was worst on Emily. She says so at least how her mother would get all tense and rigid-like. Sometimes she would have to put herself to bed Alice wouldn't even notice she blames me but I was locked out what could I do? In the barn I would well in for a penny in for a pound as they say I'd dig out my bottle of Old Gentleman from the feed bin and have myself a good old-fashioned sit-down. I've never minded the smell of animals Allure and Firebrand they would tolerate my presence that's the most I'll say. I think they'd rather I had left they had things they probably wanted to do but they understood I had no place else to go. In the morning I'd get up around five five-thirty I'd go back to the house and the door would be open. She unlocked it before she went to bed but I always waited until light. Then a lot of times I'd creep into bed with her and you know then of all times yes that was the only way she and I could be together she'd act like she was asleep but. A multitude of sins like Lebrun says love it covers a multitude of I mean maybe in his case it really was a sin since most often he was doing it with married women oh they were all married no the ones who were single I saw them hanging around him practically throwing themselves at him especially later when he had money but he had no time for them. It all had to do with the risk I guess. Like a burglar he had to break in and break out again breaking out actually I think that gave him the most pleasure sometimes in broad daylight he'd appear with this big grin on his face and I knew he didn't have to say anything that he'd just snuck a cookie out of the cookie jar so to speak. But it wasn't sin for us we were married she could only see it as sin though that was the sense I got that without sin it wasn't I don't know wasn't worth doing maybe. So in the morning she'd act like she was asleep but. I just wanted to take care of her. Emily says I was cruel but I don't see how I was cruel she Alice she set it all up to happen the way it did. Once I probably shouldn't be telling you this but once maybe she went to bed too early or was especially mad at me I don't know but she left the door locked and I had to get in so I circled the house trying all the windows and finally found the one in the yes how did you know the one in the bedroom it was open more than a crack it was practically so I climbed in there and well. It was a strange way to be close to a person because she never acknowledged it later I'd be sitting at the breakfast table and she would come out in her robe as if she had just woken up yawning and stretching. When just a minute ago we'd been. She never made reference to it not even by a touch or anything not that there was much more to say but still.

～

Higs he was a fat man he never got off his stool not if he could help it he'd spread his lunch out on the bar right on the bar not on a plate or a napkin but a sandwich a pile of potato chips once I saw him even with a pile of cold chicken right on the wood there well it wasn't a place for ladies maybe that was his point. I liked it OK in the winter it's not like I had an alternative. Ed Mosher he used to camp out there year-round no we never talked much. By then he was oh the women they still liked him the more ruined-looking he got the more they liked him but it was the way they liked him that got him all angry like a baby more and more someone they wanted to take care of and him he was still the golden boy in his eyes that's how he pictured himself. But he had let the business go all to hell he was just a salesclerk then in the same store his father had built up from nothing so he'd stay in Hig's take a long lunch hiding out from all the ladies who wanted to mother him. He'd play this song on the jukebox over and over it used to drive Higs nuts Roll Out Those Lazy Hazy Crazy Days of Summer in the dead of winter in this freezing room. I didn't mind. He'd have his little pile of quarters and feed them in one by one he'd walk over there from the corner booth I suppose that was his exercise. Me I'd limit myself I'd nurse one drink just coasting. It was mainly to warm up besides I couldn't stay long because Allure I had to leave her at the school the cemetery that lot in between it's the only place they'd let me tie her up. Once I remember it snowed while I was inside no there weren't real windows I mean there were but they were painted black he just had a few dying plants next to them I don't know why certainly not for looks. Lawrence came in and I remember he explained to me how all the trees it was some kind of code he'd read a book Druids that's right Druidology

83

that's what he called his religion he'd read some kind of book showing how every tree in the forest was some kind of code I don't really
remember code for what but he was very excited and I stayed longer
than I should have and when I came out hell maybe six inches of
snow had fallen with more on the way. Allure and Firebrand they
were both even Firebrand who was usually so even-tempered so
placid they were shaking the snow off their backs whinnying stamp-
ing their feet I got up on the bench and holy Moses they took off it
was lucky we didn't knock over the whole Hopkins family that little
fenced-in patch of stones they have right by the entrance. People
didn't care so much for Allure as time went on they kept telling me
to move her farther and farther out of town. The children at the
school the principal said they didn't like the smell or that it was a
distraction I can't remember which well just what I'd like to know is
so distracting about a horse nibbling at grass in a cemetery it's about
the most natural sight in the world. The only time they did have use
for her was when those boys came back from the war. Then Rector
Graves Rector Graves Senior father of the colored boy who died he
came up to me and asked if I'd take the boy's coffin well I couldn't
very well refuse but that started something because then each boy in
turn. Business? I wouldn't exactly call it business although certainly
I charged the army it turned out had an allowance for such a thing
so it wasn't like I was taking money from the parents. Alice ran me
up an outfit a black suit and I had these old cracked shoes that belonged to her father no we didn't put anything on the horses it
wasn't that elaborate but they looked solemn enough. A horse will
take on any mood whatever you feel inside that's what animals are
for they show you what you're feeling. Allure and Firebrand would
go at a stately pace. Well it wasn't a corpse like Cole Byron it was all
solemn and in a box there was no smell the horses understood just
the sound of their hooves on the pavement state troopers stopped
traffic for the first for Rector's boy Rector Junior there wasn't as

much of a crowd him being colored and all but it caught on you know when the others died. Maybe they didn't want to be outdone. People standing in front of shops taking off their hats flowers it was always a sunny day too figure that luck of the draw I guess. I'd go slow through town and up past the Mobil station there'd be a color guard waiting at the cemetery. Then a bugler. The army supplied that as well. Oh they're very good to you when you're dead first class all the way. Graves came up later and thanked me. He was a big man big as a house and black as the ace of spades I have no idea what brought him here. They had a place below the mill. He worked for the power company maybe he got assigned here though I doubt it he and his daughter Mary. I don't recall a wife ever. The boy Junior I don't know what kind of times they had here I never knew them all that well just to say hello. Rec came up to me after. Mary she was upset. At the funeral she'd started wailing. They had to take her away. I don't like it myself electricity. He had huge hands. I always wondered how he could touch those things I mean they say the line is dead that the power's off but how can you tell it's invisible that's what makes it so frightening you can't tell if it's on or off. I always pictured that first touch when he'd be taking the live end of some-thing and hoping they really did what they said that they really turned off the juice. He stood there not moving a muscle even when they had to take away his daughter. They give the parent an Ameri-can flag it's folded all special in a triangle tucked tight like a pillow and when he came over after the ceremony he was holding it with one hand squeezing it and I knew that something bad was going to happen to that flag or that's what I sensed anyway by the way he held it. When he got home maybe. But he didn't let on didn't let any-thing show whatever he was feeling. Father yes eventually I got him a stone Alice made me do it of all people she said it would stop him from bothering me she was surprisingly superstitious I mean consid-ering she went to a regular church and all. Reverend Berrian are you

85

out of your mind? Reverend Berrian he was for the Hollow people not. Nothing but the Episcopalians for her. In Upper Antone they like to call it up there on Palmer Ave. where the mill managers live. She thought it would stop Father from wandering that's what she said. Well yes I did see him more not just that one time once he was all covered with ice I reached out to touch him and he crinkled like he had a layer like cellophane around him only cold you didn't even realize it was there until you touched him and then of course it was a dream that still counts as haunting especially if you have the same dream four nights in a row she said she feared for her life I don't know why she feared for her life I was the one who was waking up in different parts of the house not knowing how I'd gotten there or even once in the barn hitching up Allure. If she hadn't neighed no not Alice Allure if she hadn't woken me up out of whatever I was in dream's too weak a word if she hadn't woken me I don't know where I would have ended up. He was telling me to do something to go somewhere but of course I couldn't remember where it was or what he wanted just that it was urgent. Alice thought a stone was the key that it would stop him from wandering. It sounded cruel to me weighting him down and expensive too but she it's funny she wouldn't spend money on common household products we needed even soap sometimes we did without if times were hard but on that stone we spent three hundred dollars more even to have it set in the ground right because she insisted on having her priest what the hell was his name Father John something he had to come and do it officially. That was the problem she said that I hadn't done it officially the first time. I tried to tell her how much he would have hated what we were doing how he would have rolled around in his grave but she was having none of it. It wasn't really about him I suppose. I couldn't even remember where he was I mean I went back to that church on the way to Indian Pipes and where I thought he was there was just grass which I kind of found comforting but Alice she immediately went looking for signs that priest Bigelow Father John Bigelow that was his name he just walked across the field he was this loud man one of those ones you can't believe is a priest they look like they've been out all night eating drinking doing god knows what else right up until the moment before they put on the collar and then suddenly they pull rank on you act like you're nothing while they they've got all the answers. Anyway he paced it out as if he was laying the foundations for a building this little plot. I still couldn't tell if it was right or not I didn't remember a thing. The more I studied it the less familiar it became. I thought when I walked over him my hairs would go up you know the hairs on the back of my neck or something like that but I didn't feel a thing. They said it was my fault because I hadn't gotten him a stone. I couldn't tell if it was religion or psychology they were talking about but either way three hundred dollars plus whatever Father John whatever he charged which Alice didn't dare tell me. Christian charity yes it's a funny expression well we got his name and dates that was easy enough but then they wanted me to add something to have chiseled in. No not Freddie Seaborne he wasn't a stonecutter he made fireplaces no this was very traditional with a polished face they insisted on more words something descriptive they said. I couldn't think of a thing. It's when I miss Rebecca she was the wordsmith in our family with that journal always writing things down in her journal. If you put a pencil in my hand I just go blank but Rebecca. Finally Bigelow I'm sure it was his idea even though it came from Alice he must have thought of it because it sounded just like him we put Safe in the Arms of His Redeemer whatever the hell that means. The night before we put it up I saw him one last time yes in a dream he was trying to tell me something but his throat was all clotted up with dirt all he could do was make these sounds I grabbed him by the shoulders and they came off both his arms just tore off like they were rags and I woke up and I was halfway down the drive the road that leads to the barn no I didn't go anywhere. I did look around. It was a full moon light enough so I kept expecting to see him or to see something some sign yes but.

~

Hold on a minute was it your house are you their son? Well of course I remember. Because of the hummingbird. So that was your house or your parents' rather. I spent the night there guarding it. In a way I was the first person to ever live there. Oh more than one night Lebrun was afraid I don't know what he had done to that crew or what they had done to him to make him act so nervous but. He employed at its peak Eagle Enterprises must have been using half the plumbers and electricians in the area but those Italians that was early he had me up there at least three weeks. No I never brought a bedroll or anything. I had a thermos and by the end a blanket. I'd go home at night first have dinner and then Lebrun would drive me. The horses? The horses were in the barn a horse won't just stand out in the cold all night he's a person too he'd get all spooked just like you or me. Lebrun would drive me although for a while with that arm in a sling it was quite an adventure him driving then he'd drop me off unlock the door make sure I was all set. I'd prop my feet up on that chair with the lights off you could see the sky through the glass wall. The sky and the reservoir what more could you ask well you know you've seen that view yourself. I never cared I hope you don't mind me saying this but I never cared for that rug your mother put down later yes that thick white one because it covered the bricks. The bricks the way they continued outside to make what would you call it the patio I guess it was like the floor continued from inside to out I liked that it made the wall seem not like a wall. See that's something Lebrun thought up it's not on those plans he bought. Every house he built had an individual touch. But later when I was watching the place when they were paying me to watch it your mother and father I'd have to take off my shoes because it was so white and deep it would pick up any dirt. Who ever heard of a white carpet? Well of course it was beautiful I'm not denying that. Just taking the long view though over the years I could see it getting dirtier and dirtier even though Ruth Sayheim you were too young I guess she would come over once a week even though your parents weren't there for months sometimes but she would come over and clean the hell out of the place. That carpet in particular she'd do all kinds of shampoo-ing to it. I used to kid her that it got more shampoo than her own hair but over the years well the light of course it's not just dirt with a glass wall everything fades faster it's in the light all the time. Nobody thought of that of the consequences I mean I suppose that's the price for being up-to-date. When your parents first moved in every-thing seemed so new I couldn't even tell what half the things were for. Your mother she had this sense of what was coming down the pike all these gadgets and wall hangings and music music coming out of that chair remember? That padded one that had speakers right inside the parts that came out on either side by your ears. No I never sat in it well once when your father showed me how it worked but of course I'd see it going by in my stocking feet trying not to dirty up the carpet on my way to check the traps oh in the winter I'd find mice I set traps in the back of the cupboards it was warm there because they insisted on keeping the heat on. I told them it would be cheaper to drain the pipes but they always talked about coming up in the winter. I guess they did once or twice but for long stretches you your family that is was playing host to a large section of the north country's mouse population. I would catch two or three a week clean up the droppings I didn't want to leave them for Ruth no she had a place on the other side of the reservoir this was before the days of four-wheel drive she had some little yellow foreign car that'd come slipping and sliding down your driveway she never missed a week so far as I could tell. She wore glasses kept to herself mostly she'd make no concession to the weather at all she'd come barreling from across the lake in that little Datsun that's right a Datsun Something just a toy of a car with all her cleaning supplies piled high in the back. She had other people she cleaned for too but not in the winter so much. Chopsticks in her hair that was her big thing. Instead of a pin or a rubber band I remember because I stared at her for the longest time at first I mean privately not to make her uncomfortable and finally I realized they were chopsticks yes like in a Chinese restaurant but in her hair it was the strangest thing she wasn't from here but she worked hard like the rest of us she wasn't a summer person. When she wasn't cleaning I don't know what she was doing her light was always on when I'd go by that was just a tiny house no not a vacation dwelling at all but fixed up nice from the outside at least when I went by a light was always on you could just tell she wasn't here for her health but the chair the one with the music in it yes it tilted back that one it was in the same place I sat with my feet propped up you probably saw the stars from there the same ones I did. They don't change. It was Lebrun he got me more and more of those jobs as I got older I would watch a place I would go by every week to make sure there were no leaks that no kids had broken in I'd check the refrigerator. If something went off got rotten I'd chuck it. Some of these families didn't use their houses for weeks on end. This was later after Allure had. He'd drive me or I'd walk. Since all the properties were close together I could walk from one to the other. I'd make my rounds like a watchman I suppose but in the daytime a caretaker that's what they called me. If there was work to be done I'd call the owner and arrange for someone to come out a plumber usually or an electrician. I didn't deal much with the owners well except for your parents most just left money on the table under the saltshaker usually not even a note. I remember one father a doctor down in Sparta telling his son when I was tramping back up the hill so he thought I was gone but the window the kitchen windows in back because the ground rises so fast there they're right on level with you as you pass the carport he said they could trust me not to steal because I was old. Old. That must have been thirty years ago. It's just all those years of outdoor work had left me hunched over a bit a little weather-beaten maybe but I wasn't old not then if I was old then what am I now? That's just an example of how they barely even saw who I was. Alice and Emily those are the people I was the real caretaker for. I'd come home and immediately it was about undoing the damage I could tell the minute I walked in the door if they'd been fighting they were too much alike that was the problem it was like two bulls butting in a field. Emily as soon as she got to be a teenager oh the fights they had it was no picnic I tell you and it was worse when they were quiet you could feel it this I'm-not-talking-first war just filling up the house. Not get in the middle of it? I was in the middle of it from the start I've always been the peacemaker between Rebecca and my father between Emily and Alice I can't stand it when people are mad at each other you can't have a conversation can't digest your food properly but that's where I was the caretaker really at home not those summer houses except for your place but that's because your mother and father they'd say hello stop to talk to me like I was a human being. Hell I'd sat in your house before it was done propped my feet up there just staring trying to sleep. They'd cleared the lawn what you call the lawn now all the way down to the lake. It was just a mess then all tree stumps and those tracks bulldozers leave filled up with rainwater. Of course you weren't even born. They hadn't even lit the fire in that fireplace everything had that new smell sawdust and bricks brick dust that's a smell too I liked the bricks. This is no offense to your mom she was a great decorator like I said those things she brought up what was that one she hung on the wall a tapestry yes and the rug it was comfortable even if it was hard to keep clean the way you could wiggle your toes down into it even through your socks I mean but the bricks that pattern three this way three that way and the way they kept going on out through the glass past the wall. I'd sit there in the moonlight or the starlight and it just seemed so fresh and new. *Stars Nestle in Their Mountainside Home* that was Lawrence it wasn't one of his usual editorials it was almost like he became a gossip reporter. I didn't even know I had no idea they were famous well why would a bunch of people like that come up here? I asked once I asked your father and he said they came for the clean air no I don't get it either I mean we got air here it's true but I didn't pursue it I knew better than to go on asking. Once they started spending summers though they didn't want any special notice taken they kept their lives very simple not going around in some fancy car or fancy clothes. Your nanny I suppose that was the first time we'd ever seen one of those and her being colored you'd look twice maybe on Main Street if you saw the two of you together but otherwise. That's why when Lawrence had that article editorial rather well everyone was a little surprised. I don't know what his point was I don't know what he hoped to accomplish. It was news I guess he'd say. After that your dad had to start picking up his mail at the post office because people would go through his mailbox on the road he had to get a private telephone too because on the party line people would start listening to his conversations. I don't know how they put up with it I suppose it was still easier on them here than anyplace else I think it was hardest for your mother though she was such a gentle soul when I think of that hummingbird sometimes I think well that it was like time going backward and forward I mean first I found it there and then a few months later in the same spot practically I met her she was up to her ankles in mud she certainly wasn't glamorous when I first ran across her they were moving in and that lawn it still wasn't a lawn that happened years later or over the years rather. Freddie Seaborne yes the man who built your fireplace but by then he'd been laid off at the mill so he was doing landscaping he made that whole view the lawn going down to the shore. His hands something happened to his hands that's why they laid him off they swole up like he was wearing a watch with a too-tight wristband. After that he couldn't do really hard labor not for long stretches although he worked his ass off on your place. He's the one who took that mud hole that's what it was at the time and turned it into something but when I first met your mother she was standing knee-deep in it trying to set some hammock or something into the ground probably regretting the whole thing the whole move. Your father hadn't come up he was busy I suppose and she was just stranded there while these men from the truck dumped the boxes and furniture every which way tracking mud all over the bricks. You weren't even born yet or if you were you'd have been with what was her name? Lucy something Lucy Sunshine that colored woman yes that's what she called herself Sunshine she was a follower of some Harlem minister and they changed all their last names some were Sunshine some were Heavenlyglory but she was Sunshine no you don't forget a name like that.

~

Did I who? Dream about Alice you mean after she? Like I did with my father you mean no well she was pretty securely weighted down she made sure of that she shopped for her own funeral she and Father Bigelow they took a tour of some funeral parlor down near Sparta not because she was sick it was more to pass the time kind of. Just a coincidence. I never got a bill or nothing so she must have paid in advance. She kept charge of the money I have no head for that. She and that well he was like her boyfriend at times like her playhusband I called him not to her face no none of that bothered me. What bothered me was well you weren't here of course you couldn't have known but at the funeral that speech he gave that made me want to give him a little shove backward into the hole all about how she was well never mind it's a sin against her memory to rake up all kinds of no no as you get older you realize that if you keep things inside if you don't tell and take them with you then it's like they never happened in a way they don't go on in the world. You make it like they never were. I said what? I did say that didn't I. Well that was a mistake she wasn't cremated she got buried in a grave Alice the cemetery outside of Antone. Emily goes there and lays flowers she takes me once in a while too she's got these clippers I tell her it's not worth it that it's better to have things grow over you have all these old wrinkled rotting flowers on a perfectly kept little square of grass it makes no sense but she. I did say that but I must have been thinking of someone else. Lebrun and I. I don't remember who I just remember being out in the boat yes it really happened why would I make something like that up when you get old you things get sorted differently that's the best way I can describe it you'll see. We who was it now obviously someone important to us I mean to both of us or why would we I can't for the life of me remember but yes over the town or whatever you want to call Conklingville it was hardly a town it was more like. His wife? No. That would be like poisoning the place all the fish would float to the surface. I do remember that we were on the boat and we had the ashes of who the hell was it well it'll come to me. But Bigelow he told all these lies basically about who Alice was what she did. Maybe she would have approved probably she would have. He painted this pretty picture of her you know like on a greeting card how she wanted to appear to the world at large and god knows she had a good turnout you would have thought they were giving away free ice cream. Father Bigelow he took over the whole thing he made it into this show Emily and I we were pushed off to the side her sniffling away me trying to comfort her I'd pat her put my arm around her I wish I'd had a sugar cube I guess she has her own now those sticky buns kind of although come to think of it I've never seen her eat one of those herself but anyway I kept it inside what I felt what I thought of him and acted all grateful after told him It's what Alice would have wanted. He said what's-his-name Jesus conquered death that's what really annoyed me conquered death then where was my wife up in Heaven looking down at us? She wouldn't have gone unless she could have taken everyone with her see that's the difference. Bigelow he would be waiting outside the gates and they'd open them just a crack just for him and he'd slip through and then help clang them shut behind before anyone else could get in that would be his idea of Heaven. I have no idea if he's dead or alive I wouldn't give you five cents to find out either way. Alice she well it's stupid to talk about the more you talk about it the farther away from it you get. Everything I tell you about her makes her sound bad sometimes I think that's all words are for making things out to be worse than they are because when you try to say something good about a person have you noticed it comes out all wrong somehow like you're lying or making it up. Yes like Bigelow's sermon or whatever you call it talking about her being all sweetness and light sweetness and light my ass I mean she was many things but. People always say the opposite of what they mean. But if you're quiet it's like with an animal if you want them to come close to you you have to sit quiet. When I try and tell you about her it comes out all wrong like I'm mad at her which I'm not. That's just what makes it a good story the incidents incidents yes but they were really just unusual events out of the ordinary. Oh I don't know it's like Rebecca's journal she made it out to be some kind of horror show some kind of terrible thing our family life but we were happy it's only the part that lent itself to writing down the part that made a good story. But those times were unusual see that's why what I no I never read it I told you it was under lock and key let's just say I know well you don't have to read something to know what it's like. How could I tell just from the way she wrote it I'd come into her room sometimes I was allowed I was the only one I just went into her room and she'd barely notice she'd be writing away usually after a fight with Father her pen

95

steaming along I could tell by the frown on her face and her shoulders that was the giveaway yes they'd be all tensed up just the way Father was when he worked in the fields farming rocks that's what he called it farming rocks. What's so funny is she and he they didn't get along they were at loggerheads over almost anything but deep down they were so much alike. It was Mother and me well I don't have such clear memories of her a lot of what I think I remember I must have heard later but Mother and me I'd like to imagine we were alike although once I remember Father saying that I wasn't like anyone that I was dropped from outer space. I don't know what he meant by that maybe I'd broken something or not heard what he said maybe I was staring off and he said. No the journal she took it with her. I don't think anyone read it except maybe the man she went off with I told you I never knew his name so I couldn't even track her down if I wanted to I mean where she is now I mean where she lies. Yes I know there are people that's important to. Knowing where everyone is so they can all be gathered together when what's-his-name blows his horn at the Second Coming. Maybe she wrote about Cochrane and Christopher I don't know if you're sworn to secrecy does that count writing about it in a journal no one else will read? She certainly spent enough time there it was very difficult especially toward the end when Mother was sick she spent every waking minute practically either at work or in her room with that journal her pen flying across the page she didn't have a desk really it was more like a table I'd sit on her bed. She never seemed to notice me but I think we took comfort in each other's company. No we didn't talk like I said true happiness or whatever you want to call it just being together that goes best with no words. She pressed down so hard it was almost like she was making a woodcut you know where you take that tool and gouge out the picture. Her shoulders. Well yes she was beautiful but when she frowned that way she looked just like Father it was like there was a face behind the face. Alice never knew

her they didn't travel in the same circles and there was the age difference. Her father? Why would Breckenridge know Rebecca oh because of the court case you mean well it's possible but I wouldn't
know. I was a child then I mean not a child but even when I got
older I was still I stayed a child as long as possible maybe I sensed
what came later. Once Father passed it was easier than I thought being a man although when I look back I don't know how I managed
it I mean when I think about it now there were people who wanted
to send me away who thought I was soft in the head but instead I
found the sock that was where Father's money was I got out a dollar
and. How did I know? It's like with the berries up by Indian Pipes it
was just in the air I never heard about it no not that I remember but
I went to Nell's and she decided on Gabrielle she took one look and
god knows what I looked like I was wearing his clothes a dead man's
clothes my own were too short by then and he was too tight to buy
me new ones but there I was with a shiny silver dollar and she took
me back. There was no parlor or anything no place where you chose
she decided for you or perhaps it's whoever was available. I'd like to
think it had to do with me that she sized me up and made a choice
but I don't know she knocked on the door once then opened it
without waiting. She didn't go in she just stepped aside and pushed
or pulled me in by then I would probably have given her another
silver dollar to be allowed to turn tail and run and then she closed
the door behind us and that was that. Gabrielle she was kneeling
before that picture. It wasn't a photograph I mean how could you
have a photograph He's not a real person or rather He wasn't around
when there were cameras but it was sharp-edged not like a painting
more like something you'd see in a newspaper or magazine except
of course for the barbed wire she was praying in front of and that
window-thing the prison it threw this rainbow on her I'd never seen
one before I thought it was part of her I thought it was her skin I
suppose or some piece of jewelry her praying there with that rain-

bow on her bare shoulder. No it wasn't Gabrielle in that boat I told you she went away besides what would Lebrun and I be doing with her ashes?

⁓

Now Vera Vera I still see. She's the waitress at the luncheonette. We talk about things when she can grab a moment she's pretty busy she's the only one behind the counter she's responsible for the tables up front as well so I don't like to disturb her. She has a boy just a baby practically Sam. From the way she makes it sound the daddy's off somewhere. Who takes care of him? Her mother. Her mother came with her here I don't know why. It's true I like talking to women with men it's more like a shoving match talking but you sit down with women you find out things not just about them but you hear yourself saying things. Emily no she's not a woman she's my daughter we have a terrible time finding things to talk about it's excruciating don't tell her I told you this but when she visits or takes me out I try and think of things in advance to talk about you know topics because otherwise it's just the weather and how's the food here and. With a woman there's an element of courtship to it even when you're old like me. You can still feel it. That's what's different talking to a woman. For example I said to Alice once years later Will you marry me? Because I'd never asked her right never asked her properly at the time it was more you know because we had to not that we didn't want to but so I asked her then it just came out Will you marry me? She looked at me as if I was crazy of course but that's what I mean with a woman you hear things coming out of your mouth that are just as much a surprise to you as they are to the person listening. With Emily it's a problem. I want to help her but I don't know how. Stop trying I want to say stop looking for a man stop dieting stop trying to be happy even. She's got all these books. Not from the library self-help books she gets from the mall how to do this how to do that except it's more like How to Lose a Thousand Pounds in Ten Minutes or How to Be a Goddess. There was one goddess I tried to tell her Pallas Athena the goddess of wisdom in ancient Greece gray-eyed Athena she was a real goddess you don't want to become her you want to lay down sacrifices in front of her you want to pay her off and then she'll help you out then things will start happening for you but you don't want to be a goddess yourself that's crazy. Just find something you care about I told her and forget everything else make that your number one concern and let the rest just fall into some kind of pattern around it. Well what about you she asked what was your number one concern what did you care so much about? That kind of stumped me. I wasn't thinking in terms of me. I didn't need help I wasn't spending all my spare time pouring sugar frosting on top of buns that already were so drenched in the stuff you could have used them to glue down linoleum. No of course I didn't say that out loud. Cecil asked about her just recently. Him? Well I never thought about that but no I wouldn't wish him on anybody what the hell's he doing here anyway riding herd over a bunch of half-dead seniors that's what he calls us seniors like some kind of cowboy a rancher but of dead people soon-to-be-dead people at least. I know it's a job but it's not like he's looking for something better at the same time. He's quite happy here that's my impression. As if it's his home. See he's got a calling unlike Emily just not one that you'd call normal. If I'd come across this job when I was his age I'd have run from it like the plague. I pass on the buns to him. They make him goofy with all that sugar the time I went out well I know he says he was looking after me maybe he thought he was looking after his investment you know if I fell through the ice no more sticky buns. I guess he could get them the other way for life I mean sticky buns for life but no I can't see it. She could do better. They both could do better does that make sense? In any event Vera she tells me things nothing of consequence but we talk. It makes me feel good like I'm being a good father maybe to the wrong person but who knows maybe Emily's got someone like that too some old coot she talks to though I doubt it I would have heard she would have told me she doesn't hold much back when it comes to blame. I don't mind I did the best I could. So much of it when you look back seems preordained preordained that's when yes when there's no real choice even though you think you have one at the time that's how it seems now. It's like you're a marble rolling in this groove. Lebrun are you kidding he was the most. Everyone thought he was master of his own destiny the only one from here who'd made a fortune out of nothing but I knew that he was the most stuck in a groove of all of us especially later when well you know how when you're gaining speed and you can't go right or left anymore when all you can do basically is hold on tight sometimes I think that's what all his women were about him just trying to hold on because he knew somehow that his fate was sealed. But Cecil and Emily that's an idea I'll have to keep my eyes open for that. What would that make me if they?

～

No I don't have any more. That was a long time ago. Ray Eggleston he came by one day and told me they'd determined those berries the ones I was using along with the B&B that they were illegal. Imagine that. How could a berry be illegal? I asked. He didn't really know or couldn't really say but he also pointed out I was selling liquor without a license plus it wasn't really a medicine apparently the state says what is and isn't a medicine too. The way he made it sound I was breaking about half the laws in the county a regular Al Capone he was very polite about it though more like giving me a warning. It didn't matter to me I was getting too old by then to go up there on a regular basis anyway besides I'd gotten all these jobs helping out Lebrun's customers watching their houses I mean so. The only time I might have had a sip was at that party I went to the one at the KO

Kampsites. Well not to go to the party itself but that girl Saara yes with the extra a she had been asking about Jack-in-the-pulpit you know the plant. I don't remember why I think because of the name I must have mentioned it on one of our rides when she sat up front and she asked to see it but of course you can't find them that easily they're in the woods it's not like there are groves of them or anything they're solitary. I tried explaining to her the shape of the flower it's like a man in a pulpit although why he's Jack I don't know but that just made her more intrigued more curious so she asked me to find her one. I don't think she realized it wasn't the kind of flower you pick I mean it's one of those flowers that's more part of the plant you can't separate the two like you can with a rose say or a daisy. Well I went into the woods and found one it's not that hard if you know where to look I dug around it and put it in a bag and went down to the KO Kampsite where she and those hippies were living that summer. They'd practically taken over the place I heard Ed Fullner he charged them double he was half hoping they'd go away but instead they paid in advance for the whole month so what could he do. I guess I must have known but I'd forgotten that was the night of the party the one that Swartz fellow the one with the beard had invited me to. I never thought of it at the time I mean I never thought of going but it happened to be that night when I came there with this bag that had a Jack-in-the-pulpit in it. Well I didn't want to just pluck the thing out of the ground it would have been all dried out and dead by the time I showed it to her. I was going to let her see it and then replant it maybe somewhere where she could go visit it in the woods with me I guess behind the campsite. I don't know I hadn't thought it out that clearly but when I got there it was almost dark and there were they must have had ten times more kids than usual they must have sent out some kind of alert maybe by smoke signals or something I'm telling you that boy Swartz was more organized than anyone gave him credit for he had a rock band and a table for food it was like a whole scene that's what they called it a scene and there I was walking in with my plant a bagful of dirt basically that's what it must have looked like feeling like an idiot of course the only one over hell probably the only one over twenty and by a good many years at that but I got to give them credit they were very nice to me treated me like a guest. The Horse Man they called me because they loved Allure they were the only ones who saw what I saw in her and that was late when she was almost when she was just beginning to show the first signs of but anyway I couldn't find Saara not right away and he Swartz he gave me this bug juice to drink that's what he called it bug juice not that it was really made of bugs but I took a cup and it was nasty-tasting stuff. I drank it down to be polite and then only afterward he told me that they'd made it out of those berries they picked that day the day I'd taken them all up to yes that time when we went into the woods and. Well I almost dropped the cup I was holding because I knew that like I said if you don't mix them right if you don't cook them down they don't aid the digestion they and sure enough after a few more minutes I felt I wasn't the only one people all over they were holding their stomachs going off to the bathroom or just disappearing behind a tree wherever they could find a little privacy. But the funny thing was they didn't seem to mind it's almost like they were expecting it they'd come back out all happy not smelling very good I can tell you that but with this grin on their face. Me I headed for the woods behind the campsite I didn't want to be you want to be somewhere alone not heaving your guts out right next to some longhair in a stovepipe hat or whatever they were wearing I got about two or three feet in and then just sank to my knees. You know how it is in a pine forest soft with the carpet and so I stayed a while just making sure I was all done and then when I looked up it was still light. It had been almost dark when I came came to the campsite I mean and then I had been puking my guts out for at least a half hour or so that's what it felt like but when I looked up it was lighter than before somehow and then I remembered it was the solstice the longest day of the year that's why they were having their party although still I didn't see how it could be light after it was dark. That didn't make sense. When I went back out they had strung all these power cords to the box Ed has where people plug in say a fan or an electric shaver they must have had seven or eight thick cords all leading to a clearing in the field where this rock band was playing. I never heard anything like it it wasn't even music really not so far as I could tell but there were these big black boxes the sound came out of I was right near one and it was like the music was passing right through me. I saw one of these hippies his hand strum one of those electric guitars and every note I could see his fingers so clearly somehow they were right up close closer than the rest of him and every string his finger touched I could feel the sound I could feel the molecules of me somehow got disarranged. Then all the kids were dancing hopping up and down waving their arms that kind of dancing. No not me I was feeling queer but I wasn't going to make a spectacle of myself besides I still had the plant I was hugging it I didn't even notice until Saara saw me she came out of the crowd she'd been dancing I guess and she came up to me and asked what I had and I saw I was clutching this bag to my chest guarding it like a baby. The funny thing is when she asked I didn't know what was inside anymore. That's when I realized something strange was going on. She must have seen it too that I wasn't myself because she led me away it was the first time she ever touched me she took my shoulder. I haven't read the bible Miss Dick she didn't even keep a copy in the library when I asked once she said something about not having pulp fiction whatever that is but you hear things you can't help hearing things from it and one story I knew was Moses he strikes a rock and water gushes out well that's what happened to me not water gushing out but I began to cry. It just kind of began to leak out of me this steady stream I wouldn't even call them tears really yes when she touched my shoulder to guide me to take me away it was like a chemical reaction or maybe it was just from the glare. It was I can't tell you how bright it was. It's like I never noticed before but after the sun goes down goes under the horizon that is there's all this light left behind and it was just hanging in the air shimmering like it was never going to go away. She led me up over the rise and we sat we were far enough away so no one could see us and then she sort of gently got me to open the bag. I'd been clutching it like it was this big secret I don't know why. The Jack-in-the-pulpit was so ugly I remember thinking it looked too alive like some man-eating plant I could tell she was disappointed. Maybe she'd been hoping to put it in her hair she loved putting flowers in her hair but like I said it's not really that kind of flower it's too much part of everything not detachable but she was good-natured about it as I recall and then I told her I was going to replant it that's why I'd brought it with all the dirt but then we must have left it there because. What? No nothing more happened. It was the berries see they had this quality to them properties that's what Swartz called it. Me I cooked them down I mixed them with other things so it wasn't as strong whatever they did to you it was just a feeling of pleasantness of relaxation but Swartz and his crew well they didn't know what they were doing they're lucky no one got killed they had no knowledge they just wanted to get out of their skins go nuts for one night he made it too strong he didn't cook it down enough didn't mix it. An aid to the digestion hell you practically threw up your digestion along with everything else. We went for a walk the moon was out even though the sky was bright you could still hear the music you could hear it all the way to Lake Kathan I was told later some people thought it was a nuclear attack we held hands and she told me what a hard time she'd been having this summer she said It's been the worst summer of my life. I was surprised I thought they were all having fun she and those other kids I mean I thought that's what it was all about whatever the hell they were doing here they were doing it to have fun but no she said You're the only person I've ever. Nothing it's just. Of course I'm all right. Well later I realized it couldn't have happened what I remember I realized it was the berries my mind was. But what I felt happened was that she kind of hovered close like a hummingbird and sipped all the tears from my face I mean it wasn't her anymore she had turned into something else she was flying just a little bit off the ground and well she just came so close so close to me to my face as close as you can come without touching and I know it doesn't make any sense but she sipped up all my tears drank them so when I well not woke exactly but the next thing I knew we were laughing both of us and eating because suddenly we were hungry because of course everyone's stomach was empty from that god-awful drink he'd made. They had a big table with bread and butter and honey and white wine. I'd never had white wine before. Bread and butter and honey and white wine it was I tried to tell her about my mother I wanted to tell her about my mother for some reason but there was all this rock music playing we were closer to the band then so I don't think she really heard me maybe that's why I was talking in the first place because I knew she couldn't hear me not that it would make sense if she could. It was really just me getting something out of my system I remember that look in her eyes like she didn't understand or couldn't hear just nodding her head you know bobbing it and then Swartz or some other boy he took her away to dance it didn't matter to me anymore I think I was glad in a way because we'd had this moment where there was some kind of space taken away the space between us and after it's always hard to know what to do or say when you're just getting used to being yourself alone again. Nectar that's it like she was sipping nectar my tears. Then I got it into my head to find that plant the Jack-in-the-pulpit I felt guilty that I'd left it behind like I'd left it to die which I suppose I had but what the hell it's just a plant it was just going back to being the soil it came from anyway but those berries or whatever's in those berries they had made me completely crazy and I got it into my head that I had to save this plant so I went looking for it but of course that's a big field and by then it really was dark even with the moon finally I had to sit and kind of gather myself remind me who I was my name everything about me Alice Emily like it was in danger of flying away my life. That's when I realized I had to get home. I didn't say good-bye to anyone I walked along the road it wasn't really that late even though it felt like ten years had passed. When I got back of course Alice had bolted the door so I went to the barn and Allure she showed no surprise at all just tossed her head. I said It's the Summer of Love that's what Saara had told me people were calling that summer like a blue moon like something that only comes around every so many years the Summer of Love. Allure she'd been rubbing against the side of her stall it was one of the signs of her disease. I went over and saw she had a spot rubbed all raw like a wound. I tried to comfort her and she gave this deep all-over whinny which means I'm doing something else I don't want to be disturbed. Maybe dreaming you know they dream standing up so I backed off I think maybe she was jealous although maybe it was just me imagining. The Summer of Love.

～⌒

Well there was a car yes but he wouldn't have been on that road if he hadn't been drinking. I don't blame them no. It was dark. They say he darted right out darted yes that's the word they used no there was no trial the trooper just asked questions and they. People. Strangers. I don't remember their names just passing through the trooper didn't ask where they were going he just they said the man Father that is darted out from the side of the road like he was well panicked I guess. Squirrels do that sometimes they crouch right on the shoulder and then it's like the car coming makes their muscles work they jump right into the lights there's nothing you can do. They stopped it wasn't like they tried to cover it up tried to keep going the man who was driving he must have walked a quarter mile to Irene Lassiter's house to call the police. Yes a wife and two children I've always wondered about that about the family I wonder how it affected them. Me I didn't find out until morning. Well it was already late he was coming home from one of those roadhouses walking yes I told you everyone walked in those days. For a long time after I'd wake up and there'd be half the bed I couldn't spread out over I'd still be all hunched over to one side expecting him to come stumbling in. It didn't hit me so bad at the time I mean at the time everyone well not everyone but people said Poor boy or Poor young man but me I felt like at last there were no more witnesses like it was all mine now my memories you know of the family of Mother to do with as I pleased but I did wonder about those two children in the backseat asleep probably getting woken up being told not to look then just waiting sitting there while their father went off. No I never saw him again the body you mean in those days it was all out of sight out of mind the trooper who came he had a white mustache he was an elderly type he said there wasn't much to see. I acted pretty numb they thought I was well I hadn't talked much to begin with before I mean and then people thought I'd taken a step backward that I was. But my schoolwork that's what really saved me when they tried to have me sent to that place I showed them all my reports they couldn't argue with Miss Tomlinson or Miss Ross they both said well one at least said I was promising. Then Lawyer Breckenridge came forward that's right that's where he knew me from now I remember he came one day with that same trooper the one with the white mustache and they talked to me. I didn't say much no I knew what was happening but I didn't want to let them see that I was well that part of me was relieved that it was over that everything was over that everyone had gone. I think he just wanted to get from one side of the road to the other. I didn't see it of course I wasn't there but I can see it now see it more clearly as I get older and pass through the same times of life he passed through he just got confused he wanted to join her on the other side not that they'd let him of course the church I mean not with all the trouble he'd caused them about Mother's grave they wouldn't let him anywhere near her but I just saw him wanting to get across. I didn't talk much. They thought I was slow. Breckenridge I don't know why he took an interest he fought for me to stay where I was and then he introduced me to Seraphim Washburn he got me set up on my feet. Well he was that kind of man a do-gooder a reformer that's what he called himself until whatever it was took hold of him that bug up his ass about the clinic. He was handsome too wore a vest with a watch chain the whole bit. They came to see me I don't know who the trooper was he looked like a father in a movie you know with a white mustache no he wasn't from around here I never saw him again. Certainly I tried to contact Rebecca. I went to the clinic but they gave me pretty short shrift apparently Father had been after them as well once she left. He showed up demanding all kinds of information about the guest the man who'd run off with her but Cochrane said it was confidential the records I'm not sure it's true I mean they weren't doctors not Cochrane certainly that came out later in the whole aftermath and Christopher well he turned out to be a doctor but the other kind a Ph.D. from some foreign university and after when they disappeared all the records had been destroyed but Father he apparently made a scene banging on the door in the middle of the night demanding oh yes drinking of course Dutch courage they call it demanding to know what they'd done with his daughter. Cochrane and some of those goons from downstate attendants he called them they muscled Father away from the building didn't want him to wake the patients the clientele and then well he only did that once but then he started talking to Breckenridge or maybe Breckenridge started talking to him because otherwise how would he have known Breckenridge that is how would he have known to come see me? So I went but of course I didn't bang on the door I went hat in hand like a young fool because I wanted to find out where my sister was and tell her our father was dead. Cochrane he must have been out I saw Christopher which was unusual. He told me how sorry he was. No not upstairs not that place I went to the day of the Open House that was off-limits he was in between treatments he was wearing one of those white coats and had that headlight strapped to his forehead what do you call them they don't use them anymore but anyway he couldn't spare me much time but told me how sorry he was and that he didn't know anything about my sister running off that it was all her private business and that at the clinic she'd been a model employee that's what he said a model employee. Then we got to talking and actually come to think of it when he heard I was going to work for Seraphim Washburn that's when he told me I should start bringing ice out there. Before then I don't know who'd they'd been using but I went back to Washburn and he almost dropped his fountain pen apparently he and Cochrane well no one got along with Washburn but getting the clinic's business that was a big deal it made him look twice at me. Of course with all that I forgot about why I'd gone out there in the first place about Rebecca I mean. It was for looking inside people's throats this big reflector doctors strapped to their forehead. No I never found any more clues I looked in her room or what had been her room I picked up the layer of junk we'd thrown in there and looked underneath it through what was hers but she hadn't left much. I found a prayer book that belonged to Mother. Rebecca must have hidden it because Father wouldn't have allowed her he took all Mother's things all the religious things after she died when they wouldn't let him bury her there he made a big pile sprinkled kerosene on the top and but she must have hidden this away it had some flowers pressed in it but no clues as to where she was. Then the bank sent a man to appraise everything. I had to show him around room by room show him how there was nothing of any value nothing worth selling. He sat on the bed without asking my permission spat right on the floor spat tobacco juice. I didn't say anything I didn't say anything to anyone then not if I could help it. With Gabrielle that first time you mean well I must have said something then but it wasn't like I had to be some smooth-talking Romeo she knew what I was there for. After she got me to speak up a little I told her I thought Nell smelled like mothballs she liked that she laughed but Rebecca Breckenridge made a real effort to find her he really had it out for Cochrane and Christopher Cochrane in particular and somehow he thought she was the key. He kept after me he'd ask me about her as if there was something I knew knew but had forgotten something that would help him find her. By then of course Alice and I were but he didn't know that he didn't see he was too busy it really was what you would call an obsession. He wanted to close that place down in the worst way. The funny thing is he wasn't here to see it happen. If I had to do it over again well first I'd sock that son-of-a-bitch appraiser right in the nose for spitting on the floor then I don't know I don't know if I'd do things differently. Sometimes I don't think I feel like other people feel I don't cry certainly not the way Emily she my god it's like the waterworks when her mother passed away but me I just sat there. Now good times those moments like the one I was telling you about with Lebrun say or with Saara when the gap disappears they always surprise me I'll cry I'll look down and find tears. That's part of what makes them special good times is how unexpectedly they come on you but when something bad happens that's just more mud on the road. No I never learned to drive. You see that's the thing I didn't cry but I also decided I wouldn't learn how to drive one of those things that killed Father so in a way you could say it set the whole direction of my life what happened that night even though I didn't show much outward sign.

Well at the funeral it was different the walls were caving in the sides of the hole the grave yes it was raining so hard and they'd done such a bad job somehow it didn't seem right like he was being I don't know buried alive like a cave-in not like Mother's where they put a shovelful of dirt down and you heard it on the box. With Father it was more like this mud-swirl. I kept reaching for Elizabeth and she wasn't there of course and then well one of the men he stepped back because the ground the ground right at the edge of the hole was giving way the rain I can't tell you how hard it was raining so I grabbed the shovel from his hand and tried to undo it shovel the dirt away I wasn't really trying to dig him out but it was slippery it slipped from my hand the shovel so I got down on my hands and knees and that's when they came after me and hauled me away but I still had dirt under my nails they'd look for it in school you know they'd send you home if your fingernails were dirty but of course I wasn't going to school anymore so yes it stayed there quite a while I didn't care it was almost like a badge of honor until Gabrielle she noticed it she took my hand in hers and made some joke some little remark and I blushed red. Elizabeth I don't know any Elizabeth it was Rebecca I was wanting Rebecca she should have been there with me but she wasn't. Not that she would have had such a great life up here if she'd stayed she was too good for this place but I blushed deep red and when I got home that night I cleaned them off scrubbed them. Washburn when I went to work the next day he made some comment I guess my whole appearance was different. I thought it was because I'd been to Nell's you know now I was a man that kind of thing that you could see the change. People have such funny ideas. Now I realize of course it was because I had cleaned myself up got the dirt out from under my nails cut my hair figured out how to use the straight razor just to haul ice that's all the job was. It was backbreaking work you had to use those tongs to grip the blocks. The horses he had no I don't remember their names Goddamned Piece of Shit is probably what I called both of them although I didn't even know such words then I was a very clean-spoken youth that all happened later when I began to anyway I knew nothing about horses how to coax them how to talk to them how to listen to them most importantly. We had terrible fights they used to come to a dead halt right in the middle of the road. Not that it helped what Washburn fed them moldy oats winter hay that smelled like dry rot it was quite a change from school anyone who tells you different that they'd rather be outside with a sixty-pound block of ice on their shoulder instead of sitting in a nice warm classroom well. But I was young and strong. Washburn I see now he robbed me blind sending me up into the hills up to Indian Pipes I was working from dawn till dusk I'd come home fall asleep before I could even eat dinner. Most of the money I made went to the bank. That's what he told me they were garnisheeing my wages he said. Now looking back I wonder why should I be responsible for Father's debts? They had the farm already and I was taking care of that for them too yes all the chores until they sold off the cow and some other poor benighted soul came to work the fields. Benighted it means never mind no Miss Dick wasn't there then the library wasn't I don't know when they built that. Kathan really hadn't taken off as a tourist place yet that happened later. It was hardly a town. On Sunday I'd do chores the farm chores and then go down to Conklingville. Most men they were in their dark suits their Sunday best. I didn't have to be I was my own man. I walked down the stream didn't even take the dirt road just jumped from stone to stone like it was my own private highway. A little stream it fed right into what they called the Black River although then I told you it was just you could almost leap right over it if it didn't rain for a few weeks. Gabrielle's room was in back the prison that little glass sometimes it would wink out at me. One thing I'll say for work it makes you feel good after. Tired I mean and all achy but that feeling of a job well done of having given it your all. I don't get that anymore maybe it's part of being young. All I had to do really was haul those son-of-a-bitch blocks of ice from the cart to the icebox. Fancier places had a whole separate room for the ice but it was nothing really. Mother Father Rebecca they were all gone my mind had expanded to take their places. What I couldn't do in the bed I guess you know spread my arms and legs out I did in my head and then on Sundays I'd be all tired and my muscles I could feel my shoulders growing not getting all pinched like Father's all tensed up but filling out expanding. I don't know if I was different to her to Gabrielle than any of the other men we talked but maybe she talked to the others too how should I know I'm trying to be realistic. Love? Well I was barely out of short pants you can imagine and with no one at home no one to talk to I don't know what it was I felt. Love? Like I say love it's this blanket you throw over things.

～○

Yes the stream it had all flat rocks so you could walk pretty easily from one to the next you could take it in the other direction past the farm straight up the mountainside. I used to go that way when I was younger. It was to escape Father if he saw me he'd think of some chore for me to do there was always some task he had in mind I hated it although as I got older I began to realize that maybe it was his way of well he wasn't good at communicating so maybe he wanted to work side by side with me I don't know but at the time all I wanted to do was get away of course and the stream it was this kind of hidden path I'd pretend I was an escaped convict trying to get away from the sheriff he'd be tracking me with a dog a bloodhound so if I could just stay on the rocks not leave my scent anywhere not crush a leaf or make a sound just dance up the stream from rock to rock then at the top it became a kind of swampy area the trees got spindly and there was all this standing water with tall grass. And flowers. Yes the fire tower is up there even farther but not much. I'd

113

get there all panting and sweaty. There was this big boulder in the middle I'd go for that I'd climb up to the top and sit. Rebecca no girls didn't wander around outside as much as boys they get set inside tasks women's work I think I tried to show her once but she turned back holding up her dress trying not to get it wet oh it was before pants women's pants. It was more like with the sesquicentennial when they were all wearing long dresses or when they were supposed to at least. Alice she'd run them up on her machine. Yes she was quite a sewer. Not usually for me not men's clothes but Emily she was always dressed very well. Of course she didn't like it she wanted to wear that cheap trash her friends got down at Sparta or when that mall at Breyerton opened. Breyerton it wasn't even a town it was the name of a road and even that I think they made it up I think it was some contractor's name Breyer I never knew anyone named that from around here and then they built a whole shopping mall there where there used to be fields you can still see it it's like the soil still wants to produce. Just beyond the parking lot there's this whole crop of well more and more it's just those tall reeds but you can see there's still furrows there where some poor bastard excuse my language no I don't know who but some poor bastard poured his life out anyway Alice would never let her go there well we didn't have a car so. Why should I just because everyone else did? Horses are so much better for one thing they don't kill you not unless you deserve it. Cars they're so loud and smelly and going along in them you have no time to think it's like drinking it's like people are drunk on the speed they think they're getting somewhere but really. Now in the cart I would arrive places and it made sense the time it took to get there I knew where I was going I knew what was expected of me. Lebrun would pull up in his truck which he drove like a madman by the way even when his arm healed he'd pull up and you never knew who would come out. His mind would be somewhere else entirely still having some fight he'd been in at his last stop or getting ready for the fight he was going on to next yes he still ran the dam then all his building was on the side that's the joke it was like the tail wagging the dog for a long time he still lived in that pokey little house the Authority built him down by the spillway not until his wife made him leave and even then he waited until his disability came through he was tight with a nickel he wasn't going to let anything slip through his fingers certainly not with all the years he put in checking levels so there he was with three houses going up simultaneously three crews working plus usually a surveyor or two mapping out another parcel and him driving around in that Black River Authority truck like a lunatic trying to hold about a million things in his mind at once it's a miracle no one was killed. Me I'd ride with him but when Alice or anyone else talked about us getting a car I'd just. We could get what we needed in either town Kathan or Antone and what we couldn't get we didn't really need. Emily she's a terror. One of those all-terrain vehicles like they use on the moon. It climbs well. If you listen to her it can climb Mount Antone in the dead of winter. How she paid for it I have no idea layaway probably I keep expecting to hear she turned it back in couldn't meet the payments but she's had it for a couple of years now. Town clerk can't pay that much but me no what you've got to realize is that the quality of life in this country started going down I'd say right around the time you were born. No offense. Your parents well they ended up living in Hollywood that's not a real place anyway. Out here I think that's why they came it reminded them of the good life your mother she brought that with her always trying to make things pleasant for everyone you'd never think back then that she was well who she was. With Lebrun I had to ride I didn't have a choice. That's the only time I could talk to him. Once he got rich he couldn't get away couldn't get away from himself from who people thought he was. It didn't help that he was married. What little time he had left left from work I mean and his business he had to spend with her. Sometimes I'd hint about us going up the mountain or once I think I even told him about the quarry even though that was my private place just hoping to get him there and maybe have some you know some family feeling like we used to but the only time we ever talked around then was in that truck no the new one not that old jalopy he'd gotten them to buy him the first time around. I'm telling you he was a master at milking the system he got them to buy him a brand-new truck it wasn't his technically but he used it like it was with one of those shiny horns on top and leather seats it was like lying back in a barbershop chair. Top of the line he kept saying a top of the line vehicle he even had a pint of Old Gentleman he kept in the glove compartment just for me. Sometimes we'd drive for no reason I guess it was the only way he could escape his troubles. I don't know what they were his troubles not specifically it's like he brought them on himself like he needed to have them all these troubles things weighing on his mind things that he could run away from go from one to the other women yes but the banks too he was always complaining about them Petrides in particular Petrides at Mountain Trust the Greek that's right and the Authority even though it seemed to me he was doing fine off them but he. His wife no he never complained about her. We the rest of us did but not to his face of course you couldn't say a word against her anywhere within fifty miles of here it would get back to him and he'd come looking for you but in the car I guess it freed him up driving around no one could get to him it's kind of like he was in between going from one thing to the next. Sometimes he'd take a detour we'd be on our way to a site or Mosher's to pick up an item and suddenly he'd pull us on to say Gick Road or some other little byway that basically went nowhere. Not the highway one of those roads that well once upon a time maybe they went somewhere but whatever they were following or heading toward was long gone a logging camp or a river that's all dried up we'd bounce along it's hard to drink out of a bottle in a car the glass bashes against your teeth. I'd offer him some but no he never. He could have used it just a swig his hands they gripped that wheel so tight. I asked once why he didn't just leave. He said he couldn't that Eagle Enterprises wouldn't let him which I thought was pretty funny strange I mean he was Eagle Enterprises. Then he said Anyway where would I go? It was winter so I said off the top of my head Florida and he nodded like he hadn't thought of that before like he'd consider it. Once he said to me You got the right idea William. You married a woman smarter than you. I thought that was an odd thing to say. Well it's true Alice she was a whiz at numbers and sewing at so many things but I don't know I never thought of it that way that she was smarter. His own wife was plenty smart she was always getting those college catalogs in the mail. Alice didn't ever read anything just inspirational magazines. We'd drive. He said he had to rack up a certain amount of mileage so the Authority wouldn't take the truck back. To prove he needed it. See that's another way cars take over your life I swear it's like you're the gasoline the way they use you up you can feel it when you're driving along how your life is going up in smoke getting turned into that blue exhaust coming out the tailpipe. Once we got out he had to pee and we were way up in the hills he'd taken a few turns on roads that I don't even call roads just paths showing off his four-wheel drive or whatever they call it and we were looking straight down I didn't know where the hell I was I was all turned around. Once I get in a car I stop paying attention it gets me all dizzy staring out the window besides I'm usually too busy holding onto the door handle or the side of the seat it always feels like we're about to go ass over teakettle anyway we were looking straight down at the lake but from higher than usual hawks below us riding the currents and I said Remember you said this was all going to be yours someday and now it is. I wanted to make him feel better because it was true it had happened just like he said. At first I thought he didn't hear because he didn't answer I told you if he didn't like what he heard it's like the words didn't exist like you hadn't said any-thing but then he finished what he was doing and said That wasn't me. I didn't get it. I mean I knew what I knew it certainly wasn't some-one else who had said that. Then back in the truck when we were going back down and I thought he'd forgotten he said it again. That wasn't me who told you that. Well then who was it? I wanted to ask but he took us down that mountainside like he was trying to take off in a jet airplane. Oh I don't know what he meant. He was just un-happy all of a sudden. It takes people that way sometimes in middle age they look up one day and don't like what they see. No it never happened to me not that I recall. I mean I had bad days but this was different. She just arrived. We didn't even know they were married there wasn't any ceremony not here. She kept her own name which nobody did back then painted it right on the mailbox right under his. Bud the mail carrier he was upset everyone else you see got let-tering at Mosher's you bought the letters of your name one by one and then the box number. They had stickum so you peeled off the back and applied them to your mailbox. No one painted their name it was well he claimed it was against regulations but what was he go-ing to do not deliver the mail? No one knew where she came from. He met her on one of his trips to Sparta that's where the Authority has its regional office. One day he came back with her and just kind of installed her in that house down by the spillway. She wrote her name on the box that's the first we knew about it that's how we found out Bud grousing about someone painting their name under his. He didn't take it much further than that in his mind Bud he pretty much cared about the mail and his hunting but of course ev-eryone else wanted to know what kind of name was it and when he said a woman's well you can imagine. Is it snowing again? Funny but when it snows like this that's when I see the town more clearly or imagine I can. Conklingville yes it's like all the snowflakes fit to-gether I know no two are alike but did you ever think maybe that's because they're puzzle pieces no two puzzle pieces are alike either. That's what happens if you stare long enough. Well it's not like I have a hell of a lot else to do especially now since Cecil won't let me. The porch that's as far as I'm allowed. Senior home that's a joke what it is is just a bunch of double-wide trailers put together by one of those fly-by-night contractors they use now. Lebrun his houses were built to last they stood up to whatever nature could dish out. Cement floors he'd let them set fourteen fifteen days other people you were lucky if they let them set a week you could still see damp patches but you know time is money so they'd go right on building. He'd let his set a good long time until you could drive a Sherman tank over them that's what he'd say. But this place it's built like. I try telling Emily about it but she just talks about the tax base about how the town has to spend so much on roads and schools. She says I'm lucky to even have gotten into this this what do they call it senior home. Snow-flakes if you stare well you should try it you have to have patience though if you stare and try piecing together the flakes put them back the way they were before they started falling you can look out over the lake and see the top of the church steeple peeking up over the surface. Oh I know it's not there not in the sense you mean but then you're probably seeing things I'm not seeing. Why should I believe you when you don't believe me? He never discussed it no it was just a fact about him you had to accept that he was married now like it had fallen on him from above. It didn't make him any happier I can tell you that. People said they fought the two of them Lebrun and her that they fought something awful. Maybe he thought she'd give him children if so well.

⁓

I didn't go no. I tried. Alice was dead set against it. We were just married but everyone else was either volunteering or if you waited you got something in the mail. It wouldn't have been such a bad

119

thing that's what I thought at the time you never think about getting killed not at that age but when I went to the draft board it was over in Schuyler those days they classified me as. I guess it helped that I was married most of the men the young bucks they snapped them up right away the army I mean and that was the last you ever heard of them. Oh they may have come back from the war but more often than not they ended up somewhere else. It was that bill you know the GI Bill that let them go to school and then once they went away not many of them came back. It was a boon for me though I can tell you that. With all the young men in town gone Alice encouraged me the first thing she had me do after we were married was break with Seraphim Washburn. We had money Breckenridge had set her up given her a nest egg from the sale of the house she handled that end of it and I used some to buy the rig. He was furious Washburn he said how sorry I'd be but then they took him too. Anything that could be delivered not just ice he had other customers he just didn't think I was ready to handle them yet but I'd learned I went around and gathered them all up the accounts. There was no competition. Lebrun he was essential personnel the dam was classified as a military target somehow as if the Nazis were going to pop out from I don't know where and blow it up. He got spared too people talked about that sneered said that he wasn't really a citizen or something that's why he hadn't been called up. With me I don't know why but they didn't seem to notice they took it as a matter of course. Allure well it was more like she chose me. I'd gone down to look at a bunch of different animals and she was standing there with the others. A horse will never act like you're in the same world as them they're not like you and me they're completely at peace with themselves you have to work to make yourself known to them or else they just go on nibbling grass or staring off or whatever it is they're doing. Well Allure I saw her in her stall and she was investigating something in the straw with her hoof pawing at it kind of looking down. The man he was trying to interest me in another animal but I looked down to where she was looking. It was nothing of course it never is when they do that not that you can ever see but then my eye traveled back up her leg and chest and up to her face and when I got there she was staring at me. She grunted like Let's get out of here and I told the man it was her I wanted like she was telling me what to say. Before then no I never had much of a connection with horses but. Firebrand? Firebrand was just the price he got for me taking Allure he didn't want to sell her she was a cut above you could tell Firebrand I had to take off his hands as compensation that was part of the deal but he was fine not at all like his name not a troublemaker. She calmed him down I don't know how nipped him once or twice probably. Oh she'd nip you if she wanted to make a point. Alice went to the barn early on when we were all set up in the new place she came to tell me something and then she tried to pet her. It didn't help that I laughed. Well it was just a love bite that's what I tried to explain it didn't draw blood or anything but Alice acted like she was going to lose a finger. Don't pet her I said she's not a dog. Anyway from then on our worlds were drawn up I had the barn and she had the house. The problem was she didn't have to come out to the barn that often and when she did it could be when Allure wasn't there. Me I had to live in that house which I was never a hundred percent comfortable in but I was working so hard those first years it hardly mattered. Just as hard as before yes but the money was my own. Washburn he came back after. Not to stay just long enough to see that I had taken over that there was no chance for him to pick up where he left off. He laughed at me he said that trucks were taking over. That's what he'd done during the war drive a truck I don't think he even had a gun just drove a truck he said no one needed horse carts anymore that I had gotten the last seat on the Titanic something like that I didn't care. Allure I showed her the way the first time and after that she had this sense where to go. I swear she memorized my route before

I did. Sometimes early on I'd get confused what day it was or who got what first but she well they don't call it horse sense for nothing. Mostly it was the quiet I liked. It's actually quite noisy up there I mean with the jingling of the harnesses and the load whatever you've got shifting around and then the hooves on the ground of course but you can tune it all out you kind of fall into the rhythm of it there's a kind of quiet you discover behind it all a different kind of quiet than when you're just sitting still. But I couldn't have done it without Alice she encouraged me she told me I was capable. Bricks milk newspapers. Gasoline was rationed then you could barely get any and they didn't make any new trucks during the war not for civilians so it was a paradise for me nothing but work I'd load the bricks and take them to the clinic. They were building oh I don't know they were always constructing something I think Cochrane cared more about that than anything else more than his patients certainly. The only time I ever saw him excited so excited that he was actually polite to me was when I took a load of bricks out to that hole they'd dug by the spring the spring it's up on Woodcock Mountain behind the clinic. They had plans to make baths they were going to build a kind of pool I don't know what happened. Not hot springs no cold but the water did smell funny it had a kind of color to it too that's why no one ever lived there or used it for anything the spring it stank. Sulfur I guess rotten eggs but something else too. It was a crazy idea that people would pay to shiver in a pool in the middle of the woods but no crazier than the rest of it I suppose spraying them with hoses smearing them with mud physical therapy that's what they called it that's when Breckenridge that was his starting-off point. He showed me their brochure and he'd circled the words Physical Therapy he said that's what Rebecca had done. He said that Physical Therapy was really. At first I had no idea what he was talking about I was a teenager then and well you've got to remember there was no mention of anything like that in the papers or on the radio. I mean I'd seen animals doing it of course but didn't make the connection who would I mean it's insane to connect the two when you think about it. The Greeks they had the right idea they kept all that separate the barnyard stuff from feelings. But he showed me that and said That's what they had your sister do. Well by the time I figured out what he'd been saying I was already out the door and on my way home it took that long for the nickel to drop if you know what I mean. No of course it wasn't true Rebecca she would never. The man must have told her he was going to marry her that's the only way she would have left with him. If you'd read her journal you would understand. No I never read it myself I told you no one did but you'd know I mean if you could hear it in her own words and see what a good girl she was. Breckenridge he anyway I delivered eggs bricks milk ice whatever there was back and forth from the train depot to the stores to the clinic. We beat a path Allure and me.

~

You asked me that already I told you how the horses spook if they ever catch a whiff of oh you mean from the war when they were in a coffin you mean? No that was later the Vietnam War. I was too young then I didn't have the kind of well dignity I had later when Rector Graves asked me to take his boy. Who'd want some half-wit pulling their son to the cemetery like he was a load of yesterday's milk canisters yes that's what they called me some of them half-wit touched I heard it all they didn't take too many pains to conceal it I suppose my not answering just egged them on like I didn't even understand what they were saying so they said it louder. No I never brought any boys home from that war hell they would have been my age or older it wouldn't have been right. Rector he never got over that son of his. He didn't show it at the time he didn't show nothing at the time but it took the stuffing out of him. Later I saw him at Walt's trying to bring a cup of coffee to his lips it was painful the way his hands trembled so. Mary she stayed on in that house a while after. I don't know what became of her last I looked it's still there the house but she's long gone. Maybe she had family in the south. A lot of them do you know colored people they don't like the winters. Mary Graves I haven't thought about her in a while I don't think she had one friend in this whole town growing up. The boy Junior he played sports at least he was more what do you call it more personable but Mary I remember Emily once saying that she was the only girl they picked on worse than her worse than Emily I mean at school. Well she was big even then and her father driving this cart around I suppose that made her a figure of fun. You know kids. She'd come home crying. The only one they treated worse she said was Mary Graves. I'd see her sometimes at the cemetery after her brother and father died I don't know how she made ends meet. I don't know what she was doing here to begin with there were none of her kind here. She'd been left high and dry that's for sure. Lawrence he was sweet on her. Of course he was older but that works sometimes it was just like him he always wanted to be a little different being sweet on Mary Graves that would make people talk shock them just a little I don't know if it was even legal then not that it ever came to that I don't know if they could even be seen together not in a formal way but everyone knew it was common knowledge. In fact when they found him he'd gone wandering off again out there somewhere on 9N just walking the shoulder they called Mary because he'd passed out. She might have taken him in while he recovered. Heart attack. I don't think it led to anything though. Like I said she probably went down south. Although it must have been hard leaving those two up here Senior and Junior. Senior no I didn't take him to the graveyard who'd have paid for it? Like I said mostly bricks milk the papers eyeballs that was a special case I guess they didn't want any official man looking at them a train conductor or someone. I guess they figured that if I said something who'd believe me? Oh I have absolutely no idea. When it came out later all the details well of course he sounded crazy Christopher like a mad scientist. Cochrane that was no surprise at all that he was a crook we knew that all along but Christopher I still don't believe some of the things they wrote about him the reporters I mean. How do they know? They talked to patients sure but anyone who went to that place how much can you believe what they say they were crazy to begin with the patients the clientele a lot of them and since Christopher wasn't around to answer their accusations since there were no records. What happened was this man in Sparta the one they were using for the body parts a funeral home director he talked I guess they caught him at it not burying people they opened up a box and didn't find the cadaver something like that. That's what Christopher was doing he was I don't know if he was mixing them up in a blender or what but he was injecting people with body parts human bodies kidney liver you name it. Well to make them younger to rejuvenate them or to make them better maybe to correct some flaw it was never made clear. They were never given a chance to defend themselves. The funeral home director got caught and he told them about Cochrane and Christopher and then all hell broke loose naturally although really what's so bad about it the people were dead anyway. He was in it for the money the man downstate but them I don't know. The most interesting thing is the two of them together. I mean you have to wonder if each really knew what the other one was up to. I delivered a few sacks of cement to that springhouse too. He was there Christopher he was bent over this kind of housing they'd made to pump the water into the pool the pool that never got built. I guess they ran out of money. He brought up a cup of the water it smelled like poison but he had this little electronic box he showed me. Cochrane was there too you could tell he wanted me to get the hell out but Christopher he was nice he showed me how if you held this attachment close to the water the box it had this dial and it would click make these clicking sounds and the needle would bounce very slowly in time to the clicks. It's radioactive he said. I think that might have been the first time I heard the word it was in the papers you know when they bombed Hiroshima but said out loud. The water he said it's radioactive. He was very excited. Cochrane he hustled me out of there. I don't know why they never built the pool I delivered enough material up there I don't know what happened to it it's probably still sitting there under a tarp melting into the ground. That happens the place is full of all these *Unrealized Dreams* that's what Lawrence called them once all these half-built houses and gazebos and fences fencing in nothing. People run out of money. You see all this virgin territory you want to do something with it leave your mark but really there's nothing you can do you can't reclaim it from the woods that's people's big mistake. Cochrane and Christopher people said they ran off but their car was still there the Chevrolet and no one had seen them get on the train so for a while there was this search people thought maybe they'd done a kind of lover's leap together but no bodies turned up. Me I thought they'd both taken whatever it was he was working on the elixir and turned younger and just walked right past us but in a different time in their lives so they'd be invisible to us we'd be looking for them older their older selves. Well it makes just as much sense as those two hiking one hundred sixty miles to the Canadian border which is what the troopers eventually said must have happened. *Unrealized Dreams* and then he listed this whole bunch of half-finished projects that was later when he got his camera when he learned how to put pictures in the *Pennysaver* I remember there was one of our old place where I'd grown up yes but it had been knocked to the ground and then some poor sap it's like he took up right where Father left off that spot must be cursed he started building some big house got about two-thirds done and then went broke. It was sitting there for years the insulation exposed the roof sagging a new roof yes but sagging already. I used to stop there if I was passing by. *You can see in but there's nothing to see* that's what Lawrence wrote about all those places. *The dreams are gone.* I don't know why he had it in for your mom and dad. Maybe because they were even more special than he was you know he was used to being the only celebrity around here if you can even call it that and then your mom and dad came no they didn't make a big deal out of it that's what's so funny he did that himself he's the one who had to point it out. I just thought they were summer people especially at first because they were still onstage then your father in particular I guess your mom had just had you but your father I know he went back down sometimes he'd be gone for weeks at a time but it never really registered even when I heard what he did. Later of course he was in those movies but at first when I met him what I liked was his handshake how he kind of stood back and looked at you really taking the measure of the man he was talking to. Most people don't look you in the eye or if they do it's like a challenge like a staring contest but your father he just had that quality you liked him right away at least I did. Plus of course I'd never met anyone like him I mean the way he talked and just the fact that he wasn't working like the rest of us. I'd come by to stack firewood and he'd be stretched out on a towel sunbathing or reading what was that paper he used to get the *Racing Form* that's right. He always had time for me it never looked like he was busy. My wife he said he had that funny way of talking out the side of his mouth like a gangster My wife tells me we're having company tonight so I thought I'd get in a little relaxation. Oh they entertained all the time. They had houseguests famous ones I heard later but I never knew I had never heard of them I mean. Your mother people just wanted to be around her. She had that quality she made every occasion special. I'd bring them things from the garden. Alice said I should charge but I told her they pay me enough as it is hell your dad used to pour me a drink some liquor I can't even pronounce but it was out of a fancy bottle and we'd walk down to the lake he was such a city boy he told me once he grew up on the sidewalk. Just watching him walk go down that slope was funny I mean Freddie Freddie Seaborne had made it absolutely grassy by then that's what your mom wanted it's not easy believe me to grow such a smooth lawn like that particularly on a slope going down to the water but he'd done it and even so your father would walk like there were snakes or bear traps or something hidden in there he could never get used to it. I suppose it would be like me try-ing to cross Broadway or whatever big street they have down there. Once he told me he'd lost ten thousand dollars playing pinochle can you imagine? I told him how smart Allure was and he told me about a horse that they thought could count. It would tap its hoof. They'd say What's six plus eight? and it would tap its hoof fourteen times. But they found out later of course I could have told them this that the horse was just telling them what they wanted to hear. See we're not as secret as we think we are. Around fourteen everyone watch-ing must have tensed up or held their breath. Of course a horse can tell things like that it's an animal. I told him Allure was different she'd ask you What's six plus eight? That's the difference. She'd pose the question to you. Oh he was quite a character your father so dark you know so hairy and your mom so light. They made quite a cou-ple. She'd come out it was like the sun coming out from behind a cloud I didn't even realize it was makeup it was Ruth Sayheim I think who told me. I said What's all this? I was taking out the gar-bage and this big cloud of white powder flew up and she said That's pancake makeup. Well of course how would I know she had the most perfect face so white and she kept out of the sun I remember her on the beach always under one of those big umbrellas watching you and Lucy play in the sand. No Freddie didn't have to truck it in it was under there. Like I said this was all ocean once. Just a layer of topsoil he scraped away and there was your beach like it was waiting for you plus a million rocks of course but he scattered them among those trees he planted it's all well not fake but man-made it just looks like nature. He had quite a touch Freddie not only for chimneys. But you and Lucy would play out in the sun her in that uniform of hers like she was a nurse or a maid or something and you butt-naked. Your mom would be watching you both from under that big umbrella her face as white as well I didn't realize it was powder. I brought them squash zucchini whatever we had. It used to drive Alice crazy but I told her What am I supposed to do they're always giving us stuff I have to give them something back. Whatever they didn't need. Old clothes gadgets a coffeemaker our first TV. I didn't really want it but I couldn't say no and then when I got it home Emily well she yes it was color a color TV. We turned it on and I don't think Emily did much else but watch who was that boy on that cowboy show Bonanza? I don't think she did much else but watch him for a year and a half. All kinds of guests. You don't remember? They made such a big deal out of you I don't think any of their friends had children you were the only one. They were theater people and then later there were his gambling friends too people from the track that was a whole other side to him but you had Lucy she was with you all the time she was a good solid woman solidly built I mean kindhearted too you don't remember any of those friends I'm surprised. I suppose you were too young yes by the time you were older they'd moved out west your dad was in the movies more. They came out once or twice after that but it wasn't the same he was on the phone all the time. Early on I'd go over there and you never knew who you'd run into. Once it was some old man he was roasting a lamb on the beach he'd dug a pit built a fire and had these coals working. I was walking along the taking line that's the high-water mark that was one of my jobs for Lebrun making sure all the NO TRESPASSING signs were up right where the Authority's property ended I was walking along the beach and I came across this old man dancing practically jumping in and out of this hole in the sand with

129

a fire at the bottom turning over a whole lamb and the smell I thought this is like the wine-dark sea you know from *The Odyssey* well that's Greek history too it really happened of course it did do you think you could make something like that up? When they camp out on the beach they make a fire and sacrifice a lamb and here was this old man a foreigner I have no idea where he came from not here that's for sure his name was so complicated everyone just called him Uncle. I don't think he really was anyone's uncle because they all called him Uncle you see. So how can you be uncle to everyone? But the smell. He said he was staying with your parents which didn't surprise me at all they were coming down later he said for a party. The sun was still high enough and I swear I could imagine some trireme come rowing over the horizon trireme that's a Greek boat that's how they got to Troy in a trireme. Uncle yes I'm surprised you don't remember him or didn't hear them talk about him later maybe they used his real name. No I didn't stay for the meal I had work to do besides I wasn't invited but that was the best part I'm sure the smell and the sun the wine-dark sea that's what they called it. A trireme. They would row through the wine-dark sea.

～

That's the sound of shoveling. Cecil he takes his job seriously. Well to see us through to the other side I guess. No I don't believe any of that. Other side of what? I never thought of this as a side. Allure they made her hooves into Jell-O what's she doing in horse heaven without any hooves? It doesn't make sense. Firebrand he didn't even notice she was gone. Just went about his business. Of course there was nothing more for him to do I couldn't ask him to pull the whole rig himself besides there was no call for it after the sesquicentennial after those rides that was our last hurrah. Then I worked for Lebrun did whatever odd jobs he came up with. Alice of course she began complaining to me about why was he still here Firebrand eating us out of house and home she said but what could I do I wasn't going to send him off there was nothing wrong with him. By then he was just this quiet old horse nibbling away in a field not harming anyone. He had a stiff gait always I mean but more as he aged. I don't know if he recognized me toward the end his eyes got milky she never noticed that Alice she never got close enough or else she would have pushed harder for him to be you know to be taken off. A blind horse she would have said you're throwing our money away on a blind horse. I'd lead him out. Brush him down he liked that. He was a bit vain he had this kind of prance he did when anyone was watching. Sometimes he'd stumble that was painful to see. I don't know why I didn't send him off then like I did Allure. Some animals grow old some don't. Allure the way she would pull off to the side like there was this invisible road well that was her trying to stay young trying to stay on the road of youth I think. She could see she was veering off into being an old horse and she didn't like it she kept insisting there was this other way the right way she would have said but all she'd done is by the end my god she was rubbed raw the vet said I should have done it a year ago I'd just been treating the symptoms he said taking care of the wounds but not the disease. Well how do I treat the disease? I asked. He said You can't there's no cure and charged me fifty dollars. Firebrand I never had cause to call the vet on Firebrand. He'd just stay out there all day. I'd bring him in at night. Alice never noticed. He barely moved from spot to spot that fence if he'd wanted to there were parts so rotten he could have walked right through. Six plus eight that's the kind of thing she asked me I mean not a mathematical problem but she'd pose questions just by her being there. It's hard to explain. Miss Dick told me that the Greeks had fifty-six words for riding a horse. You know like riding a horse uphill riding a horse fast slow they're all different words. She? No I never gave her a ride Miss Dick on the hayride that would have been a sight no she stuck to herself a lot of the women around here did if they didn't marry. They'd stay in their house and do god knows what Mary Graves yes Miss Dick Ruth Sayheim absolutely she was always there. You never saw her in town except to shop. I guess they wanted it that way. Not like men you know most men want to get out get out of whatever they're in being alone or being married it doesn't matter which they just want to get out. Ed Mosher people were envious of him there wasn't a woman in town he couldn't have but all he wanted to do I got the sense at least was get away get away to Hig's and sit in that corner booth and play the jukebox. That Silver-Haired Daddy of Mine that was another song he played a lot. Taking a lunch break Ed? they'd ask that was kind of a joke. He'd be there at three four in the afternoon. He started the day OK late I mean but always well dressed and friendly then around one he'd slip off for lunch and that was the last you'd see of him in any kind of condition. They kept him on they couldn't really do much else I mean it was his store partly even though they'd changed the name he still owned part of it that was the deal when the Whites took it over his father made sure of that. A job for life. And he did know where everything was Lebrun and I went in there once early enough for him still to be there and he I forget what we were looking for something they didn't make anymore and he led us in back past all the shelves it's a real maze back there and found just what we needed the last one too an old box buried under a million other things but that was at eleven maybe or noon. No all he wanted was to get out I don't know why. But the women the ones who didn't marry they seemed more content at home. I'd go by Ruth Sayheim's house the light would be on I could see her sometimes sitting at a table bent over something concentrating I don't know maybe she did crossword puzzles something like that I couldn't tell. She and I were friendly enough to say hello chat but nothing serious mostly about your parents because we both worked for them. She'd polish all those knickknacks your dad bought. That carpet she'd be on her hands and knees shampooing it scrubbing out a spot. But Cecil now he's putting sand down I suppose he doesn't want us to slip wants us to go out natural except for the pills he gives us he mashes them up in the food. That one time walking out on the lake well I'm not saying it's what I was doing but the Eskimos they put an old person on an iceberg with a day's supply of whale meat or whatever and off he goes. Emily she'd get over it. I worry about her after I'm gone though I mean we fight but well that's just the point you don't fight with someone unless you feel for them take me and Alice for instance. In her mind in Emily's mind we were always at each other's throats but really I'd call it a love story. I know it was for me I've tried to suggest that to her in a way you know just tried slipping it in but she acts like I put that woman through hell which simply isn't the case it was all her doing Alice she knew just what she wanted. Breckenridge was going on hinting at what I didn't even understand didn't even want to understand about Rebecca and Physical Therapy all a bunch of hogwash if you ask me and the sun was shining on that angle. Gabrielle yes I was visiting Gabrielle too but that was different. Well it just was. Because whatever she was feeling for me she was probably feeling for the mill boss the bank clerk and whoever else came back there as well. It was different with Gabrielle it was more like just like being alone together. Alone but with someone does that make sense? Emily maybe it'll help her after I'm gone maybe then she'll get started. With me I was sad of course but Father's death that's from when I mark my life really starting now that I look back. It's late for her to be starting out now I know and I don't see exactly where she'd end up. Town clerk that's pretty good I tell her but she acts like. Well it's all about a man I suppose without a man most women don't feel complete. That's true I take it back some women like I was telling you Ruth Sayheim Miss Dick they didn't want or need a man but Emily well. See there he goes. He's very conscientious Cecil. From the outside this place looks like a picture postcard but let me tell you at night it's a chamber of horrors. It's not his fault old people we just don't sleep or rather we don't sleep lying down most of us the ones he's doping they do but even them you can hear them make noises oh no I'm not going to imitate them he'll hear and think I'm one of them. There's others who walk around in their pajamas really they're asleep they're walking through 1920 or something looking for Calvin Coolidge it's like night of the living dead here. Cecil he comes out sometimes and puts them back to bed but mostly he just stays in his room at the far end. I think he has earphones you know playing with his computer games because hell some of them make so much noise a real racket trying to open a locked door or calling for their dog some dog who hasn't been alive for fifty years. I tell them to pipe down but they don't hear me it's like I'm the one who's dead just lying there gripping the sheet trying to pull it up high to cover myself like that's going to protect me. Violent you bet they're violent some of them the old ladies in particular I could have one of those biddies choking the life out of me and Cecil he'd be fifteen feet away shooting Martians out of outer space he'd never hear a thing. But when I tell Emily she acts like I should be all grateful just to be here. No one wants to hear about it it's true we should be grateful just to be alive when all our friends. Lebrun would have done it in style if he'd lived this long he'd have had round-the-clock nurses people looking after his affairs stuff like that but no it never came to that of course. I told him he should get the hell out if he didn't like it but instead he shows up with that wife like he's I don't know starting over or something.

～

After Alice no it never crossed my mind well I was already I wasn't that old it's true but no like I told you it was a great love anything after that wouldn't have been. See that's because you're putting the cart before the horse again thinking it's all about two people trying to take their clothes off but really that gets in the way more often than not really it's something else. After Alice no. Emily tried to keep up the garden she didn't have her mother's green thumb that kind of thing can't be taught we had worms all of a sudden caterpillars big fat green ones they got in everywhere you'd be chewing on some broccoli and all of a sudden part of the broccoli would turn into this caterpillar in your mouth it would go all squishy. She tried these tricks the same tricks her mother had taught her beer little cups filled with beer that's for slugs tin can sleeves around each individual stem for cutworms she tried everything finally I said Look at it this way we're going to have the best crop of butterflies ever this year. She didn't take to that too kindly. One day Firebrand he just walked right through everything it wasn't mean of him he just honestly didn't know where he was going he couldn't see. I don't think he even ate anything he was just trying to get somewhere with that stiff gait of his. She came back that night I had to tell her that a bear I couldn't risk having her call someone she'd be capable of that oh she loves to call people Emily the troopers the county agent the society for the prevention of cruelty she likes men in uniforms so I couldn't risk having her set some plan in motion to take him away from me he's all I had left so I told her it was a bear I'd seen galumphing off into the woods after making a mess of her garden a black bear because you get them here from time to time. I thought it was a reasonable excuse but by god she starting screaming like I'd told her the house was on fire. Before you know it we had men here with guns alerts posted on all the police radios it even made the *Pennysaver Masked Marauder Plunders Town Clerk's Crops* something like that. Lawrence he was very funny he told all about how it was a sign of the times that even the bears now were strict vegetarians. Before they'd eat meat the occasional camper he said or one of those misguided nature-lovers who smeared themselves with honey to try and get a good picture but now all they do is knock over a few tomato vines and step on a pumpkin. *Probably looking for something sweeter* he said. Everyone knew what he meant of course those goddamned sticky buns which come to think of it was probably what he was after in the first place except of course yes you're right it was just a story I forgot he didn't exist but don't tell her I made it up even now it's a tender subject because. No I couldn't send Firebrand off I couldn't do that a second time. It got so bad Lebrun and I well it was Lebrun mostly he understood. Hell he'd known me long enough and Firebrand too. Where he got it I don't know he could surprise you in that way. It was the size of a Coke bottle I'll tell you that. We had us a drink the three of us well I had a drink Lebrun he just kept me company and Firebrand he had a cough by then so I told Emily I was going to spend the night in the barn trying to clean his lungs out make a tent over his head boil hot water with some grasses that's what I told her I was going to do. So it felt like the three of us were having a drink out there but I suppose really it was just me. Lebrun knew what to get like I said he could surprise you that way but once we were there we didn't know quite how to go about it. It was almost like we were expected to say a few words but of course what was there to say there was really only that awful cough coming from Firebrand he had it bad by then. I actually had gotten some grasses together and a pot even a little hot plate I had to boil the water on yes we had electricity out there I ran a line from the back of the house but it was just for show I suppose or maybe I was half thinking of doing it up until the last minute but then why would I have had Lebrun come over with the needle? I don't know. He and I stood there. Well he said maybe you should do it. I don't know how I said. It's not that hard he said it's not like he's going to complain after that you did it wrong. Firebrand he had no idea. They understand things yes but they can't understand that. Animals all they want to do is stay alive. Believe me I see it every day here there's people here who'd be twenty times better off dead but the way they hold on every breath is like climbing a mountain for them but that's all they do every day is breathe. Firebrand he just stood there with those milky eyes of his not even seeing us I mean he knew we were there of course although who knows maybe he was living in the past by then maybe he thought Allure was in the stable next to him I took the needle and I guess I felt this time I'm treating the disease you know not just the symptoms. He reared back. He was utterly surprised. I'd known him for almost thirty years and I'd never seen him so surprised it was like something from out of his universe this needle pumping into him probably like liquid fire. I'm not going to pretend it was easy or kind. Lebrun said that's what they used vets that is. I believed him. He reared back and then his front legs they kind of buckled. Afterward Lebrun stayed with me he wanted to make sure I was all right. Once he left I heated up the water anyway put the grasses in it no I didn't put the blanket over his head I didn't go that far but it was almost like I'd committed a crime and wanted to throw them off the scent whoever might be investigating. Of course no one did. Who cares when a dumb animal passes I fell asleep and when I woke up the pot had boiled dry Firebrand he was still there he hadn't moved. A horse on its side you don't see that too often. I never knew why they called him that Firebrand he never gave me a speck of trouble. Emily couldn't have cared less she'd inherited her mother's distaste for them she started talking instead about things we could do with the barn an antique store she said a curio shop and I could be the manager the manager can you imagine? No I didn't bury him you'd need a backhoe and besides Emily would have screamed worse than when I told her there was a bear out back if we'd spent money on burying a dead horse by the kitchen window no they took him away. I had to pay. I don't know what they did with him I didn't ask it wasn't like the other time it wasn't a profit-making transaction I just wanted him out of the barn I couldn't stand seeing him on his side you can't move a horse not even to roll him over they weigh almost half a ton they're magnificent creatures. I imagine they used his hooves. The meat no that was beginning to go by then even for pet food maybe they burnt him I don't know you can burn me I'd prefer it I'd like to be blown by the wind off a mountaintop off the top of the fire tower maybe or be scattered over the lake float there for a while then drift down over town like in one of those globes you know that you shake a snow globe but it's all a fairy tale I'm not going to be anywhere I'll be gone. Whose ashes were we scattering I have no idea. It's such a clear memory but it doesn't link up with any facts. Lebrun and I in that boat of his they were blowing back in my face I remember him getting all upset because they were collecting in the bottom. He felt that was wrong somehow. I even took a little bit and put it between my lips who was it but Emily I feel bad for her visiting that grave all the time I can see her turning into an old lady before her time. What's the point Alice isn't there not really. There's none of me in her she's all her mother not that I was some big risk-taker but compared to Alice at least I questioned things. Why? I'd ask that's all. It used to make Alice so mad I wasn't trying to be difficult I genuinely wanted to know that's all. See she she took whatever she heard from people as gospel. Certain people. If they had a collar or money or if they wore a fancy suit that's all it really took. A salesman once came by while I was out and sold her seventy-five dollars worth of knives. They're so sharp she said. Sharp dresser I thought. No he was gone by then of course on to his next victim his next lonely housewife. Why is it wrong to eat people? I wanted to know. After they're dead I mean. Not that I was saying we should but they never proved that he hurt anybody Christopher he was just using body parts for his experiments. The eyeballs no I never told a soul about that so what so if he ate a man's brain I've heard that in other countries they eat all sorts of things. Washburn when he came back he said he'd eaten well I can't even bring myself to say it out loud it's so disgusting but let's just say that if that didn't make him taller nothing would. Yes brains too they eat cow brains in France so what if it wasn't a cow's if it was a person's anyway he wasn't doing it for the taste it was in the spirit of science. Alice she was sounding just like her dad railing on about how they should both be torn limb from limb. I don't like judging people I don't want anyone judging me that's for sure. So what if he put some dead man's brain in a blender or whatever the hell he did that's his funeral except of course he didn't have a funeral because. The elixir. Where are his notes everyone asked. On the one hand they were calling him Satan practically for tampering with God's plan or whatever it was that mealy-mouthed faker Bigelow said in his sermon. Tampered with maybe trying to fix it is more like what he was trying to do. That's what I said when Alice got home and told me. Trying to fix God's plan since He didn't seem to have a very good one to begin with. That's when she actually tried to cover my mouth even though no one could hear even though we were alone. So on the one hand they wanted to find him so they could kill him and on the other hand they kept asking where are his notes like maybe he found something out they could use. If I could choose what age eighteen yes that seems about right to me. I was just starting off all that crap was behind me I know that's mean to say but I was young and strong when I'd leap off one rock up onto the next sometimes I thought I could keep right on going into the air you know that I could fly that I only chose to come down. Emily she's older of course so it'll be different for her when I go but maybe I'm hoping at least that it's like I'm the balloon string that I'm just the last bit holding her down here and once I snap she'll go I don't know where she doesn't have to go anywhere physically I didn't although sometimes I wish I had but that she'll just soar up in some way leave all this clutter behind. But maybe not. She seems happy enough. That's the problem she seems just happy enough not to be really happy if you know what I mean. Not happy like I was then. Like I've been at other times too. Sitting in the quarry absolutely. Or with Allure. Or with Alice. Plenty of times. Hell I've been a happy man. But eighteen that's when it kind of existed in its pure form that feeling though it's funny if you'd asked me back then I'd have probably said I was miserable. Did I want to go away? Well everyone thinks about it from time to time what if they'd just taken off gotten on a train or gone to the highway and stuck out their thumb or when I was a kid you'd wrap some cheese and bread in a kerchief put it on a stick the end of a long stick and then go off pretend to be a hobo you know a bum it was a game we played me and Rebecca we'd go off together usually when they'd been fighting. I didn't even know what was going on just that it was terrible them yelling. Rebecca she understood that's why she got us those sticks and those kerchiefs or bandanas no we weren't running away for real it just felt that way it was kind of like practice I guess for her I mean I never went farther than Sparta but she anyway she led the way I couldn't have been more than five or six it's one of my earliest memories a sunny day both of us with sticks over our shoulders the bandanas weighing us down I don't know what she put in them walking down the main street of Conklingville Rebecca with tears streaming down her face she took everything so hard she understood you see that was her problem that's what made life so difficult for her my solution was not to understand to play dumb. We might not have even had shoes back then on a warm summer's day your feet just got black with dirt no one cared. I don't know where we ended up it was just a game. Down in the valley where the lake is now yes that's where the good farmland was not up where we were on the mountainside that's all rocks but down around Conklingville there were these fields maybe we had a picnic there I don't remember. I guess we were hoping by the time we got home it would be better that it would have all blown over. That's as far as I got in terms of going away Rebecca she got farther but I don't know if it did her much good. Emily I just want to see a look on her face that I haven't seen yet a look like suddenly there's all these possibilities. Maybe once I'm.

⁓

They called it this was just briefly after Walt passed some lady came in and tried to make it into a coffee shop. No not a diner but a place with rugs and soft chairs and music she had this music playing all the time that would make you want to go to sleep right away. Muffins no eggs just muffins. The funniest thing was the sign. She couldn't afford a new one or maybe it was hard to take down I don't know it was bolted right to the side of the building and pretty high up so they kind of stuck something over it she just had them change one word COUNTRY to CASUAL it became the CASUAL CORONER which makes no sense at all I mean less than Country Coroner which at least was a mistake but this. The Casual Coroner yes I used to see Miss Dick in there. The ladies liked it more than the men. She brought her lunch usually she was a frugal woman she had to be with what the town paid her or didn't pay her rather to keep the library going. A cheese sandwich something like that. Peanut butter I didn't really look. But she'd still take her lunch break one hour even though she'd already eaten. Close up the library from twelve-thirty to one-thirty. That's when I'd see her sometimes sitting in the bandstand just taking in the sun or in that place the Casual Coroner in the window seat. We didn't really have much to talk about besides books. She'd always ask me what I was reading. Sometimes I think I kept on reading because of that so I'd have something to answer her with. Once actually I saw her car parked in front of this old tumbledown house a shack really. There was a FOR SALE sign out front but that was about as old as the house and tilted over to one side no one was going to buy that place not for the house certainly maybe for the property. But her car was there so I stopped the rig and got out I thought maybe she needed help it just seemed like a funny place for her to be I pulled open the door and she was there with a flashlight and a big wide canvas bag like what you'd put kindling in. She must have jumped a foot when she saw me. Turns out she was looking for books. It was kind of a hobby of hers she told me she'd go into old places abandoned places and take whatever books she could find. Those are the last things to go they're worth nothing most of the time and they're heavy. I don't know what she did with them sold them I imagine down in Sparta if they turned out to be valuable or added them to the library's collection maybe I didn't think to ask it was just strange to find her with a flashlight and a bag and looking so guilty like a thief caught in the act although really who was she hurting? We didn't have any ourselves growing up. Well yes there must have been some but I don't remember any in particular. As a child Mother read to me but it didn't take that happened later when they were all when they'd all gone away. I was more your nature boy always outside either doing chores or running away from doing chores they'd have to call me for dinner they had a bell. Father would ring it. I could tell just from how he'd ring the bell if he was angry or tired oh yes all the way up the mountain I could hear it well it's an unusual sound not like a bird or anything not like anything in nature so your ear picks it out that's the point. Once I remember I was way up the hill for some reason I'd gone farther than usual maybe it was part of a game I was playing I don't know but I broke through some bushes and I was at the foot of the fire tower it seemed enormous this metal staircase going up and up and then this hut at the top you could only see the floor of. It's very windswept there just rocks. I climbed the steps or started to. There was no place else to go I was at the top of the world my knees started shaking I had never been scared of heights before but really I hadn't been that high not like this. I hauled myself up I must have been playing some game that's how I did things then there was always some story going on in my head not what was really going on but a fantasy I guess. Father would say Pull your head out

142

of your ass which in those days was very strong language not a joke it was more like a warning that the next thing I'd feel was his hand but of course that just made me want to go farther and farther off in my thoughts anyway I made myself keep going like it was a test and I got pretty high. I remember holding onto the iron rails. The whole thing creaked something terrible it's windy up there all the time I couldn't tell if my knees were shaking because of the wind or because. I'd never felt anything like that before I didn't know that's what fear did that it made your knees shake. I pulled myself up basically with my arms. I got so high but couldn't bring myself to look down and then suddenly the hut the lookout station was right on top of me I almost hit my head against it. There was this trapdoor but it was shut. I knocked several times very timid-like I was afraid to let go of the railing for very long even with one hand but no one answered. Then I tried pushing it but saw there was this lock just a hasp and a rusty old lock so no one was up there there was no point. The hardest part was coming back down. Those stairs aren't meant for coming down. They kind of tilt differently trying to throw you off and you have to look down the ground's right there kind of beckoning to you I think I almost broke a finger just holding on to the railing so hard. I was sure I was going to fall. Anyway I got to the bottom and who should be waiting for me there but Father he'd come looking for me. How he found me I don't know I guess he knew where I went all along I guess it wasn't such a secret after all. Maybe he saw me in the distance once I got high enough you know halfway up the staircase my knees flapping away. He'd been waiting for me to come down not saying a word. I thought for sure he was going to lay into me really wallop me but he didn't just as I got to the first step he held out his hand. Locked? he said. I nodded. We headed back along the path not crashing through the woods like I'd come. There was a path that led down to the road and then the road kind of spiraled around the mountain. I'd thought he was going to be

143

mad at me but he wasn't we were just walking side by side it took longer that way of course I suppose I could have told him about my secret way the stream I mean but it never occurred to me I couldn't imagine him leaping from rock to rock he wore these big clodhopper boots with steel tips. That was from when he used to work on the railroads so if you dropped a length of track it didn't break your toe. We walked side by side talking him asking questions and me barely answering because like I said I didn't talk much and he probably didn't fit into any game I had in my mind at the time any story. Then he said I was ringing that bell until my arm near fell off didn't you hear? I said I was sorry at least I hope I did probably not. Probably I just muttered something and then he said Don't you scare me like that again. Well it was funny because I didn't know he could be scared that he could be glad to see me I mean to find me up there climbing down those steps so worried that he forgot to be mad. But of course I just looked down and looked at his shoes. You never say what you want to say at the time although even now I don't know what that would be. Those shoes with the steel tips he used to take us dancing on them when we were little Rebecca and me he would take us each in turn by the hands and we would stand on his feet on the steel tips and he would dance just walk around I guess but carrying us on his shoes. He'd lift his feet way up in the air I remember Mother disapproving worried that we'd fall and him just lifting us higher and higher egging her on. Now that I think of it he'd probably had a few it was probably his way of picking a fight he liked that showing her up in front of the kids showing us another way to be. I remember her saying Herbert in that disapproving way. She only called him that when she was mad. Once he was telling me a joke he must have been drunk because I didn't get it at all it was about some man on a train and he has to go you know to relieve himself but the door to the men's room is locked so he sticks his posterior out the window of the train posterior yes it's and the train is just leaving the station I guess because the conductor comes running down the aisle and says Will the man smoking the cigar please pull his head inside the train? Well I wasn't getting it at all I was just listening and he could barely get the joke out he was laughing so hard telling it red-faced telling it more for himself I guess or maybe what he thought was so funny was the look I had and behind it all I could hear Mother saying Herbert Herbert over and over trying to stop him. Well you see it looks like he's smoking a cigar but really never mind I didn't figure it out myself until anyway we were walking along that road and I wish I'd said something but I didn't I don't even know now what I'd say. Sorry I guess. It's that spot right around there that I saw him again after he died that time with Allure that time when I realized I should get on with my life marry Alice and. What? Well that's true I only had Allure after I married Alice I couldn't afford to buy her before then Firebrand too but that is where I saw him even if the time was different. Yes you're right we were already married I suppose but what he told me was maybe it was more like he gave me his blessing I don't know. It's seeing these people that's what's important not so much what they say or what you remember it's seeing them that sticks. You see someone who's dead standing by the side of the road gesturing at you that makes an impression it makes you reconsider. Or consider I should say. That's the kind of thing Allure could do for me if it hadn't been for her he'd have never appeared my mind would have never conjured him up. But books they weren't that big on books either one of them. Mother she had her bible but aside from that and those magazines about movie stars she had those for some reason even though we never went to the movies but I don't remember anything else on the shelves just pots and pans in the kitchen and in the sitting room nothing just on the wall something she'd cut out from an illustrated section an angel but there was another name for it a little fat boy playing a guitar but he had wings a cherub that's what she called him the Cherub and President Roosevelt a photograph of President Roosevelt I don't know why. Father? Nothing maybe an almanac but where Rebecca got her taste for literature I don't know. Oh yes she had books but they were in her room they weren't ours no one else could touch them they were gifts I guess on her birthday or for Christmas. I'd get a ball she'd get a book. Whatever girls read then I don't know the titles. Later yes that's one of the major reasons she worked at the clinic besides the fact that they paid I mean but what excited her most was the books they had a little reading room there the way she described it it was like heaven on earth she'd bring one home shut herself up in her room not even come out for dinner then return it the next day for another. I don't know why she didn't contact us it's not like Father was going to come and drag her back by the hair. I used to lie on her bed while she scribbled away in that journal of hers even if she didn't pay much attention to me she knew I was there. I wonder if she kept on writing after she left if she'd look up sometimes and expect me to still be watching her. I wake up sometimes even now and think she's right past that door with one of her books or writing away in her journal off in her own little world she was so full of plans. He's excreting you see and from the outside from the station platform it looks like a cigar because yes exactly six maybe seven years old of course it's not the kind of joke you tell a kid that's what was making him laugh so hard I guess. That and the look on Mother's face probably.

～

Me and Alice? Up there under the fire tower? No. I can't believe you're still going on about that it's of no consequence it's private. No it's not because I'm ashamed. Take advantage of her I certainly didn't take advantage of her if anything it was the opposite she I told you she knew exactly what she was doing what she wanted I just went along I mean I was happy don't get me wrong but it wasn't like there was resistance to overcome. It's harder for women it's a bigger decision for them but once they decide it's like water taking you along it's like the spillway there's no resisting. Water I don't care how strong you are if a current wants to take you someplace you have no say at all in the matter. Lebrun he told me once what to do if I ever fell in there below the turbines where the water's rushing down on the other side he said Don't try and stand that's how you get hurt don't fight it just keep your head and toes above the surface and wait until you can grab onto something. That's kind of like what it was like with Alice when she got an idea in her head oh yes I was her idea the cart the business that's what she used to say later. She liked to think that it was all her doing like if she hadn't come along I'd still be working for Seraphim Washburn like the world would have stood still. I'm not sure about that I'm not so sure things would have turned out that differently not deep down oh I might have had another job or something but I would still have been me that's not how she looked at it though. She took credit for everything. No blame though she didn't take blame for any of my shortcomings. It's funny because I don't think I had much of an influence on her but who knows maybe I did maybe without me maybe she. No I never talked that way to her. With Lebrun I might have told him what I thought sure I told Lebrun a lot of things especially if I'd had a few if I'd been taking a nip from the bottle he kept in his glove compartment he always said I could see things I think that's why he liked my company. He said I could see things that weren't there you know that weren't obvious. He saw the obvious all right just clearer than anyone else. Most people they see the obvious but it's so terrifying they cover their eyes right back up and go back to dreaming. Lebrun he'd head right for it find a way to make it his own. But I think because of that because of the toll it took all his wheeling and dealing he liked to hear my thoughts they were so different. Not like Alice she'd cover her ears when I went on about what might be she'd walk away with her hands still over her ears. I'd tell him what Alice did and he'd laugh. The love of a good woman he'd say. That's what he always said about her. The love of a good woman. I guess he never experienced that certainly not with. Oh she wasn't so bad we just had it in for her I suppose. A man comes back with a new wife no one's ever met before I guess we felt like he was ours in a way and then to have this woman treat him like well like a nobody basically like he wasn't special at all you'd have thought people would be happy in a mean-like way you know him getting his comeuppance but everyone took it very personal like she was insulting them too when she'd complain at the IGA if he took too long to pull the truck up or once I wasn't there of course but she let him have it apparently at Ed and Loretta's Fine Dining they'd gone out for dinner they did that a lot I don't think she cooked much and she started laying into him about politics of all things who was going to be president senator I don't know I mean none of us gave a hoot about that it was so far away bunch of crooks basically six of one half dozen of the other but she was one of those people who took it all so serious and wanted to pick a fight with anyone who disagreed with her not just disagreed with her but who didn't agree with her one-hundred-and-ten percent. No I certainly didn't find her attractive she had stringy hair and glasses kind of a wiry woman nothing wrong with her I mean but that might have been another reason the town turned against her it's the women you know who decide all that so here was Lebrun who could have had his choice hell he did have his choice of any woman in town married or unmarried and he shows up one day with this plain-looking nagging kind of unpleasant lady who acts like she doesn't even realize how lucky she is. I don't know what he expected. Like I said he acted like it just happened to him like it wasn't a matter of choice but I wouldn't say exactly that he regretted it. He got something out of it. People make their own bed you know. Afterward no his wandering days were over you didn't hear about him jumping out of a back window or being seen down in Antone River Park at two A.M.

none of that. Maybe that's what she gave him an excuse to do nothing to stay home at night maybe he was tired. Maggie Chess. Maggie Chest they used to call her behind her back I mean because she didn't have much of one but like I said you had to be careful because he once he heard someone make a remark and slammed that fellow back against the wall so hard I thought we were going to have to call the Emergency Squad. Alice no she didn't like his wife either no one did. Looking back like I said I feel sorry for her it wasn't really her fault there was just something about her. That car she drove for example it wasn't like the others here it was a foreign car it looked like an Easter egg that was another sore spot how she drove once she got behind me on the road of course I didn't know it was her I didn't look back I was going as fast as I could it's not like you can step on the gas pedal or anything I don't know what she expected me to do pull out a bullwhip but she started honking and crawling right up my backside this was on that winding stretch right near the scenic view and then just as we were coming to the top she gave one long honk and passed me with about an inch to spare. Spooked Allure and Firebrand something awful I had to control them just to keep them from going off into the ditch plus if anyone had been coming in the other direction we'd have both. I don't know where the hell she wanted to get to so fast. Or get away from yes I hadn't thought of that but no I don't think she disliked being here not at first. She loved being with him I'll say that for her whatever chance she could get she stuck to him like glue. Not that she had that many chances I mean he was still out all the time checking levels or holed up in that little office over the spillway or out checking on his sites but when he got home boy was he home she made sure of that she must have bolted the door the minute he walked in you never saw him past sundown not alone at least they'd go out to eat not with other people just the two of them then he'd lead her back to the truck open the door for her like a perfect gentleman. Maggie Chess. I actually met her for the first time at the library that was one of the few places she went to in Kathan she and Miss Dick used to talk. I think because Miss Dick was educated and she wanted to talk to some woman who didn't spend her day slaving away over housework I guess. But most of the time she kept to herself. Bud he delivered her mail he'd complain about what she got which I'm not sure you're supposed to do isn't that like a doctor talking about his patient kind of I mean mail's a personal thing. He said she got catalogs he claimed she added thirty pounds to his route not shopping catalogs no I told you college catalogs what courses were offered that kind of thing from all over the country. I don't know maybe she was thinking of going back to school. Young. Younger than Lebrun and me I mean but not a kid or nothing. No she never did maybe she just liked to think about it going to college I don't know if she'd already been or not. Me? She regarded me with suspicion. I took up his time Lebrun's and of course I knew him so much better well for longer at least compared to her she knew him in a different way of course. She and Alice they didn't hit it off either. Nothing out loud it was all quiet at least on Alice's part Maggie would try and get her going but oh all this stuff about women's liberation burning your bra stuff like that. All you do is sit at home she'd say. Sit? Alice said. That's about as far as she'd go. Sit? She wouldn't lower herself she wouldn't bring herself so low as to answer in kind. She had a certain class about her Alice. I always liked that as long as it wasn't pointed at me. Hell it wasn't like Maggie was doing anything so revolutionary herself she was sitting at home too as far as I could tell more than Alice they didn't have a vegetable garden out back or nothing not even a clothesline no they had a washer-dryer one of the first around here. She was probably pacing the floor there not cooking either so I don't know what she did to pass the time read I guess she took out a lot of books from the library she'd talk to Miss Dick when she returned them. Evangeline she called her I don't know how she found that out I didn't even know Miss Dick had a first name much less anything so. She was probably pacing around that house like a caged tiger waiting for Lebrun to come home and when he did well it's just my guess but she took it all out on him I think. I don't know what he expected from her. Kids maybe but if so. Mean as ever that's what he'd say if you asked how she was doing. Mean as ever but he said it like it was a joke he'd laugh. That time in the library the first time I mean I was in back that's where Ancient History is when Maggie came in and said Evangeline and there was all this sort of cooing and helloing I'd never heard her be that way before Miss Dick so friendly not that she was mean or anything but she just seemed so excited I guess she'd already come in once or twice because they knew each other's names and were going on about something when I came back out and then they got kind of quiet because they knew I was Lebrun's friend. Miss Dick introduced me and I remember I dropped the book I was holding. I actually felt myself blushing hell I don't think I'd done that in maybe thirty years and like I said it wasn't that she was such a looker. I mean to each his own but it was more like knowing that she'd captured his heart I guess. Bill's my best customer Miss Dick said then she locked up the place early which I'd never seen her do before and they went to the Casual Coroner. Corner they called it though everyone but me it was like by common agreement they called it the Casual Corner like that was just an another way of spelling the word I was the only one who couldn't it stuck in my throat or my eye. I remember thinking they were almost like sisters trailing along behind them because of course she had kicked me out of there too even though it wasn't twelve-thirty yet so I was walking behind them and just the way they walked side by side and kind of bumped into each other once in a while they reminded me of sisters or how sisters would be. But most of the time she and I were just civil. It's like we both knew that we liked Lebrun that was what we had in common. I did hear not from him of course but word got round to me I did hear that she said I smelled of horse manure that's not actually the word she used but well maybe it's true it's like asking a fish what water feels like I spent my whole life around the stuff you can't expect me to horseshit she said he smells like well I guess it might have been true. Alice bless her heart she never mentioned it. And Maggie Chess she should talk. Some of those perfumes she wore I'd rather spend my life in horseshit than smell like that. But the car it was like an Easter egg light blue and round and tiny so small a kiddie car. She'd painted on that too same as on the mailbox. No not her name but a stripe a green kind of jagged line going right down the middle of the hood and on the roof too. Hand-painted yes that got people's attention no one ever painted their car up here not for decoration I mean if you wanted to paint over a rust spot that's different. See she just had this knack for rubbing people the wrong way it was almost like a gift I think it might have been her mission in life to make people sit up and take notice and then kind of grit their teeth because really what can you say it's not illegal to paint your car or your mailbox either at least Bud he could never prove it but she made the rest of us feel that we were saps somehow like we were sticks in the mud a bunch of stuffed owls she called us just going about our business while she whizzed around in her little blue-and-green Easter egg. Going where I don't know there's nowhere to go around here you can go as fast as you want but you're never going to get anywhere. I'm telling you horses are the way. Horses and walking. You go slow enough you might get somewhere. There's always places to go to if you slow down enough slow down enough in your head I mean. But everyone's speeding along already someplace else in their mind so to them the sign says CASUAL CORNER but really if you take the time to notice it says.

⁓

I didn't follow them in no they were just two ladies talking. I waited until they were settled in the window seat still chatting away then I kind of caught myself and said What are you doing here? I mean that wasn't where I was heading it was sort of like they'd drawn me along. Oh I don't think they were looking at me they were too busy ordering muffins people around here don't notice me they don't see me it's a trick I have. Cecil sometimes I catch him kind of looking twice like Are you still alive? I don't cause trouble even when the food is well let's just say the squirrels around here do real well especially around dinner time that's for sure. I left them there talking but it made an impression on me. Women they have this power even the unattractive ones especially them maybe because you can't chalk it up to looks what they do or say kind of lingers in your brain or in mine at least maybe I'm abnormal. Women have more mystery to them. To men. To other women they're just. Alice she'd sniff. She'd call her common. It's typical he'd marry someone like that she'd say so common. Common? I said Maggie Chess? That's not what I'd call her but I knew what she meant. Now here of course we're all the same men and women once you get old I mean you can't even tell us apart it's sort of like we're babies again you know when they're so little in their mother's arms and you say Is that a boy or girl? Well here you ask yourself I mean you say Was that a man or a woman? It makes you think all that stuff in between was it all some kind of big diversion or distraction but from what that's what I can't figure out. Anyway it was our lives that distraction or the bulk of it but it does make you wonder once it's all gone what it was all about. I sit sometimes at the counter and watch Vera and it's kind of like revisiting something something you're familiar with but certainly not going to do anything about. She calls me her big tipper. A dollar. A dollar plus whatever change I've got in my pocket. You can't take it with you. Alice she tried I suppose with that fancy casket polished oak or something and that stone. Why'd she do it in advance like that? I don't know she was the Egyptian type when it came to burial. You know thinking you're going to need things in the afterlife a nice cushion to lie on your body all preserved dressed fancy. Me I'm more like the Greeks. Just build a fire and pour wine over me. Like that lamb yes. They had other guests too. That man what was his name I don't remember a little man almost a midget with big round glasses always shuffling along the beach I'd meet him from time to time. He'd look at me like I was far away even from close up over the tops of his glasses you know. Ah yes he'd say and hold out this kind of dead fish hand. I didn't know what to do with it I remember the first time I squeezed it like I was wringing out a dishrag or something. He gave a little shout. After that he just nodded. He was up here a lot he was a particular friend of your mother's that was the sense I got both of them sitting under that umbrella oh yes it was big enough well he was so small. No neither of them ever went into the water they'd leave that to you and Lucy. You were scared you don't remember she would walk you in step by step. A step a day that's what she said. But he never. He was dressed like he was going out to a nightclub even sitting on the sand. Your mother would be in one of those white things like a robe kind of but fancy and he what was his name I thought he was maybe some kind of circus performer or something he'd be dressed in a little jacket a blue jacket with shiny buttons and fancy little pants and white shoes and a hat with a bill like you'd wear on a boat yes a yachting cap that's it. He asked me questions about your dad about what kind of friends he brought up did I think he was leaving your mother alone too much? A lot of kind of prying questions. I just played dumb none of your god-damned business I thought. He wasn't like that other one the old man Uncle him I could appreciate he was doing something he was making dinner that lamb you should have smelled it I can still smell it but the little man you could see he was a talker not a doer his mouth was running all the time what did I think of this what did I think of that not really waiting for me to answer and you could tell that he would never lift a finger to help. He wasn't ever going to make dinner. I told him your dad was a swell guy that's what I said.

Well yes he had that side of him gambling yes but he kept it under control for the most part. Some people drink some people run after women some people play the horses men that is I don't know what women do. Oh they do something. They're people too you know they shop I guess. And go crazy yes that's a hobby of theirs going crazy. There was that trotter track south of here Putnam Downs he used to go there once in a while but I guess he did most of it by phone that's why he had to get a private line. People were listening in. It's not illegal. Well even if it is it was with his own money so where's the harm it's what spurred him on I guess maybe that's why he was always working. Some people need that a reason to do what they do. Your mother now she could take it or leave it I guess acting or whatever it is you call it. Being in things. No I never saw her except that one time she was mostly on the stage wasn't she? Him I saw plenty once he started making movies. In the theater sometimes I'd forget myself he'd pull out a gun and I'd sort of jump back in my seat because I forgot that it wasn't real. Your mother Alice said I was in love with her which was silly. There was a theater in town sure the Star Theater. Antone when the mill was in operation when it pulled three shifts it wasn't like now there used to be a movie theater a little hotel even a Chinese restaurant the Golden Dragon with a Chinese chef but the Star Theater they'd show all your dad's movies I'd be there first night if I could. Alice didn't really approve of some of them she said were inappropriate but she was proud too that we knew them that I knew them your mom and dad no I tried to get her to meet them but she never would. Once your dad he was going somewhere and he gave me a ride home and wanted to meet the missus that's what he called her but she was shy I couldn't I tried to drag her out but she ran into the bedroom and shut the door. The Star Theater it burned. That was later not when anyone was in it not when it was a movie theater anymore no. They knocked down what was left of it it's where the parking lot is now the parking lot to the bank. The bank in Antone First Atlantic not the one outside Kathan. Petrides no he worked for that other bank the Mountain Trust he got exiled out to that box on 9N with the drive-through yes he went from that grand desk overlooking the floor to this glassed-in cage where you could see every move he made. If I was just passing by with Allure and Firebrand there he'd be at his desk trying to look important. He smoked cigars that whole place reeked of them the money too what they handed out I don't know how he managed to get it in there but you'd withdraw some cash and. No that was later Lebrun was into them for oh hundreds of thousands I imagine but that's not how he got his start they wouldn't have lent some greasy Canuck that's how they talked about him back then Petrides in particular they wouldn't have lent some greasy Canuck one red cent. It's a mystery how he got started. One day early on when we were both young men he said to me See that bit there to the right of that tree. I had no idea what he was talking about but I said Sure yes and he said I own that I bought it the other day I'm going to build a house on it. A house? I said what's wrong with the place you got now? Not for me he says to sell. Sell to who? To summer folk. See it never occurred to me. And now you've got the beach community you've got the clubhouse the Hi-Jinx. Then it was just worthless land a lot of rocks and scrub timber. Still it must have been worth something and he did not have that something on him I can tell you that. The Authority he may have played the system got them to buy him a truck but there is no way he saved whatever a piece of lakefront property cost back then plus hiring all that equipment and paying for building materials and labor. Like I said it's a mystery where it came from it's like he pulled it out of his ass that's what Ed Mosher said. Oh he was jealous everyone expected him to be the success you know handsome rich daddy biggest store in town he had it all well I guess it takes just as much concentration to fritter it away as it does to build it up. For example Ed didn't ask Higs for a quarter to play

156

the jukebox he knew better. I'm all out Higs would say after a while after hearing whatever song Ed had been choosing play for an hour or two so Ed he started coming with his own roll fresh from the bank one of those little paper tubes. He'd break it on the tabletop just like he was a cashier at the IGA all these quarters and then stack them up. Christ Ed Higs would say but there was really nothing he could do and Ed would take one quarter at a time he wouldn't load up the machine just take one quarter feed it in. That gave you three songs back then. Then you'd hear him very carefully pressing the right buttons like it was hard for him to do which maybe it was that late in the day I mean. The same song over and over. I was only there in the winter when I couldn't be outside. This dark room all those windows painted black and those sickly plants Roll Out Those Lazy Hazy Crazy Days of Summer. He'd sit back down tap his toes stack the rest of the quarters up. So I guess he was just doing what Lebrun did but in reverse you know spending it away. Him? No he never married and all the women loved him for it see that kept him pure somehow that's my theory so they could still dream about him but be pure in heart themselves. *The Adonis of Antone* that's what Lawrence called him in the obituary I mean. Obituary editorial it was the same. Wrote about him after he died whatever you call that. But Ed it was like he was carrying the weight of all their dreams I think it weighed him down whereas Lebrun he had the nerve to actually get married and not even to one of them and so they hated him for it. I'm talking about the women as a whole. I'm talking about his standing. Even though really he was a citizen here he contributed I don't mean just made contributions though he did that too Eagle Enterprises you'd see the name all over but well it all goes back to civic responsibility he cared about the town its future. Ed sometimes I think Ed would have been happy if the whole place had gone up in flames along with the Star Theater along with his store absolutely. I'd see him sometimes going into that place and it was like he was

157

going into jail. And all those women fussing over him I don't think that gave him much pleasure either. Lawrence kind of sensed that he said something like *his one true love he turned his back on.* Well it was a joke see. Turned his back on. The tattoo. But maybe there was some truth in it. He didn't even remember her hell he didn't even know about the tattoo until someone pointed it out. I wonder how can that be don't they hurt? I guess he thought he had a backache or a rash. And then to find out that way after the fact maybe that was the one he cared most about Lorene I mean he got her name written on him and then not to remember anything but they loved him the women here and he still had some kind of appeal for them right up until the end. Heart attacks one after the other. Little ones but they sapped his strength. He'd take those pills nitro and then later he'd have those things that you break open and hold under your nose. He still maintained his looks though. I don't think he ate much besides bar nuts. Just held himself kind of careful like fine china. Walking down the street. You'd watch him and realize he's not getting too far all those steps but not going anywhere little tiny steps. He's with his mom and dad now they had one of those stones that left room I used to see it when I was parked there between the school and the cemetery when I was giving those hayrides well I had to read something a book no I never took a book with me in the cart. If Allure or Firebrand had seen me back there reading a book well it is kind of insulting. I'd read the stones instead Ed Mosher's father his mother and then underneath them this blank space. Just waiting to be filled in. I don't know how they do that. The stonecutter must come up here with his equipment it must be portable unless they lift the stone up and take it to his shop then come back and replant it maybe.

～

Freddie no I told you he didn't work on tombstones he didn't have a bunch of fancy equipment he just had his eye and his backbone. He

158

worked harder than anyone I ever met always moving soil moving rocks planting this planting that. Then you'd look and say Well he didn't do anything it looks untouched. That was the point. He could out-nature nature. But gravestones that wasn't his thing. I'd go down and talk to him sometimes if I saw him taking a break. He liked his beer. He'd always have a few cans of Tail End in a cooler. Tail End it was a local brewery down in Sparta it had a bird on it with a long tail a pheasant For the Tail End of the Day. No Freddie had it whenever he took a break eleven A.M. noon it didn't matter. Just one can though. One can at a time. I'd go down and have a talk with him. He'd look over what he was doing. By then Lebrun had hired him to pretty much do over the whole mountainside what with all the properties he'd bought. He'd be working on individual houses Freddie but he also had this kind of master plan. He didn't tell Lebrun I just figured it out by the way he talked. I got this row of beech trees here he'd say and then you see that rock that's the same outcropping they got farther down at the blue house so there it's got trees above it a birch and an aspen but here it's got a row of beech so if you stand back. And I realized he meant stand back like a hundred miles like God would have to. If you stand back well I don't remember exactly but he could see it all from a distance and close up at the same time. Maybe that's where the Tail End came in I don't know. But he wasn't really a drinker he was just thirsty. Could see it all like it made a pattern. Once I remember he got mad Lebrun needed to change something at the last minute he had a buyer the man came up before the house was finished and he wanted a playground a little swing set and a slide and sandbox for his kids. So this was pretty late in the day it was too late to switch things around Lebrun just had them scoop out a whole patch right where Freddie had laid some rocks or planted bushes or left trees there I don't know but boy was he mad. He came by they'd poured the cement and put the poles for the swing set in place already I happened to be there he was ready to blow a gasket. It just ruins everything he said. I guess he had this big picture in mind but there was nothing he could do about it. His own house? His own house was normal close to town just a regular lawn garden out back. He didn't bring his work home with him I guess. He was easygoing except for that one time. He told me the only thing he shot in the war was when he was on guard duty he shot a mule a mule yes he heard it coming up in the dark and it wouldn't give the password so. Sure there's an order to my life. Pattern might be too strong a word for it but you try and have it make sense in the short term. Enough to get by. I told you I had this map in my head of all my routes where I went and when I felt it was this net sometimes holding the place together or maybe holding me together. Without work nothing really makes sense. I see these kids today they do nothing all day long they live off their parents or get money from the state I don't know how they survive I can't even imagine what it's like not having a reason to be somewhere having no one depending on you to show up. Even now in my own way I try and make myself useful well to Vera for instance I ask her about her little boy Sam how's he doing what's his favorite color stuff like that and when I'm in town I go down to that Asian man with the fruit and vegetable stand he's not Chinese I don't know where he's from one of those countries where he had to pack up and leave with nothing but the clothes on his back. I don't know how the hell he ended up here someone must have given him the wrong directions bum advice I mean because there he is with all these fruits and vegetables set out each apple individually polished it looks like everything green and fresh just sitting there waiting while people walk right by head to the IGA instead to buy that moldy crap they sell there. Yams once I asked if he had yams. Oh it took forever he barely speaks a word of English. I don't know how he gets by he's got a whole family back there too I see them sometimes scurrying around. Yams I said and then I tried to act it out. You ever tried to act out a yam I mean with your hands the shape and all? Well even-

160

tually he gets the idea but no he doesn't have any and I thought that was the end of it but a week later I'm there and he comes out of the store all excited with this whole box of yams he'd ordered. Well I felt terrible. I was asking more in the spirit of you know trying to act interested like good luck with your new business that kind of thing but there he is holding them out so I had to buy one or two more like five or six actually he had a whole box of them. I do like yams but well we have a microwave here I'd never used it before. Before after Alice was gone I mean but before I moved here I'd put them in the oven that would be my dinner some nights I didn't need much but here they deliver the meals we only have the microwave so I stuck one in there but I guess you're supposed to poke it with a fork or something I found out later because after a few minutes the whole thing blew up inside the machine. Cecil he wasn't too pleased. I offered to clean it but he said I'd done enough damage. No I gave the rest to Emily I don't know what she did with them. But the point is each week I try to buy something from Ming because I can tell that he's having a tough time. People don't trust him because Ming that's what I call him no it's not his name he told me his name but it made no sense I mean it didn't have the same sounds we use so I call him not to his face to myself I call him Ming because he's. Emily says he's a refugee and that's what he did back home he was a fruit merchant fruit and vegetables so he's good at what he does but nobody here seems to trust him I don't know why. All they eat is frozen crap. Defrost it pour some syrup on top that seems to be the main course most nights from what I can tell. What we get here oh you don't want to know. Emily says it's nutritionally balanced. Nutritionally balanced once I found a carrot that's about as close to a vegetable as I ever saw I held it up on my fork. Cecil says What's the matter? I said I'm just checking to make sure it don't have a fingernail on it. That's right. Ming. Well it doesn't matter if that's not his real name I don't say it out loud not to him. But I have my little set of chores trying to help people out do what I can. Try and do some good. Oh I'm no saint that was Alice's occupation she wanted to be a saint I just keep busy. These kids you see them sitting there with this vacant look in their eye. People say it's drugs but I think it's TV it's the same expression if you look not at the TV but at the people watching it. I do that here people think I'm watching but really I'm looking at their eyes. It's scary. Try it sometimes. They won't notice they're too busy staring at the screen it doesn't matter what they're watching. Alice once we got that TV that one off your parents she started watching this preacher Sunday mornings this man talking about the bible and pretty soon I notice she's sending mail to him. What's this about? I ask. Nothing she says she's just helping him build a church. A church where? In Mongolia she says. Mongolia I didn't even know where it was turns out she didn't either I had to get Miss Dick to show me. You talk about the ass-end of the universe. The point is she was a sensible woman but it's the TV it's evil. These kids I've seen them stare at a broken one left out on the street you know abandoned someone too lazy to take it to the town dump the landfill they call it now and they stare at the cracked screen like maybe it's going to start up again. A broken TV. The plug is just sitting there on the street but they're still expecting I don't know maybe lightning to come down and electrify it. I just get soft fruit from him because of my teeth. No more yams. Oranges that's about all he has this time of year. Grapefruit they're too big I can't eat a whole grapefruit. Every once in a while he shows me a fruit I've never seen before. I don't know where he gets them from maybe some relative sends them. One was green and pink shaped like a pear but with ridges. It was the prettiest thing but I sure as hell wasn't going to eat it. He gave it to me said it was good luck at least that's what I think he said. Ood ruck. Food truck maybe I don't know maybe he got it off the food truck. Anyway I took it I couldn't very well say no. They always make fun of me when I get back to the van. Been to see your

Chinaman again they say like I'm soft in the head. I got home and put it on my windowsill. We're not supposed to have food in our rooms but it looked so different I guess it didn't count. It didn't look real. You don't see colors like that here. I mean I call them green and pink but really the pink was more like a red-pink and the green was all lit up. Then after a while it got withered it didn't stink though it didn't rot it just got all dried out so I took it outside and poked a little hole with a stick and buried it. I figure maybe it'll grow into something. So if you're walking around here one day and you come across this tree with fruit on it that's a color from outer space that's because. I don't know why they don't buy from him. They just don't like foreigners here. Canucks it used to be and then Italians. He's out there every day polishing the apples setting the vegetables just so. I should give him something back for good luck I don't know what that would be though. A rabbit's foot no that would take too much explaining besides where am I going to get a rabbit's foot? A lucky penny but you got to find that yourself it's not lucky if someone else finds it then it's just a penny. Anyway I'm not sure luck is what he needs. Sounds like luck is what brought him here bad luck so why would you want good luck it's the same thing really just good instead of bad. What he probably wants is no luck at all for luck to leave him alone but they don't have charms for that. Alice's stone no there's no space for me there. I noticed that too not at first but later. Emily and I were there one day she was tending the grave with clippers and a new bunch of flowers and I noticed well there's no room there's a plot I mean there's room for me underground but not for my name on the stone. I wondered out loud about it to Emily and she said Mother thought you'd want to get your own. No I don't mind not really it's more that she thought I wouldn't care that she decided without even asking me it kind of leaves a bad taste you know. That's the problem with trying to be good I mean making such a conscious effort in your life you concentrate so much on being good to other people doing good all over the world and she did people came up to me after and told me people I barely knew and she never boasted about it either how much she helped and in how many ways. Not just money well it was the money her dad left her I guess the money I made we lived on this was separate but you spend all your life being good outwardly and then you do something like that kind of kick me in the teeth from beyond the grave. Things balance out. You can't be so good without being bad somewhere else even if it's private just to one person the person you're supposed to care about most not all these strangers she was practically willing to lay down her life for people in Mongolia for Christ's sake but I don't mind. I mean I mind but if that's what she wanted.

That's why burning cremation makes more sense to me. No no one was killed in the Star Theater fire. They said it was a miracle that it didn't spread. Lebrun he wished it had. Then we could have built the whole town over he said. He got it bad after a while builder's sickness he wanted to tear everything down and start over. Old was never good it had to be new I guess that's why he borrowed so much after he built the first few houses it was like new money is better than old money even if it isn't yours after a while he'd have eight nine properties going at once keeping them all in his head. And more too the whole idea of making a community that came later that was his idea a beach community so all the houses all the people there paid dues. He built that clubhouse and made the beach for them. That was Freddie's greatest accomplishment. I know what that land was like there was sand yes but it was more mud-like and plenty of trees falling over into it into the lake and these rocks no matter how far out you'd go you'd always slip and hit your knee there's nothing worse than slipping on some slimy rock and bashing your knee well he fixed all that up turned it into what you got now.

Your parents they were here earlier they had their own beach their own patch of sand but for the people who lived over a little bit where the community is Freddie said he just moved the rocks but it was more than that he fit them together like he did a chimney only lying on its side and ten times as big only with a tractor instead of his hands the way they go out into the water there and stick up high enough so they're not slippery anymore. That's why the kids are always out there on the end of that what do they call it now? The jetty. He even made that wading pool in the middle for the little ones except it looks like it's natural part of the rock formation. Well it's not a formation at all it's just Freddie. But the beach community that was Lebrun's idea the clubhouse even the Hi-Jinx the party they have every year. He became this master planner he saw everything on a map. People too I mean. He had them all spaced out Petrides and the bank over here the customers over there all his crews in various places his wife in another. Where was he? Well I don't know. I guess you're right he left no room for himself he painted himself right out of the picture. But Alice leaving me off the stone I should give her the benefit of the doubt it was probably Bigelow he probably told her it was OK that I'd make do or that he'd take care of it that's probably what he said I'll take care of it. She could be the most pig-headed woman imaginable to me I mean and then some man comes along with a collar and a bible or a fancy car and a set of steak knives and she'd be like putty in his hands. Cochrane? Sure around him she'd be all bowing and scraping even though who knows what he did to my sister. That time I was up in their bedroom I couldn't help but wonder of course I looked around as long as I was there. For nothing in particular nothing and everything yes some clue. Well it was the last place she'd been that anyone had seen her in. That other time I went they wouldn't even let me in but I knew the Open House was the one day when they couldn't stop me so yes I had it in my mind though I didn't have much of a plan really just to you know like a bloodhound sniff around search for traces. What in particular I couldn't say something left behind maybe you know they never saw her at the depot. I guess the man had a car. Cochrane wouldn't even say that much so I just thought maybe she was still there somehow not in her physical presence I mean but I thought I don't know what I thought that I could pick up a trail somehow like I said a scent find a clue no I told you I just saw their bed saw they were. I mean I suppose that was the big secret I discovered but it didn't interest me at all. Her journal maybe she'd dropped it and I would find it lying under a chair or wedged between some other books waiting for me with a leaf or two pressed inside she liked that. This world you make of it what you can. No all I ended up doing was landing in that bush picking burrs out of my behind but this business with gravestones is silly anyway. Where are your parents? They're out west I assume their resting place I mean. It was a shame when they left. No it didn't happen all at once I can't even remember the last time I saw each of them it wasn't like a grand good-bye and then of course because of the movies it was like I kept on seeing them him certainly afterward so there wasn't some final moment it was like they left slowly faded kind of. I remember once coming down from the road and thinking there they were so I went walking down the hillside in a certain way ready to greet them long time no see that kind of thing and discovering it was some friends of your dad's lowlife types I hope you don't mind my saying so. You could just tell. Those friends of your mother's even the one I didn't like the pixie man even him they all had a certain. Well these were just lowlifes by comparison they were lying there with their shirts undone their underwear showing. Fellows he met at the track it turned out. He lent them the place he was too generous your dad. Your mother when did I see her last I know one time I met her it could have been the last time she'd seen some notice in the paper not the *Pennysaver* no some downstate paper an ad from the agricultural agent saying Free

Trees something like that and I guess it intrigued her it said five hundred free trees if you're willing to plant them yourself. If you had the land you know. Well it was like someone had offered her five hundred orphans she just couldn't resist she had this heart I mean she was very impractical kind of with her head in the clouds sometimes you wondered where she came from at least I did but a heart as big as the whole outdoors. She convinced Freddie Seaborne to go down in his truck I don't know where but she called ahead and reserved and got him to go and get these five hundred free trees. Freddie he was just as helpless as I was I mean if she asked you to do something in that way she had it was like you only looked up later and thought to yourself Maybe I should have said no when you were already knee-deep in shit but at the time it was impossible to refuse so Freddie goes in his truck to this nursery I suppose tree farm and they pile into the bed of his pickup this big roll of sod but instead of grass it's got little saplings in it no bigger than my thumb five hundred of them all the same pine trees Scottish pine. Just what we need here he thinks more pine. But it's good for holding down soil they say sandy soil so he figures what the hell and drives them back. Your mother she oohs and aahs of course he's wondering he's looking at his vistas and wondering where the hell he's going to put them all. Five hundred trees. They're going to grow they're cute now but he's looking into the future he could see things from near and far and also from far off in time fifty years later he had to that's what landscaping is that's why it looks so good now better than before he had all these surprises in store things that were small when he planted them or old when he left them so now they're. But anyway these five hundred trees are just kind of staring back at him like where are you going to put us buddy and he's tempted of course to roll whole thing into the lake but your mother she's going to want to visit them the first few days at least have him point out to her where each one is so he starts planting one here one there around the property but there's too many he's still got four hundred and ninety left. Finally he just goes to that heap of dirt Lebrun's been having the backhoes make while they dig out the foundations for his other houses. It's by the water but the lake's rising since then they fill it up higher and higher each year catching all the snow runoff so they can make more power. It started out being dirt but now it has all this scrap wood in it discarded building material insulation old oil drums packing crates totally illegal of course the Authority would never stand for it but he was the Authority no one ever came here to check up on him. It was this eyesore on the side of the lake except at that time of the year it was cut off a bit so Freddie he gets Lebrun's boat that little skiff Lebrun calls it and no he doesn't get in himself there's no room he wades out pushing it with this whole roll of trees inside. Gets to this pile of gravel and dirt and sand black plastic too beer bottles whatever Lebrun was too cheap to have hauled away and he starts planting them Freddie does one every few inches until he covered the whole mound. By then he must have looked like the creature from the black lagoon but I came by the next day when he was showing her all the places where they'd been planted here and here and then he points it was way off to the side you couldn't see it from the house just from the beach he shows her this shitpile of garbage you couldn't even see them from there but he says That that's going to be your island. And your mother you know she had that perfect white skin and blonde hair and the bluest eyes I'd ever seen I mean she was just picture perfect in addition to having a good heart she got this catch in her throat she gave us each a big kiss I hadn't done anything I just happened to be there but she was so moved. I wondered later if it was because she knew she would never see it never see the trees because she knew they were going away she and your dad even though they said they'd be back and all. Freddie of course he could picture exactly how it would be. For him it kind of already existed. Me I was thinking how mad Lebrun was going to be when he found out he couldn't use his garbage dump anymore because I knew Freddie was going to call him that night and tell him but I guess what with them raising the level of the reservoir he wasn't going to be able to use it much longer anyway. You can go see it any time now it's this little island off the coast this sort of humpbacked thing bristling with pines those Scottish ones with the peeling bark it's very pretty. But your mother that might be the last time I saw her I don't know. I think there was one other time but I can't remember. Your dad I get confused because there were those types he lent the house to they came up a couple more times always around racing season I guess they went to the track they were like him without your mom. What he might have become I mean. She had this influence on him your dad she turned him into something better when you met them together they were such a good combination. I guess it was just their love you could feel it some couples are like that it kind of spills over whatever they feel for each other. With others it's more like you're running into a wall they just shut you out like Lebrun and Maggie I suppose if you ever met them together say at the IGA he had to take her shopping because that little car of hers the Easter egg it didn't hold enough bags that was her excuse I think really she just wanted him to do something with her instead of being off trying to run Eagle Enterprises all the time. I ran into them there it was like meeting a different person someone I barely knew he'd be pushing along this cart piled high with all this fruit she didn't eat much solid food just fruit she squeezed she had a machine yes a juicer that's right so he'd have twenty pounds of oranges six bags of grapefruits no this was before Ming Ming's only been here a year and then a few of those things she'd get for him frozen dinners Hungry Man Salisbury Steak crap like that. I don't think he cared I don't think he noticed what he put in his mouth. I'd go up to him but it was almost like he was some kind of undercover agent posing you know posing as someone else as this henpecked husband then she'd come by and dump something else in the cart barely notice me and go off again. Leave this trail of perfume down the aisle yes she made it herself it was one of her hobbies or projects perfume out of I don't know what coyote piss people used to say it was all some plan she had to overthrow the government by making perfume at home I know it's crazy. Perfume that was just as good as what they sold for sixty dollars a bottle in the store that's what she said so it would ruin the beauty industry she was always blaming things like the beauty industry she would say it enslaves women and another one of her things was to always put stamps on her letters upside down. That was supposed to wreck the machinery at the post office although that didn't make any sense to me because then how was your letter going to get there how were you going to pay the electric bill? Bud I asked him about it once he said he didn't care that her stamps were upside down but that if she got one more bagful of college catalogs he was going to need an operation. I don't know what that was about maybe she thought she could learn just by reading about stuff the courses I mean but you'd meet them as a couple it was like the doors of a castle with the drawbridge pulled up. Your father and mother they were different. I know it's silly to say but she was an angel. Bill she'd say you must sit down you've been working too hard I can tell let me make you a sandwich. Like I was one of her guests. And then your dad would come out always like he had nothing else to do like he had all the time in the world he'd clap me on the back and ask what was the news. It's too bad you don't remember those times I'm guessing that's when your parents were at their best at their happiest I mean. Later when they got well when he got famous I guess that was a big deal but here they were still young and loved each other and loved you. Lucy used to play with you all day either on the beach or she'd take you places. You'd be brought out in the evening all washed up and in these little outfits a sailor's suit I remember once I'd catch sight of you sometimes when I was on my way home on the beach they'd have strung the speakers from the hi-fi down there they had music drinks I kind of saw it all from a distance Uncle that man dancing in and out of the smoke that smell. Then I'd go home.

~⁓

After Allure they wanted to get me a pet a dog they said That's what you need a dog but dogs and horses they don't get along and it would be like a betrayal I thought besides I still had Firebrand even though he didn't do much he didn't go anywhere but I'd clean out his stall brush him down we'd talk a bit mostly about Allure I mean I would. Reminisce. He's the only one who really knew her how special she was. It's funny Alice and Emily they're both interested in people but not so much in animals. Like Alice when Lebrun had his accident she even befriended Maggie or tried to though those two you couldn't find two people with less in common. He got his leg and hip crushed his whole side really in one of the turbines it's not clear what happened what he was doing there he wouldn't say later. No that was a whole different deal inside the power station that was run by North Star Electric not the Authority so he had no business being there. Well they couldn't very well ask him at first what he was doing there it wasn't even clear if he was going to make it. This maintenance worker just happened on by and. Took forever to get him to the hospital that bumpy ride I can't imagine with all those bones broken. By the time I got there they'd pumped him full of morphine plus they had a tube down his throat. Maggie she clutched onto me with both hands kept looking at me trying to find my eyes like she had this question to ask but she didn't say anything I couldn't figure it out she was in shock I guess. Then Alice she just swept by us and started talking to the doctor. See with some people she could be a total boss and with others it was like she just folded her hands and looked down like she was back in school but this time she took charge asked the doctor what was happening if they should move him to a better hospital why weren't they operating. Maggie she was just. He's going to be fine I told her even though looking at him I had my doubts then Alice comes back from the doctor and takes charge of Maggie or tries to pries her off me and starts talking to her. I went over to Lebrun. His body looked all wrinkled all those years of hard living I guess or maybe it was just the water no one knew how long he'd been in there. What the hell happened? I asked him even though he was well not just the tube and the morphine something about his body made him look like he was far away. Crazy son of a bitch I said what the hell were you doing were you fishing for salmon? Because well there's a rumor at least that there's a pool down there a pool below the turbines I don't know how that place works it's noisy you couldn't get me to go in there if you paid me but there's a pool down there they say where the fish live. The spillway is closed most of the year the spillway's only open when there's runoff so they try and go through the turbines but there's a grate of course you don't want them jamming up the works the equipment Lebrun told me there was a deep pool below the grate but you couldn't get to it if you could get to it he said there were some monsters down there with no place to go it would be like shooting fish in a barrel he said I don't think he realized he was making a joke. Oh just for the sport I imagine. It's not like he especially with that woman in the house it's not like he was going to be eating fresh fish even if he could catch them. I thought maybe he'd been trying to work his way down in there somehow to stand on a ledge or something. No I didn't ask if they'd found a pole I didn't ask anything it was illegal for him to even be in there it's a restricted area there's all these signs HIGH VOLTAGE DANGER stuff like that. What the hell were you thinking? I said. Your wife's a vegetarian for Christ's sake and you you haven't had food that didn't come out of a freezer since you got married. Alice of course she got them to call in a specialist she was riding roughshod over the doctor the nurses like she owned the place. Maggie just

stood there even though she was the wife. I knew it was kind of disloyal disloyal to Alice I mean but I took pity on her she couldn't stop
trembling no one was paying attention. Then Alice came back and
told me I had to go to Lebrun's house and get everything from his
medicine cabinet. For the doctors she says so they can see what he's
taking. I don't know how she knew that he was taking anything. We
got the keys off Maggie but then well I couldn't drive and Alice was
watching over Lebrun like a mother hen over a chick this man she
couldn't stand to even hear mention of normally that's how she was
so finally Maggie she wakes up she said she'll take me there in the
Easter egg yes so I crammed in the other side. My knees were right
up against my eyeballs practically. I can't move the seat back she said
there's too much stuff and it was true the whole back well there
wasn't much space to begin with but it was piled high with boxes
with leaflets they were spilling out I could see they were all political.
Stop This Stop That. Where do you take these to? I asked. I distrib-
ute them she says. Turned out she'd just put them in piles in different places. Discreetly she said. I mean she'd dump them basically like
litter. If you ask permission then they can say no she said but if you
just leave them. I don't know what the point was I guess she figured
maybe one or two would end up in the hands of someone who
agreed with her already in which case why bother? Where do you
get them I asked you don't print them up yourself do you? She said
no she was part of an organization that's as much as she'd say. So we
were driving along and she pulls us into the driveway and she says I
hate this house I want to live in Kathan. Well you should I told her
why not there's some pretty places there and the library too you
could walk over any time instead of driving to have lunch with Miss
with Evangeline Dick. She nodded. I realized she wasn't going to
get out of the car she didn't even know what she was doing there
I shouldn't have let her get behind the wheel in the first place so I
took the keys and let myself in. I'd barely ever been there to begin

with Lebrun he was never exactly a host but certainly not since he came back with her. First thing I noticed was the front door didn't open all the way. It hit against something bounced a little and then when I poked my head in I saw it was a pile of newspapers not *Pennysavers* this paper like the *Red Banner* or something all these back issues a year's worth at least stacked in a big pile. And then when I got myself squeezed past that I saw this poster's not the right word it was this floor-to-ceiling picture of that bearded guy not Santa Claus the political one he's got a funny hat from Cuba you know Castro that's right he's holding a rifle Fidel Castro a picture of him I don't know maybe life-size maybe bigger depends on how tall he was it took up the whole wall it was like you were having him over to dinner. I almost jumped out of my skin you don't see an eight-foot-tall man with a beard every day he could have won first prize at the sesquicentennial contest oh yes they had ribbons for best whiskers best sideburns but anyway I start walking through the place it's not a big house but Lebrun always kept it neat enough when he was a bachelor I mean you could walk from one room to the next without tripping over anything but this was like walking through someone's diseased brain there were piles of paper everywhere posters on all the walls not of people necessarily a lot were in other languages these words or Chinese letters whatever you call them and from the kitchen which I didn't even go into but I mean I just glanced as I went by I could see dishes in the sink garbage that hadn't been taken out no wonder he never wanted to go home but when I got to the bathroom I opened the cabinet behind the mirror and medicine bottles practically fell out on me that's when I was really surprised. No not drugs I mean well yes drugs but pills legal stuff medications ten or twenty bottles all from Varney's made out to him Claude Brown for I had no idea for what at the time. He was a sick man that's what was obvious obvious at that moment I'd never thought so before he always seemed the picture of health to me. I took them all I couldn't even find a bag in that mess a simple paper bag I just pulled out my shirtfront so it formed a kind of catchall and walked them back to the car. What the hell's this? I asked. What's wrong with him? Maggie she was exactly as I'd left her she stared out front through the windshield like she was still driving like the road was still coming at her. Epilepsy she said. He has epilepsy. I got back in my side of the car still holding all these bottles close to my chest. Epilepsy? I said. Is he all right? He gets fits she says. When does he get fits? I asked. I never saw one. And then I thought back to that time at night when we were both in Conklingville without knowing the other was there yes the night before they were due to start flooding the place when I saw him kicking at that stump of stone that hearth. It's true when I went to get him his eyes were all. But just for a second then it was like he came to and everything was fine. Can you drive? I said and then realized I was crazy letting her drive so I made her get out we switched places. I'd seen people do it enough it's not that hard. Those pills rattling on the floor that was the hardest part listening to them roll around. I never saw him have a fit I said even though now that I was remembering there were other times times when he acted strange but I didn't think anything of it. And the way he'd disappear. He was always slipping out and then reappearing like a cricket kind of you'd see him one minute and then there'd just be this shaking blade of grass where he pushed off from. He couldn't let anyone see she said. He said if they knew they'd take everything away from him the bank the Authority. She looked at me. I think that's the only time I ever got a little bit scared it suddenly occurred to me my god you are driving a car. Forget about no license I didn't really have a clue you know the thing doesn't talk to you the way a horse does doesn't tell you what to do where to go. I reached for a knob and the radio came on by accident I almost relieved myself right then and there I thought someone else was in there with us Fidel Castro maybe I don't know she turned it off for me and showed me how to turn on the lights the headlights it was getting to be evening. He said you knew she said. He said that you and I were the only ones that did. Well hell I said I saw him act strange plenty of times but I never thought he was sick. He's not she said it's not a sickness. That's when I. That's when I heard his voice through hers. It's not a sickness. That's what he must have thought. That's why he never said to me I've got this condition or even I'm not feeling right because to him it was just a part of him maybe even a special part maybe even something not so bad. It's just like that fire-watcher the one who went crazy he said he could look at a piece of forest from up there stare at it you know and make it catch on fire just by his gaze. And right up until they took him away he said he wasn't sick at all that it was just his gift. No I'm not saying Lebrun was crazy he was the least crazy person I know but the part of you that everyone calls crazy or well say sick sometimes you cling to that like it's your private self what makes you different. The fire-watcher? He wasn't from around here he was from farther upstate. I said to him once I mean after he'd told me his big secret which didn't surprise me since I knew he was crazy to begin with oh I could tell almost from the minute I brought him his first load of supplies I said to him Well if you stare at the people instead of the trees don't they catch on fire too? He nodded like that was his biggest fear setting them on fire one of those couples. So what do you do? I asked. I stare into the sun he says cause you can't set the sun on fire. No sir you can't set the sun on fire. He had me there. Can't set fire to the sun. See Lebrun I figured maybe that was the price he paid for seeing everything so clearly seeing all our moves before we made them. He I swear sometimes the words wouldn't be out of your mouth before he'd answer them you'd be thinking something and he'd say Well maybe so but. Or with women once he kind of indicated to me that he knew before they even met him sometimes he'd see one getting out of her car just passing through or a relation of someone visiting and he knew what was going to happen that they were going to. The rest was almost like color by numbers the actual going through with it maybe that's what got him down. Color by numbers those Emily used to do them you'd have a set of colored pencils and pictures where you'd color each part in with whatever number it said on the pencil and then it would slowly take shape. But you already knew what it was of I mean you could tell. Well maybe that's what it was like for Lebrun knowing in advance and the fits they were the price he paid going a little bit off his head from seeing everyone's fate. When we got back to the hospital yes the local one here that was before they closed it down now you have to go to Sparta we found out he'd taken a turn for the worse. Alice showed the bottles to the doctor. They were preparing him for some kind of surgery. They took Maggie away to sign all these forms. Alice once they were gone once there was no one else to boss she got kind of nervous she sat with me she kept smoothing her dress it had flowers I remember daisies I said I was trying to be funny I said You're going to push those flowers right off your dress and she started wailing. I don't mean tears I mean she let out such a howl they came running from the reception desk I had to tell them it was all right that she was just upset well hell they could see that. I could tell they were unnerved because the other patients whoever else was there waiting doesn't want to hear it was almost like at a funeral like she was keening or something so I got her out to the parking lot I didn't know what to say I pointed to the car the Easter egg yes I said Look I parked that little bastard all by myself. It was a joke see because I had managed to spread the thing over about four spaces even though it was the size of a shoebox. I don't know how people fit their cars in those squares. Well she sniffles and looks around. What's wrong? I asked. Nothing she says. And then I got mad. I said For Christ's sake you don't even like him. I know she says then she goes back to wailing. I'd never seen her like that. Finally I still had the keys so I got her in the car in the passenger side just to get her out of the public eye I knew that later when she when she sort of came to she'd be embarrassed if anyone had seen her like that. Once we were in the car she stopped sniffling and looked around the way women get you know how curious they are especially about other women I told her about the pamphlets showed them to her then told her about the house too what I'd seen. I didn't tell her about the epilepsy no. Well she'd seen all the bottles but I don't think. You'd need to be a doctor to figure out what he had from those. Maggie had told me sure but she acted like I already knew so it still seemed a secret. I didn't know if I was allowed. Anyway she didn't seem all that interested in Lebrun anymore she kept poking around these piles of I guess you call it literature in the backseat reading some bits of it out loud it was pretty hard to understand. I didn't approve of that because she was just openly snooping by then she knew she shouldn't but she opened up the glove compartment going through whatever was there which wasn't much just more wads of paper when out comes this map. I said You shouldn't and she had already unfolded it onto her lap. I said again You shouldn't and she said to stop me from complaining she said Just what were you and her doing in here anyway? Like she was jealous. Well she got jealous of everyone even though I never. I think she was just jealous of the feelings I had you know feelings of friendship. For all her good works she never really felt close to anyone not the way I did. No it never led to anything physical I told you that's the last thing you want grabbing each other that just ruins all the feelings that's the end not the beginning nine times out of ten but just the way I'd sit and talk with someone she couldn't do that sit still and talk she had to be helping them or be disapproving of them or be doing both those things at the same time that happened a lot but those were the only two ways she could be friends really what she'd call friends with someone. And it's always with women she used to complain which wasn't really true. I mean I had Lebrun. But

I knew what she meant. I don't know why with women I can. They have more feelings. Or I have more feelings for them. But anyway she just throws that out there that I'd been with Maggie Chess of all people I mean it was just the most crazy thing but meanwhile she got this map spread out it was big it took up especially in that car it took up most of the room. I think she's trying to blow something up Alice said. I'll bet she's one of those you know I'll bet she's a Red. I told her not to say such things. Now you just stop it I said. Stop right there. I folded up the map put it back where we found it and we went inside. She was fine for the rest of the evening Alice. She held Maggie's hand. We stayed there until night and then Maggie was going to sleep in the room so we walked home together. Alice didn't say a word to me the whole time. She was mad I could tell. I kind of wanted to throw her a bone find something to make her smile so I told her how Lebrun would always say whenever I mentioned her The love of a good woman. The love of a good woman I said that that's what he said you gave me. I wanted to show he liked her. Then we got home and she went right on going she went out back to the garden didn't change into her gardening clothes or nothing just went out to the garden got a bucket and a flashlight and started picking away at grubs or caterpillars. I went to check on Emily. She was watching that little TV she said How's Mister Brown? I said He'll be fine which I didn't know for sure but figured there was no point in upsetting her. Your mom's out back. I didn't know what to do. I'd been so busy that whole day tending to people. I knew I should go to the barn I knew I had things to do but I couldn't it hadn't really hit me yet what was going on. That he might. Plus knowing all that time before that he'd been sick and hadn't told me. I was trying to re-see everything in light of what I knew but you can't really do that things make an impression at the time you can't go back and change that impression. I sat down with Emily and watched for a while. It was that show Bonanza. I watched it mostly because of the horses. The boy she liked he rode a chestnut mare except he'd get off it and the camera would go with him into some saloon through those swinging doors and I was still watching past the edge of the screen I was still back with the horse. Then I said Don't you ever go away Emily which I feel bad about now I feel bad that maybe she took it to heart what I said maybe that's why she's never really spread her wings. I said Don't go away but I meant don't go away like Rebecca had or like Mother and Father oh I don't know what I was thinking. Words just come out sometimes. Or like Alice out back. She had gone away from me in spirit. Sometimes I'd get this sense that everyone was speeding away from me like cars when they'd pass me on the cart hell half my adult life I'd watch some jackass in a pickup truck disappearing down the road in front of me leaving me to breathe his exhaust fumes. I remember I felt it all kind of slipping away I suppose I was afraid he'd die though I don't really know what that would mean to me except that I'd be out of work. I said Don't you ever go away Emily like I could stop it all from happening but of course she didn't even hear she was too busy watching that boy Little Joe that was his name but still sometimes I worry that it sank in on some kind of level.

≈

You can have one sure they don't stay sticky for long though not after the first day then they turn hard. Well that's the problem that's why I don't my teeth my plate I'm afraid it's going to crack if I bite down. What if she what? Now you mean? If she just up and left? Well I suppose then I'd have to go too. Emily pays for me to stay here she manages all the money just like Alice oh I trust her I suppose I'd still have something but if she took off took all the money with her I wouldn't care I'd tie a kerchief or what do you call it a bandana around the end of a stick put some bread and cheese in it and go off tramping like I did as a kid. Maybe I'd work for Ming gather berries in the forest and bring them to him. Up by Indian Pipes there must be a ton of them by now nobody picking them for so long are you all right you want some water? See that's what happens they lodge in your throat I'm surprised she hasn't had more complaints. I guess people eat them right away while they're still sticky me I leave mine out the ones Cecil doesn't take. You got to cover them though wrap them in something or else they get all. Once I made the mistake of saying If they don't work as pastries you could always get a patent for them as flypaper. She didn't appreciate that at all. It's true though. Don't worry I covered that one. If you don't if you're not careful the flies sink right in they try and take a step and. Cecil he grabbed one once before I had a chance to warn him he popped the whole thing in his mouth then said Raisins like it was a new kind of flavor. I just nodded. I don't know why he ran out and stopped me that day I guess he would have gotten in trouble if he hadn't. He was mad as hell like it was something personal like it was directed toward him. That's the thing about young people they think it's all directed toward them. How could you do this to me? he was saying well I didn't have the heart to tell him I barely knew who he was at that moment he was just in my way that's all. The church steeple it was calling me like it was a magnet or I don't know an escape hatch that I could climb down out of all this and resume. Resume it's like the path we take isn't quite right that's what Allure was trying to tell me when she went off her head at the end it's like we're living our life but then at some point we take this wrong step and after that everything's just slightly off from the true path the way we should have gone you can see it out the corner of your eye or sense it but you can't get back there you keep trying you keep running into things rubbing yourself raw trying but. No I never went in there not as a worshipper I went into the building I'm sure once or twice there was nothing special about it it was just a church but it was the tallest building you'd see it from the road as you approached that's how you knew you were al-

181

most home and if you went playing in the fields below like Rebecca and I used to when we pretended to go on the bum well then you'd look up and. From Gabrielle's room? No that faced away that faced up the mountain besides we didn't do much looking out the window we drew the blinds the jealousies she called them. I used to ask her to talk to me in French I didn't know what she said it was just soothing the sounds she'd run her fingers through my hair and talk. It was kind of like Mother when she sang in Italian I suppose. I don't know what she was saying it could have been a cup of flour a pound of butter who knows it could have been anything that's just an example you see a recipe because for all I know she could have been telling me how to bake a cake no she didn't cook Gabrielle why would she have oh Mother you mean certainly all the time flapjacks that was her specialty. They are not pancakes pancakes are flat things pancakes are thin little circles you have to pile three high just to make one flapjack a flapjack's like a bed it's soft and deep just one will take care of you and when you eat them they kind of continue to comfort you inside your belly like you've got a cushion in there to rest on with butter and maple syrup yes. We'd have flapjacks for Sunday dinner instead of meat. She made it into a treat but I see now it was probably more of an economy. Made them in this cast-iron skillet. Each one was the size of the pan. We had to wait until everyone's was done. She'd keep them warm in the oven. They were so high. They rose. Then the last one if you were lucky you got the last one because it was the hottest and the highest the others she'd put on a platter but yours the last one she'd turn right out of the skillet onto your plate. That was a sign of favor. I could eat forever then. Just wolfing it down. She'd say grace Bless us oh Lord something like that well if he'd stayed like that the God of Flapjacks then I would have been all right with him. The smell and the way they made you feel it was like you were already in bed I never had anything like that since I mean I've had pancakes Alice would make them sometimes but they're always a disappointment like a doily or something compared to. Sunday afternoons we'd do chores usually. The Lord's day it's only the Lord's day if you want to do something fun like trying to shoot bottles off a fence or teach your little girl how to carve a figure out of soap it's not the Lord's day if you're supposed to climb up on the roof and clean the gutters the Lord likes that apparently clean gutters according to Alice he did. Emily well I wanted to teach her something and she didn't like horses and Alice certainly wasn't going to let her fire a gun so. Wood's too hard you got to start with something soft like soap. Besides you don't want the blade to slip. No you never cut away from yourself you'll never be a carver if you cut away from yourself. Always cut toward yourself that way you have control. I don't know how I know that from years of doing it I suppose. I've always carved yes Father he's who I learned it from so I thought I'd pass it on to Emily. Alice said it was wasteful the soap you know even though if you do it right if you don't cut too deep it's not that much you're wasting and anyway it's just soap I tried telling her Ivory Soap six for a dollar. I think really what she didn't like was that it was idolatrous that was one of those words she used I'm sure she got it from Bigelow it sounds like him doesn't it? If you liked anything too much she'd say you were being idolatrous. We'd make these statues out of soap well I would I would try and get Emily to I would guide her hand she was scared even though I gave her a blunt blade I think she had these visions of her thumb coming off I'd say Don't start with a picture in mind just try and feel what's in there let it come out natural. My father he would do ladies mostly. He really had a talent he'd just pick up a piece of scrap a stick of kindling even if it was soft enough he always had a knife on him it wasn't like he was giving you a lesson it took me a long time to even realize what was happening he'd be taking a break or waiting on the chickens for them to all get inside and his hands would be fooling around with this nub of wood and then presto it was like a magic trick she'd be well it's like she'd been there all along this busty I always thought of them as redheads for some reason the color of the wood I guess he'd hold it up and say What do we have here? and then in the same motion throw it away let it drop. No he wasn't ashamed he just attached no value to it once it was done. I'd pick them up after he was gone he'd never let you pick it up at the time he dropped them I tried that once he slapped it out of my hand. I guess after they left him they were like filthy a little maybe but I'd go back he left them just lying around in the barn or by a fence post and I'd pick them up. I had quite a little collection at one time of course I couldn't keep them in the house couldn't let anyone discover them so I hid them up by the rock at the top of the stream. There was a little overhanging part at the bottom that made kind of a shelf I stored oh twenty or thirty maybe by the end under there. What little I learned about females what little he taught me it all came from those dolls those carved figures. Finally they got all scattered there was this storm it rained for days and then a flood it must have carried them all off he and I were down by the lower field trying to pull this cow out of a ditch it was typical bad luck the whole ditch was full of water poor creature was bellowing and he's swearing like a sailor. I noticed floating all around us all around our ankles my collection they were spinning downstream like it was a race these ladies on their backs their big boobies sticking up out of the water and he didn't notice a thing so maybe they weren't as obvious as I thought or maybe I don't know maybe they'd gone back to being wood. Me I carved horses. It wasn't a decision it was just what I had in me I was trying to carve a woman I didn't know what else to try but the wood the way it guides you with the soft and hard spots I just stood back from it at one point tried to see it fresh and realized that's no lady that's a mare. This was after he was gone of course I didn't try it while he was alive I just watched. So who knows maybe after I'm gone Emily will well not with a bar of soap I hope that's kind of silly finally all we'd do when we were done was put them in the bathroom over the sink or by the tub. We did Little Joe on his horse I did the horse of course and she made a sort of a figure. Alice she let out a scream when she saw it. I suppose he did look more like a monster I mean he was twice as big as he should have been but she got the hat right one of those Stetson hats I told Emily it was great. I thought Alice should have encouraged her more. She kept whispering to me Look like there was something to see then finally when the child was in bed she kind of hissed Look between his legs. Well then I noticed. I hadn't really before. So he's not Little Joe all over I said throw it away if you want say it broke. But she couldn't bear the waste Alice she kept washing her hands with it that night until by morning he looked more like the Mummy poor guy.

~

He was fine. They let him out of the hospital gave him a clean bill of health. His bones were broken but they'd heal. He didn't remember nothing but that's not unusual they said. He didn't remember how he got into the power station or what he was doing there. The only difference was that I knew knew about the epilepsy I mean. I did some reading kind of on the sly in the library. Miss Dick she didn't like you just browsing she needed to know what you were doing back there she kind of treated it like her own house. I couldn't say I want to read up on epilepsy because then she might have asked why so instead I stayed in my section and looked up what the Ancient Greeks thought of it hell yes they named it epilepsy it means the falling sickness they thought people who had it had visions. Some people even think the oracles those girls they asked questions to might have had epilepsy. Well no I couldn't ask Lebrun about that if he ever saw things or not because then he'd know I knew that was the problem afterward I didn't feel as comfortable with him as before and Maggie you'd have thought she'd be grateful that we'd been such good friends to her in her hour of need but instead she kind of turned on us. I've always thought it was because we saw too much those pamphlets in the backseat of the car the kind of house she kept all her secrets. No it's not like we told anyone but after the accident Maggie she would barely speak to us it was more like a cat spitting when we'd cross paths. What is it? I asked Lebrun that was about as close to criticizing her as I ever got. Did we offend her in some way? She's just going through a rough patch he said. Ten-year rough patch more like. There were changes in him all right but it was subtle like I said the changes were in me too knowing what I knew. He got more sentimental for one thing he'd say Old friend or Buddy something like that something that didn't sound right coming out of his mouth. Yes it affected him mentally not in any kind of crazy way but I think he got a glimpse of the end that he wasn't a young man anymore he'd talk about times when we were both young which he never used to do. Once he got all choked up I swear honest to god I thought it was hay fever at first because it wasn't like we were talking about anything so emotional I think I just mentioned how he had asked if I loved her Alice kind of out of the blue that one time and how I hadn't even known if I did or not until I answered until he brought it up I mean. I was kind of blaming him because we'd had one of our fights Alice and me so I was teasing him saying if you hadn't asked me that question but he took it well he got all sentimental all choked up with his arm around me I thought he was going to have one of those fits I was always on the alert for. I thought what should I do what would an Ancient Greek do? Ask him a question yes while he was still in the mood like he was an oracle but what would I ask? He said Such a long time ago and started to get all teary-eyed he couldn't control himself. What would I have asked oh I don't know. Where's my sister? I suppose but it wouldn't have helped those oracles they always answered a question with a question or gave you an answer you could take either way an oracle probably would have answered She's right here Rebecca and that could have meant right here in my heart in my memory or right here like at the bottom of the lake her bones you know. Well that's just an example I didn't mean anything by it. Anyway what he said was he was afraid Maggie was going to leave him that's why he was upset. I didn't know how to react to that I mean you don't really want to pop a bottle of champagne especially when the poor man's crying on your shoulder but on the other hand. Why? I asked. Why would she do a thing like that? Because I can't love her as a man he says. Well that was telling me something I didn't want to hear. Hell I said at her age she should just be happy she has a roof over her head. Maybe that wasn't the most caring way to put it but he laughed. I steered you right he said didn't I with Alice? Sure I said if I wasn't married to her who'd tell me to stop drinking all the time? I'd probably have to go on the wagon if it wasn't for her. Which in a funny way is true because once Alice passed the very night of the funeral in fact we got home I remember Bigelow he put on this big show of caring for us looking after us having us back to his place serving some kind of tea he said was good for nerves but when we got home Emily and I well I was ready to go out to the barn and find that bottle of Old Gentleman I kept in the oat bin bring it inside kind of inaugurate my un-happiness toast my grief but it's like I lost the urge. No I haven't touched a drop since I don't even think about it really. Of course I didn't realize any of that at the time I was talking to Lebrun it wasn't like a forecast or anything like a prediction she never did leave him no they moved to Kathan instead just like she wanted to he gave up the house gave up his position with the Authority he didn't retire he wasn't old enough it was they call it disability where you get paid because you can't work anymore. I know. It made no sense to me ei-ther I mean that happens all the time usually the person just gets fired they aren't given money for being sick. When I had no call for work anymore when the Homeowners Association informed me that they'd hired that service it's not like they said because of all your years of tending our houses we'll pay you X amount of dollars for the rest of your life. Gold watch that's a good one no just a special delivery envelope Bud had to make me sign for to prove I'd got it. I knew what was inside already they'd told me that my services were no longer required that's what she who was that woman Trinita someone what kind of name is that she was the head of the Home-owners Association maybe still is for all I know Trinita oh I'll never remember that's what she told me not to bother coming around any-more that's the way she put it not to bother like it was just this thing I did on my way to someplace else drag the garbage cans up check their traps empty the fridge if there was any food rotting in there I did stuff they didn't even know about I just didn't make a big deal out of it that was my mistake I should have made myself seem indis-pensable but instead I tried to not be there to go when no one was around put everything back perfectly in place so it seemed like it was undisturbed so they didn't realize they needed me. The service? It's just a bunch of kids a different one each time they come up in a truck from Sparta they've got this checklist of what to do what each house needs of course it's efficient but there's nothing personal about it they don't know whose garbage they're hauling what place needs ant traps in the cupboard things like that. It's a different kid each time I don't know what they do when they're not here go to other places I guess they clean too or say they do. They have women they're dropped off and picked up yes Ruth that's when she announced her retirement. She saw the writing on the wall they didn't have to fire her she went and saw that what was her name Breyer that's right Trinita Breyer she went right up to her in that little office she kept at the social hall and announced that she was retiring. Well I'm so happy for you Ruth she says. And that time your septic tank over-flowed Ruth goes on when your husband was up here alone that week to get some work done Bailor the man who pumped it out he told me it was because they found a bunch of condoms blocking the intake. Anyway for me they sent this letter I had to sign for but I wouldn't do it. I don't know why I was just feeling ornery. Yes I was still going there well those kids they weren't doing any kind of a job I thought they'd realize that you know see the error of their ways the garbage cans they weren't brought back down right away they were left by the side of the road for days sometimes same with the traps. I'd check every day you don't want a dead mouse stinking up your kitchen but instead they started to lay poison that's awful stuff it rots them out from inside burns their stomachs so they just lie there in the walls in agony you smell them sometimes for a week or two then they dry out but you can never get to them so it's like you're living in a house full of bones. Anyway my traps were still there I had to check on them put more bait in them peanut butter I always used peanut butter that's when the Breyer woman sends me this letter registered mail but I wouldn't sign for it. I was sitting out back in the garden. Emily was still having a go at it then I would try and help kind of undo the damage mostly with what I remembered as a kid. Not that Father was any kind of teacher but I was sitting there on the old apple crate if I sit on the ground now I don't get up you need a block-and-tackle to raise me off the ground and Bud comes around with this letter. You got to sign for it he says but I knew what it was so I said No why should I? He gives me this whole bit about regulations how he can't leave until Well I ain't got a pen I said. He says I do. The garden was I don't know how she managed to wreck it in a few short years she put in more time there than Alice ever did but it was like the harder she tried the worse it got. I was sitting at the very end trying to weed around the cucumbers and Bud he won't take no for an answer he's acting all official and finally I said OK then you sign it for me. He says I can't do that. I said Well I'm not signing it and he starts yelling at me telling me what a stiff-necked cuss I am. We were both too old to be getting into it that way. He retired I think the next year yes retired for all of six months then went on a hunting trip felt a pain in his shoulder where he tried to rest his rifle went to the doctor and that was that. It had spread all over his body. Anyway he has this slip of paper and a pen he's holding out to me and I never cared for Bud Johnson so much but it's not like I wanted to be responsible for his death he was all red-faced so I take the pen and lick it and suddenly I know I can't do it. I don't know when it had happened but I couldn't write my name. No it wasn't like there was any one event that's funny that's just what Doc Harmon asked the word he used I mean the same as you he asked if there had been an event when I felt funny but I told him no it just came to me that day that I couldn't sign my name or write anything for that matter it's like it came to me as a memory does that make sense? That I couldn't sign my name or take a pen in my hands or do anything with it basically I closed my fingers around it I got that far but then. Come on Bud says it's not like anyone's going to read it your signature and all I could think about was back in school they'd look at me I could feel them looking at me when I was bent over my desk taking a test and they were all thinking how does that idiot boy how can he even spell his own name? They were always so surprised when I did well because I didn't talk much or play games I was kind of clumsy too but I could answer the questions if you asked me to write them down so I was going to be damned if now if sixty years later I was not going to be able to even write my name just like they thought so then I got this idea I thought my way out of it I took the slip of paper this little green slip with my other hand and I moved it right under the pen. I started moving it sideways back and forth trying to see my name but in reverse. I can't explain it but I could I could make my name appear by moving the paper not the pen. The pen it was all I could do to keep steady it's like the pen was the paper. Of course he didn't notice nothing Bud I think he was surveying the garden because when I looked up I was drenched in sweat he had no idea what that took out of me he says Yeah she sure had a green thumb. Speaking of Alice. That was more of a what do they call that at the funeral when they talk about the person a eulogy that was more of a eulogy about Alice than anything Bigelow ever said. And I got a red nose I said. He laughed at that. It's true it's when I stopped drinking my nose got red. I think it missed the liquor my nose or maybe it was that I was out in the sun all day without a hat. Alice would always tell me to wear a hat. It's funny the things she would make me do like wear a hat I stopped doing but the things she couldn't stop me from doing like drinking that I stopped. Go figure.

~⌒

So then I'm left with this letter which tells me nothing new it says that if I go back to any of the houses I could be persecuted. I guess people were complaining. They didn't want to have to change their locks oh sure I had all the keys still but no there was no mention of disability or anything like that no check for seven hundred dollars or whatever he got a month yes for nothing for sitting on his duff not that he was doing nothing he was still running Eagle Enterprises. The house they moved to in Kathan no he didn't build that it was an old place on Pearl one street back from the main drag from the intersection it had concrete steps out front one of those turret rooms with a round roof a nice-looking place it didn't look anything like his summer houses it was very old-fashioned. Did moving there make her happy? I don't know she didn't leave him at least like she was threatening to. She could see Evangeline Dick for lunch more easily I suppose. Lebrun he still set off in his pickup every day yes he bought himself a new one finally with his own money or leased it probably I don't think he bought much outright he once explained to me how it was good to owe. The more you owe the more you got he said which made no sense at all to me. That's when he had the idea for the Homeowners Association when he was free of the dam

191

it's like he threw himself into the whole idea of a community sharing a beach and a social hall and everything that's when he had that little model built. He had an architect well an architectural student come up and take all these measurements. It was pretty accurate it was made of cork layers of cork to represent the different elevations of the mountainside and then for each tree there was a little hole drilled he stuck a little wooden dowel in there not the actual tree but a marker for it. Then you saw all the cleared plots where he was building and what stage the house was at he actually had models of the houses too at different stages of completion it was almost like a toy although he didn't think so he said it was a selling tool. I saw him once with the whole thing the whole model for the mountainside and the beach community set in the bed of his truck. Where you going with that? I asked. To the bank he said to show it off. I guess it was on the basis of that partly that they lent him all the money. Now I ask you is that the kind of man who seems disabled? Plus it's not like they replaced him with someone else instead they realized they didn't need a dam keeper in the first place they just have a kid now who comes up and takes readings maybe once a month. Economy measures they call them. Everyone just hires some part-timer no one cares there's no connection now between what a man does and why he's doing it. No not for money that's not why. You do it to feel like you're part of something. He had people too for those models Lebrun that's when it got a little odd to me little miniaturized people built to scale. That architectural student left him a catalog that sold all sorts of stuff he used to order from them yes a man a woman a child they were always the same three this happy family I guess I don't know what architects use them for I mean they're not building people they're building houses he'd sprinkle them around the model to make it more realistic. It worked I guess. You'd see them down on Freddie Seaborne's beach before it even existed these itty-bitty families they weren't in bathing suits or anything he couldn't go that far but it made it all seem like it had already happened kind of like it was inevitable at least that's what the bankers must have thought. Petrides yes at the Mountain Trust they gave him the whole kit and caboodle the keys to the kingdom. I don't know how much but for a while there it seemed like everyone in town was working for Eagle crews building supplies even the real estate agents he didn't show the houses around himself anymore he was too busy for that he negotiated a deal I hear he got a special cut a percentage of whatever commission they received. But the people the ones in the model he'd move them around like pieces on a chessboard that's what Maggie said. Not to me I told you when she and I met or Alice and her crossed paths it was like. No I was in the library in the back listening to her talk to Miss Dick complain basically which she did more and more. He spends hours she said on that model deciding where to put the people like it's so important he even has names for them. I tried not to hear I didn't want to hear I kept going deeper into the books. The problem was I couldn't make sense of them anymore. The words it was like the same as writing they just kind of swam in front of me. At first I thought it was my glasses that I needed new ones but I got those ones that magnify at Varney's Drug and all it did was make the words swim faster right at me almost I had to jerk back like they were going to come off the page. Doc Harmon said I'd had an event I just didn't remember it Well what kind of event is that? I asked. An event I don't even remember how do I know it really happened? From the results he says. Reading and writing. Your brain blew a fuse. Everything's getting rerouted. I told him about how I signed that slip of paper by moving the paper instead of the pen and he said See that's what your mind is doing it's coping it's finding new ways to deal with the situation. Will I find a new way to read? I asked. You might he said I don't know. I could see he didn't think I would. Reading's pretty complicated he said. But I can still read a little not the way I used to not whole books. I had to teach myself all over I had to move the words instead of my eyes. It's not the same but I was trying and all that time Maggie Chess going on to Miss Dick about Lebrun saying how he called them by name the figurines in his model. Are they named for people around here? Miss Dick asked. No Maggie says it's this whole other world he has they have French names Mathieu and André Gabrielle Pierre. French-Canadian names Miss Dick says. Probably children he knew growing up. The problem was I still had to take books out pretend that I was still able to. Well of course I didn't want anyone to know. Even Doc Harmon I was afraid he would tell someone. He wasn't supposed to but it's a small town there's not much going on people got to make conversation when they can. Gossip it's the stuff of life around here. I was terrified of everyone looking at me sideways thinking He can't read or write it's like all my fears were coming true it was so unfair I mean I would have traded it for a bum leg or a tremble instead I had to come up with all these strategies. Didn't you already read this book Bill? Miss Dick would say. Not in a few years I'd answer or There's something in it I want to check up on. Then I'd bring it home and have to remember when to return it again think of something to say to prove that I'd actually. No I kept going if I stopped going to the library she would have thought something was up besides I didn't want to offend her it's not like she got so many customers they were always threatening to close the place down. I still learned plenty maybe I learned more then ever in a way because I began studying the maps and the pictures those I could still look at. There was a beautiful painting I found of Pegasus the winged horse not the gas station sign this was in the front of a book about myths it was in color that special smooth paper they put in that was the only time I was ever tempted to rip something out of a book I didn't but I thought no one's ever going to take this out but me no one will ever know it's gone and if they do it's not like they won't be able to read the words just because there's no picture in front and since I can't read the words anymore it's only fair but still I couldn't I couldn't do that to her to Evangeline no I never called her that but I heard Maggie call her that enough. But when I heard Maggie say that name Gabrielle well I just noted it at first it didn't really make that much of an impression. It's true though I'd never heard anyone else called that but of course I never heard any of those other Canuck names either Mathieu or whatever. It did get me to thinking though. He's probably just trying to unwind that's what Miss Dick said he's got a lot on his mind. I was looking at this map of ancient Troy at the time it showed all these levels the same city but they kept building it again and again they had to dig so far down to find the one where the battle took place between the Greeks and the Trojans the way that map looked it was just like his relief model that's what the architecture student called it a relief model it had all these different levels and I wondered if Lebrun was kind of going back in time in his mind I mean and populating it with all these people from his youth. Before he even came here from Canadia that's what they used to call it the old-timers Canadia bringing his memories down here and housing them among us. Gabrielle did he know her from before you mean? I wonder. He wouldn't have known about us though that was private me and her she wouldn't have told him. I'd have more faith in her not telling something than I would in Bert Harmon that's why I kind of went on the offensive about reading and writing. I had Emily read me the *Pennysaver* I told her it was a good way for her to get over her shyness we were trying to figure out what to do with her. A shyer girl you never met so I thought if I get her to read me the *Pennysaver* Lawrence's editorials well then that kills two birds with one stone it teaches her how to speak out loud and makes it like I read the paper. Yes that's exactly what I thought later that I created a monster because it taught her the art of public speaking I guess or gave her a taste for it and that's how she eventually got elected town clerk going to all those meetings talking about the budget the road allowance and stuff the problem is getting her to stop and take a breath sometimes. I just wanted to be able to go up to Lawrence and say Good editorial. I was so scared that something else would go next that I'd have another event and wouldn't even know it had happened that I'd look at a chair say and it would be just this object to me this mess of wood as strange as words no clue as to what it was there for or that I'd try taking a step and my leg it would be like the pen Bud handed me completely frozen. You see people like that here people who can't do nothing. If they get too bad then they get shipped out. Cecil he may be strong but there's a difference between lifting a man out of his chair and taking care of his bodily functions if you understand what I'm saying that's where he draws the line I can't say I blame him. No it hasn't happened to me yet not that I can tell. I sit here thinking about things. What things like about you and Lucy for example Lucy Sunshine yes. Well nothing just I mean that woman she was a character and she was in charge of your education from morning until cocktail time that's when your parents took over but even then basically you and her were together every minute oh your mother and father loved you don't get me wrong but they weren't the kind of couple that take care of their child they had lives to lead. She Lucy she believed in the Second Coming she'd talk about it at the drop of a hat very natural-like she followed that man in Harlem what was his name Father Divine that's right he had them all convinced all his followers that they were going to be on the first ship out headed straight to Heaven. Once I came across the two of you down by the lake. She didn't hear me coming you were both in the water. I was surprised because it was early morning and as I got closer I saw you were dressed not in your bathing suit but in shorts and a shirt a little shirt with a collar. They always dressed you very proper like an English boy like a little lord your mother always said. Lucy she was in that uniform standing up to her knees in this dress with water climbing up the fabric. I just stopped I knew somehow this was the kind of thing you don't see regular you spy on it you watch it from a distance so I stopped and kind of crouched behind a bush. Sure enough she took this handful of water and started sprinkling it all over your head talking to you the whole time you don't remember any of this do you? You must have been at least three old enough to stand up in the lake without crying you were so scared of water at first but she cured you of that. I guess she must have figured as long as I've got him at ease in the water well it can't hurt him being baptized can it so now you you're guaranteed a free ride to Heaven isn't that what it means? I watched you from down there but I didn't say nothing. After a minute she picks you up and twirls you around like you're celebrating the two of you and then I could see you were going to go back up to the house probably to change clothes so I got out of there. Your mother she wouldn't have noticed she didn't get up till two sometimes she said the morning wasn't kind to her complexion that's what she told me. Your dad he'd be on the phone or reading a paper the *Racing Form* that's right he'd go get it he had to have it fresh every day he'd hop in his car and drive fifty miles just to get that paper. Then he'd be back on the phone. He'd wave to me while he was talking he was the nicest man. So I guess that means you're saved don't it?

⌒

Lebrun he just wanted to create his own kingdom. It's not like he wanted to run it though or have anything to do with it once it got started. I don't think it was about money in the end I think it was more like he had this vision he saw it all before it happened or he was trying to re-create something that had happened before that's why he named the figurines after people from his childhood if that's really what he did. It makes sense what Miss Dick said but no I never asked him about it he bought up the whole mountainside the beach rights from the Authority everything north of the taking line then made these parcels and the common area not just the beach but the road the social hall he even wrote this kind of constitution the by-laws for the community. Maggie said he stayed up late at night worrying about it all probably worrying about how much he owed he didn't say but I know at one point he let slip that he was into the bank for I don't know how much exactly all I heard was the word million that got my attention but it worked out there it is now across the lake you can see ads for it in magazines Private Lakefront Community Exclusive Listing. That lady Trinita I tried explaining it was just an accident but I couldn't make her understand. I could still read clocks you see the shapes the hands made on the old-style clocks not those new ones that just have numbers but I could still see what time it was and I knew the garbage pickup that day was at two so I timed it just right by my watch I got to the road at two-thirty and went to the first house went to take down the cans but they were all still full not a single one had been emptied so I went to the house and knocked on the door to ask if they'd seen the garbage truck go by you know if they'd skipped that road or maybe the truck broke down or something they're pretty reliable usually Don Byron and his son I thought maybe they'd changed the day of the pickup see I needed to know that's why I banged on the door but no one answered so I went to the next house saw the same thing no garbage pickup and banged on their door but no one answered there either so I went to the third house well you get the idea. Finally someone leans out their top window and tells me to go to hell. Well naturally I yell back I mean just because I work for you doesn't give you the right to finally this car comes down the road going real slow and it's Ray Eggleston in his pajamas he's got his uniform on but I can see his pajama top underneath like he just threw on the rest. I was about to say something make some joke when he says Bill what the hell are you doing here disturbing everyone at three in the morning?

That's when I looked up and it's like the world just clicked back into place the moon the night the stars see I knew something was wrong a little bit off I mean but I was so concentrated on my watch on getting the time right the little hand here the big hand there two-thirty it never occurred to me that it might be the wrong two-thirty that there could even be a wrong two-thirty. I mean when you think about it it's pretty silly having two times in one day with the same name. Ray says Get in. I thought he was going to arrest me I really didn't understand I was still mumbling on about the garbage about how nobody does their job anymore. It's ridiculous I kept saying It's ridiculous even though another part of me inside had already figured it out I just couldn't make my outside part stop doing what it was doing. He takes me home and sure enough as soon as his tires are crunching on the gravel a light goes on. Hell I said that's the Missus I'm going to catch it now. I knew see I knew Alice was gone but it was like my mouth couldn't stop saying what they wanted to hear this crazy old coot who gets up at the wrong time of day or night rather and thinks his wife is still alive it's like I could see myself as they saw me not as I truly was. So Emily of course he walks me to the door like I got caught playing hooky and Emily's in her nightgown when she sees Ray she gets all in a dither tries inviting him in for coffee and he's going on about how he has to get back to sleep cause he's on duty in a few hours and meanwhile no one's giving me credit for going to work for being right on top of the situation getting those cans down from the road right after they're emptied so it's like they were never there. Undoing the damage that's my job so what if I flipped over the hours A.M. P.M. it's still technically two-thirty in a way it's not my fault at all technically. So she sits me down at the table afterward. Oh Dad she says what are we going to do with you? So now I don't go there anymore especially after I got that letter I mean I just look across sometimes at your mom's island that means more to me than the house yes I know I sat in it before anyone else in a way I used to think of it as my house I mean I left my mark on it kind of before anyone else moved in staring into that fireplace with Lebrun spending the time there watching over it kind of preparing it for you and your family even though I didn't know you yet but that lady that letter she wrote just the whole way things ended kind of left a bad taste in my mouth. The island that's different I'm the only who knows what's really there that it's really garbage dirt and garbage and building supplies and then those trees your mom saw the ad for in the paper and Freddie Seaborne pushing that boat out the water coming up to his shoulders probably then scrambling over that pile of junk planting them all. I didn't see any of that no but I saw him the next day explaining it to your mom saying That's your island and her look I mean how many people have an island given to them not just given to them but made for them? She was near tears. It's the most beautiful thing she said I'm going to name it after. That's right. She named it after you.

⁓

No they don't call it that on any map those beach people the Association they don't have the imagination to name anything they just call it the island just like they call the people they use now the service. They have eyes but they don't see just a bunch of sides of beef out there broiling in the sun that's the way they look from across the lake I mean in the summer hell they got less personality than those figurines Lebrun used when he was picturing them all in his mind. Or maybe it's just that I'm old now and can't see it can't bring my own imagination to bear but that's not true because Vera for example well we just talk a little but I feel her whole life going on in her I know she's going through things that something's happening I don't know what no she doesn't tell me stuff like that but I can see or imagine I'm not blind to her state. Or even Ming and there's a man who can't string two words together not in English but hell he's got this whole other world happening inside him I mean I can tell just by the way he polishes an apple. He holds the thing like a hand grenade gives it this very careful dusting with a cloth then sets it down. He must go crazy when he sees the way people paw through them. They're always looking for stuff on the bottom like he's trying to cheat them like that's where the good stuff is. Then as soon as they're gone he rearranges the stack I don't know how he does it he can make things go so high. Me I always take the one on top it's like the cherry on a sundae. No not apples I told you my teeth. Once he gave me yes he's always giving me stuff I'm his special project I guess it's like he wants to educate me I don't know why he gave me this brown and yellow apple and says very carefully like he's reciting it Asian pear at least that's what I think he said maybe aged hair that would make more sense in a way that it's good for my aged hair so I bow that's what you do you get the feeling you should do bow your head a little with him like he does. He was so pleased when I took it. It's like we're friends now. It wasn't pretty like that other fruit he gave me the pink and green one but it was interesting. You wouldn't think there'd be other fruit that you don't know about after a lifetime. No I didn't eat it I told you it was too hard for my teeth I can only eat mush basically I kept it for a while I had to hide it because Cecil was on one of his crackdowns about food in the room so I kept it no not in my bed you can't keep anything in your bed here. I figured since it's for my hair I'll keep it in my hat my stocking cap so I kept it there for a week or two no not when I wore it that would make me look like an idiot with an apple in my hat I just stored it there. When I wore my hat I kept it in my pocket of course it wasn't like the other fruit though it began to go bad so I didn't plant it I don't know why but I put it on Alice's grave. Well for her hair that's how I explained it to Emily. She had this she'd never admit it but she had this vain streak about her hair there'd always be another shampoo bottle some special oil a new rinse or something. I don't know why she had perfectly fine hair to me it was that's right you never met her I forgot it was yellow brown I guess nothing special more yellow when I first met her yes actually the color of that fruit I guess maybe but that's not why. I told Emily Your mom will appreciate it maybe some of the special formula whatever's in there will soak down and. She looked at me as if I was crazy but really are the flowers any different? Every week a new bunch and it's not like she goes and picks them herself except in the summer if there's some growing by the side of the road then I make her stop and we pick a bunch usually black-eyed Susans or daisies or Queen Anne's lace but the rest of the year she buys them from the florist what a waste of money I have to hold my tongue every time she shows up with a bouquet of roses that aren't ever going to open. Hell fruit would be more like what she likes anyway I felt like saying and this one helps your hair. But Ming this is what I'm trying to tell you he's a person I can feel there's all this stuff going on inside him but those people across the lake maybe it's just because I got to know them first as figurines maybe that ruined it for me made it hard for me to understand them. Oh yes Lebrun he'd invite me down he kept it in his basement that's one way his moving to Kathan worked out well for us there were these steps in back leading down. He didn't have to tell me to take them it was pretty obvious with Maggie upstairs I wasn't going to ring that doorbell that's for sure ring that doorbell and risk having her show up in her battle fatigues or whatever she was doing then. Yes she went through this whole military phase the People's Army or the People's Militia he made some kind of deal with her he wouldn't bother her upstairs and she wouldn't come downstairs to the basement where he kept the model it was on these sawhorses he had this bank of fluorescent lights over it. I suppose it's true he paid too much attention to those figurines maybe not as much as Maggie made out but. Sometimes we'd hear her upstairs walking right over us. Is she wearing combat boots now? I asked. It's that time of the month he'd say makes her go a little nutty. You're one to talk I thought. I kept that to myself but I remember just when he said it he was holding this little child as I recall it was just a shorter version of the adult holding it very gently between his thumb and forefinger trying to figure out the perfect place to put it like after he let it go it was going to run off and play or something. Oh she just took it to another level she wanted to do something more than those pamphlets I guess. She kept saying Nobody listens. Well that's true I felt like telling her but the funny thing was if I had told her that she wouldn't have heard because she never listened either. Nobody listens that's the point. Taxpayer's Revolt that's what she called it since our money goes to bad things we shouldn't pay it well I'm all for that not paying taxes I mean but then who I wanted to ask her who's going to pay Ray Eggleston to come by and scare kids from throwing a brick through your window? We'd hear her above us. Guns? Sure she had guns everyone did everyone does here. It's not like a city not like Sparta where there's a policeman every two blocks traffic policemen all saying What the hell are you driving that horse-drawn cart for don't you know it's not allowed within the city limits and then they threaten to write you a ticket except it's not like I got a license plate or anything so then they'd give up let me go with a warning and then Allure if she'd bothered to take notice of what was going on she'd give him a little present a little steaming pile of hello right at the intersection where he had to stand for the rest of the day but anyway they'd take target practice she and a bunch of other misfits she managed to collect. Don't you worry about them in your house? I asked Lebrun one time when we could hear them all above us some evening having a meeting. I worry about my grocery bill he says. All they drank was soda not beer. The Taxpayer's Militia that's what they called themselves when they met even though there were only three or four of them they were younger than her a man a woman a couple yes and then another man a boy really he maybe he had eyes for her I don't know Lebrun didn't seem to mind. I think it amused him to be honest. Keeping busy he'd say that's what they're doing. With guns I'd answer. We could hear them overhead not shooting but everyone knew they went out to some abandoned farm one of them owned. And boots I'd say. She's going to change the world. He'd be leaning over his model. He could move parts of it around it was all detachable he'd try different ways. He'd ask my opinion. I don't think he listened to my answers I just think he liked having someone there. You can't take apart the mountain I said when he took off the whole top once like it was flattened he plucked the fire tower right off. Sure I can he said I can take it apart and put it back together any way I want that's the point I own it. What were they trying to do I have no idea you don't think I read those things those manifestos they'd nail to trees and such do you? Freddie he was the only one who cared he actually spoke to Lebrun about it. Driving nails I remember he said you can't go driving nails into my trees. I suppose she or her cohorts had nailed some up on the other side of the lake that was Freddie's baby nothing went on there involving a tree without his say-so. Change the world. They'd train themselves get all ready for the coming action that's what they'd call it the coming action. I have no idea it's as if there were other groups like them all over the country and they were going to come together at some signal and rise up and I mean it sounds crazy doesn't it? And they called me the Homeowners Association did when they sent that letter they called me A Clear and Present Danger that's what it said in the letter but that was just because I was getting on you see when really Maggie and her merry band of men that's what I heard Miss Dick call them once they made me look like the most law-abiding citizen imaginable. Anyway he takes the fire tower off the peak and I imagined the kid in there the one they took away no he didn't have a figurine for him by then they'd stopped using the fire tower they used helicopters instead I think that boy might have been the last one he went so crazy but I pictured him in there as Lebrun lifted it off saying Hey what the hell's happening? So busy staring at the sun he doesn't notice these huge fingers coming down and. He was placing all these people in different areas trying to reimagine it that's what he'd say. Like he had it in his head once before but then lost it the ideal place for everyone and everything. He could move the beach the land the lake even it was in sections he could build things out into it like Freddie Seaborne's jetty or he could lead it into the land like a little bay you know a cove. That was one of his big ideas at first I remember Pirate's Cove he was going to call it with sailboats stuck on top but for some reason he decided against that. The kid? You mean up in the fire tower I don't know what happened to him maybe they contacted his parents I certainly hope so he wasn't a bad sort he just thought he had this power wherever he looked. That's why he took himself away that's how he put it. I took myself away. He thought he had the evil eye that just by looking at people he gave them bad luck but then up there in the woods well I guess you can't give a tree bad luck so his mind decided it could set things on fire instead. See you can't escape what's in your head if you have this idea it doesn't matter where you put yourself the idea is still going to work itself out look at Maggie Chess maybe that's why she came up here maybe she thought far from the hustle-bustle of big-city life down in Sparta she could I don't know be normal whatever that is but instead she brought it with her the idea. It just took what was available worked with the materials at hand and hell she probably ended up going nuttier up here than she ever would have done down there you can't escape it no I don't know what the answer is. Or my father. Stopped working for the railroad bought himself a farm thought he was getting away from who he was getting away from his temper his drinking his bad luck and then what does it do it rains. Good for the crops that's what he'd say at first then it would rain for six ten fifteen days. I can't figure out if I'm Noah or Job he said to me once. I had no idea what that meant. Yes he must have had bible learning well everyone did in those days everyone but us Rebecca and me he reacted against it something must have bothered him about it he swore he wouldn't let us within fifty feet of a Sunday school. I don't know if I'm Noah or Job he had a lot of stories he could spin a yarn when he was in a good mood there was no better company he could make you laugh so hard it just happened less and less as time went by as things wore him down. Sometimes I think this is a funny picture but sometimes I think something was carving at him you know the way he used to do with those chunks of wood that something was scraping away at him turning him into I guess Lebrun would call it a figurine turning him into something he didn't want to be that he had no choice about. Maybe that's why he did it to the wood because he could feel it happening to him maybe that's why he was so good at it because he knew what it felt like.

⌐∾

A gun? Of course I do or did rather. I don't know where it's got to. I bought it from Freddie a pistol. He said he took it off a dead German officer. I don't know why I wanted it but once he showed it to me well I'd never been in the war and everyone else they all had these stories these souvenirs. I'd shoot bottles off the fence. I turned out to be a fairly good shot. If I had gone off to war who knows maybe I wouldn't have come back I mean one way or the other maybe I would have been buried over there or maybe I would have become a general and gone off and found Rebecca and started over someplace else. I tried interesting Emily in it like I told you since I didn't have a son I tried but she would have none of it she ran to Alice she didn't like the noise. Just what have you got against Dr. Pepper? That's what Alice asked me that was one of the few jokes she ever made I was shooting all these Dr. Pepper bottles I must have found a whole case of them no I wouldn't put the elixir in a soda pop bottle only in old whiskey bottles or patent medicine something more serious. Who'd drink medicine out of a soda pop bottle? She wanted me to return them of course five cents each but I lined them up all along the fence and stood maybe twenty-five feet away I was no Bat Masterson no sharpshooter but from twenty-five feet I'd say three-quarters of them went down the first time that's pretty good. What have you got against Dr. Pepper? she asked. That I didn't like. The way she would undercut me sometimes in front of the child. Undermine me. Like we were two separate people instead of one one couple I mean. Now Lebrun what he felt for Maggie yes they fought but they had something solid there. You couldn't pry them apart no not even with that whole crackpot militia she had. He tolerated that just like she tolerated him spending his nights with that play version of the mountainside. It's almost like each gave the other license to go further. Well I don't see how thinking you're in contact with aliens is so different from thinking you're in contact with the working people the working class excuse me that's what she called it. Oh she'd go on about how all over the country there were people like her the working class she said the true heart of the nation ready to rise up and take back. Take back what exactly America I suppose which I didn't realize was ever gone it's always been right here under my feet I've never left no not even to go up to Canadia that's what the old-timers called it I've never seen the point but she just wanted so desperately to shock that's what I think it came down to she just wanted to be known as someone besides Claude Brown's wife and if it took advocating the overthrow of the United States government which is what they eventually charged her with then that was fine with her that's really what she wanted was to be recognized as some kind of threat to be taken seriously not just some lady who made perfumes and left stacks of flyers unattended at the convenience store. And him well I think he was just going tit for tat. You got your secret army I've got mine except for me it's an army of well he called them aliens. It makes sense in a way his reasoning because look what happened to him look how successful he'd been this ignorant grease-ball that's another thing they called him shit-kicker too all sorts of names you have no idea the way people talk now about Ming you know foreigners that was all directed at Canucks back then. Is that your sister? they'd call if they saw one walking with his wife and kids. So how does this Claude Lebrun type turn into Eagle Enterprises which as I said at that point was employing maybe half the town it made sense in a way when he started to say he heard voices. Not in his head he was very specific about that he said he sought guidance so it sounded almost like what you'd ask a priest for but it was business guidance he got and then when you asked him from where he'd say he didn't know from where but whenever he took it he did well. So it wasn't like men in shiny space suits or anything like that it was more spiritual. That time when he first brought it up that's right it was at your house or what was to be your house when he came in all bleeding but it was only later he really began talking about it when he was well when he was sick when he knew the jig was up. It's almost like he wanted to pass it on to me his great fortune that's what he called it no not money he didn't leave me one red cent he meant the great fortune of his life how he'd gotten from here to there how he'd gotten to be what he was. It was all due to these aliens he called them who walked among us. Who I asked who's an alien? It doesn't matter he said they come and go they inhabit a person just for the length of time it takes for them to tell you what you need to know. But I thought they were voices I said. They are he said it's in the voice that's how you can tell it's different from the way the person usually sounds that's when you have to listen extra hard. So has it ever been me was I ever the alien? He was in pajamas by then and they were slipping off him half the time he was so thin so there was nothing to look at except his eyes. I didn't want to look at the rest of him because he was so wasted away. You more than anybody he said. But with you each time I had to wait through a couple of hundred hours of bullshit to get to it. Well if they told him to make a private beach community I guess they knew what they were talking about those aliens because the thing really took off. He timed it just right the highway they built the Northway that brought people from downstate up here hell they could come for the weekend with their station wagons loaded with equipment not to mention kids you never saw so many kids in your life and there were the houses getting finished one by one getting snapped up. He didn't have to truck in sand it was there naturally but somehow it got yellower not as brown as before and even the water this is my impression but it got bluer it began to look more like a resort the whole thing. That first year when he put on the Hi-Jinx before the Association had really gotten started when he kind of wanted to show them the way he spent I don't know how much of his own money or Eagle Enterprise's money I should say he got some Broadway musical put on there complete with a band it reminded me of the old days when that acting troupe took over the bank except it wasn't as friendly you didn't really feel welcome there were all these signs PRIVATE ROAD PRIVATE BEACH NO ACCESS ASSOCIATION MEMBERS ONLY. They'd put on a show every year. The rest of the time they'd have dances with a hi-fi or play canasta. I just cleaned up after them basically I didn't get to know them like I did your mom and dad they weren't as special a class of people they were more just summer folk I could tell just from the look in their eyes that I was an embarrassment. There I was hauling away their garbage and they looked at me like I was more garbage than what was in the cans. Cecil's not that way. Cecil's basically herding chickens so far as I can see that's about as much as he has invested in us as what a farmer has in mind for his chickens. You know how they're always just scratching around the yard and then it comes time to take one out to the chopping block. Sure we had chickens no he wouldn't wring their necks I know that's supposed to be the way it's done but he said it was cruel Father he'd pick one up casual the way you would a sack of flour hatchet in the other hand they don't know anything is happening they're the dumbest creatures on God's earth he'd take them out to the chopping block which was just a tree stump. A pine as I recall why do you ask it had all this sap oozing out the top even after hell it was there as long as I can remember but I guess the roots still went down I guess it was still alive in some sense he'd lay it there and then there'd be this squawk and then it's like you'd still hear the squawk even though it had stopped in the middle. Your memory would supply the rest of it. I don't know what the chicken thought they're always in a panic so it probably didn't make any difference him carrying them by the feet they probably thought the world had just gone upside down that's if they thought anything at all which I doubt. Once though he did let go I don't know what happened maybe it pecked him just as he swung the blade or maybe it was slippery but he cut off the head and then I heard him cursing I thought maybe he'd hurt himself so I ran out and there he was standing with his hands on his hips. At first I couldn't see because it didn't make any kind of sense but then in another second I realized it was the chicken running around with blood this fountain of blood spurting out its neck kind of scrambling about stopping switching direction then tumbling on the ground and getting up again all with the blood still. He was standing there he had the bucket all ready to collect it if he'd held on you know but he knew better than to try and chase it down because it had no direction it had no brain it's just muscle spasms so you can't even predict. Besides the blood was all spurting out he just had to wait until it stopped moving and then well cleaning it up that was my job of course I had to go around with a rag and a bucket of hot water. He took it as another sign that things weren't going well. Can't even kill a chicken I heard him say. Can't even kill it right he meant but anyway Cecil it's kind of the same thing when the ambulance comes it's like he's grabbing one of us by the ankles. Usually you know who it's going to be you can tell in advance. They don't of course. The person in question. They're too far gone ambulance comes and takes them down to what's it called the Full-Service Facility or something like that down in Sparta. No one comes back from there the Vegetable Patch that's what I heard one of the attendants call it once. Two for the Vegetable Patch he told Cecil. That's why I try to keep my wits about me you can't provide a fixed target for them you've got to keep.

~⁓

But that Trinita Breyer she was the worst of the bunch. One year she says Bill the Association would like you to be on duty during the Hi-Jinx. On duty well I figured sure I mean what could that entail entail it means what could that consist of the only thing that worried me was how late it would be but I had Emily fill up a thermos with coffee and then I showed up there around five o'clock by then they'd taken it over it wasn't Lebrun's deal anymore which is what he wanted he was just showing them the way now they had that committee in place that decided everything. That's when I had my first dealings with this Breyer woman she ran the committee she was the committee so far as I could see nobody else seemed to give a rat's ass excuse my French I guess you need someone like that if you're going to get anything done but god have mercy on the person they're giving orders to because a little power goes a long way goes right to some people's heads. It was the bicentennial that year no not the town's that was the sesquicentennial one-hundred-fifty this was the yes the whole country two hundred years you must remember that well they had this group of singers they'd hired Get Up and Cheer they were called it's like they had to tell you what to do because otherwise you'd just run screaming with your hands over your ears probably sixteen or seventeen of them men and women all in these matching getups the women wore red and the men wore blue as I recall and there were all these glittery white stars on them too so when they came together stood next to each other they'd kind of make a flag not a real one but it made you think of the American flag if you hadn't already because they had this curtain behind them that showed George Washington Abraham Lincoln anyone else you could think of who's American and these lights that pretty much blinded you they picked out the stars and made them shine. I got there in time to hear them practice a few songs to test out the speakers and stand on the stage it was so loud and bright I had to go down to the lake until they stopped. Bill she said this is that Breyer woman she found me right away it's like she was going to keep an eye on me to make sure I did what I was told. Bill there's not going to be any activities down here by the beach she says you have to be up by the social hall once the clambake starts there's going to be lots of garbage to take away. Sure thing I answer and then once her back is turned I kind of linger halfway between the beach and hall waiting for them to stop that noise. They came in a trailer the singers. Musicians? No it was all blasting out of speakers there wasn't a musician among them but they were all coming in and out of this trailer at first I thought they were kids but when I looked closer they were older they were all wearing makeup yes the men too in the daytime that always makes people look like they're laid out in a funeral parlor to me with that kind of dusting on them too white you know but anyway they weren't dead they were just older than I thought and these costumes they had well once they were out of the light they just looked silly like they were circus clowns almost. Then this catering truck pulls up from a place I never heard of he must have driven at least a hundred miles and starts setting up grills and unpacking lobster chicken hot dogs corn a clambake but there wasn't any clams for some reason. I had a cup of coffee from my thermos. There was a bar of course I didn't go near there all the people were coming out of their cabins by then that's what they called them even though they were houses I mean a cabin has no running water it's just someplace you spend the night when you're hunting but they like to call them cabins some even have little signs up LAZY DAYS or one it said THE BOYD'S NEST anyway they all come out the women and men in their fancy clothes still vacation clothes I guess but not what they'd wear every night and the kids some of them were still in their bathing suits running all around. The adults went right to the bar. Well the whole thing was free I didn't see any money change hands I suppose you had to pay to get in pay dues or have a ticket or whatever they all looked like they were trying to make it back however much they'd ponied up make it back in beer and liquor. Now Bill she says she could just appear beside you you couldn't tell where she'd come from it was kind of unnerving as soon as the bags begin to fill up I want you to take them up to the road take out the old one first and before you go away put in a new liner so no garbage gets put directly in the can. Like I was a child you know so I just nodded and stood off to the side. Watching people eat if you're not doing it yourself that makes them look really bad. Everyone making a pig of themselves. I felt like I was back on the farm watching the hog the way it would go at the slops I threw down like it knew its job was to get as fat as possible that's the same way these people ate they were serious about it two-fisted eaters that's what my mother would have called them she was very strict on table manners no elbows put your knife and fork down after each bite may I please be excused that kind of thing. These people they were fine I suppose I just didn't want to be there. Is this what you wanted? I felt like asking Lebrun is this what you predicted that day we were sitting on that ledge way up high looking down on the whole valley was this what you saw? I went in to replace a bag of garbage it was a big clear plastic bag and one of them a grown man without even getting up he throws in the chicken bone right over my shoulder like it's a basketball game while I'm closing it up. Two points he yells. It was like that all night. I could see because they were sitting at these long benches picnic tables lined up together I could see one group where the lady's foot was going up a man's leg no not her husband I'm pretty sure about that somebody's husband not hers but she had sandals on and she'd slipped them off and meanwhile she's eating I can see she's got this corn on the cob she's doing that whole typewriter thing going back and forth and her foot is kind of doing the same thing underneath on the man's leg and he's just shifting around looking a little uncomfortable and all the while they're talking with the others. A kid one of the little ones they can never keep still he ran up and tried to take my thermos I mean of all the things there he has to go and try and steal my thermos I don't know why. I managed to catch it back I almost brained him over the head with it and they had this bug zapper those were new then it was the first time I had ever seen one. I don't like electricity I told you even if it's killing mosquitoes. Every time it would get one it would make this little crackling sound. They were all collecting in a cloth bag underneath it. I could see how you could become a preacher looking at people from that angle thundering down about how they were all going to Hell just watching them stuff their faces getting ready to stuff each other too later on and the crackle of bugs being burnt all around me that bag getting plumper and plumper full of dead mosquitoes and I'm hauling you never saw so much trash in your life half of it wasn't even eaten a hamburger with one bite taken out of it or a lobster that still looked whole you know hadn't even been cracked open just thrown away just throw it away that was their philosophy. I guess that's what gave them the most fun yelling two points and I'm shuffling up to the road replacing the old bags with fresh ones. No I didn't see the Breyer woman sitting down she was running around organizing I can't see her ever stopping to eat she was a skinny type always on the move she was probably inside organizing the singers making sure the chairs were right so she didn't get to see I don't know how it got started my back must have been turned but suddenly these two fellows are rolling around on the ground grown men I guess you could call it a fight they didn't really know what they were doing neither one would just rear back and hit the other it was more like these little pushes they would give with their fists. A few of the ladies screamed and everyone kind of backed away giving them space in case they wanted to really put on a show but once they felt everyone's eyes on them they stopped. Plus they were panting so hard. I couldn't figure out what from but then they both got up kind of avoiding each other's eyes. At first I was concerned I thought one had blood but it was on a strange place on the outside of his shirt that's when I realized he had just rolled over some ketchup maybe on a hot dog or something anyway right around then the doors to the social hall open and that Breyer woman announces that the concert's about to begin. Well everyone gets up and goes inside they don't clean up or anything they just leave their food there half-eaten and their napkins all balled up. In about two minutes it was just me and the caterer. He packed up. He wasn't interested in any conversation I guess he had miles to go I never heard of that town painted on the side of his truck. They left the doors to the social hall open it was hot enough especially with those lights on and crammed with all those people and then that goddamned music started. I'm a Yankee Doodle Dandy It's a Grand Old Flag yes I suppose they were the same kind of songs they used to play on the bandstand in Kathan but for some reason well they were too loud for one thing and it was all on tape the music it was all prerecorded. I'm going along the tables row by row dragging a bag behind me and every once in a while there's something that hasn't been touched or barely you know a hamburger a baked potato and I pop a bit into my mouth trying to have dinner and then I look up and by god there's that Trinita Breyer standing on the porch of the social hall wagging her finger at me. No I hadn't brought a sandwich I figured well what the hell I figured that there would be enough food it even occurred to me that maybe they'd give me something anyway I go back to just dragging my bag behind me dumping it all in enough food to feed half the town of Antone. The trailer that the singers came in it was still idling they never turned off the engine so that added to the whole I guess you could call it the atmosphere and that area they have in front of the social hall it was a garbage dump the way they'd left it I even saw the woman's sandals the one who was you know climbing the inside of the man's leg she'd forgotten to slip them back on. I was tempted to throw them in the trash these kind of bejeweled sandals plastic jewels but instead I just left them there. The Breyer woman watches me a bit and then says Once you're done picking up why don't you start moving the tables back? By then they're blaring away those singers God Bless America. It wasn't any music you could work to sometimes you hear a song a tune on the radio while you're doing something and it helps even if you're not listening it kind of gets your feet going in a certain way and the time passes more quickly but maybe it was all those horns blasting away I could barely drag one table away from the next. And then this man the leader of the group I guess started giving a kind of patriotic speech with all the others humming behind him. It wasn't music anymore it was the sound of a battle or guns and then fireworks but through the speakers. Isn't that the stupidest thing you ever heard? Instead of fireworks in the air like they used to have they just had the sound of them whistling and exploding while they sang the Star-Spangled Banner and I'm dragging these picnic benches back to the storage shed when. That's when I noticed it. It was stuck on the tree. I guess they missed it setting up the people from the Association. Freddie? By then he wasn't oh no he was like Ruth Sayheim and me he was they have an expression for it he was persona non grata that's Latin. Miss Dick told me when I was explaining the situation she said Well you're all persona non grata over there. But we built the place I said not with our own hands except for Freddie I guess you could say he did but Ruth and me and Freddie we put in our time there we saw it go from nothing to something and now they won't even let us. You're persona non grata she says that was a fancy way of putting it all right. Anyway I see this flyer nailed to the big sycamore that's in the center of the cleared-out area in front of the hall. That tree was Freddie's pride and joy. He'd have gone crazy if he'd seen it with a nail driven right into the bark I'm surprised that Trinita woman hadn't caught it I guess she was too busy bossing me. It said Your Days Are Numbered. I thought it was a religious thing at first because in a way it was just what I'd been thinking myself while I was standing off to the side that all these people that it couldn't last you know that they were all on the wrong path somehow not even happy sinning I think that's when you realize that some serious kind of adjustment has to take place when you see people trying to have fun but they can't it's like they've realized even sin isn't all it's cracked up to be that's where people like Alice and Bigelow disapproving people I think that's where they get it wrong. If sin's fun then well I don't really see how it's so sinful after all what can be so bad about having a good time? But when you're trying to have a good time and can't even when you're eating and drinking and whoring when you're doing it more and more because it still doesn't feel right that's when it becomes a sin because it's so wasteful. Then I read further and realized it's Maggie it's her group the Taxpayer's Revolt or Army or whatever saying Your Days Are Numbered because I don't know why because you shouldn't be here in the first place because you're not from here that's what they were saying because you're not true Americans those were the kind of words she used. Oh yes by then her thoughts had swung completely around from when she was a communist or whatever she called herself before. Now she was against anyone who wasn't from here originally even though yes that's what's so funny she wasn't from around here either but it was all about true Americans rising up and taking back what belonged to them. So I pull down the notice but I don't have a trash bag by then not an open one so I stuff it in my back pocket I didn't want anyone to see. Maggie she'd probably be arrested if Trinita Breyer found out she might not know who the Taxpayer's Army was but she'd have called Ray Eggleston. She must have had his phone number memorized that's what he told me. Somebody takes a wrong turn he told me someone goes onto that private road of theirs by mistake and she calls like it's a home invasion situation. So I took it down but there was still the nail to consider I didn't like the look of that nail just hammered there into that sycamore so I took out my knife and was prying it loose when what should happen but. No it wasn't her for a change I don't know where she was I guess she was still listening to those singers sing Glory Glory Hallelujah but that couple the sandal woman and the man well I assume it was the same man hell how many toes could she have? I mean how many men could she be doing that to? Anyway it was her all right I could tell because she was barefoot that's why she'd come out you see early while the singers were still while everyone else was still inside she said she was looking for her shoes her sandals but I was right close to the tree they didn't see me it was almost like I was hiding even though I swear I wasn't and then before I could even do something to show I was there he grabs her and the guns are going off or explosions it's all on tape it's not real of course but those speakers that kind of excited them I could tell the noise and everyone being near but not seeing he grabs her right then and there on the porch of the social hall and they start kissing and believe me I wanted to get away it's the last thing I wanted to see but if I'd made a break for it from behind that tree they'd have seen me and also where was I supposed to go? I was still on duty I hadn't gotten paid yet I'd worked a full night I wasn't about to leave without getting paid so instead I just turn my back to them lean against the tree but I can still hear them him especially

218

they're both going at it like. It doesn't sound like fun when you hear it from off to the side that way it's like the eating and the drinking it's just a continuation they're trying to have fun but something is in the way I don't know what. And I can see her sandals that's the funny part what she came to find I can see them right in front of me catching the glare from the outdoor lights and the jewels they're shining I know they're not real they're plastic but still shining catching the light all these different colors. I felt like calling out Here's your sandals Miss you don't have to do that. Here's what you were looking for all along they were right where you left them but of course I just waited. They finished up right when the singers started in with Happy Birthday yes the song Happy Birthday. Everyone was joining in singing Happy birthday to you like America was a person and the next thing I know they're coming out of that place the social hall everyone needing to take a piss I couldn't even tell which was the couple anymore it's like they went back to being regular persons.

～

I showed it to Lebrun the flyer I mean I said Aren't you worried? They got guns and all. Your Days Are Numbered people might get the wrong idea. He said he'd talk to her I could see he wasn't pleased. No I don't know where the other flyers went I never heard anyone else talk about them maybe they got scared maybe he stopped her from putting any more up. The Hi-Jinx. They still have it I guess but I don't go there of course I'm persona non yes it's a Latin term Ruth Sayheim she took it harder than anyone you would have thought Freddie of the three of us I mean or Lebrun after all he'd created it he had the vision had the little model of it but you would have thought one of those two would have taken it the hardest when the Association made it clear they didn't need them anymore but Lebrun said that's what he intended all along he washed his hands of it he'd made his pile he said he didn't want to spend his time hearing about how people's roofs leaked or about whose dog did what to someone's flowerbed. Freddie well like I said Freddie took it a little worse when he saw what they were doing when he saw how they were kind of disregarding his plans but after a while he just shrugged it off. I told him when they were pulling up some bushes to make room for a changing area he said Well that just plain wrecks the whole thing but by then he'd distanced himself it was just a job that's what he said besides his hands were giving him trouble he couldn't do much anymore he was mostly advising his son Zeke who was a builder. But Ruth even though she marched in there and quit she took it the hardest. She'd been cleaning for Lebrun and then for the Association almost twenty years as long as me practically and she just seemed to lose her bearings. I always thought the way she was alone in her house the way I'd see that light on when I passed and her sitting there at the table hunched over I used to think maybe she was writing poetry or something doing something private that's what it looked like but when they finally found her no one had seen her for a while they broke in not Ray no I don't remember who it was but they broke in smashed the glass above the doorknob in back and she'd stopped using the bathroom that's the part everyone talked about in town she had this big enamel basin she was using instead even though the toilet worked fine. People talked about that. You know a woman without a child they said sometimes they go a little. It was funny her house being such a mess by the end because that's what she did of course she cleaned houses so you'd think her own would be. Lawrence pointed it out he wrote something like *she took in all the chaos everyone else's clutter and brought it home to herself* but I don't know. Doc Harmon said it was some kind of disease they couldn't tell at first they actually had to ship her body off to get it examined they had to take a slice out of her brain apparently before they sent her body back imagine her dying of that everyone said because the rest of her life was so you know so quiet and respectable. People said it was the chopsticks people can be so cruel but really they're just nervous I think you don't want to be serious about serious stuff because then you begin to think about yourself what if it happened to you so they joked they said the chopsticks maybe over the years the chopsticks were poking holes in her head it was just a dumb joke I may have said it myself a few times I don't know why. Evangeline Dick she was the only one who was really upset. I was surprised. I didn't even know they knew each other I mean no more than in passing but she got very upset and when the body came back and they couldn't find anyone any relative she just appeared at the funeral home one day and took it upon herself she arranged the whole thing to have her cremated and then have her ashes that's right now I remember it was Ruth Sayheim's ashes we were scattering or trying to scatter Lebrun and me of course. Well Miss Dick had arranged for her to be cremated but she wasn't going to go out in that boat I can't say I blame her it wasn't exactly seaworthy there was always water collecting at the bottom and the way it creaked you were always afraid it was going to split in half right when you were the farthest from shore. Ruth Sayheim that's right I can't believe I'd forgotten Miss Dick asked Lebrun and me. Ruth loved it here she said more than any of us. Well I thought that was a surprising thing to say but it's true in a way she came here she didn't land here because of circumstance and Lord knows she wasn't born here she chose this place that was the impression I got and then she stuck with it through all the winters and the loneliness so maybe she did love it here in a way we didn't. But I don't know if love's the right word can you love a place a section of geography? She was waiting on shore for us when we got back Lebrun was still upset because so much had blown into the boat he made us turn it over he was kind of superstitious that way he didn't want any of her left behind that's the way he put it didn't want us stepping on her. Me I guess I was more like the Greeks you know someone would die one of their shipmates they'd get drunk and talk about him cry a little and that would be that. Miss Dick she was weeping she kept saying If only I'd if only I'd. If only you'd what? I wanted to ask but of course I didn't say anything it was a very sad occasion. I'll tell you who didn't like her one bit was Maggie Chess she had a conniption when she found out what Lebrun had done how he'd helped dispose of her remains. That well she used a word I don't think I can repeat I'd never heard a woman use it in my life before the only reason I did that one time was because I went home with him that day and she must have gotten wind of what was going on she was waiting for us in the driveway. You helped Evangeline toss that I told you I can't say the word out loud toss that so-and-so into the lake? He got out of the truck like he hadn't heard turning his back on her. I tried to be more social. I could never figure out why she wasn't polite. What does it cost a person to say Hello Bill how you doing? Ruth Sayheim she says she hated me that jealous old cow and goes inside. I thought that was odd. Jealous Ruth Sayheim? Jealous of what? It didn't make sense. Lebrun kicked this case of bottles she'd left out from one of her meetings. You want these William? he asked. Oh they would go through a case of that stuff every time. Never beer Maggie was very strict she didn't want her meetings to seem like a party like it was a social event she said they were planning sessions that's what Lebrun told me. You want these bottles? he asks and kind of sets them jingling with his toe. Sure I said. So when I got them home I lined them up on the fence it was getting dark but I didn't care. Ruth Sayheim I'd known her forever it felt like even though she wasn't from around here but the more I thought about it the more I felt like I didn't know her at all. She always had that bucket full of cleaning supplies she didn't trust people to have their own and a mop and a broom. And her vacuum cleaner. Good worker. Always left that smell behind ammonia I guess but kind of piney. We'd exchange greetings small talk it was always like there was something we had in common but I don't know what. I wonder I mean I had this life a wife a child she what did she have? I'd walk by that place she'd be hunched over that table. No I never found out what she was doing. I was just shooting those bottles one after the other. Not thinking about it directly that's the key to being a good shot if you let your body kind of take over and your mind well it takes aim at something else because trying to shoot a bottle I guess your mind would think that was pretty stupid not worth its time so my mind was trying to figure out trying to mourn I guess because I hadn't been able to do it before not out on the boat that was more like a comedy scene with me and Lebrun and the grit blowing back in our faces no mourning going on there and me rolling that piece of her bones or whatever it was around between my teeth and finally swallowing. It's only when I got home and started blasting away at those bottles that I was able to. Then Alice comes out and says What have you got against Dr. Pepper?

~

Ruth's house no it never sold it fell into disrepair it got a reputation from the way she died I guess. People gave it a wide berth even the kids they wouldn't go there to misbehave. She took it the worst being told they didn't need us anymore. Then Alice asks me what I had against no I only ever used the pistol once for real well not fired it I mean but used it to wave around and make a point that was when we had that bear. That's why it's good to have around you can't depend on Ray Eggleston to come and protect you especially when you got a black bear rampaging through your vegetable garden. Emily she'd been kind of hinting that I should get rid of it but I think she was glad I had it when she came home that time and. Oh well technically I suppose yes but did I tell you that? You're not going to tell her are you? Because she'd technically it doesn't matter I mean if there had been a bear she would have been damn glad that I had a gun to defend us with but I figured it kind of added to the story if I had it out when she got home yes but no I put it away before those other people came Ray maybe he would have understood but the others. Took it off a dead German officer that's what I would have told them but it's not like I had a rifle or nothing nothing to cause alarm that's the thing Maggie and her bunch of misfits they all had permits licenses whatever it took and hell they probably were really plotting to overthrow the government or whatever that bonehead U.S. Attorney down in Sparta said about her but they were perfectly legal it turned out while if they'd caught me with that little pistol they could have put me in jail and thrown away the key. They'd have training sessions out on that farm they'd wear fatigues and ammo belts just like real soldiers. Once I asked her What kind of revolution are you trying to have? She said It already happened Bill. The executioner's sword is so sharp you don't realize your head's been cut off until you try and walk away. That's what's happened in this country nobody realizes it yet but when they try and get up and walk well then they'll see. I just nodded it made no sense at all as far as I could figure. The change has already happened she said what we're doing now is just a mop-up operation. Well a little mopping up wouldn't hurt I felt like saying if your place here is anything like that pig sty you had him living in by the dam but of course I didn't I just acted like I understood. They got themselves arrested but it wasn't for anything serious it was for Impersonating Military Personnel or something like that some law I never heard of but the penalty once they found out the guns were legal the penalty for it was nothing just a slap on the wrist but by then they'd taken her fingerprints you see and that's when it came out that it wasn't her that Maggie Chess wasn't even her real name. She'd been on the run she'd been well you know those posters in the post office Ten Most Wanted and such she was one of those sixties radicals who was part of some group I don't know which no not the Beatles one of those groups it was all years ago she'd been arrested apparently and then instead of going to trial she just up and left she jumped bail. For setting bombs but she claimed she had nothing to do with it later I mean that it was just she had attended some meetings basically that's what her lawyer said the one Lebrun got. He was a slick type a real motormouth he wouldn't let her say a word it took a real downstate smooth-talker getting paid two hundred dollars an hour to get her to stick a cork in it. How he managed to I don't know. But it was all so long ago that's the point since then she'd become she was just the opposite. That bomb they set her friends it was at some military recruiting center or whatever they called it back then where you'd go to get your physical and now here she was twenty years later she was playing soldier herself so it didn't make any sense at all them arresting her. Oh it was big news here it had the whole town talking. Well she'd lived among us we may not have liked her may not have understood her but also there was Lebrun he was quite an important man by then no matter how many people might have been secretly glad to see Maggie Chess or whatever her real name was get hers they wondered would he move would he spend all his money to get her off would Eagle Enterprises just close up shop there was a lot of worry and confusion. She'd been on the run for a while when she met him that's how I pieced it together later. She got in trouble when she was a kid practically just about to go to college but then she couldn't that's probably why she had all those catalogs just imagining her other life I suppose. I sympathized more than most around here. She had made a lot of enemies not real enemies she never did much that was so bad just her manners her attitude I sympathized you make a mistake you take one wrong step and. Yes Alice was right in a way when she saw that map in the car and said She's a Red she's going to blow things up but the funny thing is she didn't remember saying that and of course I wasn't going to remind her. No. No bail they just locked her up down in Sparta until the trial if you jump bail the first time I guess they figure fool me twice shame on me because even though Lebrun wanted to put up all of Eagle Enterprises and Eagle Holding Company he told me which I didn't even know existed even though he offered to put up everything he had to get her out they told him No thank you. He was shook up. I went by to see him. The first few times there was nobody home. Finally once I was knocking on the front door and then I hear that creaky cellar door open in back. He comes around. Come on in William. We go down the stairs just like we always do even though she's not up there obviously but still he's still sticking to the same old routine. Goddamn government he says that's about as close as he came to discussing it when I tried bringing it up. I'm about ready to join some organization myself he says. He was joking though not joking but. He was still working on the model the cove versus the jetty the access road working harder than ever this was the time of the big push when things were coming together. Well I guess they couldn't stop the bulldozers stop construction just because the boss's wife. Then I notice he's got something else a new figurine it's not like the others I go to look at it more closely oh I didn't pick it up I knew better than to do that then he'd have to wipe it off germs you know but I bend over it and it's this deer like from a kid's game or something you'd buy at a five-and-dime store a little plastic deer not like the others not from that architectural model catalog this is more like Bambi or something. What the hell's that? I ask. He says That's my fawn just the way he said it I could tell he meant Maggie even though a fawn that's about as far from the type of animal I'd pick to represent her as you could imagine. Well what's she doing in the middle of the lake? I asked I was kind of embarrassed so it was just to lighten the mood because every other figurine was placed so perfectly he'd spend hours deciding who went where but her I mean this deer was just standing in what normally would be fifty feet of water. Deer can swim he said. That's about as close as he got to talking about what he felt if you can call that talking. He just left the rest

226

to that lawyer I don't remember some name out of the newspaper or something I mean some name you wouldn't ordinarily see up here Steen-something at the end Something-steen yes. Little guy but he could be very aggressive. The most dangerous place to be I heard someone say is between Something-steen and a television camera. I guess he knew what he was doing. They didn't look at her so much the TV cameras they looked at him he was on every night once the trial started standing on those courthouse steps. But it took almost six months to get going and all that time she was in jail Lebrun he kept on doing what he was doing like nothing had happened. I wanted to invite him over for a home-cooked meal but Alice she did not forgive and forget she was Christian all right but it was not so much in her bones she had to fight against her nature and that was one battle she lost because she could not bring herself to let bygones be bygones. I don't even know what he'd done to offend her I mean except marrying that woman and hell at least he was sticking by her I tried to point out that was in his favor wasn't it but her feelings toward him or against him more like just hardened so when I suggested it I said It doesn't have to be anything fancy she got that look on her face that very stern look. He needs our help I said. I helped him once she said that was enough. Helped him how? I asked and then she got all embarrassed like she'd spoken out of turn. I'm just trying to be a good friend I said. To him or to me? she answers like I couldn't be both not at the same time. I don't know what it was they were like oil and water except that's not true because he liked her or admired her at least. The love of a good woman he said. The only thing Lebrun did that was out of the ordinary that whole time was beat the crap out of those misfits the group that had been hanging around his wife I didn't think that was really right because she had impressed herself upon them they were a weak-willed bunch but he sought them out and pretty much told them You ever show up anywhere near my house again and then the two fellows I don't think the girl did anything but the two fellows they probably just weren't quick enough saying Yes sir because he gave them such a licking no just with his fists I didn't see them they didn't show themselves for a long time but I saw his knuckles. A man your age I said what are you doing they got guns after all. I wish they had he says. I wish they'd had their rifles on them like that would have made it more satisfying. But other than that oh none of us were called to testify it was all from before it was like what she had done since didn't matter it was 1968 again they hauled people out of the woodwork hell out of retirement homes practically these middle-aged hippie types with no hair and big bellies saying Yes I hooked up the dynamite stuff like that. I followed it as well as I could I didn't go down no not to Sparta I asked Lebrun if he'd like me to come and he told me he'd prefer it if I just stayed here and kept the operation afloat that's what he said keep the operation afloat I mean all I was doing was taking care of houses basically but I guess he valued that he could trust me he wanted things to go on as normal. I did see her on TV once. They were leading her in or out she wasn't in any kind of getup no striped pajamas or anything for the trial they let you wear your own clothes well she was beautiful actually I mean in comparison all the years I'd known her before she'd devoted no time at all to her looks she was always so ragged I think that's one of the reasons the women in town didn't like her she took no care she made them feel like well why do I bother when Maggie Chess there looks like she just rolled out of bed. Would it kill you to wear a dress? I remember he did say that to her once that was about the only criticism of her looks I ever heard him say but now I mean at the trial the time I saw her on TV she was wearing I don't remember exactly but she looked totally different younger like it had just happened what she was accused of. Except in her eyes what I saw there it was the same as that time in the car when he was in the hospital I saw she was scared. I would be too I don't know how many years they were talking about but they were definitely throwing the book at her and then that lawyer gets on he just physically inserts himself into the TV screen and starts going on about the state's case. The local news they always had to break away from him in the middle of a sentence because he never actually got to the end of one he never even paused for a breath it sounded like all about how she'd proved in the time since she was a law-abiding citizen. I don't know about that I don't know how he managed to stop them from showing a picture of her in her battle fatigues holding up a rifle but instead he said she was a loving wife and a valued member of the community. Lebrun was greasing the wheels I suppose. No one from here wanted to say a word. When reporters came up everyone would go quiet she kept to herself she was a nice lady stuff like that. We kind of formed a circle protected one of our own. It's funny she never seemed like that like one of us until they took her away.

∽

I don't mind you sitting here with me. Bed's just a change of scenery I don't sleep much anymore no I don't dream because I don't sleep about all that happens is my thoughts take on a different shape. A private room sure Emily well that's what she got her degree in Accounting that's the other reason she got to be town clerk it's not just because she can talk to people at meetings she's got a good head on her shoulders. I told you Alice must have squirreled the money away she was in charge of it. All I'd do is empty my pockets at the end of the day I was happy to let her do it it weighs you down I don't mean the silver no I mean trying to figure out what to do with it where to keep it. Alice I don't know if she invested it or kept it all in the savings account or under our mattress but we always managed to scrape by even when I had a bad month and then Emily she stayed home she took classes over in Schuyler for four years we got her a secondhand car yes Lebrun taught her to drive. Only took her a few lessons. She's a natural he told me a natural driver. Just like her old man I said. He looked at me surprised. Well it's the same I said horses or cars I mean it's knowing what to do on the road. Then Alice. That's when Alice. It's like your parents in a way or how I imagine it was. Just when things are going good a person. Of course it always seems like that like things were fine before. Your mother no I didn't know anything of course I didn't even know she was sick I don't read those gossip magazines and besides people around here they had mostly forgotten about them out of sight out of mind it had been quite a few years. The last time I ever saw her with my eyes not socially it would be that movie. I went to Sparta for that nothing would have stopped me I had to it didn't play up here. I don't even know how I found out about it it wasn't the type of movie there would be advertisements for. I always kept my eyes peeled for her name. Then I saw it was playing in Sparta this movie she was in the first since well I forget but I saw they made a big deal about that the fact that she'd been away to raise a family so I told Alice I had to see this eye doctor this specialist down that way I don't know why I didn't tell her the truth I guess I thought she might have raised a stink not that that would have mattered but I didn't need to hear her complaining Going to see your girlfriend? That kind of thing. So I told her Doc Harmon said I should see this eye doctor down in Sparta. That was all right with her she said I'm glad you're going I really think it's a good idea like she had noticed something was wrong which was a little strange because I hadn't noticed anything was wrong going to see the eye doctor was just what came into my head. Lies that's where you got to go look for the truth when you reach down and come up with something a lie I mean it's usually what's close at hand what you're really thinking about but not willing to face head-on at least that's what I've discovered. So I go down to Sparta I take the bus yes and went to the theater. It wasn't a regular kind of movie house it was small and in this part of town I'd never been to it had a different smell. I pay for my ticket and then the manager he stops me before I go in and says Are you sure you know what kind of movie this is? I say Of course I do it's a groundbreaking performance by the former stage actress. I had read it out front you see while I was waiting for the box office to open there was an article a review I guess you'd call it taped to the glass. So he gives me this look but I just go in and sit back and it's not like any other movie I ever saw that article it talked all about the director I couldn't even pronounce his name but there's no story so far as I can tell it's all people talking and she's not in it not for a long time it's just these two men they're trying to oh I forget it was mostly these two just messing around I barely paid attention after a while and then the funny thing was when she did come on I didn't recognize her at first not until she opened her mouth. It wasn't just age she was a little older but it was more how she moved and what she was doing which wasn't anything I'd ever seen her do in real life. She was kind of frightened and begging. See she's the girlfriend of one and the other he's not comfortable being there but the first one the one whose boyfriend she is for some reason he wants her to go with the friend into the other room with the second man. It's not like you see anything but still. I was ready to cover my eyes let me tell you but no it wasn't that kind of film at all it was more arty she would never your mother would never. But she was on her hands and knees sometimes well you must have seen it I mean not at the time you would have still been a kid but since then after I mean you must have gone back and you can't remember? I wish I could not remember. Her voice though her voice was just the same. Kind of throaty like she smoked a lot. I didn't even listen to what she was saying it was pretty filthy some of it what they were talking about and it was in this room such a sad room not at all the kind of setting I was used to seeing her in in real life it was in a dark hotel room it was a mess and then there was this other room off to the side where he kept wanting her to go with his friend and you knew even though you didn't see it you knew that was like hell on earth in that room back there. Then the story went on and I didn't even know it was over her part I kept hoping they'd come back to that room or that she'd show up somewhere else but instead those two fellows they ended up in a cemetery looking for some watch. Oh it was the strangest movie and then someone shot them one of them this man who'd been trying to do it the whole time you never knew why. It was the strangest thing I stayed just to see her name on the screen because I wasn't sure it was her even then I mean I was of course but I just wanted to see it in black and white her name. Then I went out and read about it. I could see the manager through the glass watching like I was going to come in and complain ask for my money back but it wasn't a bad movie exactly. I thought about it on the way home it was one of those ones where you think about it later on even if you don't like it at the time. Alice she was anxious it was the first thing she asked when I walked in the door What did he say? Me of course I was still part of me was still in that room that awful hotel room and the one next to it where they'd go or where he wanted her to go. What did he say? Alice asks and I just stood there waiting you know waiting for it to come to me what the hell she was talking about it's like the rest of the world I'd kind of been holding at arm's length and then I remembered. He says I'm fine I say. He says I've got the vision of a ten-year-old. I don't know why I said a ten-year-old. A ten-year-old? she asks. Twenty-twenty I said. Oh she says and goes back to what she's doing. I could tell she was disappointed. But that was the last time I saw your mother except for pictures in the paper when she.

～

The bible? No I never read it for one thing the way it's written in columns I mean why they lay it out like that I'll never understand. But I get a sense of it by seeing others in action by watching people leading their Christian lives I get a sense of what parts are real and what parts of it are just talk. Like with Alice I could tell the parts she didn't follow in her heart I mean those were the parts she made the biggest deal about love thy neighbor all that stuff she hated our neighbors she hated everyone really hate's a hard word I don't mean that but she was naturally suspicious she wouldn't just approach anyone with open arms so that's what she worked the hardest on. Helping out always offering to come over for coffee or what a beautiful garden or how's your boy that kind of thing. But I could see what an effort it took how she'd kind of swallow hard. That was the part of her Christianity I doubted because it didn't seem to come natural to her. But the other parts the parts that me if I'd had to join I would have had the toughest time with that He rose on the third day for example yes I know all that stuff well I heard it enough you can't live around here without picking up a fair amount of knowledge the part about Him rising up from the dead that I have trouble buying. I'm fine with love thy neighbor I mean I can't always do it but I was always willing to try. Alice on the other hand I think she sincerely believed all that mumbo jumbo. More than Bigelow that's for sure he was just a salesman. She was the truest Christian I knew because she tried so hard and because there was always something about it troubling her. I don't know what I never even tried to find out it was just part of who she was it wasn't something you could undo. No I'm fine I don't need a blanket I don't feel the cold never have. That's how I. That's where I took Alice when we were courting she didn't want to be taken anywhere where we could be seen she was so shy then so ill at ease so I took her to the spring the one on the edge of the clinic's property. Well it was gloomy there it was out of the way nothing but pine trees and rocks so no one came by. She'd made sandwiches. They hadn't dammed it up yet hadn't built that housing trying to capture it the springhouse it was just a muddy spot with this kind of foul-smelling water coming out of the ground. I know it's a kind of funny place to take her but Rebecca had told me that

Christopher was always doing experiments there that it had scientific properties that's what he said. Well that kind of intrigued me so I suggested we. She didn't want to at first Alice. It's true it had a kind of reputation as a spooky place but that's good I said that way no one will be there. That clinched the deal because as I said she was shy and it turned out to be beautiful it had rained the day before but the sun was out and strong enough so it slid past the trees this colored light and there were all these needles on the ground so it was soft to sit on and no bugs. We had sandwiches. The smell it wasn't so bad. It's supposed to be good for you I said I was pretending I was knowledgeable. Breathe deep I said get it deep into your lungs. She was wearing she used to wear these frilly dresses with a million buttons and ribbons yes for everyday all women did it was the fashion then. The water had formed this pool because of the showers. You couldn't see exactly where it was bubbling out from. We sat near the edge on a moss bank and had our lunch. I asked about her dad because really that was the only point we had in common that he'd invited me over a few times and she'd brought out lemonade in the garden. School no we didn't talk in school I don't think we'd ever spoken there and of course I wasn't going anymore not since my father I was working for Washburn but we didn't talk about him not much she just said Well he's taking advantage of you I remember that when I described what I did and how much he paid me I remember because as soon as she said it I thought that's true it's like she could express things I knew but couldn't put into words when she said He's taking advantage of you I thought yes he is and I've got to do something about that but mostly we just well I don't remember what we talked about it was more than sixty years ago I can smell it though like it was yesterday I can smell that water it was so sulfurous rotten eggs they say but really it's a different smell it's almost heady makes you dizzy maybe that's why no one would come there maybe that's why there were no flies come to think of it. Everything she said it sort of became crystal clear in my mind touched a chord sort of. Maybe it was the fumes. She had this hat all women had hats then proper women hats gloves I'm telling you the factories wouldn't have stayed in business if it wasn't for that hat-and-glove trade she had this hat and I took it off I was joking being bold because she said something about her hair not faring well in the light I took it off and she snatched at it and by accident I was drawing my hand back but she knocked it loose and it fell into the lake this pool I mean the little pond the spring made. Well the wind was blowing and before either of us could get it it had blown a few feet off from where we sat and ended up plumb in the middle maybe fifteen or twenty feet off. She set up a howl she couldn't be seen without her hat and besides it was taking on water soaking it up so I didn't really have time to think I felt responsible I took off my socks and shoes and then yes of course I was going to go in but it was all mud and slime there it was a very unappealing place to step so without thinking I took off my trousers as well. She gave this little scream. I told her not to look she turned her back it's silly when you think about it it's just like I was wearing shorts short pants but in those days. She turned her back and I waded in it was freezing like springwater always is but I don't feel the cold that's the point I don't get cold all mud on the bottom like quicksand but also slippery especially when you'd come upon a rock it was covered with all that slime and the smell farther in the smell was much worse made you dizzy but I walked in and I could see her hat just ahead of me I heard her say Be careful Billy so I turned my head to say Don't worry something like that and that's when I fell my foot was on a rock and I just. That water closed over me. Only for a second. It was a different experience than that other time at Brandt Pond well I wasn't a kid for one thing but also the water itself just felt so different all velvety and thick the way it closed over my head I came up for air and the first thing I heard was her laughing but it wasn't a mean laugh no it was. That's the moment. That's when I knew. I mean not at the time it's not like I realized in my head this is I don't know what you'd call her the love of my life I suppose but the way she was laughing it wasn't mean at all Lord knows I'd heard enough of that mean laughing it was the other kind like I'd lifted something off of her. See she had the reputation of being kind of a sourpuss not from me but that was her reputation in school and in town she wouldn't smile wouldn't or couldn't I don't know which but you got the sense or I did at least that she wanted to that it was in her. Happiness I mean. But kind of kept prisoner I don't know by what like I said there were parts of her that I just didn't feel it was any of my business to go trespassing in so to speak. But I heard her laugh I broke the surface of the water sputtering a bit I'd swallowed some of that water and her laughter it was so sweet it was like it had escaped from inside her I could tell she cared about me that she liked me that's the sense I got. So then I was right by the hat and I clapped it on my head that made her laugh even harder the picture of me I guess I couldn't see it but I could imagine and then I made my way back to shore and she held out her hand she helped me up. You're a sight she said and then well. Well maybe. I'm not saying but that spring I always had soft spot for it. It's funny once I brought it up I said something like They're building this housing for it Cochrane and Christopher they're having me bring a bunch of cement and bricks up there she acted like she didn't know what I was talking about. What place is that? she asked. I said You know the spring and then she acted like oh yes I've heard about it that's not safe all the things people say in town as if she had just gone back to being one of them one of those narrow-minded church biddies who never sets foot off the straight and narrow. Where we went on that picnic I said you know when we. Well she flatly denied it acted like I was crazy. I didn't want to say Then who's this baby screaming in the corner? Where did she come from if we didn't that day? But of course well for one thing she would have hit me over the head with a frying pan but for another she would have gotten all hysterical. When things didn't go her way she could get. But also I didn't want to make it out that that's why we got married just because Emily was coming along it certainly wasn't in my case I knew knew from that moment. Not at the time I mean at the time you don't know nothing you're just in it but when you look back you think yes I knew then right then and there or you imagine you did. That's what I believe not all that hooey about Him rising on the third day that sounds like a crock to me.

～

What did I do? I went out and shot bottles what else are you going to do when your wife dies? That's when I stopped drinking I told you I ran out of empties and so I got out my pint of Old Gentleman that I'd bought special that I was holding in reserve for after the funeral I took it out I thought I was going to break the seal this was going to be my new life I thought I was going to drink myself to death basically I couldn't think of much else to do but instead without even thinking really not consciously I mean I set it on the fence and stood no not my normal distance away much farther fifty feet at least as far as you could get where the house started with my back against the wall and I aimed it took me a few shots I wasn't perfect but eventually. Emily she wanted me to set up that antiques place in back but I couldn't. Antiques. Just another word for junk. Bottles actually that was one of the things she said I could sell antique bottles she called them the old ones I'd stored the ones I hadn't used for the elixir they were still around. Then after the funeral she comes out she says Dad you've shot all the bottles. That last one it just exploded and no I never had a drink again it turns out that wasn't my new life after all. Praise God that's what Bigelow would have said that's probably what he does say when he's on the crapper trying to relieve himself I'm sorry excuse me. What's that you say what do you mean it doesn't make sense? Because when Firebrand died yes that's true Lebrun was there and we were drinking well I was drinking he never Lebrun never. It was after Alice's death of course Firebrand didn't die until. I see what you're saying. Yes and Lebrun he passed away before Alice so. No I never drank after so it must have been before. But it happened though it happened just the way I said. Well you move things around your memory does like he did with that model with the pieces I mean. It doesn't matter what order things happen in that Breyer woman for example just because they found me in her house but I was just doing my job I had the keys she screamed so loud when really she was the one who was naked you'd think I would have screamed I was the one who had the right to scream a naked woman appears in front of you blocking your path when all you're trying to do is take out the garbage well who isn't up at six A.M.? It's bright then on an August morning there's this mist off the lake it's a time to get work done before it gets too hot I was just doing my job and she. I was fully dressed yes I was decent I was the one who should have considered pressing charges no I didn't say that not out loud I let Emily she and Ray they met with the Association well they should have taken those keys away if they didn't want me to use them. Emily said she couldn't vouch for me anymore that's the way she put it couldn't vouch for me because she was busy all day but if I moved here well it sure beats jail that's what they were acting like her and Ray although I'm not really sure I can tell the difference. Maggie the one time I asked her about it she said Jail's not so bad. What did you do there? I asked and she laughed she said she cleaned toilets like it was the funniest thing like it was a novelty which I suppose it was for her. You see that mark on the ceiling? Water comes through you can't stop it not with these flat roofs they should pitch more the snow load here once it starts to melt if you don't have a good tilt it creeps into things freezes then pries them up shingles tarpaper aluminum doesn't matter what water expands when it freezes then it melts again and leaks in more and pretty soon that's when you get these stains this one here I've been staring at it for well I told you I don't sleep so. But look at it doesn't it look just like you wouldn't know I guess because you never saw it but it looks just like the valley or the way the valley used to look before they flooded it it's the same shape as the bottom of the lake that's what it looks like to me. I know it can't really be that but water has a mind of its own the same mind that's what I'm saying all water it behaves the same way so maybe it naturally forms this pattern this shape or maybe that's naturally what I see because when I lie here at night I swear I can see the bottom of the lake or what it used to be those fields yes where Rebecca and I used to be where we used to picnic. They think maybe Cochrane he was a big man six foot two at least it would have been hard for her to say no to him well of course she would have tried but I mean he wasn't the type who would take no for an answer that's why oh it was just a rumor no one thought I heard them they dismissed me they'd lower their voices when I came by they thought I couldn't they'd talk in roundabout sentences they thought I couldn't infer infer yes it means anyway they didn't know nothing it was just a rumor. That field it was going to be flooded they were already talking about it the Army Corps of Engineers but no one knew for sure of course it was just whispers all it did was add to his reputation if you want to call it that Cochrane's I mean that he might have. It made people more scared of him. Not everyone believed that's why I suppose Breckenridge he kept asking me if she'd gone you know if I'd heard from her. Of course I didn't believe it no it was all a load of hogwash I knew he wasn't interested in that kind of thing Cochrane. Now maybe if he found out she was keeping a journal maybe then but I don't know. There. You see? The map it's moving a little at the sides the way it ripples you can see it covered with water town I mean not destroyed just kind of overlaid. Maggie? She got off with time served that's what the lawyer managed. From what I hear they didn't have much of a case. People were old and forgot and besides that bomb never went off they set it but not too well because it was discovered the next day just sitting there but still she'd jumped bail she had to serve something do some time that's why they made that deal her lawyer and the prosecutors she'd already been in there for six months so they got her to plead guilty to something I don't know what so they could say we told you so but then she waltzed right on out of there with time served so she had the last laugh although it's not like they held any celebration once they got back. All I want to do is get back to normal Lebrun said but of course that was impossible and besides what was so great about normal? That's what I wanted to tell him. Maybe this will make it better I wanted to say maybe your wife won't be running around with a semiautomatic weapon now maybe she won't be dressing up like G.I. Joe either was what I wanted to say but no he and I just. He wanted to go back to the way things were but it's sad he was a broken man. I heard that expression before but I never really saw it happen until then. The first time I saw him after I mean you would have thought he'd be happy he'd won she was home they'd been talking before about serious jail time and instead there she was or at least we could hear her up above us we were back down in the basement. No just her. I told you that Taxpayer's Militia or whatever the hell they were called they were disbanded they'd been defeated in battle by one epileptic man and his two fists but instead of being happy it was like he had jumped twenty years ahead in his growth in his age. Before he always looked young compared to the rest of us and now all of a sudden it's like he got changed like someone had turned some dial inside him. I guess he used it all up the rest of his youth worrying about her. I thought he'd bounce back at first. Even after his accident even though he was never quite the same but even after his accident he bounced back he recovered it made him focus harder concentrate on the community and the buildings all those houses but after the trial or after she came home rather he let it all slide. Well maybe he didn't have to concentrate so hard anymore I mean by then things were practically complete everything was selling or sold. The big payoff that's what he called it but in a kind of bitter way. Well aren't you making a pile? I asked. Oh yes he said the big payoff and then we'd hear her walking upstairs over our heads these slow steps back and forth I don't know what she was doing pacing maybe or wandering. How's she taking it? Taking what? he says. Being out. Mean as ever he said but actually I think that was wishful thinking on his part she wasn't the same she wasn't mean at all that's what I discovered later. At the time she wasn't seeing anybody. Before there was always a chance I'd run into her at the library or the IGA now you saw Lebrun hauling home the groceries all alone and as for Miss Dick she asked me How's Maggie? Like I should know more than her. As well as can be expected I said. She shook her head. You think you know someone she said. So they weren't as close as I thought or weren't by then. Maybe they'd had some falling-out I don't know. I think he wished she was still the same old Maggie he'd brought home from Sparta kind of feisty a live wire difficult you know mean as ever but instead.

~⁀

Her real name? Oh that's not important she kept it Maggie Chess that's what we all knew her as. Like your dad I guess my god when he died and it was in the paper his real name I'd never seen so many letters no wonder he changed it. They couldn't have fit that on a movie screen. There was a time when I was walking by I was on my way home it was getting dark and they had this fire on the beach there was nothing unusual about that they'd build a fire there all the time with driftwood and old logs whatever was around but this one it made me stop it was hotter than usual it looked almost white-hot from a distance and then when they saw me they waved for me to come over it was just your mother I don't know where your dad was probably off making a movie he did that more and more toward the end before they moved out there for good and that man that little pipsqueak the one I didn't like he was visiting they were sitting in front of this enormous fire and then when I got closer I saw why it was different-looking they'd used charcoal briquettes a whole pile of them but they weren't cooking there was no grill there was nothing they were staring right into the middle of it smoking and drinking. It turns out they were making glass that's what they told me like the ancient one of those peoples I should know that ancient not Trojans ancient Phoenicians that's right they had these big fires on the beach the Phoenicians and then at the bottom of it that's how they discovered glass by accident because the fires got so hot well that's all it is glass melted sand yes they told me all about it or he did the man they were going to spend the night there your mother and him she was bundled up she'd brought down blankets from the bed not a sleeping bag no just regular blankets she was going to sleep in her chair she said and the man the little one he had this coat it was summer but he had this coat I don't know why he brought it he must have planned this before he came up I mean a raccoon-type coat all furry he was just lost inside it they were going to sit there all night drinking and staring into the fire. Make glass they said well I thought it was the funniest thing I ever heard. You're not going to get it hot enough I said. He just stares at me he has these beady little eyes. Oh ye of little faith Bill your mother said. You you were up at the house I assume with Lucy sound asleep probably Lucy she was probably reading her bible she wouldn't leave your side not for a minute and besides she never touched a drop not just liquor coffee tea you name it Coca-Cola even she said it was the devil's brew. Sit down Bill your mother said and that other one he just stares at me he was almost lost in that coat I could just see his eyes the way he huddled it around him even though it wasn't particularly cold and the fire hell the fire was putting out this wall of heat but we got to talking I think they were giving me I don't know what it was called it was always drinks I never heard of something foreign-sounding it went down easy enough though I saw the little man I caught him watching me when I was gulping it down he was kind of wincing you know because I wasn't appreciating it enough because I didn't realize how much it cost a bottle. No not your mother she didn't care she didn't think that way she wasn't a snob she didn't care we just sat there with the fire blasting away and got to talking. The little man he asked all these questions about my life he was even nosier than you. I'm just joking you're a nice person that's the difference you were raised right I can tell but he was just staring at me and asking all these questions in this whiney voice anyway he gets me talking about Lebrun and what the lake used to look like when it wasn't a lake I mean. I knew I was drinking a lot I knew I should get home to Alice but of course the longer I was there the worse it was going to be the door was going to be locked probably I'd have to sleep in the barn have to hear Allure and Firebrand saying things about me so I stayed longer than I should have and talked longer than I should have. They had this big bag of charcoal they kept adding more and more they didn't even know how to do it right I mean they should have built some kind of pyramid or something a tower so the air could get in underneath but instead they just kept dumping more on top. In the morning the little man kept saying in the morning when they woke up they were going to find this big lump of glass at the bottom. I'm going to make it into jewelry for you he said I'm going to take it to Tiffany's. Who's Tiffany? I asked. They laughed. But Bill he says it doesn't sound like she's much like you your daughter that is. I'd been telling them about Emily and I say No it's true she takes after her mother. Well that's good he says a girl should take after her mother particularly in looks and then he kind of winks and asks Does she take after her mother in the looks department your daughter? And I say Well no actually she's darker she doesn't really look like either one of us so much and then he nods nods like that's important. I'm sure Emily's lovely your mother said. No they never met I told you Alice wouldn't even allow me to introduce them to bring them over she felt I was getting above myself palling around with those types that's what she called them those types so I got up to go eventually because hell I wasn't going to stay there all night and then as soon as I step away from the fire the temperature drops around forty degrees that bastard was like an oven but still they weren't going to make glass. I don't know where they got the idea from the ancient Phoenicians my foot it was probably just an excuse to drink but as I'm stepping away the little man he calls after me It's good to have a true friend isn't it Bill? What? I ask. He says Your friend Mister Brown I've seen him around in that pickup truck he's your true friend isn't he? Your mother I could hear her shushing him I don't know why I guess she thought he was trying to get at me needle me you know but he says It's the true friends you've got to watch out for and your mother says almost at the same time I don't remember what just telling me to be careful I think walking home in the dark and did I want a flashlight something like that. Well that's what we do I call back. Me and my friend. We watch out for each other. I watch out for him and he watches out for me. Which I thought was a good answer. I showed him. No they never made nothing. I asked her the next day or whenever I saw her next she said all they got was a headache but then she showed me now I remember this was the point of it all I guess she showed me this necklace-y thing this clear piece of melted glass on a chain that he gave her he'd put it in the sand before she woke up he'd had it in readiness the whole time you see it was kind of like a blob but already in a setting that's why he'd gotten her to do it in the first place to stay up with him and watch the fire the whole thing was a practical joke he had it in his pocket the whole time in that big coat. I don't know what he meant by that that crack. I think he just didn't like me didn't like your mother liking me and wanted to make me feel uncomfortable. Friendship what does he know about friendship? He's not the kind of a man who has friends. No I don't even think your mother was one not really I think he was just playing with her putting that necklace there or whatever it was he just had to be the one who knew everything while the rest of us we were all boobs in his eyes he thought he saw behind things but Lebrun and me I don't know what he meant by that yes I watched out for him all my life and he did the same for me I don't know what good it did us in the long run but it got us through it's more than he had I'm sure in terms of friendship the little man he probably just ended up with a liquor bottle that's what types like him end up with. No that's OK I told you I never sleep I spend all night tossing and turning staring up at that map that stain I mean and every time I yawn I think well this is it I'm finally asleep but no I never do I never do fall asleep the night never really ends I carry it with me into the day sometimes sleep and waking get all mixed up as you get older they ought to have a third word for it it's like some wall has broken down some interior wall separating all the different.

⁓

Why didn't it work because they were Americans not Phoenicians I guess. See he never intended it was all so he could slip that necklace-y thing into the sand before your mother woke up. It was a lump of something I don't know if it was glass or. No not a crystal it was liquid-like. Glass is really a liquid. Lebrun told me that. At this house he took me to but that was later that was toward the end. We were driving he was in one of his moods trying to get away he started heading almost straight uphill. We went bouncing and crashing he liked that kind of drive like a carnival ride I was holding my palm over the top of the bottle I had my pint of Old Gentleman and I couldn't get the cap back on and he wasn't going to stop it wasn't the kind of incline you couldn't take slow you'd slide back down so I was just concentrating on not spilling then we get to the top and he reaches over and takes the bottle out of my hand. For medicinal purposes he said. That's when I knew he must be hurting. He took a swig maybe his first ever because Christ William he said how can you drink this stuff? Well it works don't it? I answered. Then he took another. Not as much as I'd like he said. I guess he thought it could lessen the pain. So we get out. Something was burning the tires or the engine I don't know which. There's a house up here he says. Where? I asked. Because there was nothing I mean it was a very pretty spot a little godforsaken but I like that I like it when nature leaves off trying. Everything just kind of peters out that high up. Glasshouse he says. Well I don't see no glass house I said. He laughed. Joseph Glasshouse. He had a place up here in the 1920s. Glasshouse what kind of name is that? Well it probably means something in Dutch or German he probably changed it. Like Brown I call because he's on ahead of me by then walking down this path. I follow him and about fifty yards later we're standing in front of this wreck. It was still a house I mean you could see it had been a house but there was no way you could go inside the porch was all collapsed and the roof was caved in there were all these pine needles on top the thing was practically buried in pine needles but it was big a second floor and attics two of them one on each side with little windows it was all out of proportion compared to what was around it no road no other houses no cleared land. The chimney was shifted all the way over you couldn't believe it was still standing. Look at those windows Lebrun says see how they're thicker at the bottom than at the top that's old-fashioned glass. It flows. Glass flows down if you leave it long enough it's not a solid thing at all it's really just a very slow-moving liquid. I got to admit it was a hell of a house or had been. You could still see it was green and white that's what all the houses around here used to be white with green shutters green trim. What the hell is so interesting about this place? I asked What's so interesting is that I own it he said. I just closed on it this morning. You bought it? What for? I just like to come here he says and then he gave a little cry from inside like something had bit him. It's the first time I. I knew he was looking bad well everyone knew that. Looks like he's had a load of talcum powder dumped on him that's what Ed Mosher said. I was surprised he didn't usually have that kind of a bitter tone. You could see he'd been envious all these years sitting there drinking and stacking his quarters. But it wasn't just age I realized then from the way he was holding himself it was like some string had been broken whatever it was that was keeping him together. Then the drink. He must have been in pain to take it after all those years I guess it gave him a kind of second wind because he started saying all these things about the house things he probably wouldn't have said otherwise. Used to bring girls up here he said. One girl in particular. We used to be able to go inside. That was years ago. Doesn't look very comfortable I said. We made do. He was coughing by then it took him a while to get his breath back. It had been a very grand house you could see that. So what are you going to do with it now? I asked. You can't bring a girl here anymore. He was standing back from it I was surprised he didn't want to go in. I guess even he realized it was a death trap. I'm going to knock it down and fix it up he says make it into a place for me and Maggie. Which? I asked. Knock it down or fix it up? Both he says a little of each. Parts of it we can keep the details it's got a lot of good detail inside there's craftsmanship the kind you can't get anymore I figure we can save the good stuff but obviously. I could see him trying to take it all in trying to really see it you know a new house where the old one was. Obviously we got to start over get a new foundation once the detail's been taken out. What do you think? Well I never heard him talk that way. Just him using that word detail what the hell's a detail? It's a house you can't pick and choose you can't take what you like from

one life and stick it into another that's kind of what he was propos-
ing so far as I could tell. It wasn't real that's the sense I got he was just
talking to make himself feel better like if the liquor didn't work
maybe the talking would. Letting it all out you know whatever he'd
been keeping inside him. This girl I asked it wasn't Maggie was it?
No of course not he says I told you it was long before. Then I'm not
sure how she'd feel about it I said seeing as how you were here last
with someone else. I just want to start over he says. Well that stopped
me dead in my tracks. You can't I felt like telling him you can't start
over none of us can. Of course I didn't. No I never said anything like
that. My whole life's been. It's like there's this whole other life where
you're saying what's really on your mind like the underside of a
stitched cloth. But I didn't say anything of course and then I guess he
realized he'd spoken out of turn. I don't know if I want to keep the
chimney he says what do you think? Might be nice to have Freddie
make a new one or even two front and back the way they used to
have them. Freddie? I said. I couldn't tell if he was joking. You see by
then Freddie he was incapacitated his hands no it began with his
hands but then it's a very sad story he woke one day and couldn't get
out of bed I mean he tried he pushed himself around grabbing this
and that but then his legs couldn't bear the weight on them they just
slid to the ground. His wife got the Emergency Squad they went
right to Sparta to the hospital down there but there was nothing
they could do it was in his extremities they just stopped working and
then the doctors said not to him but to his wife they said it was
creeping inward from the outer parts toward his chest this paralysis
and then when it got there of course to his heart that would be the
end. No she didn't tell Freddie what was the point he was a sunny-
minded person had a sunny disposition I mean so I could see it from
her point of view. He came back in a wheelchair but was full of this
talk about how with exercise and what did they call it therapy he was
going to be back to his old self again in no time. They even built a

248

ramp his son Zeke did so he could go in and out of the house by himself. Of course once he got out the front door there was really no place for him to go and his hands his hands were giving him trouble too they always had. That's why he lost his job at the mill all those years back. I'd walk up it sometimes that ramp just to test it out give it some use when I went to visit him yes I went there a few times I didn't mind. Alice she'd bake that was my excuse to take a plate of cookies over there that kind of thing. No she'd never bring them herself. She couldn't. Sickness she had a tough time being around people who were sick. Like she'd catch it I guess. I never minded. You're going to get what you're going to get. I'd bring the cookies we'd set them off to one side. Then I'd wheel him out the front door down that ramp out to the garden in back. He liked to sit there. We'd crack open a few Tail Ends. I'd have to hold it up for him. He knew he knew after a while but he never said. By the end he wasn't talking about exercise anymore about rehabilitation he drank his beer he had a little trouble swallowing sometimes I got him a straw that was better he could just lean over and sip. We'd stare out it was fall there wasn't much left to the garden just strings and stakes it had kind of gone to hell because he couldn't do it anymore his son wasn't interested in that kind of thing. But he'd look out over this last little bit of land he'd sculpted. We didn't say much what was there to say? How did he like the cookies? Alice would ask when I came home. He liked them fine I'd say. Where's the plate? I'd always forget the plate. But Lebrun he wouldn't go near. He if you think germs gave him a reason not to touch things imagine what a dying person no he gave the whole subject a wide berth you couldn't even mention Freddie's name he even began to insult Freddie's work like what he had now kind of infected all he'd done before all those plantings he'd say all those rows of trees and clumps of bushes the way he used to make me mound things up they don't follow the property lines the parcels. Buyers complain they say their lot extends on to the next because it looks like it does the way the trees keep going instead of ending at a natural border. Well that's the big picture I said he made it all come together. I think maybe his brain was getting a little stiff before anything else Lebrun said. He was just afraid. Nobody likes it when a man dies a slow death like that it's bad manners I guess shows a picture of what's going to happen to you and you can't ignore it. Every day you notice he's a little more progressed it made people resentful some of them. So Lebrun saying he was going to get Freddie to build him a chimney well that just made it seem like he'd taken leave of his senses. No he never did anything with that house that wreck he was just dreaming that's all just showing me something that was important to him that's why he brought me there or maybe to tell me about the girl she must have been special maybe she was the one you know. Oh I always thought there was a special woman he had early on before the others even. I don't know why because there had been for me I guess there's always that one before. The first person you feel for but you always screw it up with make a hash of things because that's what she's there for you're still feeling your way. Everyone has someone like that where they regret how it turned out someone they feel responsible for. Yes with me it was Gabrielle it was an impossible situation but I could have behaved better that's for sure I regret the way I ended it after all those things I told her the way I just stopped going. I had to once I started courting Alice. I wasn't the kind of man who visits two girls at the same time no that wasn't me at all. It was like I practiced on her that's how I felt about it later I told her things Gabrielle and even if she acted like she didn't care I'm sure some part of her. You shouldn't use a person that way. Not the other thing no that part was honest what we did together I have no regrets about that but what I said to her after and then how I turned around and said practically the same things to Alice but better you know because I'd practiced them first on Gabrielle that makes me feel bad looking back. I don't know who it was for him

Lebrun he was far better at covering his tracks than me and also we weren't friends then really that was just about the time we got to know each other. He came over to me one time I was loading blocks of ice onto Washburn's cart and he says Claude Lebrun and sticks out his hand I don't know why I guess he felt we had some kinship. Maybe because no one talked to either one of us. For different reasons of course but the result's the same. Maybe he was lonely. That's what other people don't see from the outside he looked like he was always busy rushing off to a meeting at the bank or ordering about some carpenter or romancing a lady I mean before he met Maggie but I could tell at the bottom of it all he was alone. Even the woman he finally chose to fall in love with if you can choose such a thing well I don't know how much company Maggie gave him I think in a way she just made him feel lonelier. So he wanted it and he didn't want it. Company that is. Well why else would he come up to me that way? Follow the money what do you mean what money? What it takes to keep me in here my own room? I told you Emily pays no there's plenty she said she was surprised she took over the finances when Alice passed away she was surprised at how much there was. Why do you think I busted my butt for some fifty-odd years? I told her of course we got enough. Enough she says remember she has a degree in Accounting there's more than enough here. I told her there was also the money from Breckenridge. From your grandfather I said. He gave us some to get started that's how I got the team the rig that's how we made the down payment on the house but she says No Dad it's more than that it's. And I asked What? And she says Never mind like she figured it out. I think she just didn't realize at first how smart Alice was how savvy. All those years she knew where to put it how to make it grow it was just like her garden I guess she had a knack even when I had a lean year there was always enough when those milk trucks started coming from downstate when people lost their taste for the real thing started drinking that white water basically she always found a way to get us through. Follow the money that's just what you shouldn't do it's leading you by the nose then. No I don't mean anything by it I'm just saying you've got to let sleeping dogs lie. Money only tells one part of the story. I've spent my whole life ignoring it as much as I could. I figured things would sort themselves out if I let them. I saw my father how he battled money every step of his life and what did it get him? Follow the money no thank you yes I'm sure there's a story there but I don't want to know it I don't want to go down that road. There's some things it's better not to know too much about it's like the time I found Cole Byron with half his guts strung up in the trees. The horses had the right idea. They wouldn't come within fifty feet of him. They took good care of me Firebrand and Allure. I was too dumb then to know then what I do now but they took me back home back to town that is. Eagle Holding Company how do you know about that? Oh of course I told you. But it's funny Emily asked the same question after I mean when she was going through the papers. What's Eagle Holding Company? she says. Nothing I said I didn't remember at the time it was just a chance remark Lebrun had made I don't think he intended for me to hear it Eagle Enterprises that was different that was Lebrun but Eagle Holding Company. I don't know I said. Then I remembered later and tried to tell her Emily I mean and she said Never mind Dad I figured it out on my own. Figured what out? I asked. Nothing she said. Do we owe money? I asked because he paid me toward the end he paid me even though by then I was just coming by to see him not really doing much else not for Eagle but she says No Dad it's fine. You're a good girl I said. I always had trouble telling her things I don't know why. Alice she rode her. Emily could never do anything well enough to please Alice. She'd look at her like I don't know it didn't come easy for that woman loving a daughter I don't know why. And me I knew that if I said too much if I showed too much affection if I said that I loved her she'd pay for it that Alice would make her pay somehow so that time after Alice was gone I tried to tell her but it just came out You're a good girl which is the same as what I always said. Maybe I said it a little different with more feeling I know I certainly intended to but you you you can't break habits you can't break thirty years of acting a certain way not overnight. We don't owe anything she says. That's because your mother did such a good job I said and then she began to cry.

～೨

Yes I kept getting my paycheck although all I did that month was sit with him when Maggie had to go out. She was a good caretaker. When it was clear that he was that it was over then she kind of snapped out of that funk she'd been in ever since she got back from Sparta. She even cleaned the upstairs it was the first time I'd been there since they moved in she turned the front room into a hospital practically with all this equipment a bed one of those beds that could go up and down with a little button he could push so you could be anywhere in the house and if he needed help this buzzer would go off. Some people a crisis brings out the best in them. When they told her there was no hope she dropped all that meanness and became a whole new person or maybe the person she'd been before that's what I'd like to think before all that circumstance forced her to be so ornery. Well and him it's like they switched roles he became kind of a Grouchy Gus always pressing that button that buzzer I can still hear it you'd come in and he'd say This water isn't cold or The sun's in my eyes. But the meaner he got the nicer she got like instead of matching him this time she was going to let him go as far as he needed and balance him out in the other direction. Yes the paychecks kept coming. I felt bad taking his money but I couldn't let Maggie do it alone no one else seemed that interested in helping they were still mad I guess over the publicity it's like they couldn't show it before when she was arrested we all circled around her then but after when she got off with time served then it started this sort of whispering campaign people calling her a traitor and stuff. Well also it had to do with Lebrun once people knew he wasn't going to get better they all looked ahead to what it was going to be like without him and then of course there'd be no reason to put up with her and her ways. Normally in that situation people come by with casseroles and sit with the wife and offer to help but with Maggie that house just became. People would actually cross over and walk on the other side of the street. I saw it. A boy once I was going in and his ball landed on the lawn and he was afraid to just to step on the grass and get it I could see him standing there wanting to get his ball back but he was afraid like this wicked witch lived there or something. So I tossed it to him he didn't even say thank you or nothing he just took off. Sure I'd go there most every day. Alice oh I told you she had no time for Lebrun. No dying didn't make going to see him any more appealing a proposition she didn't even bake cookies. Godless heathen she called him. Well that's not true I said he attends he goes to Saint Anthony's. They worship idols she said. What the hell are those two pieces of wood you got nailed together? I wanted to ask. There was no one else to come by. Doc Harmon he was gone by then we don't have a doctor here anymore just the Emergency Squad they'll take you to Sparta if you last that long. Otherwise your last sight's going to be some kid with pimples pounding on your chest while his partner takes a back road at a hundred-and-ten miles an hour. Doc Harmon they found him he'd taken some injection yes he did it to himself his wife Ella she'd passed earlier I guess he never got over it no no note he didn't bother to say good-bye but Good-byes are overrated that's what Elizabeth said. Who? No one. I sat with him with Lebrun watched him get smaller he got smaller all over it's like once in that stream I used to travel I found a frog skin just the skin with its eyes bugging out and its mouth open but nothing inside. Father he said it was this creature this insect with pincers that would eat from within even the bones he said. It dissolves everything digests it just leaves this sack. Well I dropped the thing before he got halfway through the description but it was the same with Lebrun he just began to shrink to shrivel up inside. Maggie she'd have a specialist come up once a week from Sparta she spared no expense I'll give her credit for that but then when the pain started he proved no help at all he wouldn't prescribe a thing. They don't want to get in trouble she said doctors. She said it like it was a bad quality not wanting to get in trouble. I could see how from her point of view well she'd been in trouble one way or the other for twenty years. So she takes all this cash I said What the hell are you doing with all that? It was more than I'd ever seen in my entire life wads of bills twenties fifties she said You just watch him I'll be right back. So I sat there. He was in bad shape I don't care how tough a man you are whatever was going through him it wouldn't quit. He was talking more in French than English I couldn't understand a word. Finally he set upon cursing that seemed to be the only thing that even worked a little he was always so proper-sounding so well-spoken didn't want to be another foul-mouthed Canuck and now it was like all of a sudden these curse words were pouring out that he'd been holding back all his life he was screaming them out. Go on I said go on if it helps although another part of me was wondering what the neighbors you know hell what the people six miles off might be thinking but no one came no one called the police just words that's all they are I don't know why they have such force but it seemed to help a little I was holding onto his hand I never felt the gap more between us between any two people I mean you want with all your heart to help and this was my oldest friend but here he was going through torment and all I could do was nothing I couldn't make his pain lessen one little bit. I even began to think Maggie going off with all that money that cash I began to think well maybe she just left me here. I started thinking well maybe she just stuck me here with him this screaming sweating madman going on in French half the time asking me my forgiveness yes my forgiveness I don't know for what saying he loved me just out of his mind that was worse than the cursing seeing him fall apart like that begging you know like I could save him me and then she comes back the door slams. Oh my god she says help me Bill. We roll him over by then he was in pajamas we just pulled down the bottoms and she says You do it I can't. Do what? I ask and she shows me. Well they're wax these wax stumps they go up his. You know. Up his. We rolled him over so I could. No I'd never done anything like that before when would I have occasion to do anything like that? On a horse? A horse would kick you from here to Kingdom Come if you ever tried to stick something up its what do I look like a goddamned veterinarian? But she held him down she was whispering to him trying to calm him and he was struggling and screaming it was quite a scene I'm telling you and then I notice for the first time I notice what they come in which is one of those prescription boxes from Varney's Drug from Doug Varney but there's no writing on it or nothing no typed-up label saying what it's for. Just do it Bill she says. He was still a strong son of a bitch shrunken or not she was using all her weight to keep him down so I take the wax thing out and yes all the way up. Now all we have to do is make sure it stays in until it melts she says until it dissolves and I think oh well that's a what do you call it that's a conundrum. I don't know how I'm going to go about doing that you know monitoring that particular situation down there but actually it turned out all right he. What's the matter? Are you? Well I'm sorry I didn't mean to upset you you didn't even know the man did you? It's all right. Sometimes that's how it hits you when it's not about you directly. It's all right it's good to get it out. Don't mind Cecil he's got his headphones on by now. No it's got a happy ending actually I mean not the whole thing but they were morphine suppositories morphine yes just like that time he fell into the turbines I guess that's what you want if you're ever in pain. She'd paid Doug Varney I don't know how much. It's a felony he kept saying. She thought it was a joke the way he kept repeating it the whole time he was getting them out It's a felony but I guess the money that's always been a tough business the pharmacy a lot of people they get their medicines at those big places out by the mall now so I guess the money she gave him. A felony Maggie says I'd like to show him what a real felony looks like. But they worked that's the important thing and she had enough of them. After that he slept more. Well no it's no answer it's not like it made him smile or anything it just kept the pain at bay. I'd watch him I'd think of that frog skin there was a little less of him each day a little less inside. She'd be with him all night Maggie sitting there I'd come by in the morning and she'd go out and shop or go upstairs get a little rest I don't think she slept much herself. Even when he was up awake I mean his eyes had this look to them like he wasn't all there. I'd help him to the bathroom he was all skin and bones by then no matter what you did you'd bruise him it was sad once he had his arm around me I don't know if his legs were even doing the walking it was almost like they were trying to remember what they were there for what their purpose was but we made it and I settled him down oh I'd never leave him alone there I'd wait so he looks up at me I don't even know if he knew who I was by then but he says She wouldn't have me and I say I know or I figured. Something like that just playing along humoring him. That was probably the last exchange we ever had and I don't even know if he knew who I was or knew what he was talking about I sure didn't. I was just telling him what he wanted to hear what I sensed I mean. I was trying to calm him down he seemed so agitated not the pain by then but in his mind. But you why are you crying? He had a good death at home with a loving wife. She did. She loved him toward the end. Well how do I know because of her actions her actions spelled it out. Ming he's the one who told me about the Chinese letters. I was noticing them on one of those wrappers the fruit comes in you know how some fruit comes wrapped in crinkly paper and this one had writing on it well not writing those Japanese or Chinese marks. I asked Ming what it meant and he said they were pictures man-walking man-woman-make-love he showed me or tried to he traced the lines with his finger and said See? So when they make love I said they're making a word? I don't know if he understood but he nodded. It made me think maybe we're always making letters in our everyday lives just by what we do with our bodies the way we twist and turn our actions maybe they spell something out. Who'd read it? Well that would be God of course. See the real book it's not the bible but us maybe we're all together one big book that's alive a kind of story and He's reading it turning the pages whoever He is and we're just words on a page. No I wouldn't tell Alice anything like that besides I didn't think of it at the time I just came up with it recently after Ming showed me that wrapper. Bigelow? Fat chance. He always thought I was such an idiot I could tell. He comes over a week after Alice passed to comfort me in my grief he says. I caught him looking around trying to size things up. Bill he says your wife loved the church so much I was surprised when they read her will. Turns out he was expecting some kind of payoff. She'd made hints or so he claimed he called them promises about a big bequest. A what? I asked. A bequest. I kept cupping my ear I wanted him to say it more I wanted to hear him say it about a million more times more a bequest a bequest a bequest but lo and behold she left his church absolutely nothing she took him for a ride. I could feel me loving her more and more as I saw how cheated he felt sitting there. No I didn't offer him nothing not even a crumb I wouldn't offer him the skin off my ass he just sits there shuffling his feet trying to ask me for. Well how much did she talk about? I finally say. Seventy-five thousand. Seventy-five thousand? I say. My god. Just having him name that number in our little house well it did make him look foolish. He was beginning to realize she had led him on. I barely got seventy-five cents I say. I could see him asking himself how could he have been so foolish she acted like she was rich like she had all this money stashed away. Then I showed him out but he was persistent I'll say that for him. Any contribution you could make he said anything at all. Well I'll think about it I said I'll do what I can. I guess he really wanted some return on his investment all that time he put in listening to her complain him saying Praise God and Amen. So the next day I come by the church with a wheelbarrow-load of manure. I didn't dump it on the front lawn no that would have been sacrilegious no I took it around back he wasn't there yet it was early I just left it for him. I guess I should have left a note or something but I figured he'd know who it was from. That's the way we do things around here everyone makes their point but quiet-like that's what Maggie never understood she was always so. If she had some thought to express she'd say it. That's not the way we do things usually. *He changed the face of our community* that's how Lawrence put it when he talked about Lebrun when he wrote his editorial I mean but he never said changed it for good or for bad. See that's what I mean he kind of indicated without saying. *The winds of change blew him here and now the winds of change have taken him away.* Taken him away straight to Hell that's what Ed Mosher said. He came late to the party kind of in terms of Lebrun just when everyone else was feeling sorry for him warming up to him you know because that's what they do when a man's dead when he can't hurt them anymore they warm to his memory that was just when Ed went on the attack kind of. Filthy Canuck he says to me of all people the man's best friend. I hadn't heard anyone use that term in years hell when all the blacks and Mexicans started coming up from the other direction suddenly Canadians sure they spoke French but compared to what came after them they were considered solid citizens and now Ed he gets this bee in his bonnet he says it to me right in front of the church in front of Saint Anthony's

like he wants to fight. I just turned my back to him what was I supposed to do? I was in my Sunday best I was as dressed up as I'd ever
been I wasn't going to ruin it by getting into a scrap right before.
Sure I went inside of course I went in I don't think Father would
have cared hell Father's been dead longer than I've been alive I mean
I know that's impossible but that's how it feels. Maggie no I offered
to take her but she said she'd rather go by herself. She was dressed up
too in a black dress I don't think I'd ever seen her in a dress before.
Would it kill you to put on a dress? he used to say and then it turns
out all it took was. Well there's a joke in there somewhere I suppose.
Alice Emily the whole town it's like all bets are off religion-wise
when it's a funeral it's a big event here folks come out of the woodwork I saw people there I could have sworn some of them had already
passed away it had been so long. What it was of course I realized later
was that I was seeing their children their faces it's like they float to
the surface you don't notice it at first when they're growing up at
first they're nothing they're infants and then after a while they look
like they're this individual person starting out like the world's never
seen anything like them before but if you catch them later in sort of
early middle age it's a face you've already seen it's like there's no real
progress at all there's just a kind of reshuffling. But anyway we went
into the church I don't know how special a service it was I had nothing to compare it to but Maggie made sure there were flowers and
those things that make smoke and organ music and a printed pro-
gram the works. Alice was uncomfortable she kept holding onto her
purse with both hands clutching it. I tried to comfort her but she
wouldn't let me. Her back was so stiff I could see the space between
it and the back of the bench the pew she wasn't relaxing an inch.
Emily she was just there because she had to be because we made her.
I don't even think she wanted to go. Kids don't like funerals I can't
say I blame them. No I didn't cry whatever I felt I felt for him before
when he was still alive. Everyone else was weeping or at least snif-

fling all around me but I was too interested in the scenery. I was finally here you know where Mother had always been. Father the last time we'd been was when he yelled at that monsignor that fancy priest Father yelling at him and then herding us out one palm on each of our heads guiding us straight out Rebecca and me that's the last time I'd been and now here I was again it was so fancy all those windows and the light and the high ceiling you got to hand it to them it reminded me of the bank the old Mountain Trust in Kathan but instead of Petrides sitting up there shaking his head it was that boy Swartz the same beard him up on the cross and those smells smoke and flowers the benches I even liked those hard benches the way they made creaking sounds how old they were I wondered if my mother had sat in one if I was actually sitting in the very same spot she. You had that look on your face the whole way through that's all Alice said afterward. That demented look. She'd been dabbing at her eyes with a little hankie just in the corner of each I couldn't tell if they were real tears or not. Well why didn't you tell me? I asked. What was I going to say that you look crazy? You want people to hear me say that to you right in the middle of a church? The burial no that was private and besides the graveyard if it wasn't good enough for Mother. You got to draw the line somewhere.

～♪

I went after though to the house I thought maybe she'd be entertaining receiving I mean people usually do after. Alice wouldn't come they hadn't warmed up she and Maggie. He was your friend she said not mine. So I knocked on the door I could tell already just from the feel of it that there wasn't anybody inside that no one had come I mean or that she hadn't answered it was so quiet but I knocked a couple more times and then just on a whim I went around back. Sure enough the basement door was open. I went down ducking my head like I had a million times before. Just the one light was on that big fluorescent lamp that hung on a chain. I didn't see her at first it only shone on the model on the mountains and the lake. When I think of all the hours he spent. You'd think you could tell. That all that concentration and attention would be soaked in that you could see somehow how he'd formed it and set it up and tinkered with it so much but to be honest it just looked dead as dead as he was. Even the people I mean by then I knew who they were these little architectural figurines hell he'd even organized them into families by the end but now they were back to being little lumps of plastic. The mountains the lake the beach the jetty it all looked so old I guess it hadn't been dusted in a while maybe that's why. Maggie she was smoking a cigarette which I thought was kind of odd and then she held it out to me which was even odder. No thanks I said but she kept stretching her arm out and kind of waggling it like she couldn't talk motioning for me to take it from her so I did. Then she lets out this breath lets out all the smoke at once. Hold it in your lungs Bill she says. Well I don't smoke I say by then I knew what it was of course I mean I'm not stupid. Go ahead she says get it deep in your lungs so I decide what the hell just to keep her company and I take a puff marijuana what's the big fuss I thought. She was grieving. Everyone would have understood if she'd had herself a bottle of wine. No not like that she says and she comes up. She was still wearing that dress. She takes it but keeps it in my hand she takes my hand and puts it up to my mouth. Now take a deep breath she says and hold it. I'd never seen her so scrubbed so plain in a way with her hair drawn back and that simple black dress she was wearing. Hold it in your lungs she told me. Smells just like alfalfa I wanted to say but she saw me about to speak and put her finger to my lips kind of sealing them and said Hold it in as long as you can. Then she smiled. When you don't talk I mean because you're holding your breath you look more at each other's face. We passed it back and forth a few times. I didn't think it was working at all I didn't feel anything but I did notice that when we exchanged it just the act of passing something from one person to another it's a kind of miracle. I was watching carefully because it was hard to see in the light our fingers the way some let go and others held on until just the right moment. She held out her hand to pass me the cigarette again and I leaned forward I guess I was more affected than I realized because we kind of bumped into each other and then we were both laughing except she was crying too so I took her in my arms to calm her down and. It's sneaky that stuff you don't feel it coming. With booze you feel it coming you kind of settle back into yourself after a few sips but that cigarette you think you're just smoking everything's normal and then you look back the next day I mean that's how long it took for me to realize and you think holy shit what the hell was I doing? No the only ones who saw us were the people on the model all the little figurines. I felt bad about it of course not then but later for a few hours I beat myself up over it and then I changed my mind again and thought wait a minute he's gone it's not like he's down in Sparta or anything it's not like I'm doing anything to him he's not here. No the only thing I regret is the stuff I said after because that probably scared her off. Yes afterward I started saying things I couldn't stop. Finally she put her hand on my mouth her whole hand flat against my mouth like a lid. I can still taste it. We were lying on the floor. I could see the underside of the mountain what it was built on. It wasn't really connected because he liked to move the pieces around yes like puzzle pieces but what they were set on was a door an old door with the knob taken out propped on sawhorses. I don't know where he'd gotten it from no. From the Glass House you think? That place he took me to? Well he could have why do you say that though? Do you know that for a fact? Sometimes you act like you know things but if you know them then why are you asking me? If you already. A wooden door yes that's right. I could see it from underneath. That's when I asked What should I call you? I mean what do you call yourself? She whispered in my ear so it was just a feeling a shiver. Oh I knew her first name was really Elizabeth it had been in the papers enough during the trial but I'd never heard her say it out loud before the way she did then just kind of formed it with her tongue whispering like it had properties. I guess she'd been afraid of hearing it for so long afraid of having someone call out Elizabeth is that you? For twenty years pretending to be someone else Maggie Chess. But the way she said it Elizabeth. See what no one understood is she was the nicest woman down under. All that time we spent together when Lebrun was sick we talked then and in the basement the day the afternoon rather of his funeral yes I know it sounds wrong but I don't think he'd have minded we talked and I got to know her and underneath she was. Well I'm the wrong person to ask everyone else found her difficult all I can tell you is I never really understood falling in love before. The expression I mean. Oh I've loved. I loved Alice and Gabrielle too I suppose in a different way maybe even Saara but falling in love that feeling like you stretch out your arms and legs as far as they'll go in any direction and there's no walls no floor you're just whistling through space I'd never felt that before and of course by then I didn't expect to not at my age. It took me by surprise. I just held onto her the only thing in the world I wanted to do was say Elizabeth. It's like I had this private name for her that no one else knew. I realized that I'd been in love with her ever since the beginning I don't know how but it was like Lebrun had brought her here for me kept her here even just for me until this moment. The cigarette no it wasn't the cigarette. That helped me see more clearly what was already there it made it seem normal. I wasn't out of my mind I was never more in my mind I was really thinking things through for once really seeing I guess it's because she was a rebel that's what I liked about her. She didn't just take it like I did. Life. She didn't just. Then she gets up. Time to go she says which I knew but I lay down there a little more.

I'm going to come by tomorrow I told her I'm going to help you take care of this place it needs a lot of work he let it go to hell. That wasn't true I was just making the lie delivering it to her so she could take it to the neighbors to explain my being there so I could tell it to Alice with a straight face. I had to believe it myself first you see. The place is going to fall down if you don't have some work done on it I said. Interior work. She didn't answer. She just went upstairs. I followed her. The bed was still there the hospital bed in the front room. I could see the sheets hadn't been changed they were still all twisted from when he. That's when I began to realize what we'd just done when it began to kind of sink in a little bit and then I had that moment of feeling bad. I remember I tried to say something ordinary as if I'd come on a regular visit with a pie or a cake about how I was sorry I hadn't had a chance to say good-bye to him and that's when she said Good-byes are overrated. No I didn't think anything of it at the time of course but the next day when I came and she was gone then I remembered. Yes without leaving word to anybody. Well that caused people to talk more than anything the way she just up and left. I think that bothered them more than finding out she was wanted by the FBI. Maybe it was because she was rejecting them rejecting us I guess. She left no explanation no forwarding address nothing it was like Rebecca all over again except this time I couldn't even ask around I couldn't even show my grief. You're taking it awfully hard Alice said you knew he was dying all along. See she thought it was about Lebrun well maybe it was maybe I was just mourning him maybe we both were maybe that's all it was but I don't think so not for me. I didn't take it personal. She just had to go back to being Maggie go back to being on the run. That was her curse her sentence I guess it's the only way she felt comfortable. Upset yes of course I was upset it broke my goddamned heart what do you want me to say? But I didn't take it personal.

I don't want to talk about that. Why because it'll make me sound. Well of course I complain about her but don't get the wrong idea that's just the stuff you can talk about that's what lends itself to words fighting and complaining people acting up saying silly things but the rest of the time the other ninety-nine percent that was just life going by and we got along fine together we understood each other we didn't need to talk. She'd be at the sink leaning over doing the dishes and I'd brush past her kind of close because of the table it didn't leave much room. Just that. From years of being together you'd brush against each other and. See there's nothing to say but it was there. It was real that was my life with her moments like that over and over. The rest was just sort of interruptions but the main part of it was good we didn't need to have some grand passion I don't want to talk about her I've talked about her enough I've given you the wrong impression obviously I can tell. She's in Heaven now. Well if anyone deserves to be it's her. Emily it's so typical the woman rode her all her life I mean all the time she was growing up nothing that girl did was ever good enough. Then she dies and you'd think Emily would be free but I can tell she's still looking over her shoulder sensing this disapproval coming from on high. Sometimes I think that's why she holes up in her kitchen at night and makes those sticky buns because she can hear Alice going Ugh. That was the kind of food she didn't like at all too messy even the name. She hated sticky things she'd always wash her hands if she touched a thing like that so Emily that's her only way of rebelling I guess she can feel her mother the part of Alice that's inside her giving a little shudder and it gives her I don't know if pleasure's the right word but you got to fight back somehow in some part of your life. But let me ask you do you really think were you serious before what you said about Emily and Cecil? Well no I wouldn't mind I'd like her to experience some joy. He can't be all bad he hasn't put me in that truck yet that ambulance I mean. I didn't know how much he felt about things until he stopped me from going out onto the lake. Did he really say that? Strongest old bastard I ever saw? Well that's. I'll take that as a compliment. It's true I felt like I was getting younger with every step I took maybe that's where Christopher's laboratory is at the bottom of the lake maybe as you get closer you. Yes it was the Breckenridge house that he was kicking at Lebrun the foundation of what had been the Breckenridge house I don't know why. What was I doing there down in the valley? Well so what if I was? Looking for Rebecca's bones her resting place that's what I've been doing all my life sometimes it feels like. I mean people talked but nobody knew for sure. I was just walking hoping to stumble upon something. Or hoping not to because then she would still be. Who knows? I was just walking looking to find her and that's when I found Lebrun instead kicking away with those fancy boots. When you're young things seem so immovable sometimes you just got to kick at them. I went up to him. What are you doing here? I asked. Same as you he says I came here for the same reason as you. Both looking for what we couldn't find I guess. That's when he looked most like an Injun to me like he was doing one of their dances the Fire Dance or the War Dance kicking his legs out. Oh sure everyone talked that way back then a Canuck is the product of a French trapper and an Indian whore that's what they'd say. No I never said that myself I heard I think heard it from Father. He'd been places he had stories. He could juggle that was one of his talents see that's what I mean I've probably only told you the bad things the things that stood out but really I haven't told you anything. Like the way he could juggle. He'd take any three objects he'd have us pick them a box of salt my rubber ball and Rebecca once she took out her hair comb she had long dark hair she'd pin it up most of the time a million pins but sometimes instead it would go down in these two spouts kind of like waterfalls on either side. She took out a comb one of those little tortoiseshell ones that held it up and he took those three things and juggled them I don't know why it made us laugh so. He was changed I guess when he did it he was light on his feet dancing around under them the opposite of how he was out in the fields. Mother would laugh. No I can't juggle. Well in my head maybe I can keep more than three things going at the same time but that's just thinking everyone does that I'm not special. Alice when she. That's when I knew something was wrong when she couldn't switch from one thing to another in her head when she kind of got stuck she asked me something I don't even remember what and then after I answered it she asked again the same question. I yelled back we weren't in the same room and then she asked me a third time. Well I came in I was mad I thought she was nagging me but as soon as I saw her she was standing kind of tilted. But in her mind she acted like she was fine like it was the rest of the world that had gone off-kilter because when I tried to help her when I tried to straighten her up she fought me she had to get back to where she was falling over to basically. Honey I said what's going on? Are you all right? And her face that's when I saw. It had gotten all pulled down on one side the same direction as where she was leaning to yes like some force was. I got her to bed but she kept asking me the same question even though her mouth was you could barely make it out what she was saying no I don't remember the goddamned question it was nothing that's not the point you miss the point sometimes miss the point entirely she wouldn't let me call the Emergency Squad she put up such a fuss when I reached for the phone. She had a horror of well like I said of sickness and ambulances no they all put the fear of God into her she'd begin to shake. I said Well what do you want me to do? She just holds me with her one good hand grips me so hard it's like all her strength was going into that one hand. But her mind had gotten stuck. She was staring past me at something. Maybe that's how it takes us we're distracted the whole time we're juggling all these things and then suddenly all the balls fall to the ground and you notice what's really there. The sunset. That's what it was in Alice's case our window faces west so she just stared. Honey I said you want me to close the shades? Because she was so focused on it so fixed on it it was shining right into her eyeball. But all she did was grip me and when I tried to get up again to call the Emergency Squad she wouldn't let go I had to sit back down. I knew what she wanted she wanted to lie there. With me. She didn't want to go anywhere she didn't want to be taken. No it wasn't anything special it was just the sun going down like it does every day. What did she ask? I'm telling you it was unimportant what's important was the way she held onto me after. Yes I had yelled I guess you could call it a fight an argument but that's before I saw before I came in and saw her standing there all confused and tilted over. It doesn't count I know what was in my heart I didn't mean anything by it it's only words. Words aren't important. No she couldn't say anything by then it was the opposite of Lebrun that's for sure it all happened so fast I was sitting with her holding her hand and I was getting more and more scared but she wouldn't let go and even if I had even if I'd gotten them to come and drive her all the way down to Sparta what could they have done? Sweetheart I said. So then just to unstick her mind kind of I started praying. I saw her lips moving but there was nothing coming out so I kind of filled in the blanks or what I imagined she'd be trying to say. Just her prayers what she said every night. Well hell I knew them all by heart it was like I was trying to be a ventriloquist just kind of breathing them out so she'd think she was saying them herself if she could still hear by then if she was even. It wasn't clear to me what was happening. All I know is the room got dark. Then after a while I said Sweetheart? But you know how you say something when you don't expect an answer when you're kind of testing to see if anyone's really at home to see if you're alone or not? Sweetheart? I said but I knew. No we sat there a while longer there was no rush. Emily was coming soon. I didn't want there to be all kinds of hubbub when she got home I wanted it to be normal one last time her walking in that door. You spend your whole life with someone and then when they go it's like you're back to square one part of you. Back to being the person you were before you met them. Like everything that happened was just a. I mean that it can end so fast. It's kind of like waking up. And then when you try to get back to her you can't the way you can't imagine yourself back into a dream. What's happened since it's like I'm trying to find a way in some entrance to the world. Well I guess not to this world but to some other. I gave him my rubber ball Rebecca she took that comb out of her hair and Mother gave him a box of salt. And we watched him. It was instead of TV everyone did something back then some people sang some played the piano people were more interesting or made an effort at least. Now they just sit and stare. Rebecca said If you ever read this I'll kill you. Her journal I mean so I never did but now of course I wish I had. If I had one change to make it's that I would be less obedient. Maybe if I'd read it if I'd seen what kind of trouble she was in I could have. She said If you ever read this I'll put a curse on you well how much worse could it have been? That's what I asked myself later. With a curse at least you know why bad things are happening to you but as it was it just seemed so. No I'm OK it's just some pain I have. You should worry about yourself what you're doing here this is not healthy you know there's all sorts of illnesses here. How long have you been here all day? Is it over? Time kind of telescopes up as you get old it starts out so slow I remember going up that stream as a kid it took years it felt like I was an escaped prisoner I'd live a whole lifetime before noon and now you blink at the breakfast table and they're telling you it's lights out that's how it feels. I can't see I can't see you in the dark I've got no one to pass things on to. Emily she's all Alice. It's better that way there's something wrong with me I even

270

said it once to Alice early on before we. I felt I had to that it was my duty to warn her. There's something not quite right with me I think that's what I said but she didn't hear. Some noise came up a man yelling a horse neighing some sound and took the words away right when I said them. I could see she never heard. I told myself it was fate. So be it I told myself. I wasn't going to risk telling her again. Risk losing all my happiness. But it's good this way. It's best it ends with me. She asked what I'd done with her hat. There. Are you satisfied does that solve the mystery for you? What have you done with my hat? she calls and I say What hat? No it was a summer's day I didn't know what she was talking about. But her tone. What have you done with my hat? she calls again and I say Nothing but louder and then when she asks a third time kind of accusing-like I don't know why but it got to me I came in and I said Goddamnit I didn't do anything to your goddamned hat what are you talking about? And she was standing there. I guess it's just what her mind was chancing on what it got stuck on when it broke down something about a hat. Yes she had a gardening hat maybe that's what she meant a big floppy one to keep the sun out of her eyes but she wasn't gardening she wasn't dressed for it she had special clothes for that old ones so she wouldn't get dirty. Besides I didn't do anything with her gardening hat why would I? Oh that hat. No the hat I waded into the pool to get into that spring you mean now why would she ask about that then of all times? See you're reading back into it that's not how life works it doesn't make sense that way. It must have been some other hat. Maybe she thought it was winter in her head I mean I don't know I'll never know. There's so much you'll never know that's what you have to accept. You think you've got all the time in the world and then you turn around and there's no one to ask questions to. You want to what? You want to go out into the woods now? Well I'm not supposed to not without Cecil only as far as the porch and even then. It is beautiful at night that's true I love how the snow

271

how it glows. I could never figure out from what miles away from any light and no moon and still it's like it's reflecting something. The lake yes there's that moment when you don't know where you're standing if you're on the shore or on the ice you're right at the border and then you take a few steps and it's different you can tell the ground's more alive under you there are these noises these groans but it's just the ice shifting don't be afraid and don't be afraid if you fall through either it's just layers there's always another one to catch you ice freezes that way it's not solid you get this moment of panic but then you hit another layer just a little deeper each time deeper as you go farther out. Sure why not we could go and smell the snow. But who are you that's what I still don't understand. You're trying to get everything out of me but there's nothing more to get. You're like that pincer creature Father told me about trying to dissolve my bones so there's nothing left well you've done your job I'm tired Rebecca she took that comb out of her hair and it all just tumbled down tumbled down her back the fire was burning a box of salt who are you?